To William Gerhardi

PART ONE

I

Walking home one night, taking a round-about route to add to experience, to stay awake a little longer and meet, perhaps, some curiosity of life not met before, Ellie Parsons, aged eighteen, independent, employed person, living in Chelsea, passed, near the Victoria Coach Station, a couple from her home town. She recognised the shape of them. She hurried. She thought herself safely past, when the husband called:

'Why, Ellie Parsons!'

His tone showed that he was struck by seeing among eight million strangers someone known to him. Ellie had not the courage to ignore him. She paused and faced them, pretending surprise.

'The Ripleys,' she said.

The Ripleys, not on their own ground, looked unsure of themselves, but they were, as usual, armed with disapproval. Overcoming his surprise, Mr Ripley asked: 'How are you getting on?' He was a lay preacher at the Pratt Hill Baptist Chapel, Eastsea, and publicly held it shameful that Ellie Parsons should have left home against the wish of a widowed mother. His face became stern: 'You're going to Eastsea for Christmas, I hope?'

Ellie, standing two yards away from him, said: 'Yes,'

then, suddenly defiant, added: 'I have a job in a studio. I'm doing my own work. It's wonderful!' Unable to control her voice, she shouted like a schoolgirl: 'I've never been so happy before in my life.'

A smile appeared unexpectedly on the young-old face of the wife. She put her hand on her husband's arm, prompting him to say 'Good-night,' then, as they moved off, she whispered: 'That girl's in love.'

Ellie heard her, and did not care. As she turned her back on them, London was about her again and she felt her own freedom.

It was a mild December night, pretending spring. The sky, lacquer-black and peppered with small stars, looked as though blown clean by a gale, but the breeze that came from the side streets was tender as the breath of a fan. The road before her was empty. At the triangle where it joined Ebury Street, it looked as spacious as a ballroom. Ellie broke into a run. At that moment it seemed to her, were she to leap up, she would rise from the moorings of earth and sail between the stars; and if she called out, her voice would fill the sky.

On an impulse, she jumped and called: 'Hey!' As she landed, the pavement smacked sharply through her thin soles; her cry came out like a mouse-squeak. She looked over her shoulder, but there was no one who might have heard her. She burst out laughing. It was true. She was in love.

That evening while Quintin Bellot and she had been gazing at one another across the restaurant table, his expression had changed. She had felt between them not merely that sharp-edged, sparking attraction, but tenderness. She had felt it like a supernatural glow in the air about them. She touched his hand with her finger-tips and he gathered her fingers into his hand, then he laughed and gave her hand an impatient shake and said: 'You must choose something from the menu.'

She tried to give her attention to the menu. It was a pity she was not hungry in the evenings. She took her main meal at mid-day and the occasional evening meal that Quintin bought her, seemed to her wasted. She wished she could say: 'Give me the money instead so that I can have a real meal tomorrow.'

He started explaining the items to her: '*Langue de Boeuf en Paupiettes* – that's ox-tongue done with a sort of meat stuffing and bacon; in *paupiettes*, in . . . oh, you know! . . . in slices. *Côtes de veau foyot* – veal cutlets done in white wine with grated cheese and breadcrumbs. Very nice. Would you like that? Or some sort of chicken?'

She suddenly became annoyed that he should take her ignorance for granted. She said: 'But all this is nonsense. These French names don't mean anything.'

'But of course they do.' He laughed at her: 'If they didn't, how could you tell one dish from another?'

Her mother, who kept a restaurant in Eastsea, was always telling her customers that the French on menus was meaningless, invented to impress simpletons. 'We write in English,' she would say. 'We've nothing to hide.'

Quintin said: 'Or would you like some kebabs – they're pieces of meat put on a skewer and cooked over a charcoal fire.'

Disconcerted, Ellie asked stupidly: 'But how do you know?'

He pushed her hand away. Still laughing at her, he said: 'Don't be silly.'

5

Suddenly she said so loudly that people turned their heads: 'How marvellous everything is!'

He raised an eyebrow: 'I believe you're the first person I've heard say that since 1939.'

'Why 1939?'

'That was when the war started.'

'Oh, the war!' – she had almost forgotten it 'I was evacuated.'

'Evacuated! I thought you girls were all conscripted.'

'I was too young.'

'So you were. So you were.' Quintin let his eyelids droop with a look of melancholy, rather comical: 'And I? Even then, I was middle-aged.'

It was for that reason, among other reasons, when later in the evening he had roused himself and said with a yawn: 'Well, I suppose I must dress and see you home,' that she pushed him back against the pillows and said: 'No, stay there. You look so comfortable.'

Not moving, he protested: 'But I must put you into a taxi.'

'Oh no.' Anything but that. Once before he had put her into a taxi and the fare had beggared her for a week. 'You just stay there,' she said.

He sighed and said weakly: 'This is disgraceful. I'm being spoilt.'

Ahead of her, traffic lights changed in an empty world. When she reached them, she gazed down Chelsea Bridge Road to observe the infernal splendour of the Battersea Power Station. It was flood-lit. The rosy cameo of chimneys, seeming incandescent against the black sky, billowed smoke wreaths, glowing, massive, majestical as the smoke of hell.

6

She loved them. They were a landmark of home. They remained at hand as she passed the cemetery. An icy dampness came from the earth where the old soldiers lay buried. She knew these old soldiers. On her Saturday afternoon walks she came here and read the inscriptions to the Master Builder, the surgeon and the mysterious Sixpennyman; to the cook who had died aged twenty-nine and the officers who had died of their wounds. She had sketched into a notebook the tomb that bore so lavish a collection of trophies of war, and had written beneath her sketch 'Decoration for a bed-head', hoping that one day at the studio she would be required to decorate a bed-head. It was familiar ground, yet now, in the darkness, she was unnerved by the glimmer of the headstones. At the thought of the dead who lay there in the cold of winter, the darkness of night, she was touched by mortality. Life was wonderful, but men died.

She looked up at the sky and was reminded of a night – she thought of it as some hour near midnight but it must have been early on a winter evening – when she had walked with her father along the Eastsea promenade. The invisible sea had scratched on the pebbles below. Her father had pointed out stars to her – Orion's Belt, the Plough, the Bear, the Dog. He had said: 'They are worlds, like ours.'

'With people?'

'Perhaps. Why not?'

For the first time in her life she had realised the sky was not a solid, light-pricked canopy, but infinite space.

The night before he was taken to the sanatorium they had walked by the sea for a little way, very slowly. He had said: 'You know, I may not come back.'

Hoping to seem courageous in her fear, she had asked: 'Do you mean you may die?'

He said: 'Yes, but it does not matter. Our destiny is not here.'

She had remembered that as she had remembered nothing spoken at the Pratt Hill Baptist Chapel.

That was ten years ago. Already she could look back ten years! How quickly one aged! She saw time stretching like a shadow behind her, like the long, dark, empty promenade on which the two figures, very small in her memory, pressed against the wind. Her father had known that he was dying. Perhaps it was death that had drawn his glance up to the stars.

The Embankment meant she was nearly home. When she neared Oakley Street, she crossed the road at a run. She lived here in this impressive street where the houses stood in the street-lights like façades cut upon solid rock. She had found her room advertised on a postcard in a sweet-shop. Who could otherwise have guessed that such houses were boarding-houses? The long, glossy, upcurve of tarmac road was deserted. Ellie began to imagine herself a spirit, perhaps isolated in some dimension of her own – but, no, there was someone else in the world. Round the corner, in Upper Cheyne Row, a door-knocker was being furiously banged against a door. The knocking stopped. There was the squeak of a window going up. A woman's voice called out: 'The bell *is* working, dear.' There was silence, then suddenly, into Oakley Street, walking on tall, thread-fine heels, a woman came as though in flight. She passed Ellie without noticing her. She was a delicately-shaped woman in a coat of expensive fur. A startling beauty.

Ellie thought: 'She must be somebody. Perhaps she's famous.'

The woman, stumbling at times on her high heels, began to run and wave and shout: 'Taxi! Taxi!' A taxi was coming up from the Embankment. It stopped beside her: she entered it: it turned in the road. Ellie watched it until it was out of sight.

Well, that was London. Profoundly satisfied by her adopted city, Ellie found her key, entered her house and climbed to her room on the top floor. When she reached it, she opened her window and gazed down on the windows of Margaretta Terrace. She was wide awake again and excited as though, even at this last minute of the day, life might extend some new experience. What lay ahead for her? Would she ever rap on door-knockers with the urgency of important emotions? and run round a corner wearing a fur coat? and, lifting a hand to an approaching taxi, impress some other girl named Ellie and fill her with envy and ambition?

Forced by the cold to close the window, Ellie embraced her own shoulders and turned round and round. The room's size did not permit a real dance but she moved as wildly as she could to celebrate the end of her virginity.

2

Half-an-hour later, when Ellie was about to fall asleep, Quintin was awake, still propped up on pillows as she had left him. The circle of light from his prune-coloured lampshade lit only his hand that held open the second volume of *The Princess Casamassima*. He was not reading.

He was not, as Ellie had been, disturbed by rapture, but by an irritation of the senses that exhausted him and kept him awake. He had involved himself with Ellie from habit, and it was a habit he would soon have to break. The very young, flinging their energy into the transports of love, were becoming too much for him.

When the telephone rang, he supposed it was Ellie again. He was tempted to switch off the bell, but, remembering the eagerness of that childish, peach-bloom face, he smiled compassionately and lifted the receiver. He spoke into it a gentle and encouraging 'Hello'.

He was answered by an unfamiliar male voice asking him if he were Quintin Bellot. He roused himself without enthusiasm. He put down his book and flexed his aching arm while the voice at the other end of the line called him urgently to a milk bar in Bridge Street. His wife, Petta, had been found balancing on the parapet of Westminster Bridge. No spark was roused in him by the emergency.

'Are you the police?' he asked, delaying the moment of getting out of bed.

'No. I was just passing. I said to her: "Don't be silly. Come down," I said, and she came down. When I found she couldn't hardly stand, I brought her here for a coffee. She won't let me leave her alone. I'd be obliged if you'd look slippy. I've got to get home tonight.' The voice was becoming exasperated as nobility of action met with so little response.

'All right. I'll be about fifteen minutes.'

'You get a move on,' the receiver suddenly shouted as Quintin put it down.

He rose and dressed, saying to himself: 'Blast Petta, and blast this busybody who's picked her up,' yet he could not blame the man for wanting someone to take her off his hands. She had no luck. Her shows of helplessness merely produced, sooner or later, a panic to escape her.

Of course, she had deliberately chosen Westminster Bridge. His flat was off Birdcage Walk. As he set out for Bridge Street, a damp, warm wind swept at him from the park. It smelt of decayed leaves, the breath of a false spring. This was the sort of night that in his youth had exhilarated him, forcing him out at all hours in search of experience – and here he was now, tramping across Parliament Square towards some tiresome situation with Petta.

The square seemed deserted. The gates to the Underground were shut. The only sign of life came from the milk bar windows that gave off a light like the glare from molten metal. Petta was sitting inside with her rescuer. Both had a gloomy look of waiting. Both, it seemed, had sunk into silence long ago. There were sandwiches and coffee on the table between them. Under the ghastly violet-white of the fluorescent strips, Petta had the pallor of the unliving. The young man got to his feet as Quintin opened the door. His look of painful impatience, painfully repressed, changed to affable relief. He was a tall, very thin young man in a shrunken raincoat. He looked at his wrist-watch and said: 'The lady'll be all right now. I'd best be getting along. I'll just catch the 12.10.'

Quintin said: 'Thank you. We've wasted a lot of your time.'

He would have left it at that, but Petta murmured something; he recoiled, saying: 'Oh, no, I'm sure he wouldn't . . .' but the young man, though he seemed on the point of going, was still there. Quintin handed over a ten-shilling note. The young man took it and went in silence as though he had been expecting more.

The food on the table was untouched. The coffee was a livid shade of yellow-green: the sandwiches looked like cement. 'Do you want this stuff?' Quintin asked.

'No. I had to buy something, sitting here so long.' She gave him a quick, uncertain glance, then, making a movement coquettish and pathetic, turned away. She had been crying. Looking down on her head, he noticed among the filmy fairness of her hair a sort of dust of grey hairs. Her whole appearance had taken on a kind of lifeless dryness as though, during the months she had been away, she had been pressed colourless like a flower in a book. Her lipstick had come off. In this light, her lips were mauve.

'Where is Theo?' he asked.

She said contemptuously: 'Oh, Theo!'

'I'd better ring him up.'

'No, Quintin, please. I've left him.'

He wondered what he was going to do with her. He was determined not to take her back to his flat.

'We must find a hotel. Where are your clothes and things?'

'Still at Theo's. I have my dressing-case.' Her voice was plaintive and barely audible. 'We had a row. I threw my latch-key at him and said I was going. When I came back he wouldn't open the door. I kept knocking, then the woman in that flat upstairs shouted at me—' she felt blindly for her handkerchief – 'I did'nt know what to do.' She started to weep and he was aware again of her old aura of desperate misfortune. He longed to leave her.

He said: 'Would you like some fresh coffee? You can drink it while I ring round the hotels.' He turned to the bar from where the girl was looking at them with distaste. She had heard what he said. She said sullenly: 'We're closing.'

Petta was gazing at Quintin. It seemed to him she was drawing up from some inner source a sadness that filled her glance and weighed down her shoulders, hanging on her like a cloak. He felt trapped. This was neither the time nor the place for an argument with her: and it was too late to go elsewhere.

He said: 'I'll get a taxi. You had better come back to my flat and I'll telephone from there.'

When they entered his flat, she looked restored. No doubt she thought she was home. Her manner regained its old vivacity. The lamp had been left on in his bedroom. She walked in there and, after glancing round it with an expert eye, gave him a grin. She picked up his comb. 'Auburn,' she said. 'Has Gem Primrose dyed her hair?'

Smiling coolly, he took the comb from her and said: 'We'd better go into the sitting-room.'

There she settled herself on the sofa. She said: 'How prosperous it all looks after Chelsea. An Adam's fireplace down in the hall; ruby carpet on the stairs.' She looked about her. 'You've brought all your painted satinwood here! I like your lime-green curtains. Sumptuous, aren't they?'

He said nothing.

Now she was safely in out of the dark, she was rapidly coming to life. She gave him a smile that would have left a stranger helpless. It roused no response in him. He observed her critically. For years she had looked much younger than her age; now the mask of her youth was fading. She behaved as though unaware of this. She said: 'Darling, give me a drink,' and kicked off her shoes and put her feet up on the cushions. She curled her toes inside her transparent stockings, laughed and said: 'Cold,' then, wrapping her coat round her, she settled into the sofa corner and smiled at him. She lifted her lashes seductively as though she were here for love.

She had with her a lizard-skin-covered box with golden clasps. She opened it and took from among the gold-topped bottles a box that had once held five hundred cigarettes. When she started smoking her movements became cramped as though she lit and inhaled her cigarette with difficulty.

He handed her a glass of gin. 'You know you can't stay here.'

'But, darling, I could sleep on this sofa.' She stretched into the cushions. 'I could sleep here for ever, for ever, for ever.'

'No doubt. I prefer to be alone here. I too have a private life.'

'Darling!' she laughed at him as though that were some sort of joke. She stretched out her hand to him, still making all her little movements of charm, perhaps knowing they had no effect upon him, yet pretending to herself they were irresistible. She said: 'You never asked me for a divorce. Didn't you want to marry Gem?'

'She didn't want to marry me. She has always been quite satisfied with Berthold.'

'You mean, Berthold is richer than you.'

'I mean, Gem and I understood one another. She said from the first: "I know what you're after, and it isn't marriage".'

Petta made a gesture of distaste: 'A vulgar beginning!'

'But a propitious one. We knew we were two of a kind.'

'Indeed! Clever Gem! She was to get you by being the one who did not want you. Yet not so clever after all. It didn't work. And there's no retreating from a line like that.'

'You're talking nonsense.' Already he was irritated by her. His natural good humour always went to pieces in her company. He said: 'Gem and I are still friends.'

Petta laughed: 'Serve her right.'

'You flatter me; but the implications of your remarks have no basis in fact. Gem is an intelligent and capable woman, an independent career woman, and fond of her husband. The question of my getting my freedom never arose.'

'After all,' said Petta, 'there are disadvantages in freedom. It leaves you open to remarriage.'

'There are disadvantages in everything,' he said more bitterly than he had intended. He moved about the room, unwilling to give her, by sitting down, excuse to stay longer. He said: 'I'll ring Worple's in Clarges Street. I know the clerk there. He'll find you a room.'

At once her front broke down. 'Oh, no—' her eyes filled with tears – 'Quintin, darling! I just can't set out again tonight. I'm too tired. And a bleak hotel bedroom, now, when I'm so depressed about things! Please! Don't send me away! Just give me a blanket and let me sleep here. I promise I'll go in the morning.'

Exhausted, knowing himself defeated, he dropped into a chair and told himself defeat had resulted less from Petta's appeals than from the lateness of the hour. If he did find her a room – and it would not be easy – he would have to escort her to the hotel: and she was quite capable of crying or making a scene in front of the reception clerk.

'All right,' he said. 'You will go in the morning. That's a promise,' as though her promises meant anything.

'Yes, darling. I will. I will.' Her face was strained with her desire to convince him. Her hand lying along the sofa back twitched nervously. It looked the hand of an invalid. It caught him, in spite of himself, into a painful pity of her. This must have been visible on his face, for at once she turned on him her gentlest smile and said: 'Had you been willing to take our marriage seriously, it would have meant everything to me. I would have been thankful for a stable emotion in my life.'

'Really! You expect me to believe that?'

He never had believed it, and he would not be induced to believe it now. When she was married to her first husband, she had racketed around with anyone who came along. She had gone off with him, Quintin, on a violent sex spree (he could think of no better term for it) without any preliminaries – and then, giving no warning, she

16

had turned up on his doorstep in the middle of the night, saying: 'I want only you. I've come to you. I know you won't send me away.'

He became increasingly angry at the memory of it. He had tried to reason with her: 'Petta, this is ridiculous. You must go back to Henry at once. You can't leave a young child like Flora. You can't just abandon your home like this.'

She said: 'I had to get away from them. I was so bored.'

'I shall ring Henry and ask him to come and fetch you.'

At that, she had started screaming: 'No, no, no! If you send me away I shall kill myself. I mean it. I shall. I shall!'

He had not known her then as he did now. In the end she was triumphant, but he had never ceased to resent the fact that marriage, a state he had long avoided, should be so forced upon him. And now the same trick (a trick that had probably been played on Theo) was being played on him again! He could scarcely speak for anger. Some moments passed before he was able to ask her:

'What caused the break-up with Theo?'

'Oh!' She dropped her hand and a weight of gold bracelets fell from her coat sleeve to her wrist. 'He behaved abominably. You know I haven't seen Flora for ages! I wanted to take her there for Christmas. Theo wouldn't hear of it. Said he hated young people. Wouldn't have one around.'

'But you know Henry wouldn't let you take Flora to Theo's flat.'

'How would he know where I was taking her? I've a right to see her sometime. I intended telling him we were going to the country, or something.'

As though she could deceive Henry any longer! Quintin

smiled wearily. And why had she suddenly decided she must see Flora? A whim, an excuse for a row, for bringing another wretched relationship to a conclusion!

Watching his face, she said: 'The truth was, I wanted to come back to you. I would never have left had you behaved just a little better.'

'I had no intention of behaving "better", as you put it. I never shall behave better, so please have no illusions about it. A person who is blackmailed into marriage cannot be expected to take marriage seriously. You are being absurd.'

'But why? I loved you. Someone must take something seriously some time, or nothing means anything.'

She smiled as though it had been an encounter of wits and she had got the better of it. He turned away from her. She said: 'How have you managed alone here in this little flat?'

'Well enough. There's Mrs Trimmer in the basement. Alma Wheeldon lives just down the road. She'd probably look after me if I needed looking after.'

'Poor Alma! I hear she's become a widow.' Petta put out her hand to him again: 'Quintin! Do believe me when I say you are the only one who has meant anything to me.'

He did not believe it. He did not want to believe it. He had no intention of believing it. He had had enough of the whole business. He said: 'I'll make up the bed for you in my dressing-room.'

'No. I'll stay here.' She closed her eyes and at once seemed to be asleep. He had often seen her collapse in this way after emotional outbursts. He felt too tired to argue with her. He went to the airing-cupboard for blankets.

While he was out of the room she had roused herself and taken her sleeping-tablets from the case. As he entered she whispered: 'A glass of water, darling!'

'You won't need tablets tonight.'

'Yes, I must take them. You see, I may not sleep – and being afraid of not sleeping keeps me awake.'

He gave her the blankets and fetched the water. As he said Good-night, she lifted her face to him. He ignored the movement, but asked suddenly:

'Why did you choose Westminster Bridge?'

For a moment she had no reply, then she said mildly: 'It has a low parapet.'

The answer seemed absurd to him and yet, he realised, it was reasonable enough. Perhaps, after all, he was wrong in thinking she had contrived the whole thing. Although more intelligent than most women – which did not mean much – she was capable of great silliness. At their first meeting he had found her mysterious. He had said to her (as he often said to women): 'You are a mystery; a delicious mystery.' In propinquity her mystery seemed merely the darkness of the void. He concluded she had no character at all. Her actions were as purposeless as the actions of a branch caught up in a gale.

One day she wanted him, the next she wanted Theo, then some other man. After years of neglecting the child, she had suddenly decided she must have Flora to stay with Theo. That was typical of her – and these whims could lead her to violent action, to rages, to attempted suicides, to bouts of despair; all meaningless.

Himself, he was a peaceful man. How could he be expected to live with a storm-tossed cipher? He knew that at the moment he was being weak with her, but not without reason. A branch flung about by the wind could blind a human being and shatter a life. He was a sensitive man. He was capable of suffering. He had no intention of provoking an action that might cost him years of remorse.

The truth was, she had once frightened him badly. Before that he had treated her threats of suicide as a joke. She had acted suddenly, without any warning, over some wretched girl in a dress-shop who had meant nothing to him.

They had been walking down Piccadilly to Gem Primrose's sherry party. The dress-shop girl had been scarcely mentioned for days. They had, in fact, walked for two hundred yards without speaking, when Petta said: 'I can stand no more of it,' and stepped off the pavement in front of a speeding bus. In the second before the bus could strike her, he pulled her back. She had been pale, but he had been much more disturbed than she. Indeed, her calm had seemed to him abnormal. As she gazed after the bus, showing no emotion, she said: 'I might have been dead by now.'

'Then let that be a lesson to you,' he said and, overriding his repulsion from her extravagant behaviour, he caught her arm and led her towards the Rivoli. She looked at him with an expression of contempt and sadness, and said: 'You are rather a stupid man, Quintin. Kind enough in your way, but stupid. You look intelligent, even perceptive, but you're nothing of the kind. You're nothing but the *homme moyen et sensuel*.'

'A very good thing to be,' he said with mock heartiness. He ordered a couple of double brandies. Apparently he needed a drink more than she did, for she barely sipped hers. In the end he drank both of them. Seated in a corner, her pale flower-pretty face enhanced by her pretty hat, she watched him with an ill-fitting gravity. Her look disconcerted him. He did not know what to say when she said: 'Death is no retaliation, is it? How could one get at you?'

Her hand lay limp on the table. He covered it with his own hand and at once her calm had collapsed. She looked as though she might burst into tears: instead she caught at his hand and held it fiercely. She seemed unable to speak for some moments, then she whispered: 'Quintin, please, no more girls in dress-shops!'

He agreed at once: 'No more girls of any sort,' for his interest was centred then on Gem Primrose, a mature woman, not to be taken lightly in any way. It was because of Gem that Petta went off with Theo.

The next morning Quintin awoke to the sound of Petta's laughter in the next room. She was charming Mrs Trimmer, making an ally of the woman, resolved no doubt to stay here until she found herself a new Theo.

Quintin, his will restored by sleep, told himself that would not happen.

Mrs Trimmer brought in his breakfast tray. He could see she was bursting to speak of Mrs Bellot. He gave her some orders for the day but made no mention of his wife.

'Isn't madam staying?' Mrs Trimmer asked.

'No.'

When he had eaten and put the tray aside, he lay for some time considering how best to deal with the situation. Because of his distrust of himself, he felt his wisest move would be to tell her he was going out to keep some engagement. He would expect her to be gone when he returned. He must arrange a genuine engagement: he could not trust his resolution if his statement were not backed by truth. How could he best engage himself?

It was Christmas Eve, nearly mid-day, so he could make no business arrangement. Then he remembered Ellie and her departure for Eastsea. He rang her at once.

He bathed and dressed and entered the sitting-room, to find Petta still on the sofa. Sleep had restored her too. Although she had slept all night in her clothes, she had still the elegance that was her one creative gift. However she lived, her appearance was always exquisite.

At the sight of him she smiled and stretched herself. 'I slept so well, and your Mrs Trimmer makes delicious coffee.' She tucked in her feet and said: 'Come and sit beside me.'

He sat in the chair opposite. 'I have soon to go out,' he said, 'but first we must arrange things for you. Where are you thinking of going when you leave here?'

She shook her head: 'I don't know.' She spoke sadly, looking at him with wide, uncertain eyes. She had made up her face with her usual subtlety. Observing the delicate rose and white of her lips and skin, the film of blue-mauve shadowing her eyes, each colour exactly toned to the ash-fairness of her hair, he thought how few of the women he had known understood this art as she did. Her beauty could still move him. He looked away.

She said: 'Perhaps one of those service flats behind Knightsbridge? But surely I haven't to go at once? You will let me take a bath?'

'Of course. Don't be silly. Go and have one while I ring up the flats.'

He went to the telephone, but she did not move from the sofa. He arranged her bookings. 'There!' he said. 'You can take a taxi round as soon as you're ready. I have to go out, so I'll say good-bye.'

She broke in protestingly: 'Oh no. Surely you haven't to go just yet. Do sit down again and talk.' As he did not sit down, she pleaded: 'Quintin! Darling!'

He looked at his watch. Thank goodness he really had an appointment. He said firmly: 'I'm sorry, my dear, I must go. I'm seeing a friend off at Victoria.'

'A woman?'

'A girl.'

'Oh!' She raised her eyebrows and tried to give a small amused twist to her mouth, keeping up a show of vivacity, but he could see desolation come down on her like a weight on her shoulders. She glanced about her with a frightened and defenceless air, like someone lost in the world.

She said: 'It's Christmas, of course. I'd forgotten. We used to have a lot of fun at Christmas when I was a child.' Her lower lip shook and she pressed her teeth against it. After a pause, she said: 'Are you going away?'

'Yes. Mrs Trimmer wants a holiday. I'm going to my club. There will be no one here, so, in any case, there could be no question of your staying.'

'I know. I know,' she assured him, tears welling in her eyes. She added quickly, as though speaking before her voice could break: 'I'll have a bath now. I promise I'll be gone before you return.' She nodded to him, smiling, but not hiding her desolation that was, he supposed, genuine enough. No doubt all her emotions were genuine, but her moods were so contradictory, each denied the other. He found it better to believe in none of them.

She went into the bathroom. As he put on his overcoat in the hall, she came out again: she had forgotten her case. In the time she had been alone, she had started crying. Her nostrils were pink, her mouth hung trembling like a baby's, she was dabbing at her eyes. He took up his hat and gloves, appearing to notice nothing. He must hurry. Exposed to the emptiness of the flat, she would fly like a bat exposed to light. He imagined she'd find some sort of companionship, somewhere.

He called 'Good-bye,' and was gone.

3

Ellie was packing her suitcase when the telephone rang down in the hall. She had nothing to hope for. She and Quintin had said their good-byes, yet from habit she followed the sound of Mrs Mackie's feet trudging up to the first floor, then to the second . . . She was coming to the top! She knocked on Ellie's door.

'Telephone,' she shouted.

'Oh, who is it?' Ellie asked, wanting her to say, as she sometimes did: 'It's a gentleman.' Instead she muttered blackly: 'How should I know?' Passing her, Ellie sped downstairs.

It *was* Quintin. Her excitement paralysed her throat. His voice sounded distant and without warmth. He asked the time she was leaving London. When she told him, he announced his intention of seeing her off.

'Oh, Quintin!' She was mazed with gratitude. After a moment she said: 'How wonderful! How kind!' She almost said: 'How generous!' but was stopped by uncertainty. Why had he suddenly decided to see her off? He was not given to caprice or change of plans. It had occurred to her he intended giving her a Christmas present.

Back in her room, she wondered what she could give to him. She was very worried. She could not buy anything.

Having paid her rent in advance, bought her rail ticket and presents each for her mother and sister, she was nearly penniless.

She had only two things she could give away. One was her reproduction of Rousseau's 'Snake Charmer' that hung over her bed. It was her richest possession. In her opinion it 'made' the room – a sliver of a room with dirty cream walls, a torn haircord carpet, and just sufficient space to permit the occupant to pass the bed and reach the window. She sat on the bed for some time and looked at the Rousseau. She would have thrust it upon Quintin had it not seemed to her an ostentatious gift, unwieldy and difficult to carry.

She would have to give him the other thing.

The glass roof of the station was dark with fog. People tore busily around one another, for there was still room to move, but soon there would not be. There were queues winding out from the platform barriers. Officially it was still daylight. The crowds and the lines of queuing people among them seemed like the darkness clotted at the bottom of a muddy pool. Then the lights came on. Distracted faces appeared, shape and impetus was given to the confusion.

Ellie, who was usually in a panic when catching trains, now cared nothing for her train. She was anxious only to find Quintin. They had arranged to meet at the buffet. As she made her way to it, she saw Quintin, in dark over-coat and bowler-hat, entering the door. A woman on her way out bumped into him, and he raised his hat and stepped aside. As he did so, two young men thrust past him with rough impatience as though his courtesy had been an interference with their liberty.

Ellie, beset with pity and indignation, thought: 'He does not belong here.' She hurried, as though to his defence, but when she reached him, there he was, standing by the counter, looking, as ever, mild and undisturbed.

He said: 'Ah, there you are, my dear! You've plenty of time. Will you have a sandwich or something?'

She shook her head. She looked up at the buffet clock, then out at the crowds, hiding behind all this display of anxiety her excitement at their meeting.

'Come on, then,' he said kindly, taking her small suitcase from her hand, 'we'll find you a seat.'

He passed quickly and efficiently through the crowd. Ellie, at his heels, felt elated by the relationship of their movement among all these people. His appearance seemed to her exactly right. This was the man she would have chosen for herself. That he should have sought her out still seemed unbelievable felicity. This was the first time he had suggested their meeting for any purpose other than ultimate love-making of one degree or another. It seemed to her their past meetings had been organised, keeping their positions distinct, while this was informal and delightful, and conveyed a sense of permanency as though they were an engaged or married couple.

The train, when they reached it, was already full. In each carriage people sat four-a-side, their outgaze smug and hostile as the ingazers went searching by.

'We'll find one. We'll find one,' Quintin assured her, but they came to the end of the train and people were standing in the corridor.

Ellie said: 'It's all right. I'll stand.'

'Oh no.'

27

'I often do.' She got into a carriage before he could walk her back again.

He said: 'Go into the first class. I'm sure it will be all right in this crowd.'

'I might get caught.' She did not say she had not the money to pay the difference. He knew her salary. He stared down the length of the train. She felt it in his mind to give her the money that would cover the first-class fare, and felt also his unwillingness to give it. She diverted him by taking a small parcel from her handbag: 'A Christmas present.'

'No! For me? How delightful!' He stood holding the parcel – nursing it, rather – and smiled as though worried by something.

'Aren't you going to open it?'

She watched him taking out the cigarette-case and thought probably she would never see it again. It had been given to her the previous Christmas by a young man in Eastsea who had imagined he was in love with her. She did not smoke. She had never used it, but she had been fond of it. It was of transparent plastic, set in a gilt frame. She had known all the time it was too feminine for Quintin.

'But it's charming,' he said. As he made to open it, the catch came off in his fingers.

She gulped in her throat. 'It's broken,' she said, knowing she should offer to take it back to some shop.

As though he knew she could not, he said quickly: 'It doesn't matter. It only needs two little screws.' He put the case into his breast-pocket and smiled at her. 'Very nice,' he said and patted the pocket. 'Now I must give you something. What can I give you?'

28

She smiled, not answering. He took her hand and held it; he moved his other hand expressively: 'I have nothing,' he said. After a pause, he whispered: 'Nothing to give you.'

Still smiling, she put his hand to her lips: 'If only I needn't go! If only I could spend Christmas here with you!'

She did not know what he was doing at Christmas, but she had in her mind a picture of him alone in his flat, and pitied him, yet felt some exasperation that he would not urge her to remain.

His lips parted; he looked at her as though he had something important to say, but hesitated, sighed, then said: 'Perhaps after you come back we will be able to meet more often.'

'Have things changed? Are they going to be different?'

'They will have to be different. They cannot go on like this,' he spoke uncertainly, as though he were very tired. In this bleak, queasy light, he might have been ten years older than his age.

'What will you do at Christmas?' she asked.

'I don't know. Sit all day in my club, I expect. I've never cared for these holidays. Such an interruption of one's life. When I was a child . . .' he broke off and pressed the base of his right palm against his brow. After a moment he shook his head slightly and said: 'What was I saying?'

'What's the matter? Do you feel ill?'

'No, I did not sleep very well. Something worried me. I'll be all right.' The whistle blew. 'Look after yourself,' he said.

The train creaked and gathered itself together for departure.

'I wish I could stay,' said Ellie, 'I hate going.'

'You'll be back in no time. I'll ring you . . . what's today? I'll ring you early next week.'

That promise for the future lessened the intervening days. The train was moving. She held to Quintin's fingers until they were drawn from her, then he put his hands into his overcoat pockets. He stood smiling rather humorously as she leant out to wave to him. He looked, what indeed he was, a man whom any woman might approach with confidence – and it was she whom he had chosen to approach.

When he was out of sight, she still felt his touch like a powder on her skin. Watching out at the blae fog on the river, through which the tower of Big Ben appeared shadowy, furred with scaffolding, she felt him still like a physical presence into which she could merge for pleasure and comfort. But the break had been made. His presence faded from her and she faced the alien days without him.

The Battersea Power Station swung past, shadow on shadow; the tower of the Brentford Gas Works; the pagoda at Kew. With gathering speed the train passed out between the backs of houses into the winter countryside where a grey light glinted on puddles and sharpened the criss-crossing nakedness of trees. A desolate world; and she was being taken where she did not want to go.

Ellie's home was at the shabby end of Eastsea front. Her mother, widowed and left without an income, had invested her capital in a small restaurant over which there were living-rooms. This property, she promised them, would be left between the girls when she died. She often said:

'Look after your business, and your business will look after you.'

The restaurant tables were set for tea when Ellie entered, but the place was empty. When a student she had painted on the walls galleons with swelling sails riding a swelling sea. Now she saw them as for the first time. They shamed her. She was suddenly beset by a powerful vision of someone from the London studio where she worked visiting Eastsea and coming in here for tea and seeing the name of Ellie Parsons boldly written on the prow of the largest and most frightful galleon.

When her mother appeared, Ellie gave no greeting but said with disgust: 'The first thing I'm going to do is paint out these ships.'

'Oh no, you're not, my lady,' said Mrs Parsons with a decided twist of the head. 'I didn't want them in the first place, but now they're there, they'll stay.'

At once their old antagonism was alive between them. Ellie felt again her mother's power and the frustration of past defeats. She would have turned and walked out if she could: instead, she forced herself to smile. 'Well, here I am! Home for Christmas!'

Mrs Parsons said: 'And about time. I'd almost forgotten what you looked like,' then she, too, seemed to remember the significance of the season. She smiled and said: 'You know you're welcome any time.'

With a sense of truce, they kissed and went into the kitchen. Mrs Parsons was a foot shorter than Ellie. She was a strong, square woman who wore tweeds summer and winter. Her clothes were spotted with grease because she felt an apron to be an indignity. She would say to her customers: 'I've had to be father and mother to my girls,' so Ellie used to wonder if that was why her mother looked so much more masculine than other mothers. Mrs Parsons's cheeks stood out like red rubber balls, her chin was a third ball stuck on below her mouth. She sweated a lot and scrubbed her face impatiently with a handkerchief. When people said to her: 'Don't you overdo it, Mrs Parsons. Make those girls of yours give a hand. You ought to put your feet up sometimes,' she would laugh and echo derisively: 'Put my feet up! Much chance of that.'

In the restaurant she laughed readily and said things like: 'It's no good looking on the gloomy side' or 'We're all here to help one another' or 'I often say we pass this way but once,' so she was reputed to be both brave and good-natured.

She looked brave and good-natured from habit in the restaurant, but as she and Ellie passed through the bead curtain into the kitchen, her face took on a belligerent peevishness. She said: 'The new girl's off to do her Christmas shopping. They're all alike. A lazy lot. They don't want to work.'

'Why should they?'

Mrs Parsons eyed Ellie sternly: 'Is this what they teach you in London?'

'I was only joking.'

'I've kept you something.'

Mrs Parsons, sitting, morosely watching Ellie eat a dish of fish-cakes, asked: 'How long are you staying?'

'I've only got Christmas Day and Boxing Day.'

'And then you're going back? Even though I've told you Emmy's getting married, you're going back?'

Ellie was astounded by this accusation. How could her mother ever have supposed anything else? She said: 'My job is there. I live there.' She added unwisely: 'I belong there.'

Mrs Parsons set her lips tightly. Ellie finished her meal in silence. She had learnt in London to eat with a fork alone and awaited adverse comment, but her mother seemed too preoccupied to notice. When Ellie put down the fork, Mrs Parsons burst out: 'You're under age. I could have you brought back. Yes, I could. I could have you brought back.'

This was a new line of attack. Ellie, looking at her mother with frightened eyes, could think of no defence against it. Mrs Parsons, seeing how effective her words had been, nodded with satisfaction and rose to pour out tea. She left her threats in the air for some minutes, then sighed and said: 'I don't know what I've done to deserve a daughter like you. Other people's daughters don't go off and get jobs in London.'

'They leave home when they marry.'

'They don't go to London. Besides, you're not married.'

'Why do you mind? You've got Emmy. She was always your favourite.'

'That's nonsense. Besides, Emmy and Joe are going to Battle. He's starting up on his own there.'

'Battle's not far.'

Ellie, tasting the forgotten iron-rust taste of her mother's tea, felt, like a burden upon her, her old struggle for freedom. The thought of returning to Eastsea suffocated her.

Mrs Parsons said: 'Miss Bird was in here only lunch-time and said: "When Emmy goes, you shouldn't be here alone, Mrs Parsons; not with your high colour. You must make that Ellie of yours come back".'

'I'm not coming back. If you try and make me come

33

back I'll . . . I'll disappear.' Ellie looked directly at her mother, longing for this conversation to stop.

Mrs Parsons slid down in her chair and pushed her hands into her pockets. She sat with her legs planted apart. She would have looked mannish had it not been for the very feminine complaint in her small, blue eyes. Her mouth with its horse-shoe droop seemed compressed by the three inflamed, damp balls of her cheeks and chin. She was not so much angry as consumed by resentment.

Ellie turned away. She knew her mother was thinking that she had had to work most of her life and now, when her daughters were old enough to support her, when her rewards were due, she was being abandoned. Ellie, beset by guilt and pity, was herself resentful at being blackmailed in this way. She said in her mind: 'Two more days of it,' and was suddenly frightened by the possibility of being forced by some accident to return here. Once back, she might never escape again.

Her mother, as though sensing advantage, pursued it. She said: 'There's no need to be in London to do your painting. That girl who was at evening classes with you, Judy What's-her-name, she's at home. She's happy enough. She's got a job with the gas company. Her mother says she paints in her spare time.'

'She can't have much spare time.'

'Well, not as much as you'd have if you were helping me here. You'd have an hour or two in the afternoons as well as after supper.'

Ellie listened restlessly to her mother's voice growing eager as though its owner really believed in its persuasive powers. In the tone of someone making an offer that could not be refused, Mrs Parsons said: 'And I'll let you paint in the drawing-room – so long as you clear your mess up afterwards, of course.'

'It's no good.' Ellie softened her rejection of the offer by adding: 'I can't work in the drawing-room. It's too small. It's dark. It's cold. I don't want to clear things up when I've finished. I want somewhere that's my own. I want to be free.'

'Free!' Mrs Parsons was suddenly roused to scorn and fury. 'Free to do what, I'd like to know?'

Ellie blushed. 'Just free,' she whispered. She too felt fury, but it was muted by the knowledge she had used her freedom to pursue not art, but life.

Mrs Parsons now spoke as though she suspected Ellie's thoughts: 'People talk, I can tell you. Why, only the other day Miss Bird said to me: "That was a disgraceful thing your Ellie did, going off to London like that! People are talking." "I know they are," I said, "but what can I do? Ellie cares nothing for me. I've no influence over her".'

Mrs Parsons's face assumed the mask of the martyr, that mask with which she had forced her daughters to obedience when they were children. Seeing it and hating it, Ellie was suddenly certain her mother sought her return not for love of her but from vanity and to satisfy the Ripleys, Miss Bird and the rest of the Pratt Hill Baptist congregation. She said bitterly: 'Tell Miss Bird there are too many old maids in Eastsea as it is.'

'Old maids? What have "old maids" got to do with it?'

'That's what I'd become if I stayed. I'd never find anyone I wanted here.'

'And who have you found up there?' Mrs Parsons stared

at Ellie with penetrating suspicion. 'You take care, my lady. You'll land yourself in trouble.'

Ellie rose and picked up her case. 'I'm going upstairs.' She was unnerved by her mother's insight and warning, yet the consciousness of danger increased her sense of achievement. It increased her determination to hold to independence at all costs.

At tea-time Emmy appeared, briefly. She pushed two slices of bread and butter into her mouth, took a gulp of tea, then, humming loudly to herself, set about preparing for her evening out with Joe.

Mrs Parsons said: 'Joe. Joe. Joe. That's all we get now – Joe.' She grumbled, but she grumbled indulgently; not that it mattered to Emmy, who neither listened nor replied. Unlike Ellie, she was able to cut herself off from her mother's presence.

She kept her make-up on a shelf in the kitchen. She curled and combed and patted her hair: she smacked on powder with a heavy puff, licking her forefinger to dampen her eyebrows and lashes, covering her upper lip with a dark lipstick and pressing it down so that the lower was also reddened. She did everything with a dancing movement, listening to nothing and no one, eager to be gone.

Ellie watched her, not without envy, disconsolate that she was to be left alone again with her mother. Business was slack on Christmas Eve and Mrs Parsons spent most of the evening in the kitchen which was also the family sitting-room. Her talk was a recalling of old grievances: 'I shall never forget the time when that women said . . .' or 'That fellow came in here and had the cheek to . . .' or 'That old chap spat on the paintwork and I said . . .'

36

After a few hours, Ellie fell into a stupor from which she could barely rouse herself to answer a question. Where Emmy would have said: 'Oh, shut up, mum, stop belly-aching,' Ellie sat bleak, bored and silent, oppressed by the weight of her mother's sense of persecution. When at last she escaped to bed, it seemed to her she had suffered through an age.

Ellie's sister, Emmy, shared their mother's sturdy lack of height. She often said: 'Men like short girls,' so Ellie had always felt at a disadvantage as they walked together along the Eastsea promenade. Although men looked at Ellie first, attracted by her colouring, it was on Emmy their eyes lingered. There was no doubt she was the girl for them. And she knew it. As she walked, she would smile into herself with satisfaction as though between her and the passing men there was some secret Ellie could not even guess at.

Emmy's success in the Eastsea world and Ellie's discontent in it had brought a division between the girls, who had been close in childhood, so when on Christmas afternoon they walked along the promenade, they walked together only from lack of anything either might do on her own.

It was a grey day with a chill and gusty wind. Here and there the flagstones were spattered with sea spray. The gulls cried bleakly as they circled in over the land, and there was no human creature in sight.

As bride-to-be, bidden that evening to supper with Joe's parents, Emmy seemed to Ellie more smug and off-hand than ever. Ellie, whose consolations were far away, said suddenly and forcefully: 'Thank goodness I've escaped this place.'

Emmy, provoked out of her complacency, replied with spirit: 'What do you mean – escaped? You were born here. Wherever you go, you'll always belong here.'

Ellie could see on her sister's face the same flush that came over her mother's face at any suggestion of slight. At that moment, as Emmy looked so like their mother, Ellie felt acutely her own unlikeness. It seemed to her she was like no one and nothing here, and she was suddenly exhilarated by her difference. She felt like someone whose stride can take them from mountain to mountain. In this state of rare and intoxicated confidence, she spoke gently: 'I do not belong, because I do not want to belong. I'm different, because I want to be different.'

'That's just silly.' Emmy spoke as though her judgement finished the matter, but when Ellie left it at that, Emmy began talking boastfully about Joe and his cleverness. By some piece of trickery he had acquired the shop in Battle at a bargain price. They were to be married as soon as he had 'worked it up.'

'Joe's a downy one, I can tell you,' said Emmy. 'He heard his boss was interested in this shop, and he went out and saw it was a snip and signed on the dotted line while the boss was still chewing it over. Joe said, when he told him, the boss looked like a sick hen. Laugh? I could've died.'

'Does mother know how Joe got the shop?'

Emmy looked sharply at Ellie. 'No, and don't you tell her.'

'Of course I won't tell her.' Ellie understood that this was Emmy's revolt against the puritanism of their upbringing.

When they reached the end of the promenade and turned, they saw coming towards them a solitary young man.

From habit Emmy quoted from a game she and Ellie used to play: 'I rather fancy him.'

Ellie said nothing.

'Don't you fancy him?' asked Emmy.

'No.' The certainty of Ellie's tone made Emmy stare at her, and Ellie blushed in agony at her self-betrayal.

Emmy looked solemn. They walked some way in silence, then Emmy said: 'Mum keeps saying she'd like to know what you're up to in London.'

'What does she mean – "up to"? I'm earning my living.'

'She's suspicious. She keeps wondering how you got into this studio. It's a bit of a step from packing furniture in a basement.'

'I don't understand,' Ellie said, understanding too well.

'Oh, you know! She suspects funny business with the boss.'

'What nonsense!' Ellie blushed more deeply. 'The boss is a woman. A Mrs Primrose. She doesn't even like me.'

'Really! Then how did you get the job?'

'I heard there was a vacancy and I marched upstairs with my portfolio. It was just luck. I was on the spot.'

'I suppose they gave you a rise?'

'No, they didn't, but . . .'

'Oh, that accounts for it. They're getting an artist on the cheap.'

Ellie felt again the power of her family to place her at a disadvantage. Wildly, she attempted to defend herself: 'But I don't really work as an artist. I'm not experienced enough, yet. I put on gold-leaf and varnish things.'

'Oh, I *see*.' And Emmy, having reduced Ellie again to inferior status, returned to her talk of Joe.

Ellie comforted herself with the thought of Quintin,

reviewing in her mind the morning when she had first seen him. Mrs Primrose had brought him down to the basement where Ellie worked as a packer. Their voices had preceded them and, as they turned the curve of the stairs, Ellie, looking up at the visitors, met Quintin's large, heavy-lidded, light green eyes and thought: 'This is the man I have always wanted.' Quintin turned to look at her. It seemed to Ellie that their understanding had been like a flash of light between them, yet she could not believe it. It was not possible. She could not be so fortunate.

Mrs Primrose, descending the stairs ahead of him, was aware of none of this. In her very low, small voice, she was saying: 'I knew you would never forgive me if I did not show it first to you.' She walked over to a commode of painted satinwood.

Quintin gave Ellie a half-smile of recognition before he followed Mrs Primrose to the far end of the basement.

Ellie whispered to Dahlia, with whom she worked: 'Who is he?'

'Shareholder,' said Dahlia. 'He's been down before.'

'Isn't he lovely!'

'Not my cup of tea.'

'But mine,' thought Ellie, 'exactly mine,' yet her reason rejected hope until a few evenings later, when she came up from her basement into the sad, autumnal twilight of the mews behind the workrooms and saw Quintin move out from a doorway. At once the sadness passed from the rose-smoky air. She paused, feeling no surprise, as he came towards her.

'Surely,' he said, 'you are the young lady whom I saw the other day bandaging table legs with brown paper?'

'How clever of you to recognise me.'

For a moment he was disconcerted, then he burst out laughing and took her arm: 'Come along,' he said. 'This will be fun. Let's find a taxi and have supper somewhere.'

It seemed they had stepped at once into intimacy; into a relationship that would last for ever. That evening they had laughed more than they had ever done since. Everything she said had entertained him, and she had been inspired by her own power to entertain.

He said: 'What a charming child you are! So fresh and intelligent! What are you doing in that dreary basement? How ever did you get there?'

She had taken the job, she explained, merely to get to London. She had come up on an excursion and gone at once to the Great Marlborough Street labour exchange and said: 'I will take any job you've got,' and this was the first one offered. She had booked a room in a church hostel and returned home to collect her possessions.

'What enterprise!' he said, gazing at her with an admiration that, together with the wine, made her feel more than human.

'But I'm really an artist,' she cried, so that the people at the next table turned to smile. She dropped her voice: 'A painter.'

'Indeed? Then we must get you into the studio. I'll speak to Gem Primrose.'

'Do you mean it?'

'Why not? I'm sure there's a vacancy.'

'How wonderful! Oh, how wonderful!' Her hands trembled; she had to look down at her plate. When she could control her voice, she said: 'I've been to art classes; evening classes at the Eastsea Technical School. They were a bit silly. What do you think they wanted me to do on my first evening? Paint a piece of white paper with the corner turned up. Just think of it! Me, who'd got the drawing prize every year at school!'

'Ludicrous!' Quintin shook with laughter. 'And did they explain this unreasonable request?'

'No. Not a word. They were all too busy getting the full-time students through their exams . . .'

'So what did you do?'

'There was a woman painting a still-life – a fan and a green ginger-jar with cape gooseberries in it – and I said: "Do you mind if I share?" and she said "No." She'd been going there three years and she said mine was better than hers.'

'Good for you.'

'And *then*, I went into the Life Class. I just marched in.'

'No! Really! Didn't the master object?'

'I don't think he even noticed. That place was chaos. The whole time I was there he only spoke to me once.'

'What did he say?' Quintin encouraged her delightedly.

'He said: "You know nothing about anatomy or perspective, you can't even draw, but you've an original view-point and these days sheer audacity can take you far".' Ellie repeated this statement with considerable pride, but added: 'I suppose he was being rude.'

'Perhaps a little rude.' Quintin leant his head back against the crimson plush of the banquette and laughed helplessly. He was holding her hand down on the seat out of sight. He squeezed it ecstatically.

'You are delicious,' he said. 'Delicious.' Then he asked: 'But why did you stay at this school where you learnt nothing?'

'Oh, but it was fun. We all understood one another. We weren't like other people. We all wanted to get away from Eastsea. We were artists.'

'I see. I see,' said Quintin, and he really did see. He had understood at once what Emily and Mrs Parsons and her friends could not understand at all – the wonder of doing the thing that meant most to one.

Remembering this as she walked with Emmy along the Eastsea promenade, Ellie laughed with pleasure to herself. Emmy, who had been observing her, perhaps for some time, said with emphasis: 'I don't know what you've been up to, duckie, but you take my tip – *be careful*!'

They had tea in the drawing-room, where the fire was lit only on Sundays and holidays. Emmy ate in a hurry. She wanted to change before leaving for Joe's house. Mrs Parsons was helping at a party, given by the church, for lonely old people. While the girls were out walking, she had been making cakes. When Ellie looked at the boxes of cakes, she thought: 'How generous she is, yet she cannot be generous to me.'

She said: 'Did Mr Ripley tell you I met him one night in London?'

'Yes,' said Mrs Parsons with sudden anger. 'That was a nice hour for you to be out alone! I don't know what he thought. He's told several people he thinks it shameful, your leaving home like that.'

'But don't you see – it's just that that I can't stand.'

'What can't you stand, I'd like to know?'

'Being criticised by people like Mr Ripley and Miss Bird. I won't have people interfering with my life.'

'Oh, won't you? You're mighty independent, I must

say. Don't forget they're your elders and they know more about the world than you do.'

'They don't.' Ellie too was angry, as she could be only with her mother. 'They don't know anything. They think everything outside their little circle is fake and phoney, but it isn't. It *isn't*. You said the French on menus wasn't real. It is real. It's just that you and Mr Ripley and Miss Bird don't understand things.'

'And you do?' Mrs Parsons enquired with ominous politeness.

'Perhaps not, but I'm *willing* to understand.'

A few months ago Mrs Parsons would have slapped Ellie's face. Now she looked as though she were about to slap it, but she did not do so. She collected together her cake boxes and said: 'You can wash the dishes.'

It was a triumph for Ellie, but a triumph that made her wretched. She realised now that her mother and sister resented not so much her escape as her wish to escape what to them seemed the common lot. They had accepted it; why should not she?

Ellie had the house to herself. When she had washed the dishes, she went up to the bedroom she shared with Emmy and opened her desk. It was a small school-desk. She had annoyed Emmy by keeping it locked during her absence; now she knew she must give it up. Her departure was final.

Inside the desk were the thick 'Page-a-Day' diaries she had kept between the ages of twelve and seventeen. The first was filled by a large, childish hand.

She opened one, written when she was fourteen, and a phrase caught her eyes: 'The strangest day I have ever lived through.' As she read the page and re-lived that summer afternoon at Vezey Park, she felt in herself the excitement of a prophecy. She and Emmy had gone with a school outing to Vezey, a Palladian house, home of a poet who had died young. The teacher said: 'It has been kept just as he left it; as a memorial; you might say, as a shrine.' This had awed the girls into silence for a while, then someone started giggling and the jokes began. Ellie fell back to the end of the crocodile, slipped down a passageway and wandered off on her own. It was, it still was, the strangest day she had lived through. She felt the lie of the house as though she had known it before. She entered alone into the long withdrawing-room and could have described before she looked at it the view from the six long windows. When she heard the others approaching, she ran from them and made her way up a stair that led to the top room in a hexagonal tower. She had not known where she was going until she arrived. When she arrived, it seemed she had known all the time. Here was the poet's bed, canopied in crimson velvet and roped off from the public. In a window alcove overhanging a lake was his writing-table and a book he had left open there a century and a half before. Opposite the bed was a tall-boy. On top of the tall-boy a looking-glass.

She skirted the glass, afraid to see in it her own inadequate face. Yet – if she believed in herself, she must face herself. She crossed the room. In the old, mottled, silvered glass she looked at herself through a silver cloud. She was almost as beautiful as she would have chosen to be. She felt in herself an inheritance no one could take from her, and she whispered: 'What am I? What will I become?'

She had written that in the diary: 'What am I? What will I become?'

It seemed to her, as she put this diary with the rest, that she had always been thrusting past the claims of her everyday life to reach some wonder that awaited her. Now she was upon the perimeter of the great heart of existence – and what awaited her?

She went to bed in a glow of anticipation, so happy she was filled with tenderness towards every living creature.

Lying in bed, she thought of the life her mother had lived for years in this congested little house, ambitious to make the restaurant pay, then to keep up the standard of food and service that had first brought success – these small ambitions made Ellie feel as though something were squeezing her heart. She thought of the house crowded about by the buildings of Eastsea; of Eastsea itself, only one small town among all the cities of this island, an island that was so tiny on the globe. As the word 'globe' came into her mind, the ball of earth shrank to a minim in her imagination and she could see swarming about it the multitudinous stars of the Milky Way that moved like a shoal of silver fish through the black reaches of infinity.

As it touched this point, her consciousness retreated, reducing its scope to smaller and smaller confines until it returned at last to the pin-point of space occupied by this house. She felt it a prison – worse than a prison, an oubliette – and she was beset by an intolerable pity for her mother. No human spirit should be forced to endure such confinement. Her eyes filled with tears.

Next morning, when she went downstairs, Ellie put her arms round her mother to console her. She had forgiven her mother, but her mother had not forgiven her.

'That's all very well,' Mrs Parsons said, moving away

from her daughter's embrace, 'but if you want to please me, you'll come back home where you belong.'

'You know I can't.'

'What do you mean? – I *know* you can't! If I had an accident, if I got ill or broke my leg, you'd have to come back. You'd just *have* to.'

'I wouldn't,' Ellie said under her breath, but she was horribly possessed by a vision of her mother falling down the steep, dark and narrow stair of the house and lying helpless for days, unconscious perhaps, breathing heavily; the restaurant not opened, the milk accumulating on the doorstep, suspicion growing, the police breaking in . . . Emmy would be a married woman and beyond reproach. The disapproval, as usual, would be all for Ellie.

Then she thought this was all nonsense. Her mother employed a girl who came every day. She would give the alarm at once if no one answered the door.

Ellie, believing herself beset every minute she was here, afraid that she might, by some trickery, be constrained to stay, began to feel a panic need to get away. She said: 'I'll have to leave at tea-time.'

Mrs Parsons stared at her as though asking was there to be no limit to her suffering. 'What's the hurry?' she asked. 'You don't start work till tomorrow morning.'

'I know, but I have things to do in London.' Ellie, conscious of the untruth, mumbled miserably.

Mrs Parsons looked threatening, but all she said was: 'Very well, my girl. You do what you like, but we'll see. *We*'ll see.'

When Ellie brought down her suitcase and put on her hat and coat, Mrs Parsons sourly watched her preparations for departure. On an impulse, Ellie flung her arms round her mother's neck and said: 'Don't be so cross, Mum. Don't you want me to be happy?'

'Happy! What's in London to make you happy?' Yet, for a moment, Mrs Parsons's face softened, and Ellie said:

'When I get a rise, I'll send you some money.'

'It's not the money I want. What I want is for you . . .'

'I must hurry. Must go now.' Ellie sped her departure and reached Eastsea station with twenty minutes to spare.

For some reason, she was certain that as soon as she entered the house, the telephone would ring and it would be Quintin. The house was dark and seemed empty. Unable to do anything but listen for the telephone, she lay on her bed beneath her coat and felt cold and hunger. When, at ten o'clock, she gave up hope, she rose and unpacked her bag and found the diaries.

Here was excuse for action. She carried the load of her recorded past down through the silent house. It was raining outside. The fine rain stung her face. She went down to the river parapet and dropped the diaries one by one into the water. The oily light dimples shook and broke over the river surface. The books went through them like stones.

She returned to her room with a sense of achievement and an impatience for what was to come.

4

When Ellie could bear his silence no longer, she telephoned Quintin. She did it one morning at half-past eight.

Quintin, awakened out of sleep, hearing Ellie's voice, felt guilty and irritated. Anyone more experienced than Ellie would have put him out of her mind.

It had not been his intention so soon to end this little affair. Circumstances had forced a conclusion. Somewhere at the back of his mind there was an accusation: he might have accorded her inexperience kinder treatment.

He said: 'Oh, Ellie, my dear, this is too bad, isn't it? I should have rung you days ago.'

Her tone was casual but it struck too high a note: 'I thought I *ought* to ring you in case you were ill.'

'As a matter of fact, I haven't been very well.'

Her voice warmed at once with relief and compassion: 'You didn't look well when I saw you last – at the station. Have you had "flu"?'

'Not "flu" exactly. I had some trouble with my lungs a few years ago. I have to go carefully sometimes.' That was true enough.

She cried out in alarm: 'But why didn't you let me come and see you? I could have nursed you.'

'How kind, my dear. The housekeeper was in and out.

She takes care of me. But when shall I see you? Are you free on Saturday?'

'Oh yes. Quite free.'

Quintin suspected that Ellie was always free. He had said to her once: 'It is so refreshing to find someone who can accept a last-minute invitation.' He had intended applause but she had seemed hurt, so now he said: 'How fortunate. Where can we meet? I've been thinking it is ages since I was last in Regents Park. Shall we take a stroll there? Would it be fun?'

'I think so. I've heard of Regents Park.'

'You have not been there? How delicious! How really delicious to be a young person seeing everything for the first time!'

'I suppose it is.'

'Well, let's start quite early. Could you manage two-thirty?'

'Yes, easily.'

He arranged to meet her at Baker Street Tube station, then he prepared to sleep again. He was unwilling to face the day. Petta was still in the flat, installed in the small spare room he used as a dressing-room. He disliked dressing and undressing in his bedroom. The dressing-room gave him space, and a degree of freedom with his clothes which he could not permit himself in his bedroom. The guest he occasionally put up for a night or two seemed to him nuisance enough; Petta's sojourn was intolerable. He avoided her as best he could. When he came face to face with her, his nerves tensed with the unspoken question: 'Why don't you go away?' but he said nothing. No doubt she thought she had defeated him.

Temporarily, she had.

The afternoon he had seen Ellie off at the station, he had returned to his flat to find Petta still on the sofa. She was asleep. The sight of her had infuriated him. This, he thought, was how she kept her promise to go. He called her; she did not move. When he shook her, her head lolled lifelessly. Then he noticed the empty pill-box on the table. At once he had felt the same fear he had known when she stepped in front of the speeding bus.

He called Mrs Trimmer upstairs and rang for his doctor. The doctor had arrived with his partner and together they had set about reviving Petta. They had (he now thought) been remarkably quick and successful. Opening her eyes and gazing up at him with an air of tragic simplicity, she had said before the lot of them: 'Darling, forgive me. It was Christmas . . . I was so alone' – voice breaking – 'I . . . I had nowhere to go.' She broke down and wept. In embarrassment, he had looked round at the audience and met the full glare of Mrs Trimmer's reproachful eyes. The doctors were trying to look like men of the world. One of them said:

'Mrs Bellot should not be moved for a day or two. This sort of thing is a strain on the heart.'

Quintin said: 'She could stay here, but there's no one to look after her.'

'Oh, I'll look after the poor dear,' said Mrs Trimmer.

'Very well.' Quintin was almost too angry to speak.

So Petta had stayed. Mrs Trimmer, behaving like an accomplice, had gone off in a taxi to fetch the luggage from Theo's flat while Petta, at the telephone, rang round their acquaintances. 'Here I am back again. Do come in for a drink some time,' she kept saying, speaking as though she had just returned from a holiday.

Several days had passed before Mrs Trimmer, giving the flat its weekly 'turn out', found a crumbling pink tablet pushed down behind the sofa seat. When she slid her fingers in further, she found a dozen more. Quintin had gathered all the pieces into an envelope and taken them to Petta, who was in bed. She opened her eyes wide and said: 'My tablets! Where did you find them?'

'I thought you had swallowed them.'

'I took six; that's a fatal dose.'

'Not for an addict. Why did you hide the others?'

'I don't know. I don't think I did hide them. They must have fallen out of the box.'

'Well, there they are. You may need them again.'

He left her, determined to have nothing more to say to her. He existed now in a state of obstinate reservation of himself. He was determined – if Petta did not go, he would. He was already planning his escape, but meanwhile he had to settle this affair with Ellie. He suffered the irritation of frustration. He had been reminded of Ellie's ardour and youth. He knew, if the relationship could not continue to its natural conclusion, he was liable for some time to be pestered with regrets for her.

Besides, he did not want to hurt the poor girl. He simply could not now carry on an affair with any girl who had not a flat of her own.

What reason could he give Ellie for the break-up? The truth was too crude. Besides, she had accepted him on the understanding that he had been abandoned by his wife. Her conscience might come between them if she were told his wife had returned. Or, if it did not, she, being young and innocent – the youngest, indeed, of many 'little girls' – might plead that to see him was pleasure enough for her, not realising there could be only one right, true end to expensive suppers in Soho.

At the thought of his predicament, he could have caught Petta by the shoulders and run her out and flung her luggage after her. When that fury passed, he reflected that only a silly, inexperienced girl like Ellie would instal herself in a boarding-house where all comings and goings were noted. Still, he liked her silliness; he loved her inexperience. He even thought of providing her with a flat – but the rent of a furnished flat these days! The cost of premium and furniture for an unfurnished one! Out of the question.

No, he would have to put her off with vague excuses. He could say the separation was temporary. If she had any sense, she would let it go at that.

He felt that, as a sort of parting gift, he should do something for the girl. Her chief need was money. It occurred to him he could get her a rise in salary. He could not do much else. He was one of those unfortunates who were being taxed out of existence; he lived on a bare minimum; he was not in a position to give anything to anyone. But he was dining with Gem Primrose that night and he might put in a word for Ellie.

As soon as this idea took hold on him, he tried to free himself from it. He had suffered enough for his folly in promising Ellie her present job. At first Gem had simply refused to consider the girl at all. Quintin moved uncomfortably as he remembered that passage with Gem. It was a memory of ignominy.

He had brought the matter up after he and Gem had dined extremely well at the Caprice. He asked her back to his flat; he had something to show her. There, with casual confidence, he had produced Ellie's untidy portfolio, saying: 'I've found you an artist – and a very charming child she is.'

Gem took the portfolio without enthusiasm. She surprised him by the gravity with which she examined the water-colour scribbles inside it.

It was clear she suspected his interest in Ellie – but did that matter? She had always said the last thing she expected from him was fidelity. It was a joke between them. She said she knew him inside and out. He had supposed she would give the girl's paint-splashes a glance, then say: 'All right, you old roué, I'll take her to please you.'

Not a bit of it. Her small, vulpine face had had the expression of someone not to be sold something she did not want. As she picked up the sheets of paper, her only comment had been an occasional click of disapproval. He felt her antagonism strongly. Perhaps he had been unwise. He had promised Ellie the job as lightly as he might have promised her a visit to a cinema.

When she put down the last of the paintings, Gem drew in her breath sharply and looked at the bundle with narrowed eyes. She said at last: 'This girl can't draw.'

Quintin had to make an effort to consider Ellie's work as seriously as Gem did. He said: 'She's not much of a draughtsman, agreed. But her work has something – freshness and colour! Don't you think? Take that fruit piece. It is dark and rich. She's looked at Gauguin and learnt something.'

'It's crude, slapdash stuff. It's not what we want. If we take on another artist, we must have someone with a knowledge of period.'

'She'd soon pick that up.' Unfortunately he could not

54

keep from his tone his contempt for Gem's ideas of 'Regency', 'Georgian', 'Empire' and all the rest of it.

Gem lifted her eyebrows a little; paused reflectively, then said firmly: 'No, Quintin, I don't think she'll do.'

He had felt that nervous drop in spirits that made persistence impossible. He said nothing more that night; but he had promised Ellie the job. How could he leave her to think his promises meant nothing?

He invited Gem out to dinner again a few evenings later. She asked him to call for her at her office. When he arrived, no doubt knowing what was in his mind, she handed him a cartoon of cupids pulling a load of flowers.

'That is nice work,' she said. 'That's the sort of thing we want.'

'It's one of the Pompeii murals.'

Taken off her guard, she protested: 'Bertie Hawkins did it. He's one of our best artists.'

'He must have found it in some book on Pompeii.'

'How clever of him.' She put the cartoon out of sight.

They went to the Ivy. When he judged her mellowed by a few glasses of vintage burgundy, he put his hand over her hand and said coaxingly:

'Give the girl a trial.'

She answered soberly: 'It's like this, Quintin. It would be unwise to take her from her present job. It's a difficult job to fill, so she's likely to keep it. If she failed in the studio, there might not be anything else to offer her. She'd be out of work.'

She spoke sense. He had been a fool. He refilled their glasses, then said humbly: 'I'm sorry, my dear; I'm afraid I promised that girl a job in the studio. If I have to tell her it's no go, I shall look pretty small.'

'I see.' Gem looked as though she did not like what she saw.

'Don't misunderstand me . . .'

'I don't misunderstand you. I have never pretended to have any illusions about you. As you wish it, I'll give the girl a trial – but don't blame me if I can't keep her. Now, for goodness sake, let us talk of something more amusing.'

In that way Ellie had got her job. She was absurdly happy in it; so happy, indeed, that he was sometimes annoyed that all this happiness had been bought at his expense. Why, therefore, had he given himself the painful task of cadging her a rise?

These reflections ruined his luncheon, made his afternoon a purgatory, and sent him to the Primroses' Green Street house in a state of anxious vexation. Berthold was on a business trip to the States. He and Gem dined alone. His appetite was ruined by the unspoken plea for Ellie sticking in his throat.

He felt guilty towards the girl. She had been a virgin. She had simply opened her arms to him. She had asked for nothing. He had been touched by her poverty and courage.

He was a humane man; emotional, even sentimental – or so he believed. If he were wealthy he would delight in making lavish gifts. But the feel of money sickened him. Beggars often roused his pity, but stronger than pity was his unwillingness to bring money into the open, to hand over to another human being some degradingly small sum. Money, it seemed to him, soiled any relationship it touched. Had Petta not had her private fortune, no persuasion could have made him marry her. Her financial independence had seemed to him an earnest of the marriage. A foolish idea, but his own. He could not change.

While these thoughts circulated vaguely through his mind, he was suddenly jerked into activity by one that put all the others out of sight. A plea for Ellie would prove to Gem that the girl was getting no financial assistance from him. With the Ellie affair coming to an end, he would be more dependent on Gem. He had better restore her confidence in him.

He blurted out: 'You know that child, Ellie Parsons – the one in the studio? She's still getting only what she got in the packing department. You probably did not realise. I think she's having a pretty thin time.'

Gem frowned slightly, but spoke with her usual cool reasonableness: 'I don't suppose she's dependent on her salary. She must get an allowance from home.'

'Not a penny.'

'But the studio salaries *are* small. It's understood. It's a luxury department. We like to get people who have a little private money.'

'She has nothing.'

'What about her family?'

'Her mother's a widow – runs some sort of little business on the south coast.'

'Doesn't she want the girl at home?'

'Clamours for her, I believe; but Miss Parsons wants to live her own life. She came here all on her own, and here she means to stay. She's determined to be an independent, wage-earning woman. One must admire her spirit.'

'She'd be better at home. And safer.'

Quintin smiled through it all. Beaten, still he rallied her: 'Let's say a ten-bob rise?'

'I'm afraid not. The firm cannot be expected to subsidise Miss Parsons's independence.'

'She does a tough job – all that "antiquing" as you call it. Labourer's work; though, God knows, the poor child imagines she's an artist. She's in the seventh heaven about working in a studio.'

Gem said coolly: 'No doubt she will get a rise as soon as she proves she's worth it.' He recognised that definitive note. Argument would get him nowhere. He looked at Gem with bleak admiration.

Well, he had done what he could. He had no parting gift with which to soften the blow for Ellie. By Saturday morning, the thought of meeting her at all had become agony to him.

It was a cold, colourless day. He awoke bad-tempered, scarcely able to contemplate that walk in Regents Park. He would have put it off, but knew it must, sooner or later, be faced.

Thinking of Ellie's youth and her delight in that arduous underpaid job in Gem's ridiculous studio, he knew himself young no longer. Was there anything that could pluck him up before he was lost for ever in the slough of increasing age?

Voices came from the sitting-room. Petta was talking to Mrs Trimmer. He imagined they were gossiping about him. Mrs Trimmer adored 'Madam'. Quintin made no protest. He had never encouraged Mrs Trimmer to talk. She was well paid but he did not trust her. He believed she cheated him on the household bills. With some satisfaction he told himself that when he made his 'get-away' and 'Madam' had to take herself off, Mrs Trimmer would look far before she found another victim as uncomplaining as he.

He had breakfast, bathed, dressed and went out. As he left the house he heard a woman's voice call 'Deena.' This was answered by the excited, shrill barking of a dog. He stood on the top step, pretending to search his pockets while the woman passed. An apricot poodle bounced about her as though on rubber feet. She gave Quintin a half-glance and laughed, ostensibly at the dog. She snapped her fingers. The dog bounced joyfully. Quintin smiled, knowing for whom all this was intended. He had seen her half-a-dozen times before. They had almost reached the point of speech, yet neither spoke. As he descended the steps, he looked after her. She was a tall woman, hatless, wrapped in a white coat of heavy wool. She had the sort of legs that could launch even a plain woman on an international career of mink and diamonds. Despite the simplicity of her dress, everything about her, the smooth bloom of her skin, the lint-pale hair severely dressed, the shoes of white lizard skin, gave off a scent of luxury. This caught at him oddly. He had grown up in a world where the insignia of money had meant a great deal. Even his grandfather, his mother's father, the master of Chudleigh Park, had married his daughters to money. First-generation money at that. The girls, Rose and Jasmin, had been too plain, too overshadowed by their lovely mother, to attract the attention of established fortunes. They had been sacrificed to the upkeep of Chudleigh. Both had died young.

Quintin's father, the son of a builder, had been a natural money-maker. He once told Quintin that by buying and selling real estate he had banked ten thousand pounds before he was twenty-one.

'It won't be far short of a million, lad, when it reaches you,' he said, but it had been a long way short of a million. The instinct that guided him, almost a second-sight, left him overnight. In the last few months of his life he lost more than he had made in the previous twenty years. On his deathbed he told Quintin: 'You'll have about two thousand a year. Not much – but I started with five pounds in the Post Office Savings. You've nothing to complain about.'

When he came to look through the bundles of dead investments, Quintin thought: 'And I've nothing to rejoice about either.'

Now, gazing after the blonde girl, who had paused to put her dog on a lead, he thought: 'I am poor.' Never before had he so regretted the fortune that had failed to come to him.

The girl went on into the grey-shadowed park; the red dog-lead danced; the dog leapt forward. The silver-gilt head and the white coat shone through the wintry half-light.

'A silken girl,' he said to himself. 'A voluptuous girl, a delicious girl . . .' He laughed at himself as she faded away from him.

The desolation of his old sobriety had gone in a moment. Petta was forgotten.

A few yards down the road, he mounted the steps of a house identical with the one in which he lived, but where his house displayed a row of new bell-pushes, each named differently, here there were only two old-fashioned bell-pulls. He pulled the one marked 'Visitors'.

The door was opened by a man-servant who greeted Quintin with deferential friendliness. Lady Wheeldon was at home. Quintin indicated he could find his own way up to the drawing-room. The man acknowledged this saving of his legs and time as he might have acknowledged a ten-shilling note.

Following the fine curve of the mahogany staircase, Quintin smiled to himself because he was once again surrounded by an ordered life. This house reminded him of his father's house in Montagu Square. Of course, when he was young he had thought nothing of Montagu Square. He used to complain that it lacked *chic*. He despised the Edwardian splendours of his father's establishment, he hated living so far from Mayfair, he envied the 'new poverty' of his friends. Now poverty, new or old, depressed him. He was nostalgic for the past.

When he reached the panelled landing, he glanced about at all this woodwork and wondered how many tins of furniture polish it consumed a week. Mrs Trimmer had a heavy hand with furniture polish. He sighed. There had once been a time when he had never heard of it. He could not doubt his own degeneration.

Alma's drawing-room occupied the whole of the first floor. It was painted green, the mouldings heavily plastered with gold-leaf, the whole rather shabby. She frequently apologised for it, saying she could not face the reorganisation of life required before the house could be redecorated. Over the chimney-piece hung a large Sickert portrait of the late George Wheeldon. It was glazed. Quintin looked into it to see the reflection of his own face, a face that had never entirely satisfied him. His full lower lip protruded beyond the upper one. His eyes, light-coloured and heavy-lidded, gave him the arrogant look of one of those Restoration fops painted by Kneller. Secretly, he thought he resembled the second George Villiers.

It was not until he smiled at himself that he could see the look of benevolence that was, he believed, one of his chief attractions. Women trusted him. He smiled again, and turned, smiling, as the door clicked – but it was not Alma; the door, which he had left ajar, had fallen to; he was still alone.

He walked round the room, observing its condition closely. He supposed it would cost a fortune to replace the gold-leaf. Alma, he suspected, could not bear to part with it, but it would have to go. The woodwork could be stripped to reduce the ponderousness of the chimney-piece and lighten the room. As for the walls? A chalky blue, he thought; rather dark. That would mean dispensing with the purple brocade curtains, the dark Empire Aubusson, and the furniture, ebonised and inlaid with brass, that he found both oppressive and trivial . . .

He paused on the words, with no time to withdraw them before they applied themselves to Alma herself. She had entered, looking a little flustered. Her mornings, it seemed, were occupied with disagreements between the servants whom, Quintin believed, he could, if they were his, control with a word.

She said: 'It's Bettina again.'

He took her hands and laughed at her, saying: 'You are a delicious silly to agitate yourself over such trifles.'

She flushed slightly and looked down: 'Dear Quintin, things are so much easier for you men. I relied on George for everything. I imagined I could not live without him, yet here I am! – left to fend for myself. And I thought you had deserted me, too. It is nearly three weeks since your last visit.'

'Yes,' he nodded; his smile died. Alma gave a little murmur of alarm:

'Something has happened? Do sit down . . . first, let me pour you some sherry, then tell me what is the matter.'

She was a large woman, Teutonic in appearance and heavy in her movements. She was only a few years senior to Quintin but gave the impression of belonging to an older generation.

'Now?' she said when Quintin was comfortably settled in an arm-chair with his drink.

He said: 'Petta has returned.'

'Oh!' Her first reaction was dismay – and not on his behalf; but this she covered so rapidly with an appearance of decent sympathy that he might, had he not been alert, have missed it. She added quickly, her breathing irregular:

'You must forgive her, Quintin dear.'

'Forgive her!' he laughed, ironical and weary. 'The question of forgiveness has not come up. She simply returned and installed herself in my dressing-room. The flat does not accommodate two people very well.'

'No, indeed. But surely she . . . surely . . .' Alma fluttered with curiosity, but her upbringing had denied her the power of the direct question.

Quintin said: 'I know I can confide in you, my dear.'

Alma pinked a little at this, his first use of an endearment, but her expression did not change. She held herself controlled and sensible, nodding occasional sympathy, as he told the story of Petta's return. He let the circumstances alone lay blame where it should lie. He told of the attempt at suicide on Westminster Bridge; her invasion of his flat; her promise to leave; the second suicide attempt with the sleeping-tablets. Only by the tolerance of his tone and one or two muted gestures did he reveal the element of blackmail.

'Then you do not think she intended . . . ?' Alma paused. She had been shocked, it seemed, at the intention, but now was more shocked at the lack of it.

Quintin said: 'She is terrified of death. Positively neurotic about it. If she has a tooth out, she fights like a tiger against the anaesthetic. That shows a deep-rooted dread of extinction.'

Alma nodded sagely, then, after a pause, moved on to securer ground: 'Poor Petta, she must feel her position keenly. Do let me arrange a little dinner-party – just to restore her *amour propre*! We might go out somewhere.'

Quintin jerked up his head. Was it possible that Alma really saw herself as a sort of Wildean heroine championing a fallen woman in a public place? Apparently so.

'Just the three of us,' she went on, 'but, no – I shall ask old Tom Claypole. You remember him? He was married to your mother's sister, Rose – such a nice girl. So tragic! She died only eight months after the marriage; he never married again. Since I mentioned to him that you have moved into a flat near here, he has asked me several times to arrange a meeting. He says he remembers you when you were a schoolboy: he thought you charming.'

Quintin laughed: 'Could I have been a charming schoolboy? It seems improbable.'

He was content now to leave the business of Petta. He had said enough. Alma was scarcely yet in a position to say more. He put it behind them by talking – surprisingly, it must have seemed to her – of his boyhood. He spoke simply, with sincerity. The time had come, he decided, to replace the pleasing but detached charm of the Quintin who had visited here when he had nothing better to do, with a new Quintin – one who could feel, who would seem to her to be within reach.

'Claypole! I only met him once – a dark, ugly, little fellow in a motoring cap. He drove about in an enormous, open Rolls. My grandmother said to my mother: "That car seems to me fast in more senses than one." My mother and I were spending the holidays at Chudleigh when Tom Claypole turned up. He was courting Aunt Rose. Poor Aunt Rose, she'd just come out of a sanatorium. She should never have married. I suppose you still remember Chudleigh?'

'Of course.' Alma smiled, looking, Quintin thought, a little like the housekeeper whose superiority stems from the 'quality' she has served.

Introducing these memories of Chudleigh, he was well aware of the value of that bond between them. He had met Alma first at Chudleigh. She had been a neighbour's daughter; a stout, good-hearted girl whom his grandmother had been pleased to patronise. There had always been a number of these girls fetching and carrying for his beautiful grandmother, most of them younger than the daughters of the house. They played tennis, strummed on the pianoforte, danced with the male visitors, and formed a little court round her. She identified herself not with her plain, dull daughters, but with a younger generation of girls, some of whom had been lovely. She had found husbands for them all.

Quintin had been much petted by the girls. He was the only member of the family who had inherited his grand-mother's looks.

Alma said: 'It seemed a great house to us, you know. I was delighted to be one of the knowledgeable ones when there was talk about Chudleigh. I never tired of describing your grandmother's famous azaleas, and the orchid house, the vinery, the stables, the electric brougham . . . They ran that electric brougham years after everyone else had cars. I thought it terribly distin-guished. We had only a dog-cart at home. I remember when George . . .'

Quintin had no intention of letting the conversation leave Chudleigh. As soon as Alma had finished her story about George and the dog-cart, he said: 'All grandfather's show, of course, was based on very little. Chudleigh was a sort of inverted iceberg – nothing below water.' Now he held the Chudleigh memoirs well centred, talking with a good-humoured melancholy of changed times and changed people. He, he said, was always afraid that one day he might not be able to pay his way – but his grand-parents! They believed no one should expect them to pay for anything. Their only fear was that some scrap of their privilege might be brushed off them by the shoulders of the encroaching mob. Quintin recalled the time when the son of the head gardener won a scholarship to Harrow. His grandfather had raged at them all through luncheon. What made things worse was that the boy was no ordin-ary 'swot'; he had a genius for games. (He later became a Rugger Blue.)

'Grandfather said: "We'll have the fellow coming to the front door and asking if Master Quintin can come

66

out to bowl for him." I would willingly have gone out to bowl for him, but I was not invited.'

The boy had to keep out of sight of the house for fear the master's anger should be turned on him. Quintin had thought his grandfather's behaviour monstrous, but now he understood it. It came of fear, a fully justified fear. 'A little air was entering the tomb,' said Quintin.

Alma looked bewildered. He laughed. 'You've heard of the body of Agamemnon, that kept its structure for centuries, then, when a little air entered the tomb, crumbled into dust?'

Alma made a movement that suggested such references were too lofty for her, then said in dismay: 'But your grandfather was a darling. I adored him.'

'So did I. When he was dying I was sent for; the only male relative. I remember, as I left the train, I said to the station-master: "My grandfather is dying", and I was bitterly hurt that the man showed no emotion. In one's school reading, the lower orders always sobbed at the death of the old master.'

Alma looked solemn: 'Thank goodness your grandmother never lived to see such changes. She would have broken her heart when Chudleigh was sold up.'

'No doubt, but my father was thankful to get Chudleigh off his hands. He'd been keeping the show going for years. He paid all grandfather's debts, and grandfather despised him. Poor father, I don't think he got much return on that marriage.'

'Quintin!' Alma was shocked, yet her eyes shone in admiration of his frankness.

Quintin smiled, then, suddenly leaning towards her, he pressed his hand down on her large, pale, soft, warm hand, and said: 'Dear Alma! Only you and I share these memories now,' and added, speaking carelessly as though scarcely aware of the implications of what he said: 'I sometimes think that the thing that makes for true understanding and happiness in a relationship is similarity of background.'

Alma blushed. Her neck – not a young neck – dyed as deeply as her face. In her confusion she said: 'Of course old Tom Claypole must remember Chudleigh, too.'

Quintin ignored that. Enough of Chudleigh for now. He said: 'Petta, you know, comes from one of those broken-down Irish families that used to live in castles yet couldn't afford sugar for their tea. I don't know what would have become of her if an emigrant uncle had not left her some money. I remember a story she told me – how she and her cousin got themselves up for a ball on the flagship when the fleet put in at Cork. The girls were invited and hadn't a rag between them. They were determined to go. What do you think they did? They took down the drawing-room curtains and made themselves dresses. They had no pretty shoes, so they bought gold paint from Woolworth's and painted right over their old shoes and stockings. Petta was eighteen. The belle of the ball.'

'She must have been exquisite. Indeed, she still is. I'm sure that means a great deal to you.'

Quintin made a sad little movement of denial. He sighed, then rose to take his departure. Alma crossed the room with him. As she went ahead, he watched her heavy face, her bulky waist and thighs, appearing and disappearing in one looking-glass after another.

When she turned at the door, he lifted both her hands and pressed his lips softly into the soft flesh. 'For me,' he said, 'you will always be part of Chudleigh. Nothing means more than that.'

5

Ellie, during the days that separated her from Saturday, suffered an excitement that was near anxiety. Had she believed she had anything to fear, she could not have suffered more. She kept assuring herself she had nothing to fear. Quintin had not rung her because he was ill. When she rang him, he had at once suggested their meeting.

Yet she could neither eat nor sleep. She realised her attitude to life was changing. She was no longer a girl with everything to hope for, but a young woman with something to lose. If she lost Quintin, then all would be lost. London, that she had thought a miracle before she met him, would be, without him, nothing but a wilderness.

For the first time in her life she looked back in envy of the past. She remembered, a few days after her arrival, sitting in a bus in a traffic jam and hearing an old man stamp his foot and cry to the conductor in desperate tones: 'Get on, can't you! Get on.' No one had shown surprise. Only Ellie had looked at him, unable to understand why anyone should so much care whether the bus moved or not.

She said to herself: 'When I came to London, I was so happy, nothing could worry me; and now I worry for no reason at all.'

Looking back to that time of innocence, not five months past, it seemed to her she had been enchanted. Life had been like one of those dreams of flying when one need never touch the ground. Now her feet seemed weighted. She passed feverishly, yet with extreme slowness, through the no-man's-land of intervening time. When Saturday came she felt suddenly intoxicated. At mid-day she pirouetted across the studio floor.

'Bless us,' said Denis, the Studio Manager, 'look at the girl. Her cheeks are like roses.'

She came to a stop in front of him and said: 'Darling Denis, can I go now?'

'Why not?'

She rushed back to her lodging to have a bath and change. She had not been able to have a bath all week. An absurd old woman, a newcomer to the house, had, apparently, taken leave of her wits. Ellie had seen her once – a little, elderly woman in a yellow kimono, descending the stairs as though she feared she might be seized by a dangerous animal. Early each evening this woman would lock herself in the bathroom and the house would become full of the sound of cisterns emptying themselves. Once Ellie, hoping for a bath, had stood outside the door and heard the water pouring away, the precious hot water, enough for two or three baths: and when the woman at last burst from the bathroom and fled, all the hot taps ran cold.

Soon there were complaints from the lodgers. Mrs Mackie spoke severely to the new tenant, then went round tapping the doors and saying she did not think there would be 'any more trouble'. The water had been hot on Friday evening, but Ellie had not been one of the lucky ones who got into the bathroom. Surely on Saturday morning, when everyone was out shopping, surely the bathroom would be free!

When she reached the first landing she heard the scurrying steps of the old woman in the dark bathroom passage, the click of the bolt, then the furious rush of water. In the bitterness of her disappointment, she sped to the basement stairs and called down: 'Mrs Mackie. Please, Mrs Mackie, that woman is wasting the water again.'

Mrs Mackie had never shown friendliness to Ellie, but in this matter she was an ally. Her short, round, flat-footed body raged up the stairs. She shook the bathroom door until the lock broke. When the door fell open, Ellie could hear above the rush of water the old woman's gasp of horror at discovery. Mrs Mackie turned the water off. There was sudden silence. She said harshly: 'At it again! Didn't I tell you all the lodgers are complaining!'

The woman said timidly: 'But there was plenty of hot water last night.'

'But not the night before, or all the week; and there's precious little now.'

Ellie, suddenly ashamed of her part in the matter, went to the upper landing so that she need not see the old woman come out. Mrs Mackie called up to her: 'You can use the bathroom now, Miss Parsons.'

Ellie said: 'I'm sorry about all that.'

Mrs Mackie nodded her acceptance of this apology. 'She'll have to go,' she said, 'I found out from the milkman she's been turned out of half the houses in the street. And what do you think she was doing in there? Just washing an old coat-hanger under the tap. Proper

looney. Oh, I said to her: "You get out of here tomorrow,"
I said.'

The bath-water was luke-warm. Ellie, who had a cold,
gave up the thought of a bath and washed in her room.
The incident had so menaced her that, even at the distance
of her youth, she felt the threat of lonely, maniac old age.
She went out depressed. It was as though anticipation had
worn out her excitement and left her too tired to feel at
all.

6

When, at Baker Street station, Quintin found Ellie by the bookstall, she was wiping her nose. She looked as though she had wiped off most of her powder; her nostrils were pink and shiny, her cheeks waxen. Why, if she had a cold, did she not ring and put off this wretched excursion? She looked plain, thin and shabby. Her manner, too, had changed. She had lost the confidence of her old happiness and seemed apprehensive. She greeted him with a nervous accusation: 'You're late. I've been waiting ages.'

He looked at his watch: 'You must have been early, my dear. I'm only a couple of minutes late.'

They walked up to the park gates without speaking. It was the dead heart of the winter. The flower beds were empty, the trees naked. The wind's edge was hard and gritty. What a day, he thought, to be dragged out for a walk! – then he noticed that over the water there was a wild circling of wings.

'What's the excitement? Oh, the lake is frozen—' his interest was roused – 'I had not realised it was cold enough.'

They stood among the group feeding the birds. Above them the air flashed with the wheeling gulls. 'This is fun! Isn't it fun?' He turned, laughing, to Ellie. She smiled, but it was not much of a smile. He could not think what was wrong with the girl.

Ellie felt herself inadequate to this occasion. She knew her inadequacy was separating her from Quintin but she could not overcome it. Her attraction had failed. She felt ugly. She could think of nothing to say. Even the sight of the birds did not rouse her. She was doing her best to reflect Quintin's enthusiasm but knew she carried no conviction.

Quintin now seemed to be enjoying himself. 'Here,' he said to a very small boy, 'that bit's too big, you know. Let me break it up.' He broke up the bread and fitted the pieces back into hands that could scarcely bend for their woolly thickness of gloves. 'Now then, throw it,' and the small boy parted his hands and let the pieces fall on to a pair of violet-throated pigeons pecking at his feet. The pigeons scattered indignantly. Quintin threw back his head and laughed.

'How nice he is!' thought Ellie. 'How wonderful to have a father like that!'

Quintin, meeting her longing eyes, caught her hand. 'Come along,' he said. 'You look cold.' As he felt her fingers stiff and frozen inside her cotton gloves, he said: 'My dear child, really!'

For the first time he noticed the cottony look of her coat, the thinness of her high-heeled shoes that were dark round the welts as though wet. 'You girls are so silly. You think more about looking smart than keeping warm. That's almost a summer coat. Come on, now, step out briskly or we'll be having you laid up.'

As they stepped briskly along the ice edge, Ellie's spirit rose because Quintin had said '*we*'ll have you laid up,' and she began to imagine herself ill and Quintin visiting her and assuring her her job would be kept for her.

Quintin broke into her thoughts, saying: 'If you were a wise girl you would spend more on food and clothing. You could save by getting a cheaper room.'

'It's the cheapest room in the house.'

'I dare say, but you could go to a different district. Why not look around World's End? There you could get a bigger room for less money, and . . .' he was about to add 'and have more freedom', but he left the thought unspoken.

She had no reply. She knew the room took too much of her income, but the atmosphere of the house and road had reassured her when she arrived. She had looked in cheaper districts and had been frightened by them. She imagined they must be those haunts of strange sins so often mentioned by the Baptist preachers. She felt safe in Oakley Street.

Her silence increased Quintin's irritation with her. Neither had anything to say. As they passed round the lake, the park, that before had seemed sombre beneath the grey weight of sky, now revealed itself in delicate vistas the colour of a moonstone. Ellie noticed on her left-hand buildings that were cupolaed, pillared, balconied and decked with statues that seemed about to take flight from the cornices. She caught her breath at them: 'But are they houses? Do people really live in them?'

Quintin gave them a critical glance. 'Yes, houses. They are much admired, but don't you think they are a little sensational?'

'No.' Ellie came suddenly alive. 'No, I like them.'

'Ah!' Quintin bowed in ironical deference to her opinion and Ellie, bursting into laughter, felt their relationship somewhat restored. She took his arm. He squeezed her hand and now they walked closely against the cold.

Beyond the island, where the lake stretched wide and light, there was a great gathering of birds. The ice was the colour of a fish's eye. In its thickness were held plane leaves and twigs, with here and there a bullet-star of cracks or a white cockle-shaped air-pocket. On the surface walked gulls and mallards and ducks with flame-golden breasts. Among these smaller fowl, awkwardly, like over-grown adolescents at a children's party, were swans that kept peering down, beak-tip to ice, as though puzzling over the disappearance of the water.

Someone had pulled a bough out across the lake. It stood in the midst of all this activity, light-coloured like a root thrown up from a submerged forest, enormous, tangled and unreal in the ice-grey air.

Under the shelter of the island was a patch of water kept fluid by the activity of the birds that crowded it like children in a paddling pool. From there the ducks managed to take off, cutting a way among the other birds, rising and whirring round, then landing dexterously, brak-ing their passage with upturned feet.

On all this Quintin commented delightedly as though he had not been so entertained for years. But beyond the lake the atmosphere darkened and grew heavy, dissolving the shapes of things in a fog that seemed a concentration of cold. Quintin retired into himself. He walked with his hands in his pockets, his shoulders contracted, as though he were shuddering into his heavy overcoat, chin down, collar up, guarding his chest against the cold. Ellie, feel-ing him withdrawn from her, let her hand slip from his arm: he did not notice its going.

When they crossed the bridge and emerged from trees into the open spaces beyond, the wind came howling at them. Ellie shivered, painfully cramped with cold – but more painful to her was the sense of Quintin's withdrawal. He frowned and kept his brows raised at the same time, looking angry, as though, were she to mention the cold, he might blame her because he suffered it.

In the open there was still a bleak, pewtery daylight. People, dark, merged yet shifting, stood round a playing-field. Here and there the red of football jerseys stood out oddly from the foggy light. There were shouts as a goal was scored. Ellie would have liked to stop, but Quintin pressed on, skirting the crowd widely and frowning down at the grass churned into mud.

'Too many people,' he said. 'Too many everywhere. The only hope for this island would be to export half the population.'

'Export them?' Ellie, hearing this theory for the first time, was astonished by it, 'Where to?'

'Plenty of room in Australia, for instance.'

She considered this for a long time, unable to accept the idea that some people, thrust out of their native land like birds from an overcrowded nest, should be sent to fend for themselves in strange lands. 'But who would be the ones to go?' she asked at last, and added daringly: 'Probably me. Perhaps you.' She smiled to show she meant no harm, but he did not smile.

He had intended pointing out to her the fantasy shapes of the Mappin Terraces, but now they had almost disappeared. He was in no mood to elucidate them. He let them pass without a word.

Half-stunned by the wind, they reached the other side

of the park. Coming into Camden Town, finding the shops open, the world busy and brilliant, he said again: 'What fun!' and, looking at Ellie with compassionate amusement, added: 'You know, I never gave you a Christmas present! I'll get something here.'

Ellie, surprised, protested: 'Oh, no, why should you?'

'But there must be something you would like – just as a keepsake.'

She surveyed her needs, too bewildered by them to catch the word 'keepsake'. 'I do need some face-powder,' she said.

'Face-powder? You shall have face-powder.' He caught her arm and guided her into a little chemist's shop: 'Face-powder,' he commanded the girl behind the counter. The girl tilted her chin, prepared to take offence, then recognising something in Quintin's expression and manner, the corners of her lips sank down in a provocative smile. Her shoulders twitched; she spread her ringed left hand effectively on her bosom. 'What colah?' she asked.

'Peach. Light peach.' Ellie could scarcely speak, stabbed as she was by the realisation that Quintin was smiling at this girl just as he smiled at her. She swallowed in her throat and grew hot. When Quintin handed the open boxes to her, she took them with agitated hands. The cheapest box was three shillings and sixpence; the dearest, fifteen shillings.

'Heavens above, fifteen shillings!' Quintin made a face, the girl giggled. 'Fifteen shillings for face-powder! What's the difference?'

'The expensive one has a lovely perfume,' said the girl.

'Is that all? Here, we'll take this.' Without consulting Ellie, he picked out a box that cost six shillings. As the

79

girl wrapped it, she gave Ellie a side-long glance of appraisal, then returned her eyes to Quintin with a look that seemed to say, given time and opportunity, she could make better use of him.

As they made their way to the main road, Ellie faced the fact that she had been jealous. She had not only been jealous, she had had reason to be. This knowledge widened her concept of Quintin. He did not exist only on the occasions of their meetings, but at other times he moved about in a world unknown to her, a world full of dangerous other women. She was caught suddenly in a fear that one of these women might desire and seize him from her, a fear so acutely real that she forgot he was there, walking beside her. She imagined him already lost. She felt relief when he reminded her of his presence by saying:

'I've heard there's a street market here: barrows and naphtha flares – the sort of things painters like. I must show you.' But when they turned into the main road no market was in sight. Quintin lost interest in it. He guided her into a tea-shop. Pushing between the packed, untidy tables, he smiled back at her, delighted by this novel contact with life. 'Isn't this amusing?' he said, glancing round at faces that were unamused: 'Isn't it?' he insisted on Ellie's agreeing.

Ellie, breathing in the stale, steamy smell of tea and clothes, the familiar under-smell of watery vegetables, said: 'Yes,' but Quintin was not satisfied. 'Perhaps you would rather go somewhere else?'

'Oh no. This is quite all right.'

They had to share a table with two other people. Quintin studied the menu: 'Very reasonable,' he said.

'Now, you must make a good tea. How about toast and jam and fruit-cake?'

'Oh, I won't want so much if we're having supper later.'

He looked a little startled. 'Didn't I tell you, my dear . . . ? I'm so sorry, but I'm afraid I shall have to leave at six. How stupid of me not to warn you. You'll have an empty evening.'

'It doesn't matter. I don't suppose I would've been doing anything, anyway.' She smiled brightly in the face of her empty evening.

Quintin put the thought of it from him in an instant. 'Good heavens,' he said, 'I haven't seen you since Christmas. And how was your mother?'

'Quite well, thank you.'

'Wanting you to return home?'

'Yes.'

'You know . . . you may be forced to do so in the end, my dear.' Quintin spoke lightly and reasonably.

Ellie stared at him: 'To go back to Eastsea?'

'Yes. This is no life for a girl, up here alone. You'd be better at home, and safer.'

Ellie was aghast. Her lips trembled: her face took on a damp pallor. She looked betrayed, yet unable to believe betrayal possible. Quintin turned uneasily away: 'What future have you here?' he asked.

'You think I'm going to get the sack?'

Annoyed by her intense apprehension, he said impatiently: 'No, no, of course not.'

It came to her that he was indeed advising her to return, for no reason, simply to return as though she were an escaped prisoner whose spirit had failed. Feeling insulted, she flushed and said: 'I shall never go back. I'd rather die.'

Her vehemence disturbed him: 'My dear child,' he protested, 'after all – one's home is one's home.'

She looked down at her plate and said nothing. She had attracted the attention of the other people at the table, but only Quintin was aware of that. He felt aggrieved, as though by obstinately staying in London she were placing him under an obligation to assist her. He knew himself unreasonable. When the silence became uncomfortable, he tried to make manageable conversation by asking gently: 'What is it you find so trying about your mother?'

Ellie swallowed some tea and made an effort to recover herself. She mumbled: 'I don't know. All sorts of things.' Contemplating the situation at this distance, she could think of nothing she could put into words. She tried to catch at something he would understand: 'She . . . she'd never let you choose anything for yourself – or, rather, you never got a chance. She'd buy things she didn't want and then make you have them. "Look what a lovely . . ." – oh, some beastly dress or coat or something – "I've got for you," she would say, and when you said: "Oh, mum, why did you?" she'd say: "Is that all the thanks I get for spending my hard-earned cash on you?" I've never had a proper party-dress. For years I had to wear a navy marocain she got at a sale for herself. It was too small for her and she made me have it. All the other girls had proper dresses and I had that dreadful marocain. They called me "Orphan Annie" and no one would dance with me.'

Quintin threw back his head and shook with laughter. What a long, mournful recital! With tears of laughter in

82

his eyes, he patted her hand and said: 'Oh, come! Don't look so tragic. I'm sure you'd find a partner whatever you wore.'

Ellie knew better. Quintin began to look bored. He felt her humourless and complaining. This was the night of Alma's dinner-party. He became restless, looking for the waitress. He would have to go, and still he had not told Ellie that this meeting must be the last.

Outside in the street, he said: 'I'll have to take a taxi. I'll drop you off somewhere, if you like. Can't take you all the way, I'm afraid.'

'Oh no,' she said in panic at the thought of an evening in her room, 'I don't want to go back now. I'd like to walk part of the way.'

'Supposing I drop you at Leicester Square Tube station?'

Looking for a cab, Quintin became irritable. He had lost interest in this seedy, cab-less district. They were almost at Cobden's statue before one came along. He said to the man: 'I'm in a hurry.'

When they reached Charing Cross Road, Quintin said to Ellie: 'I'm afraid, my dear, I won't be able to see you again,' then as Ellie turned her stunned face towards him he added: 'I mean, not for some time.'

'But, why?'

'Some family trouble. It would take too long to explain. Besides, I haven't been well – not really well. I'm thinking of going abroad. I'm sorry.' He took her hand: she let it lie in his, lifeless, as though some terrible sentence had been passed on her. He gave it a squeeze, rallying her, and let it drop. 'I'll ring you some time.'

'When?'

'Oh . . .' Looking away from her, he told himself he

must not deceive her. 'It's hard to say. Probably not for . . . well, for several months.'

'Several *months*?'

The taxi drew up to the kerb, but she sat still, looking at him, her eyes desolate. He glanced at his watch and said apologetically: 'I'm afraid I must hurry. I have to dress before going out.'

'I'm sorry.' She descended from the taxi. 'Which way do I go?'

'Why, down there, then straight on.' He gave a laugh at her ignorance, and she laughed too. 'That's better,' he said. 'Good-bye, my dear. One day we'll meet again.'

'Good-bye.'

He leant back into his corner. The taxi went on. When it was out of sight, she crossed the road and passed into the crowd that moved resplendent with light beneath the canopies of theatres and cinemas. She had never walked here at night before. She went unnoticed among a surge of people who seemed all to be companioned, mirthful and pressing towards pleasure.

Well, she had her job. She had only to exist until Monday and it would save her. She began to hurry, as though by hurrying she could speed time. Above the noise of the crowd, the noise of traffic came in a sharp-edged rattle. Beyond the cinemas, she passed windows lit with silver light, each wide and compelling as a cinema screen, drawing an audience that stood and gazed silently on giant boxes of chocolates, on green, pink and yellow fondants, on toys that moved, a boar's head covered with gelatine, grapes large as plums, an orchid in a transparent box . . .

She stopped with the rest and gazed and thought of

Quintin at his party. He had not said he was going to a party, but she supposed he must be. A cocktail party. She had never herself been to one, but she had heard of cocktail parties. She knew all about them. She was well-read in fiction borrowed from public libraries. At cocktail parties witty persons, gorgeously dressed, talked to one another in the manner of Aldous Huxley's characters. The party she visualised for Quintin was full of women, yet none was as real, or as dangerous, as that girl had been in the Camden Town chemist's shop. They were at a disadvantage in her mind because her mother and her mother's friends so often condemned them, saying: 'It's all those cocktails they drink that's the ruin of them.'

Her eyes upon the orchid in the plastic box, Ellie felt an overwhelming longing to be with young, happy, cocktail-drinking people. She felt that only a thin glass wall of not-knowing separated her from a world of such people. If she could break through it, her life would be changed.

She glanced about her as though the means of breaking into life were at hand. Some young people were pushing in through the swing-doors of the restaurant. On an impulse she followed them as though she were with them. They ran down a marble staircase beneath a sign that said 'Grill Room'. She dared not follow, but stood in the marble hall wondering how she had come there. She had imagined there would be warmth and a luxurious cushioning of sound within, but, instead, the confusion of the street had entered like the fog. Under hard, white lights, crowds of people wandered about the closed food counters. A man in a uniform was shouting directions: 'The café, the cafeteria, the Blue Room, the Pink . . .' She felt a trespasser. She had no excuse for eating again. She had had toast for tea.

She left. Ahead, a congregation of lights jerked and ran and showered out stars more dazzling than sunlight. She reached Piccadilly Circus. Here she passed a number of young men ranged against the shops. None looked at her. Some were staring avidly at passers-by as though searching for a lost friend, the rest were blankly looking at nothing. Their bodies seemed flattened back from the crowd by indifference. In the over-brilliant light their faces, gleaming sickly, seemed weary of every aspect of life. Ellie wondered what kept them there in the cold.

Beyond the lights of the Circus, there were other loiterers. Women, this time. She had heard about them. They lolled at street corners, alone or in pairs, taking the air as though it were summer. They did not glance at her. She looked at them almost enviously. They knew nothing of solitude.

Now that the crowds and lights were left behind, she suddenly began to shiver with the cold. She had been cold all day, yet it was only now she became conscious of it. It was as though the cold had turned and attacked her, and, however fast she walked, it held to her. She realised it was mid-winter.

During her weeks with Quintin she had lived, it seemed, like the 'Snow Queen' girl, in a garden where it was always summer. Now she was shut out from the summer garden of love.

'My fault,' she said.

All female gossip, all advice given in women's magazines, made it clear that a woman thrown over had only herself to blame.

She said: 'Stop feeling sorry for yourself.' After all, she was no worse off than she had been when she first arrived. She had known no one – but her solitude had had a difference. Then, as she walked about the streets alone, she walked an adventurer. The massive stone façades of the West End, shut and darkening with evening, the crowds pushing their way home, the mysterious impersonality of this city – all those had been part of the challenge she had accepted by coming here. Now there was no mystery. London seemed empty as a mausoleum.

Even Quintin did not want her here. He saw no future for her. He, of all people, had said: 'You'd be better at home, and safer.'

'Yet, I'm staying here.'

She remembered the morning after her day-trip to London – her announcement to her mother and Emmy that she had found a job in London. They had been dumbfounded. She had been braced to fight against her mother's commands and appeals. When Mrs Parsons spoke, she said only:

'I give her six months.'

'I don't.' Emmy seemed the more indignant of the two. 'I don't give her two weeks. You wait. Living in a cubicle, filthy food, no money, no friends, no fun – she'll soon be sick of it.'

'And what about her painting? All those evenings wasted at the Technical College! What's it led to, after all? A job tying up parcels.'

Ellie said: 'When I find a room, I'll start painting again.'

'A room!' Emmy shouted. 'What sort of room will you get on your screw? London isn't Eastsea, you know.'

'She'll starve herself,' said Mrs Parsons. 'When she has

a breakdown, she'll come back here expecting to be nursed. As if I haven't enough to do.'

'I won't come back!' said Ellie.

She crossed the road. She would have been glad to walk till midnight, but she had walked as far as she could. Her feet hurt; her legs felt weak as rubber. When, at the Ritz, a Chelsea bus stopped beside her, she had not the will to reject it. She decided to save money and expend more time walking from Sloane Square.

At Sloane Square, a young man left the bus behind her and, trotting at her side, murmured hoarsely: 'In a hurry, aren't you? Mind if I come along?'

At any other time she would have ignored him. Now she glanced round as though someone were offering her happiness.

'Can't very well stop me, can you?' said the young man. He gave a laugh that was dramatically sardonic. Ellie, jolted out of her gloom, told herself she must behave as though nothing could disconcert her. She enquired, with the self-conscious 'charm' of a hostess, what was the young man's profession.

He was a clerk at Covent Garden market.

How interesting! And did he enjoy his work?

He supposed so.

Where did he live?

At Walham Green.

And was he very lonely?

Not particularly.

He replied with increasing reluctance and suspicion. 'What is all this, anyway?' he asked.

'Nothing. I was just wondering.'

'You don't live with your folk, do you?'

'No. I have a room in a boarding-house.'

They turned into Oakley Street. He looked about him: 'Where are you making for? Battersea?'

'No. I live here. It was so kind of you to see me home.' Ellie held out her hand in its cotton glove. She felt she had carried things off very well, but the young man was not so easily dismissed.

'Here! You're going to let me come up for a bit, aren't you?'

'Up to my room? Of course not.'

'Oh, go on. Just for a bit.'

'It's impossible. Besides, the housekeeper wouldn't allow it.'

'What's it got to do with her? I'd soon tell her off if she stuck her mug in.'

An unpleasantness Ellie had felt all the time in him now came undisguised to the surface. Slightly sick, Ellie said with the hauteur of fear: 'It's out of the question.'

'Why did you drag me down here, then?'

'I didn't drag you. You said I couldn't stop you.' She had been fumbling blindly in her bag for her key; at last it met her fingers; she ran up the steps.

'You little slut!' The young man spoke venomously.

Heavens, suppose he made a scene! Ellie got the door open and in terror slammed it behind her.

In her room, she stared into her glass, certain some tragical change must have come upon her as a result of that day, but she saw no change. She did not look a minute older.

She said: 'Oh, Quintin!' But the sense of the young man remained like a poisonous taste in the mouth. She washed herself and cleaned her teeth. The young man slowly faded away. The thought of Quintin remained.

She sat on the end of her bed and brushed her hair and gazed mournfully at its colour in the glass. One of the Eastsea art students had said to her: 'I've mixed and I've mixed, but I can't mix a red like that.' On an impulse she took out her scissors and cut off the lock that hung beside her cheek. It lay, the colour of rosewood, like a question-mark on her hand. She put it into an envelope and next morning posted it to Quintin. She thought it would plead for her. Days passed. There was no reply.

7

After his parting with Ellie, Quintin returned to his flat. As he passed the open door of his dressing-room, that was now Petta's bedroom, the clothes thrown from the wardrobe, the ransacked drawers, the litter of shoes, told him his wife had already changed for the evening. This was the usual disorder she created about her. He frowned, acutely irritated.

He found her lying on the sitting-room sofa. She was in black. Her narrow dress, of heavy silk, was cut to mould the lower half of her bosom and reveal the upper. She had veiled her neck and shoulders with a transparent, sequined scarf.

He could tell at once from her pose, from the height of her heels, the extreme style of her little hat, the number of jewels she was wearing, that she was in one of those exalted moods he found so trying. As he crossed to the fire, she stretched out an imperious arm and said: 'You're late! Where have you been?'

'I thought we were supposed to dress?'

'No. Alma rang to say the Claypole man was driving up early on business, so he'll be in his "natty lounge".'

Quintin frowned again. The break with Ellie had left him dissatisfied. He knew he had treated the poor child shabbily – and all because of Petta, whom he found unendurable. He warmed his hands. As he was about to go to his room, she said: 'Do get ready,' restless because she was ready herself.

He paused, picked up the evening paper and leafed slowly through it. Petta held her impatience in check. She asked: 'What's Alma's idea – giving this dinner-party?'

He was silent behind the paper for several minutes before he said: 'Heaven knows. It will almost certainly be a bore. I don't want to see Tom Claypole again, and one never gets much of a meal in a big hotel.'

'Poor Alma! Now George's dead, she's no doubt going the pace.'

'No doubt.'

He threw down the paper. As he was about to take himself off, she said in a pleading tone: 'Quintin.'

He turned to look at her. She leant forward from the sofa and, catching his hand, persuaded him towards her.

Unwillingly, with misgiving, he let her pull him down until he had no choice but to sit on the edge of the sofa. She gazed at him, her eyes damp and tender, and putting her arms about him she tried to draw him down to her. The scarf slid from her shoulders. As his head approached her, he gazed into the white flesh of her bosom and saw it crinkle slightly where it had lost elasticity. He jerked away from her, saying: 'We're already late.' Her hands dropped: she let him go.

When he had lain for ten minutes in a hot bath, his tranquillity was restored. He dressed in a leisurely way, crossing to his glass and adjusting carefully every garment he put on. Petta called him, a long-drawn petulance in her voice. Mildly he answered her: 'All right. Ring for a taxi.'

At the hotel they found Alma and Tom Claypole sitting in one of the small withdrawing-rooms that were set in alcoves slightly above the main hall. She greeted the Bellots with mock severity: 'How naughty you are! Tom is driving into Hertfordshire tonight and keeps, he tells me, a régime of early bed-times.'

Quintin turned to Claypole with a contrite smile: 'How can I excuse myself?' attempting by his manner to distract attention from the fact he had no excuse to give. 'I am delighted to see you again. How many years have passed since you came down to Chudleigh in that remarkable car, the envy of my boyhood. Was it a "Silver Ghost"?'

'It was.'

Claypole spoke with satisfaction, yet a stiffness remained in his manner. When Quintin started to speak again, he smiled coldly and, looking away to where a dozen or so girls in ball dresses were ascending the main stair, he said: 'Charming! Quite charming!'

'There's a debutantes' party upstairs,' said Alma; she sighed: 'Girls dress so prettily these days, don't you think?'

'They do indeed.' As Claypole watched them, the tip of his tongue touched his lower lip. When they passed out of sight he glanced away and, catching Quintin's eyes on him, he drew down the corners of his lips. The two men understood one another, but Quintin might not yet regard himself as forgiven. Claypole first gave his attention to Petta, who had been standing a little apart.

In the indirect lighting of the hall, she looked no more than twenty-five. Quintin, watching the pair of them, supposed that to Claypole she must seem adorably feminine and alluring. The old, dark, heavily folded face melted with admiration. The black, monkey-like eyes became fixed, brilliant, acutely aware that here was no ordinary beauty.

He said: 'No wonder your husband has made so little response to my overtures. He has been keeping us apart. He wants you all to himself.'

Petta smiled vaguely.

Quintin remembered that the old boy had been regarded as something of a lady-killer in poor Aunt Rose's day. Many years must have passed since Claypole made his last kill. Anyway, Petta was in no mood to play up to him. She lifted her smile to the regions above his head and said to Alma: 'I think I'll leave my coat in the cloakroom.' The women went off.

Claypole raised his eyebrows, stuck out his lower lip and, catching Quintin's sympathetic amusement, smiled and shrugged his shoulders. The men were now in accord. They strolled towards the door of the dining-room.

Quintin returned to the topic – the safe topic – of Chudleigh. Claypole was now willing to respond. Had he been asked why he cared what impression he made on this elderly member of his own sex, he would not have known. He charmed from a habit of charming he had inherited from his grandmother. He imagined every creature he met had, up to a point, of course, a claim upon his comity.

'Those were delightful days at Chudleigh.'

'They will not come again.' Claypole gave Quintin a quick, oblique glance, then said: 'Dear me, how quickly time has passed!'

At the dining-room door they turned to wait for the women, who could now be seen crossing the hall towards them. Beside Petta, Alma looked an Amazon. Once out of her daytime uniform of tweed skirt, cashmere jersey and pearls, she seemed not to know what to wear. She had on a Dior model that would have taxed the looks of a professional beauty of twenty. She was almost grotesque. Her hair was thick, strong and unmanageable. Her petticoat dipped a little at one side. She could never keep her shoulder straps out of sight. Yet her negligence was more pleasing to him than the elegance he shared with Petta. He had, as his father had had, a pernickety sense of order in dress that he despised. Indeed, extreme elegance in women was repellent to him, invariably turning his thoughts to the mortal end of the flesh beneath.

Alma arrived at the dining-room, to be greeted as though she were a minor royalty. She leant towards the head waiter, speaking confidently of her reserved table and, moving in his protective shade, led her party across the room to a table opposite the door.

'Very nice,' she murmured, with a grieved glance at the waiter, who knew, as Quintin also knew, she preferred one of the secluded corner tables, all now occupied. The party glanced through the menu, subdued by Alma's hurt feelings. She recovered when the first two courses were safely ordered. She was a flustered but generous hostess. Old George Wheeldon, self-styled gourmet, had kept her in training. She did less well with the wine waiter. The earliest date, the highest price! And something of everything. What on earth were they in for? The eyes of the two men met in mutual apprehension. Claypole smiled and looked away.

Catching the smile, Alma felt the men to be in accord and she turned invitingly to Petta, but Petta remained remote. All Alma's efforts could produce from her no more than a delayed, vague nod or shake of the head, or that smile that was the smile of sibyl Petta, mystic-minded Petta, Petta who contemplated higher things. 'For God's sake,' Quintin wanted to say, 'forget about her.' Soon Alma did forget about her. While Petta sat on the fringe of their consciousness, picking at her food, Alma attached herself, an unassuming listener, to the men's talk.

Their conversation was more intimate than was usual between persons so slightly acquainted. Taking advantage of the fact that they were, by marriage, uncle and nephew, Tom Claypole was heading with tactful determination towards a subject that must have tantalised him for years – the failure of Quintin's father. Quintin did nothing to deflect or direct enquiries. He was amused by the devious methods of Quintin's generation. He let the old fellow recall Edwardian financiers, their fortunes and their tragedies, and when the air was full of speculation, vast wealth and curious failure, Claypole said, apropos as it were: 'I knew your father quite well in the old days. It was he who introduced me to your aunt.'

'Indeed!'

'After her death, I'm afraid I broke away from many old friends. I did not care to be reminded of past happiness.' Claypole spoke down at his plate, then, lifting his face that suddenly revealed itself as afflicted and unsure, he said: 'We were never intimate, but I remembered always that I was indebted to him. There was nothing I would not have done for him. Had he called on me . . . at the end, I mean . . . I would have made every effort.'

The sincerity of his intention brought Quintin to speech: 'I do not think anyone could have done much.'

Claypole, his moment of emotion past, cocked a black

eye, eager, yet discreet. 'Could he not have been . . . um
. . . ah . . . restrained?'

'I suppose he could, had anyone realised what was
happening, but he always had been, as you know, a law
unto himself. And it all happened so quickly. There was
no indication of any abnormality in his behaviour. Indeed,
one could not say he became abnormal – he became
normal. He lost money as I would probably lose it if I
suddenly started investing right and left. His genius, or
magic, or whatever it was, simply ceased to function.'

'Magic?'

'It seemed like magic. One of his executors said to me:
"I was always convinced your father could see into the
future."'

'Bless my soul!' Claypole contemplated the suggestion
of magic with a surprised and slightly contemptuous
amusement such as a senior wrangler might display
towards the antics of a counting boy. Quintin nodded in
sympathy. He, also, had no taste for the ebullients of life
– the eccentric, the neurotic, the outlandishly gifted. He
knew his satisfaction at an adverse judgement on his father
resulted from a certain guilt. He awaited the enquiry that
would hold embedded the accusation that, had he given
any attention to his father's affairs, he might have been
the one to save the family fortune. No enquiry came.
Claypole probably knew from experience that the sons of
his wealthy business acquaintances seldom had a taste for
money-making.

Quintin remembered with some irritation his father's
pompous, often-repeated exhortation: 'Apply yourself to
the nature of money and its reproduction.' His irritation
showed him to be still on the defensive. Years ago, when

girls at parties had teased him with their party gambit: 'Tell me all about your work. I'm so interested,' he would reply: 'I am a dilettante.' (It was at one of those parties he had overheard himself being described as 'a young man waiting for a fortune'.) Well, dilettantism had gone out of fashion about the time he had learnt that the fortune had ceased to exist. Then it was too late to start again. He had lingered on as a man of taste without the means to indulge it. He said now, accounting for himself unasked:

'I am interested in antique furniture. Occasionally make a find, but the best stuff takes some looking for, these days. Not long ago I sold some Charvels and put the money into a small interior-decorating business. A one-woman business, you might call it. Just for fun.'

At the word 'fun', Claypole's eyes lit up. Fun, eh? Quintin smiled agreement.

The waiter was refilling the glasses. Quintin lifted his to Alma: 'A really excellent hock.'

'Indeed, yes. Um, ah! Oestricher Lenchen Auslese 1934.' He spoke lingeringly, a lover of the German language. He turned to Quintin: 'Your father kept a good cellar.'

'Yes. Auctioned off with the house and other stuff. I had nowhere to put it.' He smiled ruefully, allying himself with those who had taken the brunt of things. 'Nowadays we keep half-a-dozen bottles in the kitchen cupboard.'

Claypole did not laugh: he took the situation seriously. 'We old parties,' he said, 'we can live off our fat – but you youngsters, you've never had a chance to accumulate any: mulcted from the moment you started earning.' He looked concerned, but at the same time he shifted his backside easily in his seat, aware he had had the best of it. No 'very heaven' these days!

Quintin lowered his heavy eyelids over his eyes and spoke modestly: 'I can't complain. The worst I had to suffer was a spell at the War House. It's true there's income tax . . .' He made a little move of the hand, amused and uncomplaining.

At the words 'income tax', Alma joined the conversation with a plaint on behalf of those who lived on unearned income and who, in her opinion, paid both for the subsidies of the workers and the allowances of the businessmen. 'Thousands for entertainment and travel and cars and so on. I said to my accountant, Jack Bramley: "I entertain as much as anyone. Why can't I claim expenses?" and he said: "The trouble is, you don't entertain the right people." Of course he was laughing at me, but . . .'

The men smiled gallantly, letting Alma have her say.

They were between courses. The Romanée '37 was about to appear. Let us hope, Quintin thought, it is not as time-withered as that antique hock.

Petta lent back in her chair, her eyes glazed, her nerves on edge with a surfeit of boredom. The men had been dull enough: Alma's chatter seemed to her unendurably tedious. She had been a fool to let Quintin accept this invitation on her behalf. The fact was that she had, during her months with Theo, forgotten how boring Quintin's friends could be. Especially Alma. Alma seemed to her the epitome of female stupidity; a woman so stupid she did not even know she was stupid, probably did not even notice the glazed look her chatter brought down on her listeners. Yet she had been adored by her husband, who had left her all his money, most of it locked away safe and sound in a Swiss bank. Alma spent half of each year on the continent recouping from the rigours of English life.

Alma had some crumbs of bread on her lips. Petta, watching them move as she talked, thought: 'There she sits showing all she dares of her great shoulders and breasts, imagining like a contented cat that heaven sends her saucers of cream in recognition of her immaculate merit.' Was she as complacent as she seemed? Petta could remember some time in the late '40s, when labour troubles had displaced the war in common comment, Alma, staying at an expensive seaside hotel, had sighingly confided to the chambermaid how sad she thought it that wicked men should sow dissension between class and class. The chambermaid, an old woman, had said: 'We've got nothing against your sort, m'lady. It's them middle-classes we can't stomach.' Alma had told that story around as triumphant proof of how the rich were loved.

Petta, watching the blunted and uncertain movements of Alma's large hands, listening to the conciliatory tone of her voice when she spoke to the waiter, noting the relief with which she returned to her friends, wondered if she did in fact believe in the unquestioning good-will of those that served her. Or was this 'niceness' a defence against the possible revolt of the insecure and the uncomfortable?

She turned her regard on Quintin, who was leaning back, smiling, accepting all that came to him as he had accepted it ever since he was born. Who could be more charming than Quintin? Having made no effort either to make his money or secure it, having, indeed, made no effort either on his own or anyone else's behalf during his whole life, there he was – a survival, a rare bird, a gentleman of leisure.

'I believe in responsibility, of course,' said Alma. 'George always said you can't have rights without responsibilities, but, really, when you find yourself supporting *everybody*, company directors included . . .'

At that moment the wine waiter slid round the table and, bending over Alma, discreetly recommended a change in the vintage of the Château d'Yquem that was to come on next. Apparently they were at the end of their curiosity vintage, a '29; he was pressing on her the '42 or '45.

'Oh dear!' Alma's soft-tipped fingers fluttered on her bosom. She glanced from the waiter to her male guests, seeking their confirmation of his advice, but they had taken the opportunity to regain the conversation and were not to be distracted from it. She glanced about her helplessly. She would have got rid of the man if she could, but he was determined to make her appreciate his care of her.

'Very well, the '42,' she said unhappily, plunging on the earlier date.

Petta dropped her chin to hide her smile. Alma and her lot had not even the courage of their money. There wasn't an ounce of turbulent nobility among the lot of them. They wanted to be not only privileged but loved. They wanted to be King Baby. They were to be bathed, powdered, dressed, fed, cosseted, set up in their perambulators, and then admired. And why? Just for their own sweet sakes.

And Claypole? He had no illusions about himself, of course. He just wanted to climb into the perambulator and be King Baby too. He would defend his privileges with a difference; he had earned them.

As for herself – she saw herself as apart, yet not apart.

She had known genuine poverty. Because she was experienced, she was not afraid to venture out beyond the confines of comfort. The world outside was a known world. If anyone spat at her, she could spit back.

In her boredom, thinking of the outer world, she began to feel restless, as though adventure awaited her elsewhere. The men were back on that blasted house again – Chudleigh! What a name!

Claypole enquired what had become of it.

'It no longer exists,' said Quintin sombrely. 'It was taken over for some secret work during the war. One night – when all the local fire-engines had been called to the Bath raid – the whole place went up in smoke. No one knows what happened. Anyway, Chudleigh was burnt to the ground.'

'A satisfactory conclusion!' murmured Petta.

Ignoring this, the two men shook their heads. 'What a tragedy!' said old Claypole. One might suppose that Chudleigh had nurtured both of them. In fact, Quintin had gone there occasionally during school holidays, while Claypole had put in a brief appearance as the husband of a plain, despised daughter of the house. Petta reflected how fashionable it was to attach oneself to some relic of old decency, some fantasy with which to outface the shabby present.

Quintin sighed: 'And so nothing remains but our memories.' He glanced round to include Claypole and Alma; not Petta. Petta had never seen Chudleigh. She was not in on this.

He said: 'I am not one of those fortunate people who think in pictures, but, at times, there flashes into my mind, just for a second, the corner of a room, or the rose-bowl that stood on my grandmother's writing-desk, or the damasked pattern of the yellow silk curtains in the drawing-room . . .'

These memories (that Quintin, for some reason known only to himself, was protracting beyond all reason) seemed footling to Petta. She had half a mind to break in with a farcical description of her own family house, but so deeply entrenched in boredom was she, she could not make the effort to speak. After a conducted tour of house and grounds ('Let us do your appreciation for you'!), Quintin had paused to mourn over an old Russian leather writing-case that had belonged to his grandfather and which he now kept like a scent-sachet at the bottom of his handkerchief drawer. Cuir Russe. The manly scent.

'. . . a faded plum-pink: worn out now, but of that perfect workmanship he demanded in everything. Whenever I open the drawer and catch that musky smell, I am returned to my grandfather's study. A flash of memory. Everything is there. If I could only hold it long enough, I could even read the names on the books: but each year it is a little more difficult to recall them.' He again sighed. '*Timor mortis conturbat me.*'

At this, Alma flung herself back into the conversation, scattering Quintin's pleasantries as a porpoise might scatter a play of flying-fish.

'Time!' she exclaimed as though the word itself were a witticism, 'The other day I met Juliet Duff's girl – Quintin, you remember Juliet? She's about your age. Now this girl of hers is a woman, a grown-up person!' She looked round for their astonishment and, meeting none, explained: 'This girl was born in 1935. Think of it! When we were in our heyday. Doesn't it make one fear one will never be young again?'

Petta raised an eyebrow at the inclusive 'we'.

Claypole, noticing Petta's expression, opened his lips with a waggish smile, but Quintin got in a second before him:

'I won't pretend, my dear, that we are young.' He gave Alma's hand a pat. 'But women like you and Petta here—' he smiled at Petta, not excluding her this time – 'women like you have nothing to fear. There is a sort of beauty that ends only in the grave. You will always receive homage. But for us men, alas—' he glanced amusedly at Claypole, whose eyes between their wrinkled lids, aware and admiring, glittered like jet – 'our virility is our happiness. When we lose that, what is left to us? Nothing but an occasional mood of complacency when we see in the future no immediate cause for anxiety.'

'Oh dear!' Not realising she was meant to smile, Alma looked concerned.

Quintin responded seriously, with the tenderness of an old friend: 'There are consolations. People, seeing the marks of age upon one another, begin to pity where they used to envy, and so are drawn together.'

Alma looked at Quintin with damp wonder. Claypole nodded in sympathy.

Petta thought: 'This old man is no fool, yet Quintin has fooled him.' Seeing Quintin and seeing through him, she felt a pang of possessive love for him. She looked away, not willing to recognise that their life was what it was.

Quintin, his hand still covering Alma's hand, thought of the girl born in 1935. He smiled into himself because the birth-date of Ellie, who adored him, was even more recent than that: 'And not the last of my little girls! Not the last, by any means.'

Alma gave Petta a worried glance, then twitched her fingers underneath Quintin's hand. He took his hand away. Petta seemed to notice nothing.

A waiter came to inform Alma that Mr Claypole's chauffeur, in accordance with Mr Claypole's instructions, wished to inform Mr Claypole that they should be on their way. Claypole began at once to get to his feet.

'Oh, no, no, no!' Alma touched his arm. 'You must have coffee first.'

'I never drink coffee.'

'Brandy, then, or a liqueur: or some of this excellent . . .'

'No, no,' Claypole seemed suddenly on edge, as though beset by anxieties. He disengaged himself rather irritably from Alma's hold and stood up. 'I would rather start back now. It's a longish drive. I make a point of being in bed before midnight.'

'A very good habit,' said Quintin, seeing Claypole was intent on going.

'Doctor's orders.' Claypole smiled an elderly, tetchy smile that warned them not to detain him.

'Dear me, then, of course . . .' breathed Alma.

Claypole said his goodnights, with a special salute for Quintin, and made his departure. Before he could be quite out of ear-shot, Quintin said: 'Really delightful, seeing him again.' When Claypole had passed out of the room, he added: 'I suppose he takes good care of himself.'

'Poor dear,' said Alma. 'He's not a young man. He's been a widower for nearly forty years. I often wonder why he never married again. I suppose he was devoted to his Rose.'

'And who, do you think, will come in for all that money when he dies?'

Alma laughed nervously, disconcerted by this direct question yet beaming at Quintin who asked it. She giggled and tried to copy his daring:

'Who knows. Maybe he has some little milliner or seamstress tucked away in a bye-street.'

Petta stared at her. When she decided Alma had spoken seriously, she tried to catch Quintin's eye, but Quintin would not let it be caught. What was he up to now? In the past he had been ready enough to make fun of Alma. Those had been the days when Alma had tried to make a friend of Petta, and Petta, impatient of her archness and idiocy, had discouraged her. Alma had been no easy woman to discourage. Invitations had been forgotten, excuses given had been inadequate, apologies casual, yet Alma had taken no offence. She owed so much to Quintin's family, and only he remained to be rewarded.

Quintin, who had always declared the Wheeldons were ridiculous, was now devoting himself to Alma. Why? Petta watched him touching Alma's hand, gazing into her face, talking directly at her while his eyes watched, his voice held that emotional note he could emulate so perfectly. She had seen this act often enough before, but never performed for a plain woman of fifty odd. Petta began to believe his behaviour was a deliberate attempt to torment her.

And there was that ass, Alma, taking it all seriously: looking pink, confused, excited: giving Quintin warning glances, withdrawing her fingers, but lingeringly, from the amorous touch!

Really! It was Alma's caution, rather than Quintin's incaution, that maddened Petta. She saw no reason why she should endure it. They were supposed to be returning, for a 'night-cap', to Alma's house. Well, not Petta. She would make her escape somehow, and Quintin would be left to carry on his act without an audience.

She rose and announced: 'I'm going to the loo.'

'Oh, shall I . . . er . . . would you like me . . .' Alma fumbled around for her bag.

'Don't bother. I'll go alone.'

Crossing the enormous Aubusson carpet, beneath the glitter of chandeliers, Petta moved with the elation of pure anger. In this mood she felt, as she could so seldom feel, freedom from all restraining fears, especially the fear of solitude. She was self-sufficient, as independent of the world as a disembodied spirit. She ran up the stairs like a girl. On the upper floor she was caught up among other girls, the young and delicious creatures who had drawn Claypole's eyes earlier in the evening. They seemed to be everywhere. They crowded the cloak-room. The air was heavy with the scent of their flowers and powder and young, warm bodies. Ball dresses fluted and swayed about them like the skirts of a *corps-de-ballet*.

A whisper of laughter moved among them like electricity in the air. Petta caught their excitement. By the door a girl was re-arranging gardenias in the dark hair of a friend. Passing them, Petta smiled and they smiled back, eagerly yet shyly. Petta looked round, smiling, at the smoothly curved, rose-petal youth of all these faces. Her own face seemed to her reflected in theirs, a white rose among pink roses. As the skirts parted to give her space beneath the make-up lights over the dressing-tables, she moved forward confidently, unprepared. As she met herself emerging from among the petal-smooth girls, her smile went. Flushed and moist from the heat of the room, she seemed to have grown old in a moment.

Her face shocked her. It had an appalling pathos. She looked round at the girls as though there might be explanation of this change in her. They showed no surprise. She was a middle-aged woman. They accepted her age, just as they accepted their own youth.

She slapped her puff over her face, trying to obliterate it with powder. Lifting her chin, she gave herself a brief glance through half-closed lids, then left the glass. No more smiles for the girls. She collected her coat and went.

Out in the street, the cold air astringent on her cheeks, she began to recover. The heat, of course, had puffed her skin. She was herself again.

She walked down St James's Street and wandered into the Mall. The blackness of the sky seemed to hang like a canopy just above the street-lamps. Rain, fine as a web, began to fall aslant the car lights. It blurred the pink surface of the Mall: the cars cut ribbons upon it, and soon all was glistening with damp. Her self-sufficiency faltered in the cold and lonely dark. She did not know where to go. She might not be at home among the limited, retrogressive possessors of unearned money, but was she at home anywhere else?

There were no pedestrians in the Mall. Only the indifferent traffic moved. Beneath the trees, she was alone. The Palace, in a blear of light, looked untenanted, all blinds drawn.

As, in this solitude, her old desolation came down on her, she was troubled by a memory that had often recurred since that night before the war when, the centre of a party of friends, she had gone to the Chelsea Arts Ball. It was the usual crowded, noisy occasion, when you might glimpse a person on the floor or in a passageway and not see them again all evening. She had been oddly haunted all night by a woman, dressed as a Pierrot, wearing a green wig. It was the wig she had noticed when she first saw the woman getting out of a car beneath the Albert Hall portico. Petta had glanced back at her and seen the green woolly wig, the large ear-rings, the satin suit, the red balloon in hand, surrounding, with a sinister incongruity, a despairing face – a face of lost beauty, peaked out of recognition by discontent. As she and her two companions, a man and a woman, followed Petta's party up the steps, Petta heard the woman's voice, tiny, tinny, querulous, demanding some attention of some sort from the man.

Petta, unaccountably disturbed, moved for comfort into the midst of her crowd of friends, among whom she was the beauty, the spoilt and adored one. She was dressed as a late-eighteenth-century marquise: her dress and looks caused people to step aside for her and gaze after her and speak their admiration aloud. After midnight, when people were reeling madly around the floor, a student had climbed up to her box and handed her a rose.

For thanks, she said: 'My dear boy, it's faded.'

He smiled, saying as he jumped back to the floor: 'They are all faded, except you.' As she watched after him, she saw the woman in the green wig breaking in between her two companions, who had been dancing together. She was scolding them, and crying aloud. Petta thought: 'There, but for the grace of God . . .' She, who could have asked for nothing that could have added to her life!

The last time she saw the woman was towards daybreak when the company was falling to pieces in an atmosphere of melancholy squalor. Crowds of people were lying in heaps on the floor: a few couples remained, the partners propping one another up, trudging about as though in delirium. Her party was leaving, yet she looked back, seeking something, and saw what she sought: the woman in the green wig moving alone among the dancers, fluttering her hands and singing to herself in a voice like a wail.

Now Petta asked herself: 'What had she to do with me? Why have I never forgotten her?' A stranger had entered her mind years ago and now had permanent place there. She wondered what had happened to the woman. No doubt she was dead. All she had lacked of the suicide was courage to end herself. But perhaps she was alive, an old woman, a wreck of a human creature.

Petta caught her breath, her thought checked abruptly as though she had bitten on a nerve. She came to a stop and looked about her. She was standing on an island opposite St George's Hospital. Her fur coat was heavy with rain: she felt like a wet cat. She had no memory of leaving the park, of negotiating the traffic and reaching this point of safety.

What was the matter with her? It was as though some dark area of her mind was derelict, peopled by ghouls. If she were not always vigilant to skirt it, she stumbled in and was lost.

She wondered where she had been going before that excursion into her mental slums. She thought: 'The important thing is not to be alone.' With some idea of visiting a bar where she was known, she found a way through the traffic stream and started along Knightsbridge. She shook her coat. The rain had stopped. Passing the lighted windows of shops, she saw glances drawn to her, men fingering their ties at her approach. Their eyes met hers. She smiled into herself. It seemed to her now that somewhere near, just within reach of her hand, there was the solution of her whole life. She began to hurry as though the solution lay in a region just ahead of her: in a moment she must come on it. At times she ran a little as though she were a young girl impelled by the excitement of life. The sense of life about her was a delicious sweetness she could taste with her whole body. In delight at her own existence, she could have flung open her arms and embraced anyone she passed. She looked into her own mind for the face of love and, parting her lips, she said: 'Quintin', but at once she looked away. No more Quintin. Suddenly she whispered: 'Why, Theo!', greeting her memory of him as she might greet a friend found amidst chaos.

Of course, she could return to Theo.

She began running along the kerb, waving and calling at cabs until one drew in beside her. She entered breathlessly, several times telling the driver her destination.

'All right, lady: I know.' He pulled the glass screen across to silence her.

She sat on the edge of the seat, restlessly watching the road, scarcely able to bear the delays at traffic lights, corners and pedestrian crossings. Once she called out: 'I'm in a hurry.'

'Can't do it any quicker, lady.'

At last they reached the King's Road public-house where Theo spent most of his evenings. She paid off the cab and entered the saloon bar. When she saw he was not there, she had the illusion the place was empty. She left at once.

She was not really perturbed. If he were not there, she knew where he would be. She walked to his house in Upper Cheyne Row, all fears and indecisions gone. As she neared the door she anticipated their meeting with such longing that tears filled her eyes. She knocked impatiently. The ground and first floors were in darkness. He usually worked at the back of the house. No sound came from inside. She knocked louder. When there was no answer, she pressed the bell of the upper maisonnette, determined somehow to get inside and wait for him. No one answered the bell. She put her finger on it and held it down, whispering: 'Hurry, hurry.'

Not a sound from inside.

Her excitement failed. The house stood back from the road, one of a row behind gardens. In the dark, damp garden that smelt of sooty earth she stood shivering, bleakly lost, as though she had been rushed excitedly to a promised appointment only to find nothing. What could she do now? Where go?

After standing about for some minutes, she searched in her bag for her diary that had a pencil in its spine. When she found it she tore out a page and wrote: 'Theo darling, why have I heard nothing from you? I must see you again.'

She heard someone coming from Oakley Street. A woman's step. Her hands trembled. There was something she had wanted to write, but now she could not remember what it had been. In panic, she scribbled her name and thrust the note into Theo's letter-box. Someone came in at the gate. A woman's voice enquired behind her: 'Looking for Theo?'

The bland insolence of the tone restored Petta. She turned, smiling, to ask: 'How ever did you guess?'

The woman from the upper flat returned smile for smile. 'Didn't you know he had been invited to lecture in the States? He left three days ago.'

'Oh!' Petta was not equal to this information. She had to swallow an impediment in her throat before she could ask: 'How long will he be away?'

'Several weeks.'

'Thank you.'

She kept up a show of sprightly unconcern until she gained the cover of Cheyne Row: there she stood still. It seemed to her that in the whole world there was no one who would welcome her, nowhere she could go, nothing she could do. She felt paralysed by lack of cause to live. She had not even cause to move from the spot where she was now. She might have stood there indefinitely had not a cat come up from the basement of a house and pressed itself against her legs. She picked it up; a small, warm, living creature pulsing with pleasure beneath her chin. She thought: 'I must have a cat of my own.' She looked into its dark, pointed face and said: 'I love you.' The dynamo in the cat's throat whirred louder. She brushed her chin over its head. Then, suddenly, she dropped it. As she walked towards the river, the cat followed her. She hurried to get away from it.

Of course she could not have a cat. An animal, any animal, was troublesome. She had no settled home. If she kept a cat in an upstair flat, she would have to have a box of earth for it. The box would have to be emptied and refilled. A cat had to be fed. The house would smell of boiled cod, a most disgusting smell. She would never be free to go away.

To be free to go, even though she never went, seemed to her now the first need of life. Yes, children and pets were out of the question. They interfered with life.

'I must go away.'

She began to think of places she knew on the Mediterranean. Her mind became full of the dazzle of sunshine on painted houses, of flowers and the peacock sea. She thought: 'I'll go tomorrow. Or the day after', and then the fancy disintegrated into heat, dust, mosquitoes, flies, the tedium of travel, of finding sympathetic accommodation, and the strangeness of strangers who seemed always critical, antagonistic and dull.

She had travelled enough. She felt the effort of change beyond her.

In Cheyne Walk she wandered over to the river. She had some idea of walking to Chelsea Bridge, but the sharp wind tired her. Before she had reached Albert Bridge she came to a stop, scarcely able to move further, so weighted was she by an oppression of boredom.

Once she had said to Quintin: 'I don't suppose I shall have to live in this world many more times. They could not ask it.'

'Who could not ask it?' He was amused, yet curious. 'What are you talking about?'

She knew he was laughing at her and said: 'Why trouble to explain? I'm beyond your comprehension.'

'Are you, now?' He could never hide his contempt for

her absurd femininity. 'Then why didn't you leave me in peace?'

'I mistook you for someone else.'

'Oh? For whom?'

'I don't know. Just someone different: someone who would understand me.'

Someone different! Not that she really wanted someone different: she simply wanted Quintin to want her.

She crossed the road to a public-house and bought a gin as an excuse for sitting down. She had spent a lot of time in bars with Theo, but she was not a natural drunk. She became sleepy long before she could become merry. She thought enviously of those to whom drink was a refuge. 'If I could get really drunk,' she thought, 'I'd never be sober again.' From the distance of her sobriety, she saw the crowd about her ridiculous and unreal.

A man carrying a glass of stout came over to her table: 'Mind if I sit down?' He sat down and offered her a cigarette. She took it. He was a strongly-built man in early middle-age, prosperous-looking; a shopkeeper, perhaps, she thought, someone on the up and up. She watched him evaluating her fur coat and rings. He looked down at her shoes, then, lifting his eyes and catching hers, he laughed: 'Got a Rolls outside?'

'A what?'

'You didn't walk here?'

'I walked part of the way. I was feeling depressed.'

'Depressed!'

She knew exactly the effect her frankness and simplicity of manner had on this sort of man. She noted the drop in his assurance: his approbation taking life as though a fog were clearing and he realised that here was something remarkable. When he spoke again, it was with respect: 'I wouldn't think you'd any call to be depressed. What is it? What's the trouble? Could I help you?'

'No. It's just – life's too familiar.'

He was startled, then, deciding she meant only what she said, he agreed: 'It gets a bit familiar at times, but if you've got what it takes, the world's your oyster – of which, I may say, I've had a good few lately.'

'A good few what?'

'Oysters. You shouldn't let things worry you, you know. Tell yourself, like I do: "We'll soon be dead."'

'I often do.' Indifferent to her effect on the man, she explained herself deliberately as a means of dealing with her own mood: 'When I have to face myself and know there's no one to blame but me, and there's no hope because I cannot change myself, then I understand the purpose of death. It's reasonable: it's desirable: it puts an end to failure. I know then we're not required to suffer for ever.'

He moved uneasily. His expression forced her to smile. He said in a warning mumble: 'You're getting morbid, girlie.' His respect was waning.

She burst out laughing. In an instant her mood had turned and now it was as though she had been given control of the world.

She said: 'Don't be frightened,' not that he looked frightened: he suspected someone was making a fool of him.

She crossed her legs and looked down at her narrow ankles, her neatly shaped calves. He looked, too, but without satisfaction. He knew they were not for him. He did not speak as she finished her drink.

'Well,' she said, 'I must go. Thank you for your company. You have cheered me up.'

'Always glad to oblige,' he said ungladly.

Out again on the riverside, she walked until she found a taxi. When she arrived at the flat and was paying the driver, she saw Quintin coming down the steps of Alma's house. He hurried towards her and said in a wrathful half-whisper:

'Really, Petta! Your behaviour was, as always, impossible. What do you suppose Alma thought?'

'What do I care?' she tipped the man extravagantly, threw the rest of the change into her bag and ran up the steps. Before she entered the house, she said in her most penetrating tone: 'I've no use for the English middle-classes. They're so bloody vulgar.'

Quintin gave Alma's windows a glance of apparent concern, but he was in no way displeased that she should experience for herself the eccentricities of Petta's behaviour.

PART TWO

I

Ellie did not tell herself she would soon see Quintin again. Self-deception would not bring him back. Instead, she turned herself from the thought of Quintin, telling herself she might live for half a century more and all that time without him. 'My life must change. I must find myself friends.'

That was no easy matter. Her life had broken in half. In one half there was Quintin: in the other, no one at all. First she had to cure herself of the habit of thinking of him as the only companion she needed or wanted. Every time his name came into her mind, she said: 'He has given you up. Forget him.' The trouble was, she did not believe that. Whenever the telephone rang, she imagined it was Quintin, to say he must see her again. One thing helped her through the first bleak days: her cold grew worse.

On Sunday morning she awoke so muffled and hot-eyed, her mental misery could scarcely make itself recognised. Out of doors there was a little pallid sunshine. Sunshine should never be missed. At least she could wear away part of the day's boredom by walking in the park.

When she left the house, she found the brightness was hard and cold. There was spite in the wind. All the wonders she passed – the façades of Oakley Street, the houses of Cheyne Walk, the iron swags of Albert Bridge, the river's sleek and glossy folds pressing between the pylons – all had lost their magnificence. A dust lay on life.

She took the long walk round by the lake and stood among the Sunday people throwing bread to the water-fowl. Yesterday, she thought, yesterday . . .

'Here,' she said to a small girl in pink. 'That's a bit too big, you know. Let me break it up for you.'

The little girl seemed to resent this service. She took the broken bread with a fierce look and flung it towards the ducks. 'Not those, not those,' she said, kicking up her pink feet at the interloper sparrows.

'Yes, let the sparrows have some,' said her mother, 'Here is another piece for the ducks.' The child took it and threw it with a great effort and it landed at her feet.

Ellie, watching and smiling, became aware that some-one was watching her. She looked round into the face of a man in a wheel-chair who had come so close that one wheel was brushing her skirt.

He said: 'Isn't it a lovely day!'

She stepped from him as though repelled by a physical force. At once she tried to make amends for her move-ment. She agreed the day was lovely. She looked up to where the branches rocked stiffly in the wind as though too cold to sway: 'Almost like spring,' she said. Then she tried to escape: the chair moved with her. When she looked at its occupant, he was still watching her, smiling up at her face, a thin, middle-aged man with a clever, perky face, not ill-looking. He spoke with a slight Cockney accent: 'Do you come here often?'

'No.'

'I've seen you before, you know.'

She blushed as though she had been accused of lying. As she lowered her face, he bent to look at her. 'I've often noticed your hair,' he said.

She did not reply but quickened her step: he kept beside her. 'Come and have Sunday dinner with me,' he said.

She looked at him, surprised, and, meeting his coaxing, confident smile, felt a frisson of pure dislike. 'It's impossible.'

'Do come. I live alone, you know. I have a little room off Battersea Road. I do everything for myself. Come and help me.'

So he could leave the chair! 'It's quite impossible—' she backed from him – 'I have to meet my fiancé – over there.' She waved in the direction of Cheyne Walk, having in mind a restaurant where, in the evenings, she had seen through the window people dining by candle-light. 'As a matter of fact, I shall have to hurry. He'll be waiting for me.'

'What a pity! You looked so nice.'

She went off, nearly running, afraid he might pursue her, but now the wheel-chair remained still.

'Nice, nice!' she cried to herself. 'What good is it looking nice if the only people who want you are horrible young men and men in wheel-chairs?' She hurried all the way as though she had indeed a fiancé impatiently awaiting her, a fiancé who looked exactly like Quintin. The fantasy almost carried her in through the restaurant door. Steering away in time, she went to a snack bar, where, in the belief that one should feed a cold, she allowed herself soup as well as poached egg on toast.

* * *

123

On Monday morning, in a stupor of headache and fever, she put her coat on over her pyjamas and went downstairs. She imagined if she took some aspirin she would have energy to go to work. She called down into the dark and silent basement, but Mrs Mackie was out.

Ellie went back to her room and managed to dress: then, with some idea of lying down to recuperate for five minutes, she dropped to her bed and went to sleep again. She awoke at mid-day with her breath burning her lips. The girl who did the rooms had been and gone. Ellie wondered on whom she could call for help. She felt no great sympathy with herself. She knew that those who chose to earn a living in London should do so on the understanding they were never ill. Other people, living alone and working as she did, were so organised to deal with a difficult life, it was unfair to ask assistance from them. Besides, whom could she ask?

Her chief sensation was fear she might lose her job. If she rang and asked help from someone at the studio, that would prove she really was ill. But how could she let people like Denis, Bertie and Rhoda know she lived in a room where no artist could work, a room as narrow as a slice of bread?

She thought, at last, of Miss Senior, secretary to Mrs Primrose. Of course, Miss Senior was the one. She had interviewed Ellie for the packaging job, and brought her the news of her advancement to the studio. Miss Senior's manner was nervous and unpretentious: the thought of it reassured Ellie. Besides, Miss Senior was at the elbow of power. When Mrs Primrose said: 'Dismiss that girl for malingering', Miss Senior could say: 'She really isn't fit to come to work. I've seen her myself.'

Miss Senior, when Ellie got through to her, seemed surprised and flustered by the call – but, yes, she would come. She would be round about six o'clock with food and aspirins. Meanwhile, had Ellie not better return to bed?

Ellie slept heavily until late afternoon. She was awakened by the distant ringing of the front-door bell. She switched on her light and looked at her alarm-clock. It was nearly six. That must be Miss Senior ringing below. Mrs Mackie was out, as usual. As Ellie put on her coat, the ringing changed to knocking. She felt a sort of love for Miss Senior that she could persist so, standing in the cold porch, all to help Ellie who had been fool enough to fall ill.

Ellie sped downstairs, switched the light on in the bare, yellow-brown hall, and opened the door. Then the cold came in like a blow. Outside stood a small boy with a brown paper bag: 'Name of Parsons? Sign here.'

Inside the bag were five oranges and a note: 'I do not think I should risk catching 'flu' but these will tide you over. Stay in bed tomorrow if you are no better. I will explain to Mrs Primrose.'

The last sentence was all Ellie needed. She would survive. She spaced out the oranges so that they would last until Tuesday evening. On Tuesday morning the girl who did the room brought her aspirin and hot milk. During the day of half-sleep she found herself again in the park with Quintin. Together they drifted silently, covering vast areas of green, through a strange and deepening twilight. As the light failed, Quintin's figure wavered, became less than a shadow . . . She tried to touch him. He was not within reach. She called to him.

He disappeared. Seeking him, harassed by glimpses of him that came and went, she passed at last, alone, into a black emptiness of sleep.

Awaking next morning, clear-headed and hungry, she felt the exhilaration of recovery. After all, Quintin had said that one day they would meet again. And she was well, more or less. Anyway, she was alive. And she was in London, where she had always wanted to be: what was more, she worked in a studio, an artist among artists. She had achieved so much, why should she, in the end, not achieve Quintin, too?

2

The day Ellie was sent to 'Primrose's' by the labour exchange, she had entered mistakenly through the main door. That never happened again – but she saw the showrooms. For the first time in her life she saw painted furniture and furniture ornamented with gilded brass: a purple carpet – *purple!* – silk and velvet curtains of remarkable colours; wall-paper embossed with gold.

When Miss Senior came seeking her through the alcoves, she found her pulling out the drawers of a writing-desk that was painted yellow outside and pink within. She called reprovingly: 'Miss Parsons?' Ellie, swinging round, dazzled and alight, said: 'Isn't it all wonderful!'

'What?' Miss Senior was more bewildered than annoyed by Ellie's behaviour.

'All these things. I've never seen anything like them. How lovely to work here!'

'I'm afraid you won't work here.' As though Ellie had trespassed, Miss Senior said: 'You should have come in by the staff entrance in the mews.' She took Ellie out to the new, brick factory at the back and interviewed her in the porter's office. She was given the job without much questioning. No one else had applied for it. When Miss Senior had approved her, she was taken beyond the porter's room to the office of Mr Daze, the accountant and chief of staff. She was less than a minute with Mr Daze, whom she was to see again only twice in her life.

When she arrived the following Monday morning, the porter took her down to the factory basement, a chilly area, green-painted, cement-floored, lined with pipes, ventilators, fuse boxes and power switches. Dahlia, whom she was to assist, said: 'Lucky for them they got hold of you. I wouldn't have stuck it down here alone another week.'

Dahlia was a thin girl with a face like a whippet. Her hair, yellow and long, with the texture of hemp, hung over one eye. She was seldom silent. 'What do they think we are, I'd like to know. I wouldn't keep a dog down here. No proper lighting, not to speak of, that is, and cold! Why, last winter when the boiler broke down I nearly died. I said to Klixon – that's the bottom-pincher with the red moustache – I said: "You get me some heat here, or you'll be packing your own furniture." He tried to make a joke of it, but I wasn't having any. "I mean it," I said, and what do you think he sent down? An oil-stove! Would you believe it? "I'm not standing for that," I said, "You get that boiler mended double quick, or else . . ."' She gave her head a threatening twist and fixed her visible eye on Ellie.

Ellie said automatically: 'I don't blame you.' She had learnt in her mother's restaurant several idioms of least resistance. They were to serve her now. Dahlia nodded satisfaction.

At one o'clock Ellie asked where she could eat a mid-day meal. Dahlia, who lived at home, said she had brought sandwiches, but the Primrose employees were permitted to use the canteen of an electrical works in the mews.

'Do you never go there?' Ellie asked.

Dahlia expressed fastidiousness with a gesture: 'I don't fancy it.'

When Ellie returned from her canteen meal, Dahlia said: 'What's it like?'

'Jolly good,' said Ellie, at which Dahlia seemed suddenly resentful that Ellie should be familiar with the canteen and she not. The next day she told Ellie she would go there with her.

The canteen, large and noisy, smelt of stale food. It was decorated with anti-waste posters, very old and tattered. As Ellie and Dahlia queued for food, Ellie saw Dahlia look about her and distaste appeared on the lean, whippet face. Dahlia's seeing eye fixed itself on the nearest table, at which four people sat hemmed in by dirty dishes and the tin covers used to keep the food warm.

Ellie said: 'The food is all right.'

Dahlia swallowed in her throat. 'I never did fancy this place,' she grumbled. 'When I told my mum I was coming today, she said "What do you know about their cooking-pots?"'

The queue moved. At last they were served with food and wandering about among the tables looking for free seats. They seized on two as they were vacated and cleared a place for themselves among the discarded plates. Each had been served with a slice of grey mutton and a ladleful of grey sauce. The mutton took up no more than two inches of plate, which was given a look of plenty by a wedge of dark green cabbage, two mounds of mashed potato and half-a-dozen baked potatoes. Dahlia poked at the baked potatoes and said fretfully: 'What are these made of? Cardboard?' She crumpled the paper-thin meat and ate it in one mouthful. 'I'd rather have a sandwich,' she said. 'At least it tastes of *something*.'

'Then you'd need another meal at night.'

'Don't you have one?'

'I have tea. They let me make it in my room.'

'That's big of them.'

Ellie ate everything, gulping down water at each threat of nausea. This food was part of the challenge of life here. She would not be defeated by it, but she felt some guilt about Dahlia. She said: 'Yesterday there was cottage pie: it's easier to swallow.'

'That muck! It gives me flatulence.'

It was Dahlia, unfortunately, who found in her cabbage a piece of coarse string bag in which cabbages came from market. She held it up to the two women who shared their table. One woman said: 'I got a black-beetle once, right in the middle of my fried egg.'

'I got worse than that,' said the other, 'but I wouldn't like to put you off your food.'

Dahlia lit a cigarette and her ill-temper began to dissolve. When the trolley girl came to clear the dishes and scrape the waste food into a bin, Dahlia, handing over her plate, said: 'If you didn't want it, why did you take it?'

'What?'

Dahlia pointed to the anti-waste poster on the wall.

'Oh, that! Let them make it so you want to eat it, I say.'

Ellie, who, the day before, had heard the same girl say: 'Where do you think you are? The Ritz?', was impressed

130

by Dahlia's influence in the world to which she belonged. She complained, as Ellie would not dare to complain, and her complaints were accepted or treated as a joke. Ellie wondered if she herself would ever find an environment where everything she did or said was accepted and right. She had reached London – yet she had not moved very far. Shut in all day with Dahlia, she might have been shut in her mother's restaurant. Dahlia's company was much like that of her mother's customers. It imposed the same restrictions and prohibitions. One was supposed to accept the limitations on speech and conduct set by powerful insiders like Dahlia. Ellie had long ago discovered that if she ever made any comment other than 'That's right,' and 'I don't blame you,' she would find she had somehow upset someone. She was determined to escape. She belonged elsewhere.

Sometimes later when Dahlia had discovered all of Ellie's background, she said: 'You're loopy, you know.'

'Why?'

'Leaving a good home, and living in a bed-sitter and eating that stuff in the canteen. Whatever made you do it?'

Ellie smiled, but did not try to explain.

Dahlia said: 'I thought at first your mum and dad must be dead, really I did. And then when I asked you and you said your mum was alive and wanted you home, I thought you must be loopy. Why, when I think of all I've got – a good supper waiting, and a big fire, and Ty-rone dropping in, and mum putting me to bed with a hot-water bottle if I sniff a bit – why, you're loopy, that's what I think.'

Ellie smiled, knowing that all that was nothing compared to her own freedom to live differently.

'What do you do on Sundays?'

'Nothing much.'

'Well, one Sunday you come and have tea with us at Hammersmith. We always have hot buttered scones and fruit-cake on Sundays.'

That was Dahlia in a mellow mood. Soon after, her mood hardened and Tyrone, so tenderly mentioned before, became another cause for complaint. 'That Ty-rone! He's that soppy! The other night at the Palais a chap came up to me like this:' she bent forward, waving her backside, on her face a ghastly leer before which she waggled an upraised forefinger. 'He said: "Hello, Hep-cat, dig that down beat. On your tootsies: I'll give you a creep." The nerve! "I've brought my partner with me," I said, very dignified, and I looked at Ty-rone – and what did he do? He just got red in the face and looked the other way, pretending he hadn't noticed anything. "Why, Ty-rone," I said, "you make me sick. You'd let that chap steal your girl right under your nose."'

'And be so rude,' said Ellie.

'Rude!' said Dahlia, made indignant by the suggestion anyone dare be rude to her.

'I mean, calling you a "hep-cat",' said Ellie.

Dahlia's face collapsed in an expression of utter weariness. 'Don't you know anything?' she asked.

'I'm sorry,' said Ellie. 'Do go on. What happened after that?'

'Nothing,' said Dahlia; but after she had brooded a while, she spoke again: 'He thinks I'm going to marry him, but I said "You watch your step, Ty-rone. There's plenty more where you come from."'

'That's right,' said Ellie.

Then it was Mum who was 'that fussy' and Dad who took off his collar and tie as soon as he entered the house: '"For God's sake," I said to him, "why don't you take your shirt and vest off, too? Always undressing – what does it look like if I have callers?"'

Dahlia had been employed at 'Primrose's' for two years. She knew the names and occupations of everyone in the the building. If Ellie singled out a face among those she saw in the canteen or on the stairs, Dahlia would pin down with a word the individual to which it belonged: 'daft', 'shifty', 'barmy', 'soppy', 'cheeky'.

'What about Mrs Primrose?'

'Stuck up.'

'I'd like to see her.'

'You'll see her soon enough.'

'And Klixon? What do you think of him?'

'Downy!' Dahlia sniggered. 'He's a one,' she said.

Ellie felt no surprise at Dahlia's respect for Klixon, the Staff Manager. She herself was fascinated by his ebullience, fearing that by sheer inability to resist such force of character she might be one day driven to respond to him, or someone like him. How terrible to end up as Mrs Klixon! His habit of touching her waist or patting her backside if he slid round her heightened his aura of danger. He was a tall, large young man who, at their first meeting, had stood with his head thrown back and looked down at Ellie from under his thin, reddish lashes. 'If you want to know anything, come to me. If you want any help, I'll see you right.' He suddenly expanded his mouth in a significant smirk. She was appalled. She said to herself: 'Please, God, not Mr Klixon.'

He had the air of an important person who would

become more important, but he despised no one's admiration. His bright blue eyes, glassy as dolls' eyes, bulged unblinking and expressionless on either side of his scimitar nose: he was always laughing. He could be heard stating loudly 'Ha, ha, ha!' from every part of the building. As he went through the upholstery room above, there came down to the basement his 'Ha, ha, ha! Hello, girls. Ha, ha, ha! A good time being had by all. Ha, ha, ha!'

Even when he was not talking or laughing he would keep his lips stretched open to show his large, white teeth: but sometimes, when his attention was distracted from himself, his mouth snapped back and shut into a very small pocket, like the mouth of a crab.

It was odd that, although he was so affable with all of them, the upholstery girls, when they chatted in the cloak-room, usually spoke of him with suspicion, even dislike: and odder that, although they disliked him, they could not cease to speak of him. He was so constantly discussed that the girls did not trouble to name him. Klixon was 'him', as though there was not another male in the building.

'Him! He'll get on all right. He knows all the tricks. But it was the war made him. He was nobody till he got in the Army and turned into an officer and a gent. Don't ask me how. He'll own his own place one day, see if he don't.'

One of the older women broke in to say: 'Catch him young, girls. Find yourself the boss's boss one day.'

'Him! I wouldn't marry him . . .'

'No fear! Any girl that got him'd earn her keep.'

Ellie asked Dahlia: 'Would you marry him?'

'Who?' Dahlia pretended bewilderment but her cheeks grew red.

'Klixon, of course.'

'Him!' Dahlia's voice rose in scorn, then subsided into spurts of laughter. She said: 'Seeing as how you're a friend, I'll tell you something. Klixon waited for me one night in the mews.'

'Did you go out with him?'

'Not likely.' But again Dahlia's scorn collapsed in giggles, and after a moment she added mysteriously: 'Not so's you'd notice.'

That was the only time Ellie heard any girl claim that Klixon had made any sure advance to her. She doubted it, yet the claim reduced Klixon's power. She began to see him as rather ridiculous.

Some weeks had passed since Dahlia's mention of tea at Hammersmith, but Ellie had not yet been invited. As her appetite grew keener with the autumn cold, she became haunted by the thought of hot buttered scones and fruit-cake. At the end of the week made notable by the fact Dahlia had described her as a friend, Ellie diffidently asked her: 'Do you think I could come to Hammersmith on Sunday?'

'What, you mean to tea? Not this Sunday.' Dahlia spoke with decision. 'My young man, Ty-rone, 's coming in.'

Ellie had to realise that a young man, even a young man as faulty as Tyrone, was more important than a friend.

Ellie left one luncheon time behind three people – two men and a girl – who looked and dressed unlike anyone else in the building. Their freedom of manner touched her acutely. Something moved in her as though, on a voyage, she had glimpsed her destination without any certainty of reaching it. When she returned she asked Dahlia about these people.

'Oh, them! They're the artists.'

'What do they do?'

'They do that stuff.' Dahlia pointed to a white table on which was painted an urn enclosed by a wreath of flowers.

'What are they like?' asked Ellie.

'How should I know! They're artists.' To Dahlia, it seemed, artists formed a section of the community no normal person would expect to understand.

'Where do they work?'

'Up in the studio; next to the paint-shop.'

Ellie watched for the artists, gazed after them and avoided being seen by them – all with an anguish of envy, longing to be disclosed as a member of that body which was beyond the range of Dahlia's criticism. Meanwhile she could not bear that they should observe her in beggary in the basement. She believed so completely in her right to be in the studio, she was certain that sooner or later she must go there. It was as though all the forces of her life were propelling her there, but, in her impatience, she wanted to hasten things. What should she do? Show her portfolio of work to Klixon? Ask Miss Senior to show it to Mrs Primrose? It was while she was considering these moves that Quintin presented himself to her.

With Quintin, everything fell into position. It was his arrival, of course, for which she had been waiting all her life. When he promised to arrange her move to the studio, she knew it would be arranged. When Miss Senior, bringing round the tray of pay packets, said casually one Friday evening: 'Miss Parsons, you can start on Monday in the studio,' Ellie was transported as by the fulfilment of a premonitory dream. Everything at last was hers.

Dahlia said pityingly: 'What made them think of sending you there?'

'I want to go. I used to be an art student.'

'Did you!' Dahlia looked narrowly at her. 'I'm not surprised. I said to myself when I first laid eyes on you: "That one's potty".'

Dahlia hardly spoke to her again. During the months ahead, if they came face to face in the hall or entrance, she moved away quickly with the look of someone who feels she has been injured but has no wish to make the matter public.

Ellie, ascending the stairs on her way to the studio on her first day, met Klixon coming down. He stopped, keeping at a distance from her, throwing his head back, expanding his mouth in no semblance of a smile, and said: 'So you're moving to the studio!'

Ellie was too frightened to answer. Her fear had nothing to do with Klixon. Now she knew Quintin, Klixon meant nothing. His disapproval affected her less than Dahlia's had done. He said:

'You should have consulted me. You're taking a risk. I hope you don't regret it. That packing job was a safe job. You might have been in it for years.'

Having said what he had to say, he motioned her to pass on. She went, her fear heightened by a new sense of risk. Not that she risked anything. She had never intended to stay in the packing job. As for her new position in the studio – had she not been recommended by Quintin Bellot, a shareholder in the firm? It was the drama of risk, hazard deified, that caught at her throat.

In the paint-shop the men, recognising her, shouted to her: 'Hello, ducks! What are you doing up here?'

Near tears, she croaked: 'I've come to work in the studio. I'm looking for Mr Plumley.'

'Mr Plumley? That's him. Tall bloke at the desk there. Him with the golden curls. Here!' they directed her. 'Get round here. Mind the wet paint. There's a girl!'

She reached the studio. It was a white room full of white furniture lit from a dozen windows by silver daylight. Denis Plumley, sitting at his desk, showed no awareness of the uproar in the paint-shop. He was in young middle-age, his pallid, melancholy, classical face hung over with limp, black hair. Ellie, unable to speak, stood for some time beside him. He was filling in a cross-word puzzle. When he glanced up and pushed away his hair, he noted her with surprise. She managed to say: 'I'm Ellie Parsons.'

'Oh, my dear, *yes*. What are we going to do with you?'

Ellie looked round the gathering of white furniture, in the midst of which a youngish woman was cleaning a palette and a short, stout man painting cupids on a commode, and said: 'I've come here to work. I've brought some designs.' She had spent Saturday afternoon in the Manresa Road library copying urns, flowers and swags from books on period design.

Denis Plumley asked: 'Can you put on gold leaf?'

'Yes.'

'Can you do "antiquing"?'

'Yes.'

'Can you varnish nicely?'

'Yes.'

He smiled. He was not deceived. He stood up, as tall as the wardrobes, and called out pleadingly: 'Rhoda darling, show this child how to do something. I don't mind what.'

When Ellie had learnt how to make a thin mixture of black and umber, to wash it over the white paint, rub it off, then brush the patina till the crass white surfaces seemed bloomed with age, she covered wardrobes inside and out, tables, bed-ends, commodes, cabinets, writing-desks, chairs. She had never worked so hard in her life before. In the evenings she left half-sleeping from exhaustion and the fumes of turpentine and new paint. When Quintin spoke with concern of the state of her hands, she said: 'That's nothing. I love being there.'

'What about the other artists? How do you get on with them?'

'They take no notice of me, but I don't think they mind my being there.' Ellie, who had had two glasses of wine, added: 'I don't think Mrs P. likes it, though.'

'Likes what?'

'My being there.'

'Nonsense. I'm sure she loves having you there.' Quintin turned his face from the subject and Ellie knew she must leave it.

During her early days in the studio, with Quintin behind her, Ellie had felt secure. The first time one of the painters put his head in and hissed: 'Mrs P. coming,' Ellie watched eagerly to be acknowledged by this important woman who knew she knew Quintin.

She had, of course, seen Mrs Primrose before. Now, as

she stood in the doorway talking with a mysterious and intimate quiet to the painters' foreman, Ellie looked at her newly. She was a neat, dark, miniature woman who wore on her tailored suit a brooch flower of diamonds as large as the lapel. Ellie gazed and gazed at Mrs Primrose's small, dark, hawk's face, catching the flash of diamonds as she moved, but when Mrs Primrose turned from the foreman and looked into the studio, her eyes passed blankly over the space where Ellie stood. It seemed she did not see Ellie now, any more than she had seen her in the basement. Yet Ellie felt awareness, and, with it, enmity. Some instinct made her move out of sight. Hiding behind a piece of furniture, she glanced out cautiously. Mrs Primrose was talking to Denis in a voice no more than a whisper. They were going through the work-sheets. Denis could not keep his tenor down to her level. Ellie heard him say casually: 'She is quite useful', and was sure he spoke of her. Ellie was grateful to him.

Mrs Primrose crossed to where Denis's friend, the stout, short man, Bertie Hawkins, was decorating a wardrobe. Ellie could not hear what she said, but her movement expressed admiration. Bertie, indifferent, smiling from politeness only, fingered his brushes and waited for her to go.

She passed Ellie, leaving on the air a scent of gardenias, and paused by another wardrobe on which Rhoda was drawing bamboos. She smiled at Rhoda and at her work, then left the studio without speaking again. She had not recognised Ellie's existence.

Ellie, chilled by the certainty she was not wanted there, no longer felt secure. Whenever warning was given of Mrs

Primrose's approach, Ellie would hide behind the largest piece of furniture and hope to be forgotten.

In time she began to think she had been forgotten. Weeks passed and she was still in the studio: her confidence came cautiously back. She learned to put on gold and silver leaf: she could 'antique' and varnish. As she became skilled, Bertie let her fill in with flat colour Greek key and acanthus borders, later even to shade them.

She was useful. She was progressing. Secretly, she came to regard her work with admiration, believing herself more than useful. She was becoming valuable. When she contemplated some massive piece 'antiqued' and varnished by herself she felt love for it, and pride in it. She was beginning to believe Mrs Primrose kept her because she was too good to lose. It even entered her head to ask for a rise, but she put that thought from her. Mrs Primrose had expressed no satisfaction. She had expressed nothing, but somehow she had let Ellie know she was not wanted.

3

Recovering from her cold, putting Quintin behind her, Ellie returned to the studio in a state of emotional and physical emptiness that surely betokened a new beginning.

At least she could work.

More than that, she had nothing and, having nothing, she could hope for everything. To begin with, there were Denis, Bertie and Rhoda. When she had had Quintin, she had been content to remain out of their sight. Now she would make herself known to them.

She came, she knew, from the darkest outer rim of provincial ignorance. She had trained (of course, now, she realised she had not trained at all) for six months in the art classes of the Eastsea Technical School. She lived in a room so small it contained no table on which to put a drawing-board: she had no drawing-board: she had no money with which to buy paper, canvas or paint – but Quintin had said to her: 'You are a remarkable girl! A unique girl!' and when she spoke with envious respect of Denis, Bertie and Rhoda, he had laughed at her, saying: 'Really! You are delicious!'

Abandoned by him, but still the unique and remarkable Ellie, here she was, back at the studio, dry-eyed and determined to live again. She found that the table she had been 'antiquing' had disappeared. One of the painters had varnished it. Disconcerted, feeling less unique, she asked Denis: 'Was Mrs P. cross at my being away?'

'She said nothing to me, darling.'

Ellie caught her breath and asked after a moment: 'She doesn't want me here, does she?'

Denis looked up from his crossword puzzle and said with a not unkindly exasperation: 'How do I know? If she didn't want you, would she have taken you on? It's her firm.'

This was no doubt meant for reassurance. How could she explain why she was employed there! Her arrival in the studio had probably mystified Denis, Bertie and Rhoda. When she said nothing, Denis said:

'Why don't you speak to her? Chatter gaily. Be ingenuous. Put across your girlish charm.'

'How can I? She never looks at me.'

'Well, push into view. Ask her how she likes your work. She's all right, really. You'll soon win her over.'

Ellie, contemplating the monstrous impertinence of pushing into Mrs Primrose's view, said faintly: 'I couldn't.'

'It's up to you, darling.' Denis dismissed her with a flick of one of his long, white, unused hands. 'Get to work on Bertie's last piece. Don't stand there wasting my time.'

Ellie thought: 'If I hadn't my job, I would be so unhappy, I would die.'

But she had her job and did not die.

During the middle of the morning Denis finished the crossword puzzle and came to lean against a wardrobe, on the twin doors of which Bertie was limning a shepherd and shepherdess surrounded by flowers.

Looking at this work, Denis said: 'Ah, Rex! What an artist he was!'

'Really, Denis!' said Bertie.

Denis touched the rim of the wreathing flowers, and said: 'The old boy who wrote "fringed grot, grass plot" knew a thing or two, or didn't he? What do you think, darling?'

Bertie giggled in spite of himself, then said primly: 'Don't be naughty, Denis.'

'Now, what I don't understand is censorship. If I find I've doodled a three-leafed clover, I know what I have in mind – but, knowing what I have in mind, why a three-leafed clover?' asked Denis, touching with the point of his finger the clover on which the shepherd was pressing his foot.

'Really, Denis! I have to draw *something*. What do you expect me to draw?'

'I don't know, dear. You're doing quite well. It is a bedroom suite. But I sometimes feel you're still in the cloisters.'

'Do the Time Sheets,' Bertie commanded, with mock sternness.

'I hoped you would finish them off this afternoon.'

'Oh, Denis, really!' Bertie seemed both cross and pleased at the same time. 'You expect me to do everything.'

'Not everything, darling. Tell me what you think of Leslie.'

'As a designer, or a cup of tea?'

'Tea, darling, tea.'

'I'd say she'd had it.'

'Had it! Too true: too often. Never was one myself for the wide open spaces.'

Ellie turned to look at them, hoping for some clue to Bertie's yelp of laughter: she saw none. Bertie, catching her eye, became prim again. He said: 'We're shocking baby.'

'You're not,' said Ellie regretfully, 'I haven't understood a word.'

When, between eleven and mid-day, tea was made in the paint-shop, it was Ellie's task to collect four cups for the studio and distribute them. Then, if she had the courage, she would have opportunity to talk to someone – but to whom? It seemed to her that only Rhoda was possible. An attempt to approach one of the men might be misunderstood.

Rhoda made no move, at any time, to talk to anyone. If she caught Ellie's eye, she smiled, but without encouragement. She was a large plump woman, claiming to be delicate. She was always asking the painters to shut windows, or move furniture, so that she might be screened from draughts. On cold days she wrapped a rug round her legs. Shut in by furniture, wrapped in her rug, she would perch on a high stool, surrounded by her materials – her crocodile handbag, her crocodile court shoes (she changed into sheepskin slippers), her box of biscuits, her cigarettes, and the novel she read while she drank her tea – a small island on which she was marooned for most of the day.

Denis never went near her. Bertie occasionally strolled over to her, and when this happened Ellie would try to overhear their conversation. A conversation between painters might prove as dazzlingly strange as were most conversations between Bertie and Denis. Unfortunately it did not, but Ellie learnt something about Rhoda. Rhoda lived in a place called Golders Green, a place so remote she had to have her own car in which to drive to and from the studio. From her mention of the lily-pond, the big lawn, the little lawn, 'Mummy's awful plaster gnomes' and Daddy's irises, Ellie came to believe Rhoda lived in the country. That might prove a hindrance to friend-ship between Rhoda and Ellie. Still, when Ellie brought in the tea, she served Rhoda last and lingered to look at the jointed stems of bamboos, the pointed leaves, the little figures, the 'Willow Pattern' bridges and so on, all, in some odd way, associated with the studio's pet period, Regency. She said with Bertie's intonation: 'Very nice.'

Rhoda smiled, saying nothing.

Ellie asked: 'Did you understand what Bertie and Denis were talking about this morning?'

'I wasn't listening.'

Ellie attempted a version of the conversation. At the end of it, Rhoda said vaguely: 'I don't suppose it meant anything much,' and she opened her novel and glanced at it several times as though she could not keep her atten-tion from it.

Ellie went away, wondering whether the conversation between Denis and Bertie had meant anything. Her mother would have dismissed it at once as 'a lot of nonsense.' For that reason, Ellie was unwilling to dismiss it. 'I must understand everything,' she decided, 'Everything.' But she need expect no help from Rhoda. She feared she would never get to know her at all, and there she was right. Rhoda left without warning a few weeks later. She sent a note to Bertie which he read aloud: 'My daddy thinks work in the studio is too much for me.'

'I can't bear it,' said Denis, and neither mentioned Rhoda again.

4

When Ellie realised Rhoda had gone for good, she thought: 'I may be promoted to her job.' Hope spiralled up from the pit of her stomach and, like a spring, shot her into a state near hysteria. She had swallowed back so much dejection that here it was, leaping out at her with a different look. She eyed Denis and asked herself why she should not fall in love with him. The fact that no one wanted her need not deprive her of the excitement of wanting someone.

At the thought, she suddenly rushed across the studio, flung her arms round Denis and said: 'Darling Denis, will I get Rhoda's job?'

Denis, a gold cigarette-holder between his teeth, looked down on her and opened his eyes in astonishment: 'Heavens above! What has happened to baby?'

Ellie let her arms drop but she kept her manner up as best she could: 'Tell me, tell me, tell me – will I get Rhoda's job?'

'It is most unlikely.'

'But why not?'

'Don't be silly. Could you do Rhoda's job?'

'Yes.'

'Of course you couldn't.' Denis sat down to his paper, not bothering to say more.

A little deflated, Ellie said: 'Well, I'm jolly glad Rhoda's gone. Now we'll get someone different. I love change. I feel something wonderful's going to happen.'

Denis looked across at Bertie: 'Do you feel something wonderful's going to happen, Bertie?'

'No.'

'Alas, we've done everything, seen everything, heard everything – even that "most melodious twang." Nothing wonderful can happen again.'

'What "most melodious twang"?' asked Ellie.

'Go away and find out for yourself.'

Even when irritated, Denis's manner was tolerant. He gave a sort of comic act of irritation. Ellie felt she could say anything to Denis, but to Bertie she could say almost nothing. She often told herself: 'I like Denis,' but she could not change this to 'I love.' It was not Denis's face that came into her mind when, between sleeping and waking, the guard slipped from memory.

For three weeks she was the only woman on the first floor. With Rhoda, some restraint went from the air. Not only was Ellie in an odd fever of excitement at this time, but she sent out her excitement like an emanation, and only Bertie was not amused. The painters and carpenters called after her: 'Come here, duck!' 'Hey, sugar!' 'Hey, strawberry!' and tried to catch her as she dodged from them.

Denis she thought a brilliant wit. When he held up her pen-knife to Bertie and said: 'My dear, look! An edge like a consumptive's temperature-chart,' Bertie gave a pallid smile, but Ellie, intoxicated by all the attention she was receiving, leant her head against the wall and wept with laughter.

All went well for two weeks and two days, then Denis's mood changed. It changed overnight. One day he spent leaning against Bertie's wardrobe telling stories about a friend called Edwin who was a tolerable companion so long as one could listen, at any time, in any place, to the story of his constipation: the next, he was silent at his desk, not working on his crossword puzzle, but gazing, head pressed to hand, at a sheet of blank paper. When Ellie crossed to him, as confident as ever, and said: 'Denis darling, let me decorate the little desk that's just come in!' Denis replied coldly: 'Certainly not.'

'Oh, Denis!'

Looking over her head, he said to Bertie: 'For heaven's sake, give this girl something to do. Don't let her pester me.'

This, unlike most of Denis's shows of annoyance, was not good-humoured. All Ellie's dash was gone in a moment. Bertie set her to work. He gave his instructions in whispers. A mourning chill hung over the studio.

After a while Ellie found courage to whisper to Bertie: 'What is the matter with Denis?'

Bertie whispered back: 'He is writing a film script.'

This made Ellie feel a little better. She had gathered from conversations that Denis had once been employed by a film unit, but the slump in British films had thrown him out of work. It was Bertie's influence that had found him the studio job, but he could not take it seriously. He was waiting for the film world to need him again.

That day, and for the rest of the week, Bertie received no better treatment than Ellie had done. He accepted it in the manner of a loyal wife respectful of her husband's humours. He tip-toed about, doing Denis's work as well as his own, and it seemed to Ellie he looked rather smug, as though he thought it as well she should have discovered the realities of Denis's temperament.

The studio employees were allowed to take off one Saturday morning in three. Denis took his that week. On Monday morning he arrived looking wan and sombre, but with head lifted, again aware there was an outer world. Ellie felt he would now like to be questioned about his script, but she was taking no risks. Bertie also kept silence. In the middle of the morning Denis crossed over to where they were working. There was a long pause, then Bertie asked with casual gentleness: 'How's it going?'

Denis shrugged his shoulders. His face was ghostly, his eyelids pink. He said: 'I've given it up.'

Bertie clicked his tongue and sighed: 'But why?' He looked as though all his efforts had been wasted.

'Unsaleable subject.'

'What was it about?'

'The future; push-button warfare; lots of maniacs shut up in towers madly pushing buttons to destroy each other's toy cities and aircraft and ships. The ordinary human beings going about their ordinary lives, and the little groups of loonies who want war isolated, and fuming and pissing themselves, and issuing bulletins no one reads, and pretending to one another they're important.'

'In towers,' said Bertie, making a mental effort. 'How did they get there?'

'They've been put there: perhaps they're lunatic asylums – that's an idea. The normal human beings have realised at last how crazy these power-mad loonies are. They've collected the lot of them together, stuck them inside and told them to get on with their wars on their own. The rest of the world simply goes on living a normal life without them.'

'Um.'

'Not saleable, eh?' Denis suddenly swung on Ellie: 'You wouldn't go to a film like that, would you?'

Ellie blushed with pride that her opinion should be sought, 'That's just the sort of film I would go to. I always go to the Classic.'

'Oh, well!' Denis turned away. 'I might take another look at it.'

Bertie said: 'What you've told me is simply an idea. Where's the story?'

'There's plenty of story. Think of all the conflicts among the button pushers – the establishment building, the jealousies over promotion, the pretensions, the lies, the vanities, the rows. They imagine they're the real world, and, of course, they're no longer anything.'

Bertie said quietly: 'Still, that's not a story.'

'I suppose it isn't.' Denis was biting the side of his finger-nail; he paused, wry-faced, as though his nail were bitter: 'Have to think about it.' He wandered back to his desk, pulled his newspaper over his manuscript and bent over the crossword puzzle. That, so far as Ellie could tell, was the end of the film script.

Later that day Mrs Primrose came into the studio and talked to Denis for some time. A communication of importance. Ellie peered anxiously out from her hiding-place. When Mrs Primrose left him, Denis smiled over to the others, recovered, apparently, from his creative attack. 'A new young woman, my dears. A little playmate for Ellie. A brilliant girl – scholarship to the Slade, and such *brilliant* flower designs!'

'Did you see them?' asked Bertie.

'No. I'll see them soon enough.'

On the following Monday morning Miss Nancy Claypole started work. She was a tall, thin, bespectacled girl with a prudish appearance. Ellie thought she looked even more discouraging than Rhoda.

With Miss Claypole on his hands, Denis gazed vaguely round the studio, then led her over to a notorious chest-of-drawers, a large Edwardian piece on which Bertie had refused to waste his talent.

'There, darling,' said Denis, 'This delightful commode has been specially reserved for you. It is a genuine *Bête Blanche* and when in the possession of Madame de Montespan was one of the *sensations de Paris* – or so we've been told. It is mentioned in the works of Kirchenbaum and is believed to be the very commode in which Napoleon kept his socks.'

'What am I to do with it?'

'Oh, just pretty it up. Sprinkle it with forget-me-nots.'

Ellie, who had watched Miss Claypole's entry with a certain sulky envy, glanced out now to see how she was facing up to Denis's humour. Denis, seeing Ellie, seized her arm – 'Here's our junior, our odd-job girl. She'll show you where everything is,' and made his escape.

Ellie grew red at Denis's description of her. She could not be more than three years junior to this young woman. Ellie looked at her, smiling grudgingly, and met the eyes of an ally.

'What am I to do with this thing?' Miss Claypole asked as though she believed Ellie could advise her, 'I bet the *bête* was an elephant.'

Ellie's eyes widened in admiration at Miss Claypole's wit, and Miss Claypole, conscious of having made an impression, started to giggle. Her small, ginger-brown eyes, pinpointed behind spectacles, jigged about, giving her so mischievous a look that Ellie giggled, too. Ellie did not know why Miss Claypole was laughing so much, but the extraordinary naughtiness of Miss Claypole's expression, compared with the propriety of her staid body, her severe features, seemed to Ellie unbearably funny. She almost wept as she laughed. Suddenly the two girls were caught up in a madness of giggling. Each time each caught the other's eye, their giggles were renewed: they became convulsive, wild, almost sick with laughter.

'Really, girls!' said Bertie.

Bertie, pained and unamused, seemed to them funnier than anything else. Miss Claypole said pleadingly: 'Oh, no!' and Ellie sank to the floor and leant helplessly against the chest-of-drawers. Denis raised his head and watched them with a mild smile.

'What *is* the joke?' Bertie asked with patient impatience.

Neither could answer, but, looking affectionately at each other, they felt the alliance of their femininity, their girlhood and their understanding of each other. They had fallen into friendship, immediate and complete. This friendship started fully grown; later it was confirmed by the similarity of their circumstances.

Nancy came from Bleckworth, a small Midland town, where her father was a bank manager. She had overridden her parents' plan to make her a shorthand-typist and talked them into sending her each day, by bus, to a Birmingham art school. From there she had taken a scholarship to the Slade. The grant that went with it had been so small that she had, during her first year in London, to sleep in a hostel cubicle. After that an uncle had made her an allowance and she could afford a room of her own.

Ellie was impressed by Nancy's scholarship to the Slade. Nancy, too, was a unique and remarkable person. Ellie asked: 'Were you miserable at home?'

'Not miserable, exactly; just bored. Bleckworth wasn't my world.'

'Nor Eastsea mine.'

'How lucky we've been to escape.'

'And how did you get into the studio?'

'My uncle told me to ring Mrs Primrose. He'd met her somewhere. I think she was quite glad to get me. It's not everyone who can manage on her idea of a salary.'

Nancy's salary was higher than Ellie's: she still had the allowance from her uncle, but most of her money went on the large bed-sitting-room she rented near South Kensington station. It left her as poor as Ellie. This fact drew them closer. They shared the triumphs of economy.

Nancy went to the canteen on her first day and said: 'Thank God for it.'

When they had eaten, she asked: 'Do you ever lick your plate?'

'Good heavens, no!'

'I do. When I'm hungry.' Her eyes danced at this victory over respectability, a victory that went further than any of Ellie's victories.

Dumbfounded, Ellie asked: 'Here? Would you do it here?'

'Perhaps not here. The plates don't look too clean.'

Faced with the queues, the heaped dishes, the dirty

tables, the food; entertained by tales of black-beetles and cord in cabbage, Nancy said: 'Who cares! It's cheap.'

Ellie glowed as she looked at Nancy's plain, long-featured face. Here was a friend and comrade; an equal in daring; a girl who had appetite to lick a plate.

Nancy said: 'Even if we're not paid much, we're doing our own work. I've heard of art students washing dishes in hotels, cleaning windows, acting as waiters, scrubbing stairs in blocks of flats. Some have even had to go into advertising. We can't complain, really.'

The girls took to meeting on Saturday evenings. Usually they went to the Classic Cinema, but if one or other was saving for some necessity of life, they would walk to Knightsbridge and look in the lighted windows of shops. Sometimes they went as far as Regent Street. Then they would visit an Espresso bar for coffee, talking long after the coffee was drunk, aware that they were grown-up, responsible and independent persons who stayed up as late as they thought fit.

On Sundays they would meet in the afternoons and visit the Victoria and Albert Museum. When that became over-familiar, they went, at the cost of a weekday meal, the long bus ride to the British Museum. After that a desire for discovery came down on them. They would walk, quite late at night, through Tottenham Court Road, Charing Cross Road, Shaftesbury Avenue and Soho, defensively, but, when the danger was past, congratulating themselves on having no such fears as their mothers would have had.

'The truth is,' said Nancy, 'we are natural Londoners.'

Their evenings together had a quality of recklessness that kept them in continuous, giggling excitement. At the sight of a dark and narrow street, they would say: 'Let's explore,' hoping they were taking a risk. There was no knowing what they might do, or see, or discover: or, when they later talked, their spirits heightened by adventure, how their thought might be revolutionised by speech.

It seemed to Ellie that Nancy surprised her more often than she surprised Nancy. Nancy, after all, looked so unlikely to surprise. Despite the jigging mischief of her eyes, she surprised Ellie most by her continual interest in the male sex. At the smallest blink from a young man in a café or a cinema queue, Nancy would flush and grin in delight of the chase.

Ellie supposed herself aged by experience. How could she, who awaited Quintin's return, be conscious of ordinary young men in queues? She longed to tell Nancy she had touched the ultimate of experience in such matters, but she doubted the wisdom of doing so. Nancy might disapprove of the ultimate: or, if she approved, she might be envious and their friendship suffer from an inequality.

Here, again, it was Nancy who was to surprise Ellie. It was a Saturday night. They had seen at the cinema an old film called 'Mayerling', then gone to a snack bar for coffee. Ellie, wrapped still in the fogs of romantic tragedy, of illicit but enduring love, of snow-bound palaces, of luxury and death, forgot Nancy's presence and let her head droop and her eyes swim with tears.

'Who was he?' Nancy asked. She allowed herself four cigarettes a day and had just lit the last of them.

Ellie gulped. After a moment of snuffling into her handkerchief and pretending to blow her nose, she said, husky but defiant: 'Who was who?'

'Whoever you're mooning over.'

Ellie, able to look up at last, caught the glint of Nancy's mocking eye. 'Come on, now,' said Nancy. 'Did you go the whole hog?'

Ellie's lips parted: she blushed more in astonishment than guilt. 'Why? Did *you*? Ever?'

'Of course. Lots of times.' While Nancy's thin, soft mouth stretched complacently, her eyes showed their triumph at Ellie's surprise. 'What did you think?'

'I didn't think,' Ellie untruthfully murmured. She looked down again, ashamed that her own experience had been so slight. After a long silence, having swallowed back her tears, she said: 'There was someone, but I'm afraid it's all over now. He said he wouldn't be able to see me for some time.'

'And you haven't heard from him since?'

'No.'

'Hah! Trying out some new female. Trying to keep you in reserve.'

'Oh no!' Ellie grew pale at the thought. 'It couldn't be that.' And yet, what else could it be?

'Forget about him,' said Nancy.

'I am forgetting about him,' Ellie said meekly. When she could, she smiled and said: 'Tell me about yours.'

'Oh, I could never be bothered mooning after just one. I like lots.'

'Goodness! And have you someone now?'

'Not exactly now. At the moment, as a matter of fact, I'm bored with men. I was thinking only tonight how much nicer it is to have a woman friend. Don't you think we have much more fun together, enjoying things, saying what we think, being free, instead of each trailing around pandering to the vanity of some stupid man who expects you to be grateful because he buys you sardines on toast?'

Ellie's eyes widened and shone: her cheeks glowed as she considered how they were constantly amazing each other with the originality of their ideas, the breadth of their concepts. She said: 'You're absolutely right.'

Nancy gazed at Ellie. From pleasurable emotion, she glistened pink as a peony, her eyes were no more than intense sparks behind their spectacles, and at last, as though her heart were breaking open with a fact she could no longer suppress, she said: 'I have a rich uncle in the country. Not far from London.'

'Have you?' Ellie was not certain what was expected of her.

'Next time he asks me for a week-end, would you like to come with me?'

'But I'd love to.'

Ellie was surprised Nancy could have any doubt about it, but later she began to suspect Nancy's doubt was of her own wisdom in inviting her. As time passed and the invitation was not repeated Ellie began to fear that, like the hot buttered scones, it would disappear altogether. She kept it in view by asking, whenever there was an opening, questions about Nancy's rich uncle.

She learnt he was called Tom Claypole; his house called Clopals. The eldest of a large family of brothers and sisters, he alone had been sent to a university. When he had taken a degree at Oxford, he went to London, wrote occasionally to his mother, but came home only once, to attend her funeral.

'He just despised the lot of them,' said Nancy, 'and I'm not surprised. Sometimes my aunts would go to London to shop or see a matinée. At first they used to ring him up and get invited to lunch, but he always had other people at the same time so that he wouldn't have to talk to them. They got awfully offended and stopped seeing him, but they found out all they could about him. They were always telling their friends how he'd made money and married into a county family. I can't tell you how ghastly my relatives are.'

'Mine would be, too, if I had any.'

'I made up my mind that when I came to London I would look him up and let him see how different I am.'

'And what happened?'

'It took me ages to track him down. He'd retired and gone to live in the country. He lives alone. His wife is dead.'

'And you went to Clopals? – the place you thought we might visit?'

'Yes.'

They were walking in Kensington Gardens. They walked two hundred yards in silence before Nancy said impetuously: 'Look here! If I take you down there you must promise you won't vamp him.'

'Vamp him!' Ellie was astounded. 'Vamp him, for goodness sake! Why, you said he's nearly a hundred.'

'Yes, but he's rich as well.'

'*Nancy!*'

Nancy glanced sideways at Ellie, then said contritely: 'Well, I've suffered . . .' She glanced again and said: 'I'm sorry. I should have known you were different. But he's susceptible.'

'Do you mean he's a menace?'

'Goodness, no. He's terribly old-fashioned. You even

have to go carefully with lipstick. As for . . . well, if you ever let him know you'd . . .'

'As though I would!'

'Well, don't! And the next time he invites me, I'll ring him and ask if I can take you there with me.'

5

Tom Claypole's invitation to Nancy came in early March when winter was breaking and the cool brilliance of spring was lighting the evening streets. Tom was willing that Nancy should bring her new friend. He asked for Ellie's address and sent her a separate invitation. To Nancy he sent their railway tickets.

Denis agreed they could take their free Saturday together. They left on Friday evening. Passing from the clutter of London to the country horizon, they saw, among the placid and spacious curves of the Chilterns, bursting tree buds and hawthorns sprayed with white. Primroses opened in safety on the railway banks and the sunset still lingered at six o'clock.

Ellie said: 'What will happen to us this year? What will we do? Who will we meet?'

'We may get married.'

'I don't suppose I'll ever marry. Quintin is married already and his wife won't divorce him.'

'That's an old story.'

This was no time to argue with Nancy. Ellie, alight with spring and the visit ahead, put Quintin from her and so concentrated on her good fortune at meeting Nancy that she said: 'How lucky it was you who came to the studio!' and she might have flung her arms round her friend had the lights not come on suddenly and made her self-conscious.

As soon as the sun slid below the horizon, darkness fell. When they arrived, they stepped out into a cold sharper than mid-winter. Above the station, with its two little oil lamps, rose the deep, surprising blue of the country sky. A shadow on the platform approached the girls and touched a cap.

Nancy at once took on the manner of the employing class. She smiled down on the little chauffeur and said with polished cordiality: 'Good evening, Partridge. Very nice to see you again.'

'Very nice to see you, Miss,' said Partridge.

Under the first lamp, Nancy winked at Ellie. As they sat on the broad, pneumatic back seat of Tom Claypole's car, she whispered: 'You wait till dinner. I bet there'll be at least grouse.'

Clopals, when the headlamps picked it out of the darkness, showed white, a low-built, weather-boarded house in colonial style, over the front of which a climbing-rose ran like a plan of the nervous system. The door opened as they arrived. From the hall came a red-golden glow as from the heart of a fire. Ellie, passing from the night cold into warmth, as into safety, was touched suddenly as though by a memory of some past happiness, acutely sweet. She groped in her mind to account for it but could find nothing. She was distracted by the appearance of Tom Claypole, who came from a room to greet them.

He took Ellie's hand and looked intently into her face: 'How kind of you to visit an old man!'

'How kind of you to let me come.' After a moment she thought to add: 'Besides, you're not old.'

His face broke into a smile. He patted her hand approvingly.

The girls had been given adjoining rooms that shared a balcony. The housekeeper, Mrs Fitton, moved between the rooms, simpering, giving Ellie inquisitive and critical glances that sent her at last out on to the balcony to await the woman's departure. There was silence like cosmic silence. She held her breath and felt the silence, filled with tenderness for the countryside lying about her like a dark-furred creature, asleep, wild but gentle.

Suddenly she burst in through Nancy's door and said: 'How wonderful it is, the country!'

'But you can't see it.'

'I mean the silence. The smell and the silence.'

The drawing-room at Clopals was curtained against the night. The area around the fire, to which three arm-chairs had been drawn, was screened into a small stronghold of comfort. A butler's table, put down among the chairs, held decanters and glasses. When the girls came down, Tom poured them sherry, then, sitting back with his cigar, he said to Ellie:

'I hope, my dear, you will find it tolerable here. We are not at all grand. It is a small household. I've only the Fittons and Partridge to look after me: but they manage, they manage. Food simple but good; that sort of thing.'

Ellie replied that the house and everything about it seemed to her wonderful. While Tom questioned Nancy about her work in the studio, Ellie, with some caution, looked about her. She was willing to admire these surroundings, but not to seem unused to them. Beside her, where she sat on one side of the fireplace, the firelight glanced over the brass and tortoise-shell framework of a glass cabinet. It held a collection of figures that minced and gesticulated like the figures Bertie drew – valuable, no doubt, but they meant nothing to her. On the lowest shelf, leaping like spray in the moving light, was a cluster of white coral. It saddened her, set there, so far from its own sea. She felt the pang of the deserter.

'And you also work in this studio?' Tom asked Ellie.

'They only let me do "antiquing".'

'"Antiquing"! Dear me! No deception intended? Is it hard work?'

'No, it's fun. I enjoy it.' Ellie started to laugh. 'One day I was "antiquing" a wardrobe: I was working inside it. The paint was new, of course, and the smell was so strong that everything went black and I fell out on to the floor.'

'Bless my soul! That doesn't seem to me work for a young lady.'

'But I love it.' Ellie was suddenly afraid that Tom might protest to Mrs Primrose. 'We're lucky to be doing our own work,' she said. 'We're lucky to be there.'

Ellie looked at Nancy. Nancy, sitting with her feet under her, smiled and was complacently silent, watching her uncle and friend as though conscious of being the begetter of all that passed between them.

When they went in to dinner, Ellie noticed the fire at the other end of the drawing-room. It burnt there all by itself, picking out the gilt on picture frames and the spines of books, forming a genial little world that no one troubled to inhabit. There was a log fire in the hall and another in the dining-room. There had been fires in each of the girls' bedrooms. Ellie contemplated this extravagance with wonder. At first she was disturbed by it, then it seemed as it should be: 'For goodness sake,' she told herself, 'let us have fires everywhere.' For a moment she exulted over the cheeseparing life of Eastsea; she felt angry with her mother, who had never secured for herself the warmth of wealth: then her anger collapsed, leaving her silent and guilty as Fitton took away the soup-plates and cut up two roast chickens.

Nancy grumbled skittishly: 'And I betted Ellie it would be grouse.'

Tom turned on her with unexpected irritation: 'My dear girl, *grouse!* At this time of the year?'

Nancy made a comical face, but Tom was not appeased: 'If you wish to be accepted among civilised people, my dear, you must learn not to make these ridiculous mistakes.'

'Won't do it again.'

'I hope not.'

Tom looked at Ellie and, meeting her worried gaze, smiled, relaxing, and ordered Fitton to open another bottle of Meursault-Perrières.

He said to Ellie: 'A rather nice burgundy, don't you think? Unfortunately I've come to the end of the '47.'

'I think myself,' said Ellie, quoting Quintin with an air, 'that the '50 is just as good.'

Tom leant towards her: 'You may be right,' he nodded gravely, his small black eyes bright with amusement.

Ellie drank off her glass and let it be refilled, but already there was a division between herself and the material world. She was beginning to float on that sea of exalted benevolence she had almost forgotten since

Quintin had ceased to take her out to dinner. An old sense of luxury and ease pervaded her, but she refused a third glass.

Slowly, with the intent appreciation of a man used to dining alone, Tom drank most of the second bottle himself. The conversation was still restrained. Ellie, when Tom looked in her direction, smiled but had little to say.

With a hint of aggression in her tone, Nancy asked: 'Has Maxine been down lately?'

Tom replied in an off-hand way: 'Yes, a couple of weeks ago.'

'How is she?'

'Very well. Very well indeed.' He fidgeted with his glass.

When the girls withdrew to the main room, Ellie asked: 'Who is Maxine?'

'Ah!' said Nancy as she poured the coffee. 'You may well ask.' She looked dramatically severe. 'She was – *was*, mark you – a friend of yours truly. I knew her at the Slade. She was quite a bit older than me but we had digs near one another in Gower Street and we gradually got pally. I thought she was a wonder in those days. I wanted to show her off to Tom. I brought her here – and she just annexed him.'

'How?'

'I don't know. She made a set at him: he loved it. After we'd been down once or twice, he invited her but not me. Then she brought down her cousin, Erica, who was looking for a house in these parts. Erica didn't cut much ice, of course: Tom's not interested in married girls. But she lives in the village now and she's always ringing up. She keeps a look-out for Maxine. She lets her know everything. If Tom's unwell, Maxine's down like a shot. If she knew you were here, she'd try and winkle you out like a pin. That's our Maxie.'

The telephone rang in the hall.

'There!' said Nancy.

'But why all this? What do they want with Tom? Surely he's too old . . .'

'Oh yes. Too old to be a nuisance. It's just a Beautiful Friendship. Maxine has her eye on the cash.'

'She thinks he'll leave it to her?'

'He'll leave it to someone.'

'Why not to you? You're his niece.'

Nancy's colour heightened. She looked down at the carpet, but said only: 'I'll never get anything. I can't go on doing and saying the right thing for long enough.'

When Tom joined them, Ellie saw him as though a new dimension had been added to him. He was not merely a human being: he was a rich man, aware of the power of his money; generous to those within the area of his power: perhaps less generous to those outside it.

Fitton added a brandy decanter and liqueurs to the tray by the fire.

Tom said to Ellie: 'Well, young lady? Crème de Menthe, I suppose?'

'I prefer green Chartreuse.'

'Indeed!' Tom raised his brows approvingly.

'It's a much nicer colour.'

This entertained him as it might once have entertained Quintin. Ellie felt a little of the elation she had felt with Quintin when he had laughed so much in acknowledgement of her wit, making her feel no commonplace, temporary partner in this game, but a natural player. She had had some opinion of herself in those days. For goodness sake, was she not someone? Where had her brilliance gone?

As the Chartreuse added to the warmth of the wine, her confidence picked itself up. Couldn't she defeat a dozen Maxines? She leant towards Tom, smelling about him the scent of cigars and a little sourness of wine: the scent, it seemed to her, of an earlier, richer generation.

She said: 'You know, you look like an Edwardian roué.'

'Dear me!' He smirked into his brandy glass. 'I suppose to you young things I'm just a period piece?'

'You're a darling,' said Ellie.

She put out her hand and touched the garnet-coloured velvet of his frogged smoking-jacket. As her hand moved away, he caught it and held it a moment, then let it slide from him. His smile surprised her. Disconcerted, she retreated into the depths of her chair and made no further moves that evening.

6

Next morning the girls had the little breakfast-room to themselves. Tom took his breakfast in bed. When Nancy was staying there alone, Tom usually spent the morning in his room. With mischievous smiles, Nancy predicted that he would this day make an early appearance.

The breakfast-room overlooked the great lawn that dropped in a long, slow slope down to a stream. Beyond this rose the boundary woods that tossed, stormy black, against a wet sky. Here and there in the grass a few daffodils were opening. They, too, tossed in the wind, yellow as yellow light in the grey, gusty, bitter brightness of the morning. To one side, hiding most of the Partridges' cottage, three trees stood dark and stiff-boughed, their foliage lifted about them like iron wings.

'What are they?'

'Cedars.'

Ellie looked out at them as she ate, content that she had added cedars to her experience of the world.

The fires were alight in the drawing-room. Three french windows, opening on to the lawn, quivered in the uproarious wind. Ellie gazed longingly into the unexplored garden, but Nancy said: 'Not today. Let's be comfortable while we have the chance.'

When, about eleven o'clock, Tom appeared, he said: 'Have you shown Ellie my roses?'

'I shouldn't have thought there was anything to show.'

'Of course there is.' He turned from Nancy with scornful impatience and called Ellie over to a portfolio-holder. 'I have a few prints and water-colours of roses here. What do you think of that? "The Celsiana Rose".'

She peered into the faded silver-pink of the petals, the faded silver-green of the leaves, then took the drawing over to the light and looked again.

'Shall we go and see them?'

'I'd love to see them.'

'Not me,' said Nancy, 'I'll stay by the fire.'

When Ellie came downstairs dressed for out-of-doors, she found Tom waiting in the hall. His fur-lined great-coat of Donegal tweed reached to his ankles: his tweed cap had ear-flaps: he carried a shooting-stick.

Ellie had imagined they were about to visit a hot-house where roses bloomed all the year round. Instead she was taken beyond the cedars to an arrangement of rose-beds, grey-earthed and exposed. Here, standing in a wind that turned as it blew, tugging her clothes this way and that, spattering rain in her face, she wondered why the rose-shoots did not shrink back into the stem.

Tom, propped by his shooting-stick, ignored the edgy wind, the blae, changing sky, the sting of the rain's attack, and gazed at his roses with love.

'Look there! Aren't they pr'y?'

Ellie, following his outstretched hand on which the blotched and yellow skin was wrinkled like an old glove, peered down at the spiny wood. Yes, leaves, tightly wrapped but green, their outer edges curling back, had broken forth like little sweet-pokes made of jade.

'The rose,' said Tom, 'is white and flat like a gardenia. Here is a red one of the same order, Roseraie de l'Hay. When one of the old poets likened a girl's lips to a rose, he meant, don't you know, this sort of rose. Nowadays, girls looking as they do, he'd no doubt mean one of those new hybrid-teas coloured like a boiled lobster.' He gave Ellie's lips a swift, critical glance and, seeming satisfied by what he saw, returned to his rose-bed. He moved round it slowly. As he went, he talked of roses – burgundy-coloured, bloomed like velvet; roses grey-mauve like tissue-paper, purple at the heart; the Zepherine Drouhin, the thornless rose, as pink as pink china; the Jaune Desprez coloured like an apricot; blush roses, moss roses, musk roses . . .

Ellie, catching her breath against the onslaught of the wind, thought of the summer, the mild air of June, the branches weighted with roses. She was filled with longing – but for whom? There was only one name in her mind. She said to herself: 'I will not think of him,' but of whom else could she think?

Tom straightened himself uneasily: 'Ah! Um!' he said, 'My lumbago putting me through the hoops.' He pressed a hand into his back and, looking at her wind-whipped cheeks, said:

'You are like a rose yourself.'

She protested, rather crossly: 'Oh no. I'm ugly.'

'Silly!' He drew out a silk handkerchief and wiped his eyes and blew his nose. 'You're quite a little beauty, you know.'

She did not believe it. She would have chosen another face. She said: 'No one at Eastsea ever thought so.'

Tom laughed. He raised his face to the sky: 'Bit dicky overhead. Still, care to risk a stroll?'

He took her arm. They went down through a shrubbery sheltered by a wall of laurel. Ellie burnt with the remembrance that she had been called a beauty. Though she could not believe it, she could not resist asking: 'When you said I was quite a beauty, did you mean it? Or were you pulling my leg?'

Tom squeezed her arm tightly. 'Don't you have any doubts about yourself, my dear. I still have an eye for beauty even though I'm only an old materialist with one foot in the grave.'

'Really a materialist? Do you mean you don't believe in any sort of a next world?'

'Not in any sort. We're just machines. When we're worn out, we're done for: thrown away: finished: *kaput*.' He made a gesture of finality, but Ellie was too concerned to leave matters there.

She said: 'Don't you ever *feel* immortal?'

She glanced askance at him, seeing at the same time his age and his unbelief. Because he thought himself mortal, he seemed to her a clay man, the dust of mortality lying in the folds of his skin. It was almost as though he had about him an aura of decay. Repelled, she would have moved from him if he had not held her arm: yet she felt compassion.

'But haven't you ever been in love?' she asked.

'Of course.' He was slightly impatient of the question. 'You must surely know that a man of my age has been in love many times.' He sighed, and after a long pause added: 'Many, many times.'

'And even then you did not feel immortal?'

He laughed: 'Even less than usual.'

She wanted to ask if he were not afraid to die, but the question seemed too cruel. After reflecting for some moments, she said simply: 'I am sure I am immortal.'

'I envy your conviction. I am afraid I cannot emulate it.'

The dry remoteness of his voice silenced Ellie for so long that he started to speak, as though to make amends: 'As you grow old, don't you know, your ideas change. When I was young, I used to plot against death – how I might live to be a hundred or more. Or I used to think that, with all the scientific discoveries, the world progressing as it seemed to be, some means of defeating age and death would be found long before I became old. My father often said: "Ah, my boy, we're on the brink of great discoveries. There will be wondrous changes. I won't live to see them, but you will." I used to think how fortunate I was. Now I realise life changes: it doesn't improve.'

'Oh, I don't know!' said Ellie. 'Rationing stopped.'

'Rationing!' Tom threw back his head and gave a bark of laughter. 'That didn't last long.'

'Long enough. I didn't remember not having it. When mother said "Sweets weren't rationed before the war!" I could scarcely believe her. But then, I didn't believe in "before the war" either. I thought the war was permanent, like the Government or the town council or the rates, or one of the other things people grumble about.'

'What a baby!' Tom's arm weighed heavily on Ellie as they walked down the slope between the trees. He moved stiffly, trying to hide his age and keep his shoulders square. 'We all grow old,' he said. 'I've grown old, just as my father did. Indeed, at my age, he looked a lot younger than I do. There's no need to envy the young. It's all over too quickly. Ah!' He shook his head. 'You're eighteen? Nineteen? When I was eighteen it seemed we were reaching the Golden Age. Horror, cruelty, injustice – all those things were being left behind.' He turned his head and looked directly into Ellie's face: 'Was it a great shock to you to discover the present is no better than the past?'

'I don't think so. I grew up during the war. I didn't expect much.'

'So you've no cause for complaint?'

'I'm not complaining.' Ellie raised her chin a little. 'I think I'm jolly lucky.'

'Do you read the newspapers?'

'Not often. Denis does, at the studio. He says we're just waiting for it.'

'For what?'

'The bomb, of course.'

Tom stared at her a moment, then laughed in his throat. 'Yes, quite so! The bomb!'

They had come to the end of the shrubbery and, as the trees parted, they could see the wet sky lifting like a canopy to reveal the wet light of the west. As it brightened, the day changed from winter into spring.

Tom, looking about him with a gratified expression, said: 'Dear me, yes, the bomb! Not much future after that!' He smiled into himself, but suddenly turned to Ellie and seemed concerned for her: he squeezed her arm again. 'Surely you don't worry about atom bombs?'

'Hydrogen bombs!' Ellie automatically corrected him. 'No, I hardly ever give them a thought. Besides, they're a sort of insurance against getting old and not marrying and having no money and perhaps dying alone of starvation in a basement, the way old people do. I just tell myself: "Don't worry, we'll all be dead long before that happens".'

'Upon my soul!' Tom stared at her, astounded. 'Do you mean to tell me that's the way young people look at life these days?'

'Of course not. Only when they stop to think about it – and how often is that?'

'You're a frivolous lot.' Tom spoke severely but smiled as he spoke. 'Follow my example, my dear. When I was at the 'varsity I did two things: I opened a deposit account and I took out a subscription to *The Times*.'

Ellie laughed. 'I read a lot,' she said, 'I borrow everything I can get from the library. When I read Defoe or Dickens, I think "Things aren't so bad now." If I read the papers, I might think they are worse.'

Tom squeezed her arm. 'Quite a fresh little mind,' he said and, moving his hand down her arm, he squeezed her fingers: 'Cold fingers! Here!' He stopped and pulled from his pocket a pair of rabbit-lined gloves: 'Put these on.'

As her hands sunk into the fur, she was touched by his kindness. She thought that a girl might marry for kindness and count herself lucky, but there was not much ardour in the thought.

Taking her arm again, Tom smiled into her face and said: 'You'll think I'm a bit quizzy, but – you asked me if I'd ever been in love. You didn't tell me whether you had.'

Startled, Ellie gave him a guilty look, blushed and said: 'No.'

'Young woman, do you see any green in my eye?'

Not understanding the question, Ellie looked into his small, black eyes, saw he was laughing and laughed herself.

He seemed satisfied. As they walked down to the stream, he said: 'A warm, sympathetic nature like yours cannot help being attracted by the opposite sex, but I am sure you are not the sort of girl to do anything foolish.'

Ellie truthfully replied that she did not think she was.

By the stream, Tom took his arm from Ellie's and paused to wipe the wind-tears from his eyes. Ellie was glad to be released from him. She deliberately went where Tom would not wish to go – down through the long grass where primroses, each as large as half-a-crown, had reached the air on the end of long, hairy, water-pale stems. Here there were larches. Sheltered and river-fed, they were putting out their first fur of green. She pulled a branch down, the colour flashing with electric brilliance as it brushed her cheek. She breathed in a scent of citron sweetness, so pungent that her eyes filled with tears. She whispered: 'Quintin.'

Tom called her: 'You'll get your shoes soaked.'

Reluctantly, she let the branch go. When she reached Tom she said: 'The larch smells of spring.'

'No doubt. Everything smells of spring.'

Perhaps he was annoyed at being left. Contritely, Ellie slipped her arm through his: he smiled. As they turned to walk back to the house, he gazed into her face with an affection that was near tenderness.

Nancy said as they entered through the central french window: 'Maxine rang. She's coming here this afternoon.' Her glance at Ellie said: 'I told you so.'

Tom was disturbed: he lifted his arm so that Ellie's hand slipped away. 'Is she now?' he said, speaking nervously as though there were a dozen things he must do and he did not know on which to start: 'I'd better see Mrs Fitton.'

Nancy said: 'I've told Mrs Fitton. She said: "Miss Maxine's room is always ready".'

'Yes. Yes, it is.' He glanced about him, distracted completely now from his interest in Ellie. Suddenly he began to hurry from the room. 'I suppose she'll remember to put a light to Maxie's fire.'

Nancy, looking after him, nodded significantly: 'You see!' she said.

At luncheon Tom looked out from his preoccupation to say: 'I know you girls are great ones for seeing a picture on Saturday evenings. I thought tonight we might go to the little cinema. How would you like that?'

Nancy asked which film was showing. Fitton was sent to find the local paper. The name of the film meant nothing to them; no one showed enthusiasm. Tom's question was left unanswered. Indeed, Tom seemed too distracted to remember, when a few minutes had passed, that the subject had been discussed at all. As soon as luncheon was over, he said he would rest in his room. He spoke like a man preparing for a difficult time ahead.

While they drank coffee alone, Nancy said: 'I'm blest if I'm waiting here to welcome her. We'll go for a walk and come back late for tea.'

The pall over the sky had thinned: the light fell more richly, giving an illusion of warmth. They walked for a long way, skirting the ploughed, chocolate-coloured fields where the white-flowered blackthorns were singled out from anonymous hedgerows. The sun broke through as the girls returned up the lawn. At the sudden brilliance, the certainty of spring, they started running, laughing to one another, Maxine forgotten until they burst into the drawing-room and found her sitting there with Tom.

She was sitting in the chair where Ellie had sat the night before. She gave Nancy a faint smile of recognition but seemed not to notice that Ellie was with her.

'So you're back,' said Tom with some annoyance. 'I was about to ring for Fitton to take the tea away.'

'We went for a long, healthy walk.'

'Did you! Um. I've told you before, Nancy, that I prefer you to stay inside Clopals. I'm responsible for you girls while you are here.'

'I forgot.' Nancy spoke without apology. 'Can I cut this chocolate cake?'

'It's there to be cut. Mrs Fitton will bring you fresh tea.'

Tom gave Ellie a look of piqued interest. She realised they had regained his attention by their independent action. He wanted to keep them about him, to possess their interest, to know them dependent. He said to Maxine: 'You have not met Ellie before?'

When Ellie looked round she found Maxine was observing her. Without smiling or moving, Maxine said: 'How do you do?' then lifted her face as though absorbed in thoughts remote from anything about her.

Lolling in her chair, one arm drooping over her head, she looked to Ellie like one of those jointed figures that display clothes. She lolled – but stiffly. Her legs were stretched out, crossed at the ankles as though to show to advantage her expensive shoes. All her clothes looked expensive, glossy, new.

'Where did you go?' Tom asked. Nancy described their walk.

When Ellie looked at Maxine again, she saw Maxine's eyes fixed critically on her hair as though she were seeking some point on which to disparage it. She herself was dark-haired. Her eyes were dark brown, the large, clear eyeballs very white, so that they reminded Ellie of those china eggs used to trick hens.

Ellie had imagined she would find herself outfaced by a vivacious and dominating beauty. Instead, Maxine was not even much of a beauty. She had a strong, full-bosomed figure, but her features were set in heavy cheeks joined by a heavy chin that gave her face a fleshy look. While the girls ate tea, she lolled there, inert and silent, yet she outfaced them with her silence. They were all changed by her presence; Tom most of all. He no longer gave Ellie warm, admiring glances: no longer implied, by the deference of his manner, that she was a privileged and exceptional guest. Instead he kept his face turned from her.

When, some time after six, Tom was called to the telephone, Maxine, left alone with the girls, looked at Nancy and said: 'So you two are off to the cinema?'

'Are we?' Nancy looked at Ellie and began to rise as though, if Maxine wished it, she would be off to the cinema that very minute.

Ellie kept her seat. She said: 'I thought we were all going.'

'Oh!' Maxine stretched her muscles without moving her position. 'I get enough of cinemas in town.'

'We would not want to go without Tom,' said Ellie. 'After all, we came here to see him.'

Tom entered the room as she was speaking. Erica was on the telephone, he said: she wished to speak to Maxine.

Maxine began by moving slowly, then suddenly was out of the chair and crossing the room with an alert, swinging walk that seemed the walk of an altogether different person. As the door closed after her, Tom bent towards Ellie and asked: 'What was that? The cinema? I like to see a picture now and then. Shall we go?'

'If you come, too.'

'Very well, then.'

Maxine's conversation on the telephone took some time. When she returned, Tom said: 'I think, my dear, we might all go to the cinema.'

'Oh no!' Maxine's brows met darkly over the bridge of her fine, straight nose. She threw herself back in her chair as though too much were being asked of her.

'If you do not feel up to it, of course . . .' Tom spoke with a rather cool solicitude that seemed to bring Maxine to her senses.

She sat up, smiling, and said: 'If you want to go, dear, of course I'll come.'

It was arranged that they should eat sandwiches, go early to the cinema and return for a late supper. Maxine accepted these arrangements with a bland, bored smile. Ellie, feeling she had scored a point on Nancy's behalf, began to chatter about Denis Plumley, who had written film scripts for a famous unit in the days before the slump in British films. Denis, she said, lived only to return to script-writing. She described his frequent cry at the studio: 'How long, O Lord, how long?' and his crossword puzzle which he tried to solve in under ten minutes, after which successful solution he was bored because he had nothing else to do.

'And he says terribly witty things,' said Ellie.

'Indeed?' Tom smiled a smile of unbelief. 'What has he said that has particularly impressed you?'

Maxine closed her eyes, excluded but seeming to wish for nothing else.

'He's always saying things that impress me.' Ellie looked round the room in an attempt to catch her own wonder at Denis's wit. She breathed at last: 'You know . . . well, you know T. S. Eliot?'

Tom, restraining himself, nodded gravely.

'Well, I always thought everyone thought Eliot so frightfully good, no one would dream of criticising him. But Denis criticises him.'

'Um. And what does he say about Mr Eliot?'

'He says . . .' Ellie, remembering what Denis had said, started to laugh: it was some time before she could speak again. 'Denis went to Eliot's plays – I've only read them, of course, but Denis saw all of them. He was talking about Eliot's humour, and he said Eliot was like someone up from the country uncertain about tipping, and so does it very punctiliously, very exactly, putting the money down on the table and nodding to the waiter: "That is the tip, you know", and with Eliot it is: "That is the humour, you know".'

Tom gave a little shout of surprised laughter: 'That's quite good, and true. And true.'

Encouraged, Ellie recalled more of Denis's remarks that, as she read her way through the public library, were becoming more comprehensible to her. While Ellie talked, Maxine became sunken so deeply into her black silence that Tom could not help but notice it. Aware of his power among the girls, he began to withdraw his attention from

Ellie and bestow it upon Maxine. When the sandwiches arrived, he offered the plate first to her.

'You're very quiet, my dear.'

'Am I?' She spoke as though half-asleep. She stirred lazily, hiding resentment under an air of lethargy. She smiled, but it was an injured smile. Tom frowned down on her as though his affection were, at that moment, being unwillingly dragged towards her: then, suddenly intimate and anxious, he bent over her:

'How about a little b. and s., eh?'

'You know I never touch spirits.'

'Oh! Oh!'

She jerked herself upright and began patting her hair. Her irritation escaped into her voice: 'Really, Tom! I don't mind the odd gin, of course, but . . .'

'Odd! What's odd about gin?'

She gave him a look of naked exasperation which, almost at once, she covered with a smile.

Tom coaxed her: 'Just a little one.' He put his hand on the decanter.

She started 'Definitely . . .' then corrected herself as though the word were a bad habit: 'Certainly not. Bad for the complexion.'

'A sherry, then. That's harmless enough.' He poured her a glass of Amontillado. 'Ellie here likes very dry sherry,' he said. 'She has a most cultivated taste.' He smiled down on Ellie as though they shared a secret. She returned his smile but looked away, become shy, wary, unwilling to join in this game.

They drove the three miles to the village cinema with Tom beside Partridge and the three girls silent on the back seat. Maxine remained silent until the return journey, when Ellie, feeling in some way responsible for the evening, said: 'I'm afraid it was a pretty awful film.'

'I enjoyed it.' Maxine's tone reproved Ellie's ingratitude and discourtesy. She leant forward and put her hand on Tom's shoulder: 'Thank you, dear, it was sweet of you to take us.'

Tom patted the hand on his shoulder. He said: 'I'm glad someone enjoyed the evening.'

He may have meant no more than he said but Ellie felt as though a weight had fallen within her and was dragging at her bowels. She could not overcome the sensation. She could not speak. Tom, not noticing or not caring, did nothing to comfort her.

The film may have wearied him, or perhaps he needed his evening meal. When he entered the house he looked exhausted, withdrawn and old.

This fact, it seemed, gave Maxine her opportunity. Her manner changed. She no longer sulked. Suddenly she was a mature woman, an adult at home in an adult world: and she was willing to talk. When they took their places for supper, her glance round the table affirmed the fact that she would now compensate Tom for the absurdly juvenile conversation Nancy and Ellie had forced upon him.

Her full, over-cultivated voice dominated the company. Sitting upright, one elbow on the table, her bosom outlined by the taut silk of her dress, she disported a regal manner.

Ellie thought: 'This now is Maxine; a Maxine who gets what she wants.'

She first brought up the subject of some wild land which lay on one side of the Clopals garden. Tom had been approached by a farmer who had offered a good price for it. Maxine advised him to accept. Tom thrust out his lower lip with a certain hauteur, seeming to suspect the farmer of impertinence. What made the man suppose Tom would sell his land? The land, Maxine thought, lay outside the natural contour of the garden. If Tom did not intend to cultivate it, it would be no loss to him.

Nancy, seeing Tom's reluctance to part with any of his property, tried to join the discussion but soon found she was defending the wrong piece. She retired in confusion and did not speak again.

Maxine, having made her point about the land, next asked if this were not the moment to sell some shares she had bought on Tom's advice. If she sold now she could pay off her overdraft and have something in hand.

'No, no.' Tom spoke with decision. 'Don't sell. There'll be a bonus issue soon and I've been tipped off they'll go higher yet. And don't worry about the overdraft.'

Nancy turned her head sharply and gave Ellie a look. The look conveyed much to Ellie: it would have conveyed more had she known what an overdraft was.

Maxine said: 'I'm so sorry, Tom darling, to worry you about so many things when you're tired, but . . .' she glanced round as though to say she had been given no previous opportunity to speak, 'but I have just been offered such a dear little house in Knightsbridge; such a pet of a place. It would be so nice to have a place all one's own. It's been an ideal of mine for years.' She spoke as though there was virtue in aspiring towards such an ideal: she sighed: 'One gets a little weary of a flat, don't you agree? Well, I thought if I sold the shares and had something to put down, I could take out a mortgage on the house and pay it off gradually. It would be so *worth* doing.'

'Um.' Tom did not respond at once. After a long pause, he said: 'That's flying a trifle high, don't you know. You've got a charming flat. A house is a great responsibility. We'll have to chew this over.'

Nancy winked at Ellie, yet, despite discouragement, Maxine seemed satisfied. She now let these affairs drop and started praising Mrs Fitton's chocolate mousse, looking first at Nancy then at Ellie, as though convinced they could not appreciate it without her help.

Ellie went to bed in a low mood. Having observed the grave and informed assurance with which Maxine met Tom on his own ground, she felt young, ignorant and defeated in advance. She was deeply envious of Maxine, who, no more than six or seven years her senior, had the knowledge, confidence and income of a much older generation. She longed to be as grown-up as Maxine: to enter the great world of mortgages and overdrafts.

7

Maxine came down late to breakfast: Ellie and Nancy were finishing their meal. She did not serve herself from the row of silver tureens on the hot-plate but rang for Fitton, then sank into her place at the table as though exhausted by the effort of descending from bedroom to breakfast-room. She pressed to her nostrils the lace edge of her handkerchief.

When Fitton entered, she pleaded: 'Oh, Fitton, just give me a little piece of bacon. A very little piece. I seldom touch breakfast.'

Letting the bacon grow cold before her, she gazed out at the cedar trees. She seemed upon some remote verge of tears.

With a raucous cheerfulness, Nancy asked: 'Got a splitter?'

'No,' Maxine murmured vaguely, 'no.' Some moments passed before she was capable of saying more, then she spoke in a small voice, occasionally sniffing: 'I've been so touched.'

She had kept her right hand in the pocket of her quilted dressing-gown; now she drew it out and placed on the table a small fob-watch of enamel and gold.

'Isn't it exquisite? French, I believe. I have never seen

anything so lovely as that tiny scene painted on the face. And the pink enamel bow, and all those little diamonds! I'm afraid it's valuable, too.' Her voice failed with emotion.

Ellie looked at Nancy. Nancy's eyes were fixed on the watch. She said nothing.

After another pause, Maxine said hoarsely: 'I've always admired it. It belonged to Tom's mother. Last night, when he came into my room to say good-night, he put it on my bedside table and kissed me on the forehead and said: "This is for you, my dear." I was so touched! I couldn't speak. I just started to cry.'

Nancy stood up: 'We're going out,' she said.

Ellie followed her from the room. Outside the house, Nancy said: 'What did you think of that?'

Ellie felt bound to say: 'I think, you know, she'd quite forgotten Tom's mother was your grandmother.'

'Yes,' said Nancy angrily, 'she had forgotten. That's just the point. She's displaced me so completely, she's quite forgotten that I have any rights here at all. And Tom – he's forgotten, too.'

'Oh no . . .'

'If he hasn't, would he have given it to her while I was in the house? Or, if he did, wouldn't he have had the decency to say: "Don't tell Nancy anything about it"? My father would be hopping mad if he knew. As for Aunt Isobel and Aunt Mabel . . . *well!*'

'How did Tom get the watch?'

'He went home for the funeral. I suppose he asked for some of his mother's things: he was very fond of her.' Nancy brooded for a time, then added bitterly: 'Yes: so fond he gave her watch away to the first little bitch who sucked up to him.'

'Is she really a bitch?'

'I can jolly well tell you, if he knew as much about her private life as I do, she wouldn't be queening it here. But she'd better look out. She's had it all her own way so far: now I think he's pretty taken with you.'

'I don't really think so.'

'He is. I know he is.'

Nancy, smiling again, turned on Ellie the full stare of her mischievous fox-brown eyes. For the first time Ellie realised she had been invited here not entirely from friendship. She was here as Nancy's candidate for Tom's favour: a candidate who was required, in return for hospitality, to prove herself Nancy's champion and support. Out of the muddled emotions formed about this knowledge the thought came clearly: 'I am Nancy's friend.'

She put her hand through Nancy's arm and said: 'You never told Tom anything about Maxine?'

'Lord, no. She knows too much about me.'

Ellie said: 'We're free. We could hardly accuse her of freedom.'

The sun was shining. When the girls returned to the house they found Maxine had had chairs brought out to the terrace. Still in her pink satin dressing-gown, her black hair tied with a pink ribbon, she lay in a sheltered corner where the sun was warm. She made a lazy gesture towards the girls. As though defending an eccentricity, she said: 'I love the sun.' Lifting her face to the light, her look acquisitive rather than appreciative, she stretched and relaxed and moaned a little. She said: 'Do you think Mrs Fitton would bring me some pineapple juice?'

'I'm sure she would, if you asked her.'

As Nancy walked past her into the drawing-room, Maxine made a murmur of hurt protest.

Ellie asked: 'Does she do nothing but lie around all day?'

'Nothing but that.'

'But in London? I suppose she has a job?'

'Yes, a wonderful job. She's art editor at Topham's. Tom got her in, of course, but I must say it for her, she's a brilliant draughtsman.'

'I suppose she's well paid?'

'I'll say: and she has private money. She's a South African: terrifically snob family – so she says. You should hear her going on about the natives. I bet she had a Kaffir grandmother, or something.'

'She's clever,' said Ellie unwillingly.

'She's no fool,' Nancy bleakly agreed.

At luncheon Tom asked: 'Who's coming to Erica's for tea?'

Ellie and Nancy looked blank.

'Hasn't Maxine told you we're going there?'

'We are,' said Maxine, 'but not the girls. We couldn't expect Erica to ask everyone. It wouldn't be fair to her.'

'She knows they're staying here.' Tom looked displeased: he thrust out his lower lip, then said: 'Supposing I give her a ring?'

'Oh no, it would make such a crowd. And it's Sunday. She can't get extra cakes or anything.'

'We might take a cake with us.'

'We can't ask her, Tom. She has other guests coming and her drawing-room isn't very large.'

Ellie and Nancy sat in silence, looking at Tom, wondering if another victory was about to be theirs. Tom looked at their bright eyes, then said: 'I'm not over-eager to go myself.'

'But, *Tom*,' Maxine broke in sorrowfully, 'Erica will be so disappointed. She has invited that new friend of hers, Lady Roberts, who so much wants to meet you. You promised. We must go: but we won't stay late. Anyway, I have to catch an early train.'

By the time the car was at the door Tom had been persuaded. When the car had driven off, Nancy said: 'Did you hear that? She's going on an early train. And I bet I know why she's going early.'

'Why?'

'She must have a date with that fellow of hers.' Nancy paused, then said with an accusing intensity: 'A married man.'

Ellie's lips parted. She blushed so deeply she wanted to cover her face with her hands. She said: 'But Quintin is a married man.'

'This one lives with his wife. The poor, stupid woman is being deceived.'

Ellie, growing pale with relief, said: 'That's different.'

When Tom and Maxine returned, the house seethed with Maxine's departure. She ran repeatedly up and down stairs. She tore through the drawing-room and went out through the french windows murmuring something about 'Mrs Partridge.' Soon she was back and hurrying to the kitchen, her colour heightened, her glance inward.

Tom seemed distracted and concerned for her. He said: 'A glass of sherry, my dear, before you go?'

'No, no, Tom dear: I'm sorry. No time.' She brushed past him, speaking lightly, scarcely aware of him now. She hurried out to the hall, where she could be heard making her demands on Mrs Fitton. A little later she called to Tom to join them. Her voice, animated and appealing with an ornamental appeal – for who could refuse her anything! – was begging for some of the more valuable plants in the hot-house.

Ellie, feeling Maxine's intense excitement, could not doubt she was about to meet a lover. Ellie recognised the key of her anticipation. Dashing about, too eager even to be cautious with Tom, she left upon the air the scent of her desire.

Her voice rose: 'But I must have an amaryllis, Tom darling. I love them so. I won't let this one die, I promise you. I'm having a few friends in tonight. I want the flat to look pretty.'

Nancy's eyebrows went up. She glared at Ellie, whispering: 'Listen.'

'I am listening,' whispered Ellie.

When, at last, Maxine was standing in the porch, on the point of departure, her voluptuous vitality sparked from her like electricity. In her high-heeled shoes, taller than the girls, much taller than Tom, she cast about her an atmosphere disturbing and dominating. She held in her arms a sheaf of flowers and beech-leaves. Partridge was packing into the car, beside her small piece of aeroplane luggage, a basketful of home-made jams, curds and pickles, a box of geranium plants, some flowering shrubs and plants, and a canvas bag, well packed, from the top of which protruded part of a plucked chicken.

Ellie asked innocently: 'How ever will you carry all this when you get to London?'

Maxine gave a short laugh of naked contempt. 'I won't carry it. A porter will carry it for me.' As she glanced at

Ellie her contempt took on for a moment the quality of cool and contemptuous enmity. It was gone in a moment. It left Ellie chilled, but Maxine had melted into smiles for Nancy and Tom. She flicked a commanding finger at Nancy:

'Ring me up sometime and come to supper.'

Nancy, as though hypnotised, took a step forward and said eagerly: 'I'd love to.'

Maxine lowered her cheek to Tom's lips. How could he not sense, as Ellie did, the aura of her desire for someone else? But he smiled as before, seeming only fearful that he might not fulfil all her needs.

'Have you everything you want, my dear?'

'Yes, Tom, I think so. You've been so kind, as usual. Good-bye, my dear.'

She entered the car among the plants and flowers, then smiled out with such evident happiness that Ellie was shot through with envy of her: 'Oh, Quintin! Oh, Quintin!'

The car drove off. Ellie scarcely saw it go. As she followed the others into the house, she caught her breath and stood still, transported by memory so that Quintin's presence seemed tangible. She almost lifted her arms to curve them about him: she raised her face and smiled into the empty air.

Ahead of her, Nancy was turning back from the drawing-room door. Ellie quickly covered her rapture with a question: 'What did she want with the geraniums?'

'Window-boxes. From now on Clopals keeps her supplied.'

Ellie made some excuse to go up to her room. As she went, she heard Tom asking: 'Where is Ellie?' She ran to her balcony to think of Quintin, but the thought had emptied itself. She felt only cold and lonely. Soon she went downstairs again. Tom said: 'Ah, here she is!' and took her hand and led her to the fire. Now his attention was all for Ellie. He sought to draw her back from the remote place to which memory had taken her. He rubbed her cold hands and said: 'Brr!', shivering through all his old bones: 'Cold outside. What will you girls have? How about a martini? Warm you up.'

Ellie smiled wanly, not certain Tom would not change suddenly into the old man of guarded looks and worried manners who was under Maxine's spell. He took the seat beside her and held her hands while Fitton mixed the drinks.

Ellie's martini tasted like fire: 'Goodness!' she said.

Nancy's cheeks grew very pink and her eyes danced madly. Ellie gave a spurt of laughter. Nancy lay back in her chair in a state of incipient giggles. Tom, delighted by these results, began to make mild fun of Erica's tea-party and Erica's husband, Peter.

'After tea,' he said, 'Peter, doing the heavy, produced a bottle of cooking sherry. When I'd tasted it, he said: 'What do you think of it, sir?' I said: 'Rum! Very rum!' 'Oh no,' he said, 'it's sherry.'

The girls collapsed: 'Oh, Tom, you are funny!' They laughed helplessly, wiping their eyes. Ellie said: 'Really, you are wonderful!' and Tom smiled his satisfaction.

'What does Peter do?' Ellie asked.

'He's a Civil Servant: one of those fellows in bowler-hats who catch the 8.55 every morning. But that's merely his bread and butter. By inclination he's a numismatist. I dare say you girls don't know what that means? He collects coins. He comes sidling up to you and slips you something that looks like a bad halfpenny and says: "Babylonian: tenth century".'

'Babylonian!' squealed Ellie, as though the word itself were born of Tom's wit.

When their laughter subsided, Tom said: 'Dear me, the world would be a dull place if it were peopled by numismatists.'

'Do you often see Erica and Peter?' Nancy asked.

Tom answered dryly: 'Erica is always on the telephone.'

Nancy and Ellie exchanged glances. They saw again the possibility of victory.

At dinner Nancy, sighing that next morning she must return to work, began complaining of the fact she was paid less than Denis and Bertie. She was as much use as Bertie and much more use than Denis, who now spent his days doing nothing at all. Recently she had spoken to Daze, the chief of staff, and had been told that there was one wage scale for men and another for women.

Tom nodded his approval: 'Men need more money.'

'They don't need more,' said Nancy crossly, 'they just get more, that's all. Prices aren't reduced for me because I'm a woman. You bet they're not.'

'Surely, my dear girl, you've discovered by now that you're living in a man's world. You must try to gain things by your charms. We men are delighted to reward you, but we won't disarm ourselves in your favour. Why should we? Eh?'

They were uncertain whether or not he was laughing at them. Nancy said: 'What happens to women who have no charms? They have to live.'

Tom smiled and shrugged his shoulders as though the answer must be obvious. After some moments, he said: 'I believe in the male heir. Let money and the power of money pass from father to son. We'd be a nice pack of fools, wouldn't we, to put power into the hands of you giddy girls!'

The girls did not find this funny. Ellie said in support of Nancy: 'If we have no money, how are we to live?'

'You'd manage all right. The world is different for you.'

'Different, perhaps, in some ways, but just as hard.'

'Harder,' said Nancy. 'For instance, because I'm a woman they give me smaller portions in restaurants. They don't charge me less.'

Tom laughed and looked over her head: 'You should lodge a complaint,' he said. It was obvious he found these wrongs too remote and finical to be taken seriously. He turned to Ellie and smilingly filled her glass, as though to say: 'There, that will make everything all right.'

Realising how easily they could bore him, Ellie glanced a warning at Nancy and received her acknowledgement. They knew themselves a penniless feminine combine, in no position to quarrel with benefits received. Ellie leant coaxingly towards Tom: 'You wouldn't really want to deprive us of money, would you?'

'I once thought that way, I must admit: but age has mellowed me.'

Fixing him with a brilliant, mock-offended, flattering stare, Ellie said: 'Men are dreadful. They've imposed on women for centuries, pretending to be strong and superior. In fact, they're weak: they're positively fragile. They're – they're over-sensitive.' Two martinis and three glasses of wine had made Ellie slightly hilarious. She ended on a high, accusing note: 'They're neurotic.'

Tom smiled with a mild shrewdness, his lips turning down. 'But you do not wholly disapprove of us? I mean, you would let us exist?'

'Oh, yes. You're quite necessary, of course.' Through a mist of wine, Ellie remembered a need for caution. Her mouth stretched in a smile, broad, innocent and admiring: 'As Nancy said, you have more money than us. Besides, you're rather nice.'

Tom's smile widened: his old sunken cheeks grew warm: his stiff, elderly body and his face, dark, monkeyish, that could never have been handsome, seemed imbued with so complete a certainty of masculine ascendancy, disputation could only be in joke. Whatever Ellie might think she was talking, he knew she was talking nonsense. Aware of this, she became more daring: 'And all this about men being terribly promiscuous and needing lots of women – that's just to flatter themselves. I think polyandry is much more natural than polygamy. Don't you, Nancy?'

Nancy's lips parted in terror. Her eyes signalled wildly.

'The fact is,' Ellie concluded, having recently read a book by Wyndham Lewis, 'the fact is, man is revolting against his inferior rôle: he's becoming feminine.'

'Dear me!' Tom examined his hands as though the change might even then be manifesting itself. 'I wonder if you're right?'

Ellie lay back in her chair, convulsed with laughter, and Tom, setting his lips, half-hid his gratification at her amusement.

As the girls rose to retire, Ellie caught Fitton's eye and as he smiled, subservient in his look of indulgent good-cheer, she knew Mrs Fitton would hear all that had passed.

In the drawing-room, she gasped: 'Oh dear, did I say too much?'

'I think he loved it, really – but do be careful. *Do* be careful!'

Ellie dried her eyes and powdered her nose. 'How wonderful to have such an uncle,' she said. 'Almost as good as having a father.'

'My father,' said Nancy, 'is the world's most excruciating bore.'

When Tom came into the drawing-room he gave Nancy a ten-shilling note. 'Take a taxi from the station.'

Nancy looked doubtfully at the money. 'It's a long way to Chelsea,' she said, 'and I'll have to give the man a tip.'

'You want to give him a tip and he's paid more than you are!' Tom sounded on edge with ridicule. With a scoffing gesture, he added five shillings to the note.

As they sat waiting for Partridge to bring round the car, Ellie felt Tom withdraw from the absurdity of their youth, poverty and femininity. Her own excitement had fallen. They were leaving the shelter of Clopals, the secure centre of comfort. She saw them journeying out again to their precarious perimeter. Looking ahead, she saw the smallness, chill and discomfort of her Chelsea room. For the first time she wondered if the step that had taken her there from Eastsea had been much of a step after all. She fingered her purse, to find if she had a shilling for the gas-meter.

The car awaited them. At the last moment Nancy ran upstairs to find a book she wanted to borrow. Tom, who had been standing a little aloof in the hall, crossed over to Ellie and took her hand. 'I shall look forward to seeing you again.' He turned Ellie's hand round and pressed the finger-tips of his left hand into her deep, soft, pink palm.

'Girls,' he said quietly. 'They are the doves of Venus . . . little soft white doves . . . silver doves that carry our thoughts – where?' He touched his lower lip with the tip of his tongue, then he looked up smiling, an odd light in his eyes. At least, Ellie thought it odd, but it was gone before she could interpret it and later she believed she had imagined it.

Nancy appeared on the landing and started, noisily, to run downstairs. Tom, his voice screened from her by the noise of her feet, said: 'Dear me, Nancy is plain. She'll never find a husband.'

Ellie said: 'People like her. She has her own attraction.'

They were ready to depart – but, no. Nancy had left a handkerchief in the drawing-room. Tom, standing close to Ellie, looked sideways at her feet. His smile, sardonic yet indulgent, grew as he lifted his eyes to her face. 'You also have your attraction,' he said. He took her hand quickly, then dropped it as Nancy returned.

'Well, you young creatures,' he said, 'you've raised my spirits. When will you come again? Week-ends are so short. Why not come for Easter?'

They accepted this invitation without a pause. Tom bent and looked into the car and took their hands in a last good-bye. He held to Ellie's fingers lingeringly, then, as the car moved away, had to let them go.

8

When Ellie remembered she had promised to go home for Easter, she did not withdraw her acceptance of Tom's invitation. There was always time to do that. Somewhere at the back of her mind was the certainty she would go to Clopals. Yet she did not write to her mother. She told herself: 'If I can save my train-fare to Eastsea, I must go,' knowing how difficult it would be to save her fare.

When her mother wrote, 'Looking forward to seeing you at Easter,' Ellie would not believe she was looking forward. She told herself: 'She has Emmy. She does not want me. She never did want me.'

With a sense of guilt that somehow enhanced the attraction of Clopals, she remembered the smallness and discomfort of her own home. Now it seemed to her scarcely possible that people could live out their lives in rooms as small as that. She thought of Tom's mahogany dining-table. Nancy had said the table was two hundred years old. For two hundred years people had been polishing it until its surface had a depth like the depth of a pond at night. Once or twice, when she could do it unseen, she had pulled her finger-tips across it. Now, touching it in memory, she felt instead the dry, flawed surface of the table where for years she had eaten every meal.

Nancy, who had made no promises elsewhere, talked freely of Easter at Clopals. She had spent the previous Easter there while Maxine was making her second visit.

'That's when she jolly well began patronising me,' said Nancy, 'but she won't do it again.'

And Clopals at Easter? What was it like? Nancy described the rooms in the long spring twilight, a-glitter with lamps and filled with the scent of lily-of-the-valley. In the garden the double lilacs bloomed – the dark, grape-purple bunches; the white sort like clotted cream. The pink chestnuts carpeted the lawn with pink and the late-flowering double cherries put forth blossoms so tender they wrinkled like Jap silk.

As they talked, Clopals encompassed them. For Ellie, Eastsea lost all substance: her promise became less than a shadow.

'Why did Tom never marry again?' she asked.

'He's too selfish.'

'But he's terribly kind.'

'Yes, if he wants to be.'

'Well, he does want to be.'

'He likes girls.'

That was a fact Ellie could appreciate in a region beyond her own advantage. For her, it gave Tom a poetic quality, almost a sort of youth. If he liked girls so much, how could they help but like him in return. Before she eventually spoke of it to Nancy, she thought many times of how he had described girls as the doves of Venus.

She thought of all the girls she had known – some too fat, some too thin, some plain and bespectacled like Nancy, some stupid, some dishonest, some mean, some cruel: all given, at times, to giggling, sniggering, sniffling, smelling of their under-arm smell – and yet, somehow, they were all transmuted by Tom's admiration into unearthly creatures, silver-white doves, delicate, diaphanous, lovely as female gods.

At last she had to tell Nancy what Tom had said.

'Doves!' said Nancy. 'It's true doves are sacred to Venus, but so are lots of other birds. Sparrows, for instance.' She started to giggle. 'He might have said we were sparrows flying to Clopals for crumbs.' Later, having reflected on Tom's remark, she said: 'I sometimes think he's a naughty old thing.'

'I think,' said Ellie, as one in a position to judge, 'he's really terribly innocent.'

When these conversations had been going on day after day until the days became weeks, Denis said: 'Chatter, chatter, chatter. I suppose you girls do do some work?'

'We never stop working,' said Nancy.

Ellie said: 'Oh, Denis, will Easter never come?'

'It will come. It will come and go and be forgotten. One day you'll say: "Why, it's forty years since that Easter I longed for so much. Then I was a girl and now I'm an old, old woman".'

Ellie said: 'How silly you are!'

'You think you'll never grow old,' said Denis, 'but you will. We can't be sure of much, but that we can be sure of. We grow old.'

Bertie crossly asked: 'What is the matter with you, Denis?'

'Nothing. I'm just wasting my life here. What would be the matter?'

'You could fill up the time-sheets,' said Bertie, who, each evening when his own work was done, filled the time-sheets with the speed and competence of extreme irritation.

9

Easter was late that year. The light grew tender, the air warm. The sun did not set until nearly seven o'clock. In the new sweetness, the new brilliance, the girls were like prisoners released from winter confinement. They could not bear to return to their rooms. They would walk together to the river or the park, moving quickly, their spirits seeming about to rush from their bodies.

One evening Ellie persuaded Nancy to go to St James's Park. They took the bus to the end of Victoria Street, and there Ellie manoeuvred their direction so that they must pass Quintin's house to reach the park. The sun had set before they arrived. Through the clear twilight the lofty, languid plane trees with their mottled trunks shook from their buds leaf tassels delicate as flowers.

When they turned into Quintin's road Ellie became faint with excitement. Nancy, unaware this place had significance for Ellie, talked as before. Always at the back of Ellie's mind had been a sort of dream-belief that, were she to pass Quintin's door, he would come from it. It was a magical certainty, but she had not dared test it alone. Nancy was her shield and talisman.

They reached the house. Ellie was near collapse – yet nothing happened. No one came from the door. There was no face at the window. She saw nothing and she passed, no doubt, unseen.

In reaction she felt a wretched emptiness. Nancy, aware of none of this, talked on about Maxine and Tom – Maxine's guile, Tom's money and the power it gave him. Ellie suddenly found this talk unendurable. She was repelled by the thought of Tom's money. She felt she could scarcely bear to hear another word about it.

She despaired now of ever seeing Quintin again. Only the portfolio remained. Surely the time had come to make use of it? As soon as she returned to her lodging she rang Quintin's number. A woman's voice answered. Ellie could not reply. The voice, speaking to silence, called urgently: 'Hello, hello, hello.' Ellie said at last: 'Is Mr Bellot there?'

'He's out at the moment,' said the voice. 'Who's speaking? Can I give him a message?'

Ellie had recognised the woman's anxious jealousy. 'It's not important.' She put down the receiver before further questions could be asked. She went to her room with a pain in her breast. She said: 'I must forget him.'

10

Easter was nearly upon them when Maxine rang Nancy from Clopals. Tom had had a slight stroke a fortnight before; nothing very serious: he was recovering, but in a day or two he was flying to Menton, where he would spend the summer. She was afraid the girls would be disappointed.

They were stunned.

They walked slowly to the river, no longer fearing their spirits' escape, and tried to concoct for themselves some compensating occupation. They were already sufficiently Londoners to dread bank holidays in London. Ellie had not saved any money for her ticket to Eastsea. She was not likely to save it now. Added to that, she had sent her mother a letter of apology and explanation, not to be retracted.

The next day word came from Tom. He enclosed railway-tickets and suggested they should spend Easter Monday at Clopals. The Fittons would be away and the house shut up, but Mrs Partridge would open up the drawing-room for them and make them luncheon and high tea.

'That's not bad,' said Nancy. 'We'll have some fun.'

Suddenly expansive, she invited Ellie to take tea in her

room on Good Friday. That was the first time Ellie had been invited to Nancy's room. Nancy always spoke of it as somewhere mysteriously private, as though accessible only to herself. When the front door of the house was opened to her, Ellie was surprised that the caretaker permitted her to go alone to the first floor and find Miss Claypole's room number.

Nancy opened to Ellie's knock, grinning not so much, it seemed, in welcome as in anticipation of Ellie's wonder at the room. Ellie's wonder was all that could have been expected. With lips parted she looked at the vast bay window which formed an area itself not much smaller than Ellie's own room. There were two arm-chairs, a sofa, books in a white-painted book-case, a writing-desk, some early flower paintings framed in white, linen chair and bed covers which Nancy had hand-blocked, and a white Indian carpet she had brought from her bedroom at home.

It was the carpet, its size and whiteness, that made Ellie realise how Nancy's home must differ from her own.

Nancy said: 'The room's a bit expensive, of course, but it will pay for itself. When I'm settled in, I'll be able to work here. I'm doing some book jackets now.'

Ellie said: 'This is not just a room of one's own – it's a world.'

Below the rear window there was a small acacia tree. 'A poor thing,' said Nancy, 'but a tree.'

Nancy made tea on a gas-ring. Ellie wanted to help. 'Shall I make toast? I'm good at that.'

No, Nancy did not want her to do anything: 'It's all organised. Sit down.' She went to a cupboard. Inside were small quantities of provisions put into pots, tins and boxes, labelled and set out in alphabetical order. On the lowest shelf was an oven that could be placed over the gas-ring.

Seeing Nancy organised in this small organised world, surrounded by so much that was her own, Ellie felt subdued. She had supposed she and Nancy knew all there was to know about one another: each knew what the other knew: and much of their knowledge they had discovered together. Now it seemed to her that Nancy had a whole life unknown to her, sorted away into containers, placed in some private cupboard that Nancy kept beyond Ellie's reach.

She remained subdued throughout the visit. For the first time in their relationship a hint of boredom floated in the air. Ellie was not invited to the room again.

Somehow, meeting and taking walks, eating their mid-day meals in small snack bars, they lived through the desolate row of Sundays that was Easter in London and came to the holiday Monday when they were expected at Clopals. It was a brilliant morning. The train was crowded. Partridge, at the station with the car, carried them out of the uncertain straggle of picnickers to the spacious seclusion of Clopals that, during the weeks of their absence, had come into flower.

A certain loftiness of manner had come upon Nancy during this transition. She became hostess and leader. At moments in the past Ellie had caught in her face and movements recondite resemblances to Tom. Now, as she talked to Mrs Partridge, she talked in imitation of Tom.

Mrs Partridge asked when they would like luncheon.

'Oh!' Nancy raised her eyebrows, drawing out the word in enquiry, 'I think one-thirty would do excellently, Mrs

Partridge. We'll go for a walk first, just to get an appetite. Eh? What do you think, Ellie?'

They walked up into the beech-wood where the Venetian red glow of the leaf carpet was broken by new spikes of green. Now the leaves were large enough to form a shade: they dappled the air, a waxen green transparency.

'It's not the same without Tom,' said Ellie.

Nancy said: 'I'm not sure it isn't better.'

In a hollow of the hillside the bluebells had opened and their colour flowed like water between the trees. The girls stopped to admire. Nancy's admiration had about it a slight air of survey and satisfaction such as Tom might have worn. Ellie, watching her, suddenly knew that in one of the hidden containers of Nancy's nature was belief that Clopals would one day be hers.

There was a sense of division between them for which Ellie could not account. The visit, so long looked forward to, seemed empty of all excitement. Nancy was unusually silent. It was as though she had retreated into a world of private hopes. As for Ellie, her hope had almost gone: she did not know where to look for its renewal.

Before luncheon, the bright day clouded over. The rain started: it chilled the air. When they had eaten, the girls sat before the empty fireplace and read Tom's books, saying little. Perhaps Nancy realised how bored Ellie was with the talk about Maxine and Tom. Now it seemed that, if she could not talk about them, she could talk about nothing.

In the early evening, when it seemed there was nothing to do but return to London, a glow of sunset appeared. The rain came slowly to a stop.

The girls hurried out, their mood changing. A pink light, strained through thinning cloud, washed the garden with a supernatural sheen. Dazzled, as though some spell had come upon them, they linked fingers and ran down the lawn. Their lifted faces were rosy from the sky. The sodden beds of lily-of-the-valley filled the air with scent.

By the time the girls had reached the stream, the colour had gone from the air. In the milky sheen of evening the trunks of the apple trees were luminous, bloomed over with copper-green. Among the trees the water flickered, the links of a silver chain.

Ellie, pulling her hand from Nancy's hand, ran ahead, suddenly aware of her own separateness, wanting to move alone. It seemed now her problem imposed solitude. No companionship in the world could solve it, not even the companionship of Quintin. During the months when she had thought only of London, then only of Quintin, the problem had been forgotten. Now it assailed her, possessing her mind with a bitter-sweet force like the scent of the young larch – a problem that a year before she would have called the foremost in the world.

How could she, in the instant of its changing, catch this light, this damp and leafy evening – not as a dried leaf or a pressed flower or a glimmer in the density of paint, but moist with life, moist-smelling of wild mint and earth, with the water glinting, the trees a cloudy darkness upon the mist and silver of the air?

She brushed through the riverside trees, paused on the bridge and gazed into the green-black lustre of the water. When Nancy reached her, she said: 'What will become of us? Will we ever do anything?'

'We've already done things. We've come to London.'

'But that's only a beginning. There are so many other places.' She felt the compass of the earth and its wonders. 'I want to go everywhere. I want to see everything.'

'You want too much.'

Ellie broke away again, this time harshly, with impatience: 'You can't want too much. I want everything. I want the whole world.'

She flung herself with a violent effort up the lawn, tripping and regaining herself, flinging herself forward and away from the limitations of herself, until she came to the terrace. She stood there trembling and panting until she heard Nancy's approach, then she entered the empty house.

11

That spring in London there was neither sun nor rain.
The parks were hung with a green gloom of leaves. Ellie
and Nancy no longer left the studio together to walk in
the sad, pearl-grey twilight. Nancy had fallen in love.

Ellie never knew when this happened. She was not told
at once. She wondered if it had been the cause of Nancy's
preoccupation at Clopals. Several times Nancy was not
free to meet Ellie on Saturday evenings, then at last she
explained: 'I have to meet my man-friend.'

'You have a man-friend?'

'Of course.' Nancy spoke as though only Ellie could
be so foolish as not to guess that.

'But . . . but where did you meet him? How long have
you known him?'

Nancy giggled: 'Oh, some time now. He has a room in
my house. We met one evening coming in the door. He
asked me to go to the pictures.'

'Why didn't you tell me?'

Nancy shrugged her shoulders, her eyes mocking, as
though she had reason to keep this matter from Ellie.

After that Nancy would make casual mention of the
young man, whose name was Terry. If Ellie tried to
question her, Nancy, with the most provocative glances

and murmurs, refused to tell her anything. Unquestioned, she made such revelations as: 'Terry wears spectacles, too. It's terribly funny to see the two pairs cohabiting on the mantelshelf.'

'But why do you take them off?'

'Can't you guess?' Later, she added: 'You've no idea the fun we have.'

'But where? Where do you have this fun?'

'In my room. His is a poky little place at the top of the house.'

So Terry had the freedom of Nancy's room! To Ellie this seemed a final exclusion.

Soon the Saturday nights were given up. Nancy was never free now. Oddly, as though it were Ellie who was to blame for this lapsing of friendship, Nancy had less to say in the studio and what she said could be harsh and critical. She said: 'You'll really have to get yourself a new coat. That coat looks awful.'

She said: 'Tom says he thinks you're attractive but it's a pity you dye your hair.'

'I don't dye my hair. When did he say this?'

'That last evening. When you went upstairs for something. You know how stuffy he can be.'

'But you know I don't dye it. I couldn't afford to.'

Nancy was convinced. 'It's that bitch, Maxine, of course. Tom believes everything she says.'

'Surely you told him I don't dye it?'

'I thought you gave it a rinse or something.'

'I couldn't even afford that.'

In this matter, Ellie realised, Nancy had not defended her. It was not important, but it increased her sense of insecurity at a time when security was low. The spring, it seemed, was rousing expectations only to enhance deprivation. Not only had she lost Nancy, but Denis – who was a friend of sorts – chose this time to disappear.

For weeks his boredom had been such that it had taken on a quality of physical suffering. Even his crossword puzzle could not absorb him. He pushed it aside and sat in the lassitude of despair.

As for Bertie – it seemed that at any moment he might burst into tears. Anxiety so weighed on him now that he sometimes talked to the girls. Glancing askance at Denis as though Denis could be bothered to listen, he murmured: 'He wouldn't come at all if I didn't drag him out of bed. Literally *drag* him out. I don't know what's going to happen. He must earn some money somehow.'

When Mrs Primrose came in, Denis pulled himself to his feet. He stooped over her vacantly, leaning on his desk, his cigarette hanging from his lower lip. Though it was evident to the others he did not hear a word she said, she seemed to notice nothing wrong. Though he kept on his feet with an effort of such tedium that it seemed at any moment he might drop from sheer lack of will to stand, Mrs Primrose murmured on, her eyelids lowered as though to protect herself against any disturbance of her tranquillity.

When she went, Denis would look round blankly and ask: 'What the hell was she talking about?'

Bertie attempted to overhear her instructions – no easy matter – and those he heard he carried out. It was those unheard that bore on him most cruelly. In his anxiety he would go round the studio crying: 'You'll get yourself the sack, Denis. I know you'll get yourself the sack.'

Yet Denis remained, as Ellie remained. There was only

one indication that Mrs Primrose was not mocked, and that came at a time when it no longer mattered.

A grand pianoforte, like a white whale, had come into the studio from the paint-shop. Bertie and Nancy were unwilling to tackle it. Denis took to playing inaccurately upon it bebop or boogie or 'Mortify us by thy Grace.'

He was playing one day when Mrs Primrose entered. Unaware of her, or indifferent to her, he continued to play. She raised her eyelids and from under her black brows she fixed on him eyes that were grey and bleak as rain-wet slates. Ellie knew Denis was doomed.

In a little voice, meek as the bleat of a lamb, Mrs Primrose said: 'Mr Plumley.'

'Sorry,' said Denis, but before he rose he struck out in execration a row of consecutive fifths. When Mrs Primrose had gone, Bertie ran around, marking the new furniture, his soft backside quivering with indignation.

'It isn't fair,' he said tearfully, 'it just isn't fair. Haven't I enough to do?'

'But I thought you loved it, darling,' said Denis, back at the pianoforte, 'Bertie, my Busy Bee. You believe genius is one per cent inspiration and ninety-nine per cent perspiration. If you perspire enough, you're ninety-nine per cent a genius.'

'Get out of my way.' Bertie pushed Denis off the stool. 'If you won't help, please don't hinder.'

Denis went to the window and stared out into the mews. Bertie, bustling about, sorely tried, kept up a run of comments: 'It's hopeless.' 'I can't go on like this.' 'My own work's suffering.'

In the midst of this, Denis roused himself suddenly and left the room. When, an hour later, he had not returned,

Bertie said with tense satisfaction: 'There! Now he'll expect me to clock out for him.'

Denis did not return the next day, nor the next. Bertie, who had a cold, was sometimes seen to wipe not only his nose but his eyes. Nancy and Ellie treated him with great consideration. At the end of the week one of them ventured to ask if Denis was coming back. Bertie shook his head.

On Monday morning Mr Klixon appeared. He said: 'I'm fitting in Plumley's work. Don't suppose it will take long. Can't see why she keeps this place open. Orders don't justify it. No use even as a shop window. Out of date, all this painted stuff. Just ruining good furniture. Look at that piano! Did you ever see anything like it?'

Mr Klixon went through the time-sheets, costed the pieces that stood finished, ordered their removal, cleared up the papers on Denis's desk, came round, hands in trouser pockets, chest thrust out, and looked at the designs in progress as though they had meaning for him, then went. He had not given Ellie a glance. In three-quarters of an hour he had completed work that Bertie and Denis might have muddled through in a week.

When he had gone, Ellie, choking with anxiety, said: 'Will he persuade Mrs P. to close the studio?'

Bertie replied irritably: 'Of course not. While there are orders, the studio will be here to carry them out.'

Grateful for their sympathy, gentle in his unhappiness, Bertie began to show the girls a new friendliness. Ellie was so far encouraged that she confided to Bertie her fear of Mrs Primrose.

Bertie said vaguely: 'She's always been very nice to me,' but the next time a small table came into the studio, he passed it to Ellie, saying: 'You can decorate this when you've nothing else to do. If it's good, I'll show it to Mrs P.'

Ellie received the table as though it were compensation for all else she had lost. She designed for it a cornucopia from which poured every sort of exotic fruit and flower. When she transferred this to the table-top, she asked Nancy's opinion of it.

'It's flamboyant,' said Nancy, whose own designs were anything but that. 'It's too big.'

Ellie had no use for such criticism: she was looking for praise. She was in love with the design herself and spent hours in the library seeking some new beauty to add to it. She admired it so much that she longed for others to admire it, too. When she started to paint it, she asked Nancy:

'Don't you like the feeling in this line?'

Nancy laughed at her: 'I adore the feeling of uncertainty in this one.'

Ellie would not be discouraged. She believed that when the table was finished, her abilities would be recognised, her position confirmed, her salary raised and Mrs Primrose astounded.

12

One morning Nancy arrived late at the studio. Her eyes were pink-rimmed. When she hurried to Ellie, she could not speak for tears.

'Is it Terry?' Ellie asked.

'No. My mother.'

'Not dead?'

'No. Oh, Ellie, I have to go back to Bleckworth.'

Her dejection was such that Ellie asked: 'But surely not for good?'

'I don't know. She has to have an operation. Father says he can't afford a housekeeper. I must go back. Just when I've found Terry.' Nancy threw her paint-box and brushes together, moving about blindly, scarcely knowing what she was doing. Once or twice a sob broke from her and she said: 'It isn't fair.'

The sense of division was gone from between them. Ellie was near weeping with her. 'Is she very ill? Is there any danger?'

'I don't know. I'm worried about her, of course: but my life is here. Supposing I get trapped there. I may never get back. If I were a man they wouldn't think of dragging me back. They'd have to find someone else – but because I'm a girl, I must give up everything and go.'

'Supposing you didn't go?'

'How can I get out of it?' Nancy spoke despairingly, tears trickling down her cheeks.

Ellie knew the sense of ruin that had come upon her. She knew and dreaded it. She watched Nancy's departure with sorrow. The studio seemed empty when she had gone. Work was slack. Nancy's job would be kept for her until the autumn. If she did not return then, another designer would be employed. Meanwhile the two widowed figures, Ellie and Bertie, worked alone.

Bertie, resigned, it seemed, to Denis's departure from the studio, was withdrawing again into the consolation of his art. He had scarcely a word for Ellie.

The summer came suddenly. In a night spring's damp penumbra lifted to reveal a brilliant sky. Heat poured down into the London streets. The dusty smell of cars and melting tarmac recalled to Ellie her innocent first weeks in this city. How she had lived since then!

Returning in full daylight, she found her room stifling and was restless to leave it again. She bathed her aching feet, drank tea and, aimless and companionless, returned into the open air. The heat mist filled the streets so that they were golden, opaque as sun-filled water. Weary and eager, she was impelled by certainty that, turning some corner, she must come upon Quintin. Again and again she saw him down the vistas of the evening streets, but as she ran his likeness melted. She had pursued a stranger. With the failure of the light, these visions passed. The air grew cool. Among the ghost shadows of dusk, she was oppressed by solitude.

The doors of public-houses were propped open. She could see inside where people were crowded together –

all seeming to know each other, all friends – and from the doorways came the smell of hops and sawdust.

In Eastsea once she had visited a public-house. A young man, walking home with her from the Life Class, had invited her to have a drink. When she later mentioned the fact with a triumphant casualness, her mother had been aghast. With impressive severity she commanded: 'Never – *never* let me hear of you entering a public-house again.'

'But it was only a little bar marked "Private" and there was no one else in it and I only had ginger-beer.'

Halfway through this defence Mrs Parsons gravely raised a hand. As Ellie's voice tailed off, she said: 'Your father drank.'

'I didn't know.'

'I think you are old enough to know now.'

'But did he die of drink?'

'He died of T.B. accelerated by drink.'

Ellie had looked so appalled that Mrs Parsons merely added: 'So never enter a public-house again.'

Glancing nervously into the Chelsea public-houses, Ellie now felt the fascinated dread of one foredoomed. What would happen were she to enter and order – a cocktail? Would she be seized by an unendurable craving? – something that could be satisfied only by more and more cocktails: cocktails for which she had not the money to pay? Would she pawn her winter coat and her spare pair of shoes and her suitcase and her Rousseau reproduction? Would she give all, all for cocktails? Such a downfall had its attractions. At least it gave one something to die for.

In the late evening an enormous moon, red-gold like a guinea, came up in a satiny glow behind the trees of

Battersea Park. Her walk, that had taken her along the Embankment, up Beaufort Street into the Fulham Road, through Sydney Street and down Flood Street, had brought her back into the little gardens in Cheyne Row. There, exhausted, her feet sore, she sat down. The noise of the Embankment traffic seemed muted as though the heat were a thickening of the air, but it was cut through by a car radio, a baritone singing an old popular song:

'Al-ways, al-ways.
Not for just a day, not for just a month,
Not for just a yee-er, but
Al-ways.'

'What a ghastly song!' thought Ellie, and her eyes filled with tears.

Somewhere in the gardens there was a syringa tree in flower. She remembered those evenings when she had walked home from the art class and breathed the summer scents of flowers. Then she had believed she could achieve so much, she had been so exhilarated by the sense of the future and her own achievement, she had thought she might at any moment fly into the air. But now she did not feel like that. Sitting on the garden-seat, half-sleeping from exhaustion, she felt, even in her finger-tips, the weight of her own body. She could scarcely face the effort of moving it.

The two people sharing her seat murmured together. Others walked through the gardens, couples caught closely together. No one else was alone.

Every now and then a taxi would stop: there would be a sound of voices, sometimes laughter, then the voices were cut off; there came the ping of the taxi flag adjusted, the taxi starting off. People were arriving for a party.

Ellie got to her feet and walked to the end of the gardens. Returning along Cheyne Walk, she passed the house that was alight for the party. No one she knew was entering. She returned to her room. At least she had a room: she had a bed: nothing could deprive her of sleep.

The weather held until the week-end. Saturday came, brilliant and empty. King's Road was full of girls in new summer dresses, all moving as though they had somewhere to go. Ellie moved in the same way, pretending a whole week-end of amusements. She visited the library, walked to Sloane Square to buy a quarter of a pound of tea, walked as far in the opposite direction to buy a pound of sugar, then, looking purposeful and excited, she sped back to her room. When she reached it, she could not bear to stay in it.

In the evening she set out to walk to the Chelsea Pensioners' Hospital. To get there, she went first to World's End and turned through Riley Street to the river. Halfway along Chelsea Embankment, she saw Quintin.

This was not an illusion. This Quintin really was Quintin. She came to a stop, as frightened as if she had conjured him up by witchcraft. For several moments she felt too sick to move. Of course it could not be Quintin. Such meetings did not happen. She walked forward slowly, keeping her eyes on him. He was leaning against the Embankment wall, elbow on the parapet, chin propped on hand, gazing down on the gilded river.

She paused beside him, staring at him, unable to speak. He glanced round. His expression changed from surprise to delight:

'The very person! Do you know, I was thinking about you?' He caught her hand and held it and looked at her as though he had had no means of finding her save by chance – and chance had brought her here!

'Why, this is delicious!' he said, and he gave his old laugh of pleasure. 'You must have known I was here? You must have come to look for me?'

At the first sight of him she had grown white with cold: but now her cheeks were burning. Of course she had come to look for him. But to find him! – that was more than she had ever hoped for.

She nodded, still unable to speak. He gave her hand a shake: 'Say something, you silly girl! Where have you been all this time?'

She could only smile at that. With the forefinger of his free hand he touched, very lightly, the bloom on her cheek. He said: 'A short time ago I passed a girl with cheeks like yours, and I thought of you. I thought: "That's what I want – a young, young girl with skin like a peach." I kept thinking about you. I rang your number but there was no reply, so I took a taxi to Chelsea Bridge and walked down here looking at the river, and I thought: "Perhaps I shall see her".'

She swallowed in her throat. 'Did you really come to look for me?'

'Yes, yes, I did.' He gazed into her face, smiling, assuring her, and catching and squeezing both her hands he held them together between his. Her finger-tips showed between his hands and he put them to his lips. Then, holding both her hands in one of his, he cupped the line of her jaw. 'You are so young,' he said. 'How exquisite – that line of youth, that delicate skin!'

She said lightly: 'I shall grow old.'

223

'No. You'll never grow old. You'll never change.'

She smiled, yet that was just what she believed herself. Youth was a part of herself. To be Ellie was to be young.

As she smiled, he said urgently: 'But you'd forgotten me, hadn't you? You do not love me now? I said to myself: "That young, brilliant, romantic love of hers – it couldn't last. I should have drunk it off like a hot posset. I shouldn't have left it to grow cold."'

She protested: 'But it hasn't grown cold. I've been thinking of you all the time. I couldn't forget you.'

'My dear!' He gazed at her, then he asked anxiously: 'You still have that studio job?'

'Yes.'

'That's good. I'll always know where to find you.'

'It's seven months since we last met. You said it wouldn't be long.'

'I know. The whole thing was unforgivable, my dear. I could not help myself.'

'But shall I ever see you again?'

'Of course. We are friends. We shall be seeing each other all our lives.'

'I mean – soon?'

'Yes, soon. Why not?' He laughed as he spoke. 'When my affairs are settled, I will telephone you. Straight away. There, that's a promise!' He gave her arm a shake to confirm it. He was in his most delightful mood, seeming to put from himself an enchantment so that she believed she too possessed his charm. She thought: 'This is life – this very moment. I am not thinking of the future, or the past. I am alive now.' Believing herself irresistible, as he was, she caught his arm: 'Let's go into the park. It's so lovely when the moon rises.'

He glanced at his watch and looked startled. 'You bad child,' he said, 'you've made me forget the time. Good heavens above!' He broke from her and looked about him. He signalled a taxi. Before it could stop, he had opened the door and jumped inside. He called to the driver: 'Straight ahead. I'm in a hurry,' then waved at Ellie from the window: 'Take care of yourself, my dear.'

He was gone. In a few moments the taxi had turned a corner and was out of sight. She touched the parapet where he had been leaning: it was cold. She stood for several minutes, then there was nothing to do but walk on.

13

When Ellie reached Chelsea Bridge Road, she looked down it as though the taxi might still be in sight. She crossed the road and was jerked to consciousness by the noise of brakes. Denis, putting his head out of the car, shouted: 'Idiot!' When he saw it was Ellie, he asked:

'What is the matter with you? You seemed to be sleep-walking.'

She shook her head in apology.

'Where are you going?' he asked.

'Nowhere. Just for a walk.'

'Get in, then. You'll be safer inside.'

They drove on eastwards, following the river. As they passed the Tate Gallery, she said suddenly: 'This has been the most wonderful evening of my life.'

'Really,' said Denis without belief or interest.

His tone restored her. Her mistake had been in speaking of herself. She knew what passed for kindness in her chosen world: 'I will save you if I can, but first I must save myself.'

She asked: 'Have you a new job, Denis?'

He answered abruptly: 'Yes. Script-writing. Hack stuff.'

'Perhaps you'll write something terrific. The sort of film they have at the Academy.'

'No living in that stuff. Give the bastards what they want: and damn them to hell.' Driving the wrong way, at speed, down a one-way street, he said: 'I hate their guts.'

'But whose? Whose guts?'

'How do I know? Whoever it is that's buggering the world up: whoever it is that wants trash, and whoever it is that gives it to them. Me, in other words.'

They arrived unchallenged on Victoria Embankment. At the first traffic lights the car before them drew up. Without slackening speed, Denis cut round it and crossed as the amber changed to red. Ellie had the unfearing faith of the non-driver. 'Where are we going?' she asked.

'I don't know.'

He pulled up on Waterloo Bridge without comment. They went across to the balustrade. Ellie gazed with him at the broad river that, pearl-coloured beneath the pearl-pale light of the low sun, looked motionless as a lake. The city was washed in the same pearl pallor. Only the dark church spires reflected the smoke streaks of cloud that rayed from the horizon where the night was.

Ellie, gazing round the great chrysanthemum of sky, noticed above the cross of St Paul's a gnat-sized plane that, rising, drew across the glassy empyrean a frayed, frost-glittering scratch.

She said: 'A cherub returning home.'

Denis nodded seriously: 'Might fit that in.' He took out a notebook and scribbled something. Content, Ellie let her head fall back and stared into the sky above her. It seemed that a name was written there in a line of light – it flashed an instant, then the blue closed over it like water. There had not been time to read it but she knew whose name it had been.

Denis said: 'Come on.' They went back to the car. He turned in the face of traffic, shaved a bus and bolted for the Strand.

'I suppose at your age,' said Ellie, 'you've been in love a good many times?'

'Do you!' Denis took a short cut northwards and was stopped by a policeman on traffic duty. 'Oh, Officer!' he called in the accents of the Deep South, 'I just can't get wise to your English traffic laws.' The officer put him wise. They reached Fleet Street.

'Love!' he suddenly spat the word with disgust. 'A trick to keep the world populated. Working so well that we're over-populated. Swarming masses of human beings. Love begetting hatred. World famine. People gnawing at each other's thigh-bones.'

'No.'

'Just wait. You'll probably live to see it.'

That kept her quiet until they reached St Paul's. She had not been so far east before. From the lifeless, shadowed city the cathedral rose into sunlight as from a depth of water. Denis gave no sign of hearing Ellie's squeaks and 'Ohs'. He drew up in Lower Thames Street and jumped from the car in a businesslike way.

'Now! A shot of that!' He waved his notebook to where Britannia, in the glow of sunset, bent attentive over Billingsgate. 'And through here.' They stood at the gates and peered into the glass halls which, wet, empty and smelling of fish, reflected the pink sky.

'What is this film about?' Ellie asked.

'I don't know. Haven't written it yet. Hitchcock stuff, I suppose. Criminal or political. Ending with a chase. Through here, over the river. What else could we use around here?'

'Oh, that.'

Denis looked critically at the Monument and after a pause conceded: 'We might pan past it.'

They were driving towards Tower Bridge when suddenly its delectable oddity was rapt from Ellie's sight by the turn of the car. 'An Underground station!' said Denis, speeding inland: 'a good one. Not one tarted up with strip lighting. And how about a gin palace! Teddy boys, chromium, pin-tables. Might make something of this after all.' He took tickets and hurried Ellie down a moving staircase. 'We want a very long staircase – shoot it so it looks longer. Dropping down, down, down. Passages: more passages. A figure disappearing round a corner: run after him – no one there. Dead end.'

'Where has he gone?'

'God knows. Look at that!' Denis caught Ellie's arm and stared across the line to where the daylight, a silver verdigris, struck through a vent on to a clotted mass of cables bloomed by a decade's dust. 'Magnificent.'

'Will it be a colour film?'

'May be.'

As twilight came down in a greenish fog, they crossed the sleek, green river and drove about among the riverside lanes. A bridge rose above them. 'Out again,' ordered Denis. 'Now, up here.'

To reach the bridge road they climbed a circular staircase enclosed in iron. He shouted 'Hello' and his voice spiralled round the walls. With satisfaction he said: 'What do you think of that? Hitchcock? More like Eisenstein. Imagine footsteps coming up there; only footsteps – flagging. Flagging's the word. That ringing echo. A figure stumbles at the top: falls: a hand spread on the pavement.

Picks himself up; pretty well had it. The lights coming on along the river bank . . . This is where it ends, of course. Drops into the river. The white face going down . . . What do you think of it?'

'Wonderful!' said Ellie. 'Most wonderful film I've ever seen.'

Denis laughed: 'Where's your Wullie Shakespeare now?' Ellie looked up at his face that, pale as a drowning face, gazed down the river with a look of satisfaction.

Had he been Quintin she would have said: 'Who is Hitchcock? Who is Eisenstein? Why Wullie Shakespeare? Tell me what it all means,' heightening with her youth and ignorance the sensual excitement of their relationship. She knew better than to play that game with Denis. She had flirted with him, but it was an odd sort of sexless flirtation. It was not to be relied upon: his exasperation might break through the spell to say: 'My dear girl, don't you know anything?'

Now, because she hid her ignorance, the spell held. He said: 'Let's drink to it – a great film.'

He drove back to Chelsea. They entered a crowded public-house in the King's Road.

'What will you drink?'

'A cocktail.'

'What! My dear girl, no one further in than Pinner even speaks of cocktails these days. Besides, you don't get them in pubs. Have a gin?'

'I'd love a gin.'

When Denis had brought the drinks he said: 'Over there,' and led Ellie to a corner where there were three men, two seated at a table, the third standing. He knew them all, it seemed, but he did not bother to introduce

Ellie. She felt that, so far as Denis was concerned, she had now dropped out of sight. One of the men seated on the bench moved up so that there was room for her. She sat down, effacing herself, watching but saying nothing. She noticed that Denis's manner had changed. He was no longer authoritive and clipped of speech but had returned to his studio manner of languor and endearments. He sat on the edge of the table and gave his attention to the man standing up. This was a very large man who, swaying slightly, held a small round glass in his hand. Denis sniffed the glass.

'Brandy, darling,' he said. 'In the money at last?'

The large man gave a deep titter, then grunted and said: 'Yes . . . um . . . yes. Got an advance. Ghosting a book of memoirs. Chap knew all the right people, all the best times. Last days of Oscar: Ronnie under the table at the Eiffel Tower – "Look at my white hands" etc. Then South of France stuff. Scott Fitzgerald, Paris and so on.'

'Those were the days, darling. The conscience-stricken '30s. They did themselves well.'

'Before the war,' said the large man, 'you'd only to publish a book and they kept you in drinks and parties for the rest of your life. Nowadays it's like dropping a stone into mud.'

'Lot of stones dropped, nevertheless,' said the young man who had made room for Ellie. She realised he was speaking to her rather than to the others, his tone implying some sort of confederacy. She turned to observe him: his square, fair, good-humoured face seemed to her pleasing, but it did not mean much. He said something quickly, seeming to snatch at her attention – but already she had returned it to the large man, dazzled by his cross-talk

231

with Denis. His appearance seemed to her spectacular. She had never before tried to embody the word 'intellectual' and now here it was embodied for her – a man with a large, pale, aquiline face, seeming at once aloof and piteous. A black Homburg hat was pushed to the back of his head. Under his arm, at a dangerous angle, he held a broken-down, black cotton umbrella. He swayed a little as though he were unsubstantial, an inflated skin, huge but tender, that was stirred by every current of air. Occasionally, it seemed, he doubted his power to stand alone, for he would glance round for support and depress on to the table-top the fingers of one hand. It was only in the heat of talk he took the risk of lifting them.

He said: 'Even the artist these days is being cut down to the common man. The local's good enough for us. No one wants to applaud. No one records on shirt cuffs. Why, in this very pub I heard Dylan talk his head off, night after night, and no one remembers a word of it.'

'Too much talk, darling, too much drink . . .'

'How else can we forget our enemies?'

'Enemies, darling? Have you enemies?'

'Indeed, yes. Three. The psychiatrist, the mad-house and the grave.'

'Oh, my dear Arnold.' Denis caught his arm affectionately. 'Let me buy you a drink – a beer, I mean. I'm not standing for brandy.'

Ellie watched Denis go to the bar. How wonderful to be Denis and on such terms with such a man! In this interval of silence, the young man at her elbow tried to distract her again. What was her name? What did she do? His was Simon Lessing. He was an architect, but painted in his spare time.

Simon? 'Simple Simon' was the unfortunate correlation in her mind.

'I've often seen you in the King's Road,' he said.

'Have you?' She was surprised that anyone, even this young man, had noticed her in the King's Road. During the months of her loneliness it had seemed she must be invisible.

She looked into his face and, recognising in his intensely watching eyes the reflection of her uncommon attraction for him, she could only pity him. He had made himself known to her just too late. Before this evening she might have been glad of him, but what hope for him now that she was restored to Quintin?

She smiled briefly. Discouraging him, she looked away to where Denis was returned to converse with the writer. Simon started to say something, but Ellie shook her head and kept her face from him as though he were interrupting a performance upon the stage.

The large man, Arnold, was saying: 'The '30s, of course, were pretty well taken up with their own doom. The poetry was in the self-pity. The young today are different. They haven't grown up blaming everyone but themselves. They don't see themselves as the helpless victims.'

'No, they've simply gone underground. Every man his own deep shelter. They're just not interested. Here—' he turned on Ellie – 'what do you believe in?'

She was too startled to answer at first: she blushed and asked miserably: 'Do you mean God?'

'Not necessarily. What about politics?'

'I don't know. I can't be a Conservative because my mother was. I suppose I'm a Socialist – but I can't see how they differ.'

'There you are,' said Denis. 'And when I was her age I wanted to fight in Spain.'

'But then we knew how they differed. Since then there's been a clash. Black and white have mixed. Everything looks grey.'

At that moment Bertie came in and gazed feverishly about him. Ellie caught his eye, but he seemed not to notice her. When he saw Denis he cried out accusingly: 'So here you are! What became of you? I wasn't more than a second late.'

'Late?' Denis looked coldly at him. 'Late for what?'

'Weren't we meeting this evening? At the "Passport to Fortune"?'

'Were we?' Denis turned away and asked Arnold what he had been saying.

Bertie, ignored and wretched, stared at Denis's back. After he had stood for some time, Ellie tried to distract him. 'Hello, Bertie,' she said. 'I do think your writing-desk design is terribly good.'

'What?' Bertie looked at her as though he had seen her before somewhere but could not place her in this setting. He shook his head slightly.

She repeated her remark.

'Oh!' he said blankly, then returned his gaze to Denis.

'Have a drink?' Simon Lessing invited him.

He looked round again with a pained frown as though these attempts to console him were agony to him. When he realised what had been said, he replied: 'Don't bother. I'll get one myself.' When he came back he sat on the edge of the form beside Ellie and watched Denis as a dog, trained to patience, watches its master.

Now that this interruption was over, Ellie could hear the author again.

'. . . isolated and done for,' he was saying. 'Life has us surrounded. I've done my best to identify myself with it, but I know I can't.'

'Retreat into literature,' Denis advised him. 'Write a great book.'

'Literature's down the drain. As for great books – there's one published every minute.'

Denis, on his third drink, was losing his languor; he was becoming dictatorial and fast-speaking, his white, tensed hands swinging about. 'Not that sort of "great book" – give your time to it, give ten years: write *Bovary* or *War and Peace*.'

The large man shook his head in a defeated way. 'When Tolstoy spent ten years, or whatever it was, on *War and Peace*, he believed when it was finished society would still be there to read it. I don't know where we'll all be ten months from now.'

'Why did you ever write at all?'

'I started young. When we lived at the peak of civilisation. Remember those times? A few years later we went to war. We had not, after all, inherited a world of light.'

'Six bloody wasted years,' said Denis.

The large man laughed. He made a movement, deprecating Denis's vehemence. As he talked, his manner implied that nothing he said was to be taken very seriously. Occasionally he glanced about, observing his neighbours and the people at the bar. When the newcomer was a woman his eyes, shy and enquiring, would rest on her until she looked at him, then he turned away.

Denis said: 'We grew up believing in progress and civilisation, then found they didn't exist.'

Arnold nodded: 'That's our trouble. We live in an age to which we do not belong.'

Ellie had heard something like this from Tom Claypole. She was bewildered by the dissatisfaction of her elders. Did she, she wondered, live in an age to which she did not belong? She thought not – but then, she had no clear memory of growing up in a belief in civilisation and progress. When the war broke out she was an infant. Mrs Parsons had gone with her young children to a cousin in Staffordshire. She still spoke with wrath of the years of squabbles and hatred that came next. Ellie did not remember much of them, but she remembered their desolate return to an Eastsea restrained by barbed wire; bombed, silent and shut. Her father had been invalided from the Army. He lived for three more years. During that time her education had been sketchy. When they moved into the restaurant, Mrs Parsons had been too busy to worry much about the girls. What Ellie had learnt, she learnt in spite of circumstances. Perhaps she had missed something.

'Man,' said Denis, giving an imitation of a famous political figure, 'set in a world rich and beautiful, expends his infinite resources upon means to exterminate himself. What is this instinct that forces him to destroy his own happiness? Is it the Divine Will that, having ordained a hell upon this planet, economises by setting the silly bastards to make it for themselves?'

Arnold started to laugh, then stopped to watch the woman who had just entered the bar. She let the door bang behind her and crossed the floor, frowning, looking about her in a distraught way. The others watched her, too. There was a stir as she sighted someone in their group and smiled with relief. She had singled out a man who, sitting next to Simon, had had nothing to say. He saw her, but neither moved nor smiled. He still said nothing. The woman was driven to whisper to him: 'Theo, I must speak to you.'

He gave a sigh of annoyance, then, looking about and finding himself observed, he rose and went with the woman to an isolated table.

Arnold Valance watched them go.

14

There were two chairs. Petta sat on one of them. Her companion stood some moments, then dropped impatiently into the other. He looked away from her with an expression of long-suffering, waiting for the interview to come to an end.

Petta said: 'I've rung your number every day. I thought you were never coming back from wherever you were.'

'I'd've stayed if I could,' he said.

Petta smiled gently. As she watched him, her eyebrows a little raised, her face and body leaned towards him in tender appeal. She said: 'I've been so miserable without you. Take me home with you.'

He gave her a shocked stare, then said: 'You're crazy.'

'I'm not, Theo.' She slid her delicate hand and forearm across the table and touched his wrist. She slipped two fingers up under his shirt-cuff: 'Darling,' she said.

Abruptly, he pulled his arm from her: 'You're being ridiculous. All that's over. I suffered enough: we both suffered enough. It would be lunacy to start it up again. It's out of the question.'

He spoke with decision, but a sulky decision. She was not convinced. 'Theo, look at me,' she said pleadingly, and when he looked she lifted a hand as though to say: 'I am helpless and defenceless.'

Turning from her, he said: 'Don't be silly.' She watched him, believing still in her old power over him. She knew this peevish resistance too well to take it seriously.

She begged him: 'Get me a drink.'

He rose with a sort of sullen obedience and went to the bar. The centre of the bar was crowded. Between the heads moving this way and that, she could sometimes see Theo's side-face as he stood waiting to be served, too absorbed in his own thoughts to press for attention. He was ten years her junior. His smooth, regular face was still a young face. Now it was the face of someone cornered and resentful. The weak down-droop of his lips filled her with contempt. He did not belong to her world at all. He was a journalist: the sort that fills the picture weeklies with re-writes of old murders, haunted houses, great loves, famous trials and curiosities of history. He started thumping this stuff out at nine in the morning and went on till five. He was becoming well known. He earned rather more than a cabinet minister and could have earned much more had he been ambitious. He was content to spend his evenings here, drinking beer by the pint glass. Petta had disturbed him by widening his life. She had refurbished his sitting-room, given parties, improved his dress, put him on to an agent who marketed his stuff abroad, arranged lecture tours, travel-film scripts and documentaries. He had accepted what came, but resentfully, finding this extra work an intrusion upon the daily life he had organised round his typewriter, his *Encyclopaedia Britannica* and his public-house evenings. He had found a formula for life. He did not want it changed.

When he returned from the bar, he put her gin down before her with the air of a small boy who has unwillingly performed an errand.

She said: 'How did you enjoy your trip to "Sunny Honolulu"?'

'Cuba,' he corrected her, and left it at that.

'I'm glad you're still getting this film work.'

'The Cuba film was the last of the contract.'

'Will you get another contract?'

'I don't want another.'

The end of the contract. The end of her interference. The return to a routine life. His clothes were becoming shabby again. She felt her old exasperation with his lack of ambition. She wanted to overwhelm him with her own fervour, to set him to do her work for her – but this was not the moment for that. She asked him in her subdued, suppliant's voice: 'What are you working on now?'

At the same moment she looked up and found Arnold Valance's eyes fixed on her. He looked away at once, but his expression had told her he was hers for the taking. She knew who he was. This was not his home ground, but she had seen him in here before.

She looked at him again. Again his eyes were fixed on her and this time they remained for several seconds in the long look of recognition. She noted that when he returned his attention to Denis Plumley, he was smiling.

She sat back in her chair and looked at Theo. Already his face was coarsening. For years he had been swallowing beer as though life owed it to him. Soon his youth would be gone. And what would remain? His selfishness, his ignorance and his vanity.

He had answered her last question, but she had not

been listening. She broke in on something he was saying to ask: 'What on earth is going to become of you, Theo?'

He looked up, startled by her change of tone. She had been suddenly restored to her old, magnetic vivacity. The ridicule in her glance made him shift uneasily in his seat.

'Don't worry about me,' he said. He jerked up his beer-mug and tried to empty it in a mouthful. It was too much for him.

Now, from among the crowd in the centre of the bar, a figure dodged warily into sight – an old man, keeping an eye on the barman and holding open a decayed rain-coat beneath which he displayed, like a hand of cards, some paper-covered booklets.

Petta watched him as he edged round Denis's party. No one there gave him a glance. Denis and Arnold, it seemed, were absorbed in an argument. The girl with a face like a powder-puff was gazing at them, a-gawp and a-glitter. The young man beside her was watching her with a world of meaning in his face. Lucky girl. Petta thought: 'If I were starting my life again, that is the sort of man I would get for myself. I would live in a cheap Victorian house and have a dozen children and never have time to wonder where my looks had gone.'

The old man, his white hair starting up from his head, his beard frenzied as the beard of a prophet, noticed Petta and made his way towards her. As he drew near, his surface broke up. He lost his seer's look: he was dirty: his teeth were black, his eyes were full of guile. He brought with him a stench of old urine as he bent over her. 'Spare a copper, lady.'

Theo moved his face away. The man, taking no offence, moved his display of books round so that Theo found himself looking at them. He was about to shift again when one caught his eye. He pointed imperiously at it. The old fellow, in his eagerness, nearly fell on top of him.

'Here y'are, guvner, "Fortune by the Stars"'; the book shook between his fingers. As Theo took it, the man pulled the corner of another one from an inside pocket: 'Brochures,' he whispered.

Theo shook his head but held to the fortune book: 'How much?'

'Two bob.'

Theo tossed the book back at him and looked away. The old man, scrambling to catch it, said: 'A bob, then, guv. A bob—' he trembled over Theo – 'it cost me that. All right, a tanner. A tanner to you, guv, just to make a sale. Just to change m'luck. God's truth, guv, what can you get for a tanner these days?'

Theo brought out a handful of change and examined it. With a fastidious forefinger and thumb he picked out six-pennyworth of coppers and threw it on to the table. The old man scooped it up with a businesslike gesture and went. Theo glanced idly about him, then, when it would seem he had forgotten the book, he picked it up.

Petta had watched his movements closely.

The truth was she could not remember now whether she had ever been in love with him or not, but to heighten her contempt for him she asked herself, had it been insanity, or what, that had possessed her? At her age still not to know herself, still to be gullible, still to be capable of the self-hypnosis of passion that could cause her to mistake this boor, this prig, this carping egoist for a man!

He was holding the book open at his own birth date. She said: 'Come on. Read it aloud. Give us a laugh.'

He ignored her. Something he read brought a simper to his mouth but he bit it back. He pursed his lips, expanded his nostrils, lifted his eyebrows and gave an approving nod . . . Petta snatched the book from him. He made to snatch it back: she held it out of reach. His expression became angry: he was about to catch her wrist when he realised people were watching him. He sat back, motionless in anger.

Petta read aloud: '"People born under this sign are lovers of everything beautiful." (Well, what d'you know!) "They possess strong family ties, pride and love of home. They are generous and high-minded." (The author of this *feuilleton* must have known you personally.) "They desire to lead and are fairly successful, but never originators." (Oh, bad luck, little Theo!) "They . . ."'

Theo rose and tried to strike a way through the people packed in front of him. They did not move. He was forced to go round them.

'Theo.'

He turned.

'Your book, baby boy!'

He took it from her. She watched the fretful push of his shoulder as he broke into the crowd. He passed out of sight. Petta wondered how long it had been since she said to him: 'I cannot live without you.'

She looked over at Arnold Valance. As she did so, he turned his head away. Something in his movement told her he was a man who might expect too much of her. She had intended to join Denis's party as soon as Theo went. Now she sat uncertainly, conscious of his vision of her – a delicate beauty, the faultless possessor of a faultless face. She understood that rôle, but too long had passed since

243

anyone had asked her to play it. She remained alone in her chair, in a dream of existence where nothing would be expected of her – no effort, no movement, no wit, no virtue, a relationship with sleep. She propped her head on her hand and returned unawares to memory. She found herself in a summer afternoon so long distant she did not at first relate it to herself. The two little girls were little girls seen in a picture-book. In the distance was a picture-book lawn where ladies in summer dresses sat at tea. It was not until she smelt the honeysuckle that she identified herself with the girl astride the garden wall. This was the colonel's house: the ladies had come with the newly arrived English regiment. The little girl standing on the grass below the wall was the colonel's daughter. Although she had almost forgotten what was coming next, she suddenly resisted the memory, but now its impetus was too great for her.

The English girl said 'Hello! Come down here,' and, eagerly and fearlessly, Petta had jumped at once down into the summer garden. They walked together round the stables, where there was a carriage but no horses. Petta climbed on to the dusty leather of the coachman's seat and pretended to drive. She shouted: 'Sit up here beside me,' but the English girl in her white gossamer dress said: 'Mama says I mustn't.' Petta swung round the stable wall from hook to hook. She walked along the partitions between the stalls and climbed into the mangers full of straw. The English girl laughed at Petta's wild energy, but she kept out of range of the dust and straw and said: 'Oh no, Mama would not like me to do that.' Petta's antics flagged at last and the girl said: 'I'll show you my rabbits.' When they came into view of the tea-party, the colonel's wife called: 'Joan, come here, darling,' and Joan had crossed to her mother and been introduced to the party of ladies. She behaved with a charming shyness, already an accepted personality in the world because she was just what a little girl should be.

The ladies did not seem to see Petta, who was also a little girl – but an untidy, dirty little girl who probably had no right to be there. The grown-up Petta could now see herself as she had been then, standing on the fringe of the party, brushing her hair away from her brilliant eyes, smiling and smiling and waiting to be noticed, like a friendly puppy that cannot imagine it will be overlooked.

No one could have ignored a puppy as she had been ignored. Only Joan's mother looked at her, giving her a frown, no doubt wishing her out of sight. Petta, of course, did not move. She was waiting for her new friend. At last Joan was released. The girls started to run off together, but when they had gone a few yards, the colonel's wife called her daughter back again. She whispered – in the quiet of the garden her whisper filled the air: 'Who is that girl, darling? Wherever did you meet such a person?'

Joan tried to move away. 'She's nice. She's very clever.'

'I dare say, but she isn't clean.'

Although Petta heard all this conversation it did not take shape for her until she remembered it years later. She was too full of her new friendship, of the garden, of the silken ladies. These things crowded out resentment. Their contempt, if it was contempt, was some silly mistake. Aware only that they were wondering who she was, she ran across to the tea-party and said: 'I am Petronia Berengaria Vanessa Kilkane, of Kilkane House.'

Joan's mother looked round her guests with a splutter

of laughter: 'And no doubt,' she said, 'descended from the Irish kings?'

'Oh yes,' said Petta.

The officer's wives found this delightfully funny. Petta watched them. It seemed to her then that she felt nothing, understood nothing – but now she knew their laughter had struck against the blank wall of her innocence and left something dark there.

Remembering this, she could have put down her head and wept for her own innocence – then, in a second, the whole incident had swept back into absurdity, into darkness, into complete forgetfulness. She was suddenly revived. Looking about her, she met the anxious, longing eyes of Arnold Valance.

She finished her drink. Then, as though making a leisurely way from the bar, she passed Denis's group and paused. Arnold Valance seemed not to exist for her. Her eyes, their silver colour clear and gleaming between her darkened lashes, were only for Denis. She spoke in a low voice sweet with sex:

'Why, Denis darling, I haven't seen you for so long.' The confidence of her vivacity had a hypnotic force. It dominated them all, but it was Denis whom she held by the arm, possessing him with her look as though she had been searching for him down the centuries. She turned to the three at the table – Ellie, Simon Lessing and Bertie – gave Arnold Valance a casual glance, then said: 'You must all have a drink with me.'

'No, no,' said Arnold, 'this is my round. Please allow me.' He started out for the bar.

Petta, like a fire lighted in its midst, was the centre of the company. Everyone looked at her, expecting a revelation,

246

but now that Arnold was not there to listen she had nothing to say. Her hand fell from Denis's arm. Her colour seemed to fade. The others realised she had not brought new entertainment: she had merely halted the old.

Petta smiled at the three at the table, but already Simon's attention had returned to Ellie. Bertie was taking this opportunity to attract Denis's attention. He stood up and whispered fiercely to Denis, who replied: 'It's no good, darling. I've got one of my normal phases coming on.'

Petta looked about her, smiling vaguely, like an actress who has forgotten her lines. Turning his shoulder away from Bertie, Denis said to her: 'Have you come back to live among us?'

'Not yet – but I feel at home in this part of the world.'

Arnold returned. He had been lent a tray on which to carry the drinks. His hat had slid to the back of his head: his umbrella was still clasped by his elbow: he held the tray at eye level to safeguard it from the crowd. Before he could get to the table, the umbrella escaped, clattering down somewhere beneath the feet of the crowd. He returned to retrieve it and brought it back crushed and dusty. When the drinks were distributed, he stood beside Petta, leaning slightly over her, giving her contented glances but not speaking to her, as though, having been safely captured, she could be kept in abeyance. He looked to Denis to continue the conversation.

It was after ten o'clock, not yet closing time but people were sensing its approach. There was an urgency in the drinking: they looked uneasily about them through the smoky air. Those who had cars were planning to make their way across the frontier of some borough where licensing hours were longer. Glasses piled up among a litter of cigarette ends and cartons. The tables, wet with beer, fogged with ash, gave off a rancid smell. Manners, conversation and sense were all failing with the failure of oxygen.

Denis said: 'They say one day the sun will expand and envelope the whole solar system – all the planets just cinders, stuck like currants in a suet pudding. Who'll care then? Take this star, Betelgeuse . . .' Denis drank from his glass, then gazed into it for so long that Arnold said:

'Betelgeuse? What did you say it was?'

'A star.'

'I don't think I've heard of it.'

'It is two and a half million miles across.'

'Dear me! Rather large.'

'The earth is eight thousand.'

'Are you sure?' Petta interrupted. 'Only eight thousand?'

Ellie shuffled forward in her seat, touched now with an eager excitement, feeling that in this matter of the stars she was on her own ground. She listened to Denis as one expert to another. He said:

'When the sun swallows up the earth and Mars and Venus, and Neptune and Jupiter, and all the rest of them, who'll care whether you were Wullie Shakespeare, or just that chap who wrote – what-was-it-called? – "How to make friends and influence people without actually cheating"?'

Ellie, her mind upon the great star Betelgeuse, herself a familiar tenant of the stars, spoke suddenly and said: 'But our destiny is not here.'

The three standing turned as though a bird had spoken.

Arnold Valance smiled on Ellie's behalf, but Ellie remained solemn. She had meant what she said. Simon Lessing was solemn for her sake. Slowly, beneath the scrutiny of her audience, she flushed and looked down at her glass.

Arnold Valance said: 'This is an age when a writer lifts his eyes from his work and looks straight into the face of death. And he faces it in cold blood. He's not drugged by faith or hope or heroics. He is forced by his own nature to see it clearly. Perhaps our destiny is not here, but we have no proof of that.'

His intense, almost emotional manner forced Ellie to raise her flushed cheeks. He was looking at her and she looked back, moist-eyed in sympathy as though she had been listening to poetry.

She said: 'But I feel immortal. I know I'm immortal.'

'That's an illusion of the creative temperament. I take it you are creative in some way? An art student, or something?'

'She's a full-blown artist,' said Denis, 'a member of the Cape Gooseberry school of water-colourists.'

'The defeat of time,' said Arnold, 'that's another illusion. But time is advancing over you, an avalanche moving quietly but much more quickly than you think. It will bury you in the past and your poor little talent with it.'

Ellie looked down again. She had thought the writer was being kind to her, and now she knew he was not being kind. He was not even laughing at her: he despised her. The young man beside her, Simon Lessing, held her arm to comfort her and said: 'Let me get you another drink.'

'I don't think I should have another.'

'One more won't do any harm.'

He took her empty glass and went away. She kept her head down, distrustful of all of them, and thought: 'But I have Quintin.'

Outside, a thunderstorm was roaring and clashing. Denis went to the window: 'No rain,' he said. 'A costive show. A case of cosmic collywobbles.' Before he could return to the table, Bertie had jumped up and hurried to him. Denis listened to Bertie as though he were being told something he could not understand.

'Well, that's the position,' Bertie ended on a high note. He glanced about defiantly. 'And now I'll go.'

Denis made no comment. Bertie went. When Denis returned to the table, he started to do a step-dance, pretending to play a banjo and singing:

'Under the A,
Under the B,
Under the Atom Bomb.'

'Bravo,' said the writer, patting the palm of his hand.

'Do you know my modern child's alphabet?' Denis asked, 'A is for Atom Bomb, O what a bang!'

'Already out of date,' said someone.

'Here's a new one.' Denis went into his dance routine to sing:

'I'll love you atomised,
I'll love you pulverised,
I'll love your outline on the pavement.'

Petta looked aside at Ellie and, meeting the girl's eyes, said: 'What do you think about it all?'

Ellie shook her head vaguely. She had suddenly become appalled, as though she found herself stepping over a chasm which was revealing itself as much wider than she would have thought possible. As she drank her third glass of gin, she began to retreat from this company. All her senses were functioning as though at a distance from her. She seemed to be deep in a well round the rim of which buzzed a swarm of bees. When Simon spoke to her she could not reply.

Watching her, Petta thought: 'If I still had that look of innocence, that smooth magnolia face, yet knew all I now know – I'd give them hell. I'd win every trick. But as soon as you've learnt this game, you're out of it. Your place at the table is wanted for a newcomer. And I suppose this is the newcomer, this silly innocent!'

A wreck of a man, thrusting his thin, damp nostrils in between the swing doors of the bar, began a starved quaver:

'I love you: yes, I *do*,
I love you.
It's a sin to tell a lie . . .'

Listening, Petta told herself this sing-song was typical of all she had ever been offered of love in these cold islands. Men here understood nothing of passion. Few men had been able to draw her from the prison of herself. Her first husband, Henry, looking down on her blank face, had asked her: 'What do you think about at such a time?' She said: 'I design clothes for myself.'

Denis said: 'The trouble is, we invested in war. We didn't provide for surviving it. We've left ourselves intellectually bankrupt. Now, the next war . . .'

Petta lifted her face from the next war and noticed Ellie again. As she saw the girl, pale and unmarked, her youth all newly taken from tissue paper, she thought: 'The last war did not touch her – but, my goodness, the next one will land her a whanger.'

Ellie, who had been breathing-in Petta's dry, heavy scent, looking at the lace handkerchief in her hand, at her expensive suede handbag, her coat of geranium-pink, thought: 'If Quintin ever met a woman like this, I'd never see him again.' As she raised her eyes in admiration, she met Petta's scrutiny, cold as the look of an enemy.

At that moment the lights went out. A voice began bawling 'Time.' One white globe was lit behind the bar: it cut through the smoky gloom. Shadows moved oddly. People seemed to draw together for comfort. The voice of the barman changed from appeal to command, from command to anger. Ellie, lost in the darkness among strangers, thought: 'Supposing nothing ever does happen to me! Supposing there is nothing to hope for! Supposing we do no more than die!' Knowing the situation beyond her, she dropped her head on to her arms and, sobbing, whispered to herself: 'Quintin! Quintin! Quintin!'

Denis said: 'That kid's squiffy. I must get her home.'

Simon Lessing had a car outside. Together they took Ellie away.

15

The rain came down as the last dawdlers were pushed from the public-house. The doors were locked behind them. They stood against the closed door, pressing away from the downrush of water.

Arnold put up his umbrella and looked at Petta. She moved under it.

'It won't be much,' he said. They could see the edge of the storm like a wall across the street: 'Have you far to go?'

'I have nowhere to go.'

She wanted him to accept her statement as simply as she made it, but he said: 'Are you serious?'

'Of course.'

He took her arm. They walked together up the King's Road and turned into Sydney Street. 'I live off the Fulham Road,' Arnold said. 'My place is pretty dilapidated; not even very clean. My char leaves things much as she finds them.'

'It will do.'

She could feel his nervousness, his desire for an explanation. She would not make one. She felt irritated because he could not accept their impending relationship as she accepted it. Like everyone else, he wanted the conventional preliminaries.

Now they were alone together, he had become tongue-tied, uncertain of himself. She glanced at his big belly, his vague handling of the umbrella, his limping foot, and there came down on her a chill distaste for the night ahead. Could he have responded to her own recklessness, nothing else would have mattered. Now she anticipated nervous fidgeting in a dingy setting.

She thought: 'If I see a taxi, I'll call it and say it was all a joke. I'll say I must go home: my husband is expecting me,' but at the thought of Quintin's frozen presence in the flat her resolve failed. She had known from the first she would have to find some other refuge. She could bear no more of life with Quintin. Even Arnold Valance was to be preferred.

This was the extremity to which her need had reduced her. She sighed. Arnold, bending over her, put his hand to her elbow and said: 'We are nearly home.'

Next morning, while Arnold sat in bed with the Sunday papers spread over the soiled counterpane, Petta made coffee. The flat comprised two rooms. The kitchen was a large cupboard in the sitting-room. The bathroom, on a lower landing, was shared by the tenants of the floor below.

The sitting-room, filled with forlorn junk-shop furniture, smelt of the books that were stacked everywhere. The dirt and untidiness of the place did not worry her unduly, but she found the cupboard-kitchen distasteful. It held a sink, gas-stove and provision shelves. Unventilated, it gave out a strong smell of old frying fat and a leak in the stove. She threw away half a tin of fungus and poured the last of the sugar into the cracked basin. As she made coffee, she felt the peace of domesticity. She might have been living here with Arnold for twenty years.

When she carried in the breakfast, he looked at her with satisfaction and held out his hand – a gentle and undemanding man.

He would do. He would have to do.

He sniffed at the coffee jug: 'I say, this is something like.'

She was in her most tender and compliant mood, as sweet as he believed her to be. She remained so all day.

She explained that her life with her husband had become impossible. He was a philanderer and indifferent to her. She had been intending to leave him for some time. She could bear no more of it. Arnold held her hand as she talked, looking aside with his shy, pale eyes that were every few minutes drawn to her face. He seemed scarcely able to bear this record of her sufferings. In protest against it, he said once or twice: 'My dear girl, my dear girl,' and at moments he seemed to be feeling acute pain.

Talking or reading the papers, they sat around until evening. Then they went to a restaurant near South Kensington station.

Petta's mind was made up. She would move her belongings from Quintin's flat. She had reached at last the moment when she could say: 'This time I am leaving you for good.' She intended going on Monday morning to the flat alone, but she made the mistake of mentioning this to Arnold. He insisted that he must accompany her. He was an honourable man. He was not afraid to face her husband. She might have dissuaded him, but at the risk of rousing his suspicions.

Well, he was presentable enough! He even looked impressive.

When they reached the house, Arnold took the stairs slowly. Petta ran ahead with some idea of facing Quintin. 'Tell him nothing. Give me a chance,' she would say; but when she called 'Quintin,' there was no reply.

The flat felt empty. She looked at the letters on the hall table. One was addressed to her in Quintin's hand. She could hear Arnold at the second landing. With her anxiety choking her, she shut herself in the dressing-room and read the letter:

'Saturday.

'My Dear Petta,

'I am about to leave for Switzerland. I have been threatened with a return of my old chest trouble and advised to see a specialist in Berne. For both our sakes I shall remain away for some time. The present situation is intolerable and I hope my absence will give you the impetus to remake your life with someone else. The rent of the flat is paid until the end of the quarter. My solicitor will then arrange for my belongings to be moved. You can take it on if you wish. I shall not return to it.

'I have instructed my solicitor to start proceedings. I am sorry, dear Petta, but our marriage has come to an end and official recognition of the fact will be best for all concerned.'

'Quintin'

'For *all* concerned!'

Petta could hear Arnold Valance puffing in the hall.

She wished she could tell him to leave her in peace. She bolted the dressing-room door. She heard him go into the living-room and, finding no one there, come out, calling: 'Where are you?'

She burnt with anger against him. Could she not be alone to realise and absorb the finality of solitude which Quintin's desertion had brought upon her?

She shouted: 'Go into the sitting-room. I'm making coffee.' She heard him blunder off again.

Switzerland! The name of the country brought another name to her mind. Alma! And only Alma had enough money there to keep him 'for some time'! But it was unthinkable. Above all things, he wanted youth in his women.

After some minutes Petta regained herself enough to emerge, but she did not go into the kitchen. She went into Quintin's bedroom and dialled Alma's number. The butler answered the telephone. Her ladyship has gone to Switzerland. When did she go? On Saturday evening; the seven o'clock plane. Still she could not believe it.

The bedroom looked out on to a well. With its wine-coloured walls, ceiling and curtains, it was almost dark. She switched on the lights and went through the drawers of his writing-desk. She found some cheap cuff-links, a plastic cigarette-case, a lighter, a metal pencil and half-a-dozen trinkets. She recognised them for what they were – tokens of affection. She threw them into the waste-paper basket.

She went to the hanging-cupboard which held some of his old suits. Striking at the neat row of sleeves, she said savagely: 'Damn the lot of you!'

When she went into the sitting-room, Arnold turned,

his smile diffident yet expectant. She took no notice of him. She looked into the cupboards beneath the large Georgian book-case which covered one wall. These had been kept locked while Quintin was here: now the keys were in the key-holes. She flung the doors open. In her anger she breathed as though near to choking. She found nothing but books and empty folders, and a large portfolio. She dragged this out into the open. There was a system and fury about all her movements that caused Arnold to follow them with a perplexed look of enquiry. 'Anything wrong?' he asked. 'Anything I can do to help?'

She pulled at the portfolio tapes, impatiently breaking those that would not untie, and threw open the boards. Within were shabby sheets of drawing-paper, each heavily painted in pure colour.

'For God's sake!' she said with seething disgust.

'What is the matter?' Arnold lifted himself in his seat: 'Whose are those? Yours?'

'Of course not. They're signed "E. Parsons." There's a name for a genius! "Miss E. Parsons, Eastsea Technical College, Eastsea" – I ask you!' She ran through the paintings quickly, then, with sharp and violent movements, picking them up in twos and threes, she tore them into pieces.

Arnold raised himself again, a thing he did not do easily, and protested in a mild, hurt way: 'You shouldn't do that.'

'Silly little bitch!' – Petta ripped up the last of them – 'Probably saw herself as a *femme fatale*. One of those emotional, frustrated little pieces on the look-out for someone else's husband. Quite ruthless, but treating it all as a Great Love, something Too Big for Both of Them.'

'But you shouldn't tear up her work. She may want it back.'

'She may – but she won't get it, will she?' Petta, white, with a fierce and wild look of rage, gathered up the pieces and searched for the waste-paper basket: then she noticed the empty grate, in which lay the gas-poker. She dumped the pieces in the grate and lighting the poker thrust it, flaming, among them. Arnold watched, still pained, still dissenting, yet alarmed and fearful lest he be made to suffer, too.

Petta went back to the portfolio. A white envelope remained. It was addressed to Quintin. She lifted it, looked into it, then shook out on to her hand a lock of hair. Satin-shining, it curved like a question-mark, the colour of rosewood. As though it were infected, she looked at it with horror then threw it on to the burning papers.

'What was that?' Arnold tried to see for himself, but it was too quickly consumed.

'Hair,' said Petta. 'Disgusting.' A feel as of silk still lay on the palm of her hand: she rubbed it violently against her thigh. 'To think of Quintin sentimentalising over things like that! I would not have thought it possible.'

For a moment she stood holding to the chimney-piece, supporting herself against the certainty that Quintin had roused in someone a romantic, magnanimous, despairing love – the sort of love no one had ever offered her.

'Curse him,' she whispered.

Arnold sank back into his seat, seeming dazed as though hit by a storm. 'I don't understand. Whose things are you destroying?'

'Nobody's. They've been abandoned. This was my husband's flat. He's cleared out and now I'm clearing out.'

Against her will she touched her own hair and felt it, as she knew she would, as dry as straw. She moved towards a wall-cupboard, but the ringing of the telephone distracted her. She snatched off the receiver and spoke breathlessly into it: 'Hello. Who the hell is that? Hello.'

Mrs Primrose wished to speak to Mr Bellot.

'Put her through.' Petta turned, glittering, towards Arnold: 'This is another of them.'

Arnold drew his brows together in expectation of further assault, but Petta's voice when she spoke again was dulcet and suffering: 'Gem, my dear, is that you? Yes, it is Petta speaking . . . But I've been back a long time. You did not know? How like Quintin not to tell you. I'm afraid I have some bad news for you . . . Poor Quintin! . . . Yes, his lungs again. He has been flown to Switzerland to see a specialist in Berne. We had to charter a special plane . . . Expense, indeed! But it was an emergency; a question of life and death . . . I know . . . I . . .' her voice broke and failed her: she paused, then whispered: 'I must be brave, but his doctor here did not offer much hope.'

Arnold murmured solicitously: Petta turned her back on him. She said into the receiver: 'I shall go when . . . if . . . I'm needed, but, for the moment, I'm forced to remain here. Flora needs me . . . Flora, my daughter, of course . . . yes, a child . . . Dear me! Poor Gem! Quintin does not seem to have told you anything . . . I will ring you, of course. I will let you know as soon as I know myself.'

She dropped the receiver and turned, smiling, to Arnold, suddenly pliant and sweet. In a little voice she persuaded him: 'Come and help me pack. I'm so tired of this place.'

Arnold remained where he was. She went to him and lifted his hand, pretending to pull him up – but he pulled his hand away. He still looked confused – but he was recovering. He was emerging into disillusionment. The expression of his eyes had changed. He was on guard against her. She moved impatiently away. Was she never to find a man who could accept and understand her moods?

'What is this about your husband?' Arnold asked.

'He has some lung trouble. He has gone to Switzerland. I found a letter from him when I came in.'

'Has he gone alone?'

'I would like to know that myself.'

She stood looking out of the window. She heard Arnold sigh, then he said weakly: 'I don't think you should have destroyed those paintings. They probably meant a lot to someone.'

'Oh, nonsense.' She lifted the ragged home-made portfolio: 'Look, it's falling to pieces. It's covered with dust. It's been here for months. He probably gave some student ten bob for the lot. Let's get rid of it.' She broke the rotting cardboard into pieces and stuffed them in with the rest. The poker was still alight.

'Look.' She showed him her dusty hands, then wiped them on his corduroy trousers.

'Hey,' he protested, but weakly: his defence was falling. She sat on his knee and put her arm round his shoulder.

'You can't realise how thankful I am to be getting away from here.'

Arnold smiled. Petta was glad Quintin had not seen him. He had the slightly disintegrating appearance of a man who drank too much. His skin was puffy: his eyes seemed too small for their sockets. He moved them round to watch her as she fingered the soft, fine-textured skin beneath his collar. He had the look of a baby, half-rebellious, yet delighting in the power of its nurse. As she felt his surrender, she started to giggle.

'Let's finish it,' she said.

'What?' He became uneasy again. 'What?'

She jumped from his knee and went to the telephone. She dialled and asked for Mrs Primrose. The secretary was on the line. Mrs Primrose had just left for a tour of the factory. The telephonist would have to ring round for her.

'No,' said Petta. 'Just give her a message. This is Mrs Quintin Bellot speaking': she paused and her voice became lachrymose. 'Please tell Mrs Primrose . . . please break it to her that Mr Quintin Bellot passed away in Berne this morning. Tell her I am flying to Switzerland at once—' she caught her breath, then mumbled: 'Thank you. Thank you. I am sure everyone will feel the same.' She put down the receiver.

Arnold said in bewilderment: 'But is he dead?'

'No. That's just to give a jolt to one of his prize bitches.' She hugged herself and asked suddenly, in high excitement: 'Shall I put a notice in *The Times*?'

'I don't think they'd accept it without a death certificate.'

'I suppose not. Well, Gem Primrose won't find it easy to check up. Quintin's secretive about his movements; and there'll be no reply from this number. Come. Come and see where I've had to sleep alone for six months or more.'

This time he rose, grinning. She pushed him ahead of her. Watching, as he went, the expanse of his back and buttocks that broadened down pear-shaped from his drooping shoulders, she knew him a failure, too slow in combat with the world, too sensitive to succeed.

PART THREE

I

On the following Monday morning Bertie was himself again: a self-sufficient Bertie, retreated into the stronghold of his own talent. Ellie had little to do in the studio at this time. Bertie was too absorbed in his own work to keep her occupied. She was content, imagining that any day now Quintin would telephone her. Meanwhile she was creating tiger-lilies, moss roses, carnations, grapes, strawberries, pomegranates, butterflies – all flowing from a silver cornucopia amidst stars of gold.

After a few days Klixon had begun to relent towards the studio. His laugh came in with him from the paint-shop. He and Bertie exchanged 'Primrose' gossip. Having found that she was useful and showed no improper pride, Klixon also relented towards Ellie. He sometimes even included her in the conversation.

Before the war, in the days when painted furniture was 'the rage', Bertie had been a young designer in a Mayfair firm called Kelvin-Frinton and Frost. He liked to talk of those days to Klixon, who listened with an air of concentrated observation, learning, it seemed, everything there was to be learnt about this, as about everything else.

'There were always twenty artists at Kelvinfrintonfrost, sometimes thirty. A huge studio. And we'd quite wonderful furniture: Regency and Georgian and Om-pere, and even earlier, even Queen Anne, though people didn't like it much: vanfuls of it bought from the Caledonian Market. For a song, my dear; for a song. The buyer would go to Italy, too, and bring home boat-loads. The stuff we'd strip! Wicked, it was, really! I saw lovely bits of satinwood, wonderful old mahogany, walnut and rosewood – straight into the acid-bath, and then white paint, a few swags and urns, a lick of antiquing, and you'd get any price you liked for it. Not that anything cost much those days. Artists didn't cost much either. Some of the girls worked for thirty bob a week. And when we had a piece of Om-pere with real marble, we'd paint over the marble and then paint on new marble. No one liked real marble: too Victorian – but they loved my painted marble: we did it in such delish colours: grey, pale blue, salmon-pink.' He sighed. 'We did it with a feather.'

On Monday morning, Klixon broke into Bertie's chatter to say: 'What do you think?'

His dramatic tone brought Bertie to a stop. Klixon put his arm round Bertie's shoulder: he flapped a hand to Ellie and, when she approached, put his other arm round her shoulder. Then, holding their heads so that they almost touched his winged moustache, he rolled his eyes and whispered: 'What *do* you think?'

'What? What?' they questioned. Ellie began to feel unreasonably anxious for her job.

'The boy-friend is sick unto death.'

'Who? Not the shareholder?' Bertie seemed delighted. 'Not that fellow Quintin?'

'The same. I happened to be in our lady's office this morning, making a query, and she said "Half a mo, I'll ring the paramour', and who did she get? *His wife*! The wife was in tears. It seemed the shareholder is like that famous Chinese invalid Mr Wun Lung, and that one not too good. The wife didn't hold out much hope. As a matter of fact, he's dying.'

'No!'

'Our Mrs P. looked as though someone had dropped a brick on her.'

'But what shareholder?' asked Ellie.

'You don't know him,' said Bertie. 'A fellow called Quintin Bellot whom she used to drag round the factory. Always giving the girls the eye.'

Ellie might have learnt more had Mrs Primrose not come into the paint-shop. Klixon broke away at once. He bent in a businesslike way over his desk. Bertie returned to his work. Only Ellie remained where she had been standing when she heard the news. She was shivering. She had not the sense to push her table out of sight.

For the first time, she received from Mrs Primrose a direct stare. This brought her to her senses. She picked up an 'antiquing' brush and brushed over a finished job. The handle of the brush slipped about in the sweat of her palm. She did not hide from Mrs Primrose, but watched her as she moved round the room. This woman knew what had happened to Quintin.

When she came to Ellie's table, she said: 'And what is this?' Her face and voice were expressionless.

'Oh!' Bertie looked crossly at the table. 'That's just a little piece I'm letting Miss Parsons practise on.'

Mrs Primrose said nothing. She passed round the table and was gone.

'Why on earth did you leave that there?' Bertie was angry. 'You are a silly little fool.'

Klixon asked: 'What happened to that place during the war?'

'Kelvinfrintonfrost? It stayed open. I was allowed to stay in the studio. They said I was psychologically unfit. I kept it going, with a couple of kids. In the end there was no furniture, but we did repair jobs for customers. We just named our price. We never closed!'

'Ah-ha,' said Klixon. 'We never closed!' He shook a finger in the air, rolled up his eyes and started to sing: '"Give me that old soft shoe, tra-la, give me that old soft shoe. Ta-ra, ta-ra, ta-ra-rah-ra-rah-ra-ra".'

Ellie watched him. As soon as he stopped, she said: 'Is Mr Bellot going to die?'

'It looks like it.' Klixon gathered his papers, said 'Cheerio, chums,' and left the studio.

Ellie stood out of Bertie's sight and wondered what she could do. She could ask Miss Senior for the truth of Klixon's story. The fear it had roused in her destroyed all other fears. She left the studio at once and went to the secretary's office, but there was no one there. She heard a typist in the next room. She looked in to ask where she could find Miss Senior. 'She rushed after Mrs P.,' said the girl. 'If they're not in the factory, you'll find them in the shop.'

Ellie returned to the studio.

That evening, to allay her agitation, she walked to Westminster. At the back of her mind was the thought that when she came to Quintin's house she might learn something. She imagined a procession of nurses, doctors and specialists passing in and out. Perhaps among them there would be some humble person to whom she could speak. When she reached Quintin's house, she saw no activity at all. The house might have been empty.

She stood for some time in the evening light on the opposite pavement and gazed at the dark windows of his flat. She tried to imagine him lying ill in his bedroom, but when she pictured the bedroom in her mind, it was empty. She did not know where he was.

Then she went into the park, where people were moving quietly in muted air. The stretches of water beneath the trees reflected the tea-rose pallor of the sky. The water-fowl floated becalmed where the light struck between tenuous, drooping branches. She could believe in nothing. This beauty had no more substance than an image in poetry: the passers-by were shadows. Only she and her anxiety were real.

She wandered between the crowds until she came to the lake's end where the windows of Buckingham Palace looked over the bushes. Now the rose of the western sky was a pink rose. Its colour tinged the air, heightening and clouding the green of foliage. The couples beneath the trees merged and emerged, distinguishable only by their movements.

She sat on a seat by the water's edge. The gnats dodged about her head. The air was full of the muddy, weedy smell of lake water. This was a summer of her life that would not come again: a year of her youth that would not come again.

From somewhere near, a park-keeper blew his whistle. From the distance another whistle answered, a thin and anxious cry.

A keeper passed, holding a dog by the collar. 'Come along now, Miss,' he said, 'I want to get home to my supper.'

She went at once, taking with her a memory of those evenings when she had hurried home to supper. She sniffed at fried sausages, strong tea, grilled kippers, toast . . . She had forgotten to have tea. When these memories passed, there remained in her mouth hunger like the taste of a copper coin. She said: 'I chose to be different. I'm not sorry for myself.'

The park gates were half-shut when she went through them. The last of the courting couples were leaving.

'Come along there,' shouted the keepers.

The couples strolled out. The gates clanged to, clipping the heels of the last to go. A group of ejected boys stood in the road. Ellie quickened her step to pass them.

'In a hurry, Miss,' they shouted after her. 'Going somewhere special?'

She sped away, in a hurry, and going nowhere at all.

2

The next morning Ellie was called to the office of Mr Daze, the chief of staff.

'What does he want me for?' Ellie asked Klixon.

Klixon shrugged his shoulders. He looked preoccupied, as though he preferred not to make even a facial comment upon the summons. Ellie was terrified at first, then suddenly she became excited, thinking perhaps Quintin had sent her a message through Daze. This hope, absurd though she knew it to be, made her rush, pink-faced, up the stairs and into Daze's office. He looked at her sourly.

'Now, Miss Parsons,' he said in a quick, businesslike voice. 'Mrs Primrose wants to put you on to a special job. She thinks you'll be more use on this than in the studio.'

Ellie did not speak.

'We're putting you into J50 by yourself.'

'Why?' she asked too sharply, bewildered and agitated that this change was being thrust upon her at this time. She wanted to say: 'I can't attend to this now. I must go away and worry by myself,' but the threat in Daze's manner kept her silent. He was demanding her whole attention for the new project. He looked annoyed at her question: he might lose his temper and dismiss her out of hand. He repeated loudly, a vulgar tone coming into his voice:

'Mrs Primrose is putting you on to a special job. You're to move out of the studio into the small basement room J50.'

'But must I move out of the studio? Couldn't I do the work there? I've been happy there . . .'

Mr Daze interrupted dryly: 'I'm afraid this is a job of work, Miss Parsons. You're earning a living, or you're supposed to be! It's not a question of whether you're happy or not. You're under orders. You have to go where Mrs Primrose wants you to go.'

Mr Daze was a small man in a pin-stripe suit. He had a small, reddish face from which jutted a beak of a nose too big for his other features. His small mouth and chin were enclosed by anxiety lines. He met Ellie's distracted eyes, then looked away.

'Better go straight to J50,' he said. 'Mr Crump will bring your things there. He'll tell you what to do.'

He spoke more gently, but made it clear that Ellie would gain nothing by wasting his time.

J50 was a small room, cellar-cold, windowless, lit by a single bulb. It had been a store-room when Ellie worked in the basement. Now the stores had been moved out: a chair and trestle-table had been moved in. On the table was a heap of pseudo-Italianate writing-cases and cigarette-boxes. They were cheap things, covered in imitation leather. She had never seen anything like them at Primrose's before.

She knew Mrs Primrose was playing some sort of trick on her. She did not know the purpose of it, but she was afraid. Her instinct was to run to Quintin for protection

274

and reassurance – but he was ill: he was out of reach: he must not be troubled.

Bertie brought her belongings down from the studio. He also brought two cans of white paint and materials for 'antiquing'. She was to paint, 'antique' and varnish the boxes and blotters.

'But why here?' she asked. 'Why in this miserable little room?'

Her apprehension and bewilderment seemed to irritate him. He shrugged his shoulders: 'She says you're a new department.'

'But why? When can I come back to the studio?'

'My dear child, how do I know? Better ask Mrs P. yourself.'

'You know I can't. Where did she get these things?'

'She picked them up in a sale. They went with some curtains and odds and ends she wanted. She thought they might sell if they were white.'

'Have you heard anything more about Mr Bellot?'

'Mr Bellot? No. Why?'

'I just wondered.'

When Bertie left, Ellie gave him time to return upstairs, then she set out again for Miss Senior's office.

Miss Senior looked shocked when Ellie entered the office, then relaxed a little, as though realising that only the most extraordinary circumstance could have brought her there.

Ellie was aware of the enormity of her visit and its purpose. She went close to Miss Senior's desk and held to its edge to hide the shaking of her hands. There was a swelling in her throat. Miss Senior, waiting patiently for Ellie to speak, held up between her thin, knotted fingers the sheet of paper she was about to put into her typewriter.

'Could you please let me know about Mr Quintin Bellot? Someone told me he's ill.'

'Mr Bellot?' Miss Senior's narrow, pale, long-nosed face took on a curious look of unbelief and suspicion. She waited for a confirmation of one or the other.

'He's a friend of my family.'

'Oh!' Miss Senior lowered her eyelids and began rolling the paper into the machine. After a long, reflective pause, she said: 'I don't know that I ought to tell you. Why don't you speak to Mrs P.?'

'I can't. Please, Miss Senior, *please* tell me. He isn't going to die, is he?'

There was another long pause while Miss Senior fidgeted with the paper, releasing it, straightening it, releasing it again. 'Well,' she said slowly, 'I don't want to tell you this . . .'

'What?'

The agony of anxiety in Ellie's cry caused Miss Senior to look up. For a moment she stared at Ellie coolly, in judgement, displaying the fact that she, Miss Senior, who lived so satisfactorily within her emotional and monetary means, thought Ellie a muddled, silly, hysterical girl.

Ellie was checked as though she had been hit in the face. She looked at Miss Senior and waited.

Miss Senior said in sombre tones: 'I am afraid he has passed away.'

'Passed away?' At first Ellie could not relate these words to the fact of death. 'Do you mean he is dead?'

'Yes. He died in Switzerland.'

'But he can't be dead. How could he have died in

Switzerland? I saw him on Saturday evening. He didn't tell me he was going to Switzerland.'

Miss Senior kept her face lowered, but her brow grew flushed. She said sternly: 'It was Mrs Bellot who rang up. *His wife*. I take it she knew what she was talking about. He went to Switzerland on Saturday evening and died on Sunday.'

Ellie was bewildered. 'But he wasn't ill.'

Miss Senior clicked her tongue impatiently. 'Mrs Bellot said he had a haemorrhage. That can happen in a minute. If he's a friend of your family, I don't see why you can't ask her about it.'

Ellie stood silently, holding to Miss Senior's desk and looking at Miss Senior, until Miss Senior said: 'I'm afraid you'll have to go. I'm busy.'

'Yes.' Ellie turned and tried to find a door on the wrong side of the room.

Miss Senior said: 'It's over there.'

'Oh yes. Thank you.' Ellie spoke calmly. She found her way outside and went calmly to J50. What she had been told was held obscurely in some pocket of her mind waiting to be sorted out. She knew she was going to suffer, but not yet.

Testing herself, she said deliberately: 'So he is dead. I shall never see him again.' She felt nothing.

In a businesslike way she started work on the boxes and blotters. She sorted out her brushes, pitying their outcast look in this wretched room. Something trembled within her. She said: 'Don't be a fool.'

When she had removed the varnish from the boxes, she covered them with white undercoating. Cut off from the other employees and unaware of time, she worked right through the luncheon hour. During the afternoon, she said again: 'Quintin is dead,' and this time the jolt of her nerves brought her to a standstill. She tried to work again, but she could not hold the brush. She let it fall and her eyes filled with tears. She dropped into a chair, made suddenly incapable by grief. Tears streamed out of her eyes and down her cheeks: she began to sob. Once she had given herself to tears, she could not control them. She buried her face in her arms and sobbed in paroxysms of helpless weeping.

At first she could hear nothing outside herself: then she heard someone pass the door. Afraid that Klixon or Dahlia might come in, she ran through the basement to the cloak-room. There she hoped to cry in peace. It seemed to her there was nothing she could do but cry. For the first time in her life, she knew despair.

Feeling herself safe, she leant over a wash-hand basin and wept without restraint. She put her hands over her face and felt the tears roll, scalding, through her fingers. She was so obsessed by her own weeping, it seemed to her something set apart from its cause. Now she was scarcely aware she was weeping for Quintin dead. She wept in a region beyond hope. Could she go further than that, she too would be dead.

Someone came into the cloak-room. Without looking round, fiercely resentful of the intruder, she flung herself into a water-closet and bolted the door. There she stood, swallowing her sobs, her palms pressed into her eyes, and waited for the girl to go. There was no noise from the cloak-room. She imagined the girl was silent, holding her breath even, in order to overhear her grief, but after a while she began to think the girl must have gone. She emerged from the water-closet – and there was the girl sitting on a chair reading a letter. She lifted her glance, as though casually, and gave Ellie a look of experienced awareness.

Ellie wept the afternoon away in J50. No effort, no thought could stop her tears. She left her work exhausted, her face swollen, and had scarcely reached Oakley Street when calamity swept over her and her eyes swam again. It was then she saw Simon Lessing, the young man whom she had met in the public-house with Denis. He came straight towards her, smiling, imagining she would smile back at him.

Unhappily, she looked at his face – not the right face – then looked away. Her tears flooded down. As he started to speak, she moved round him and took to her heels. He called after her. A concerned voice. She wanted only to get away. When she reached the safety of her room, she threw herself on her bed and wept until her pillow was soaked.

The week dragged on. She was thankful now for the privacy of J50. She worked on the blotters and boxes, crying all the time. She lived on cups of tea. Not only was she nauseated by weeping, but she turned her back on food as though life had injured her and she repaid it by rejecting its sustenance. At night she slept heavily from exhaustion. Waking next morning, she remembered and wept again.

By the end of the week she had no tears left. A cold tranquillity possessed her. Contemplating existence, she contemplated nothingness. Traffic moved about her without purpose. The human beings who passed her were unrelated to her. It was extraordinary to hear them laugh.

Their speech was like the chatter of another species. Only when she passed someone maimed or wretched or very old, she would pause in her indifference to think bitterly: 'He is alive, but Quintin is not alive.' It seemed this bitterness was now the only emotion she could feel.

On Saturday evening she sat for a long time in Cheyne Gardens. A large dog came and nuzzled into her hand. Looking into the liquid adoration of its eyes, she said to it: 'You feel sorry for me,' and she was flooded with pity for the dog. When its owner whistled it away, she looked down at some zinnias that grew beside her seat. As though she had some new power of sight, she saw them hard and bright and minutely detailed. It seemed to her, secure as she was from all distraction, that she could see and hear the process of their growth. She watched an ant climb the stalk of a flower and make its busy, complex journey about the petals. When it had moved out of sight, she continued to watch the petals without will to look elsewhere. She thought: 'I could paint a zinnia,' then she remembered the portfolio she had left with Quintin. Suddenly it seemed to her it had been part of Quintin, a part she could regain. She jumped to her feet and started out for Quintin's flat. She felt a wild sort of happiness, as though out of the very heart of despair she had snatched hope.

She reached the flat in the late blae twilight of midsummer. Somewhere from the gardens of Birdcage Walk a bonfire was sending into the air intimations of autumn. The whistles were blowing in the park. The heavy foliage was dark. Ellie, caught up in the purpose of her visit, cared for nothing. She went straight to the door and pressed Quintin's bell.

Klixon had said that Quintin's wife, that cruel deserter, had answered the telephone to Mrs Primrose. She must be in the flat. Ellie pressed the bell again and again, but no one came to the door. While she stood there the twilight darkened: the street-lamps were lit. When it seemed there was nothing to do but go away, a woman came out into the area and lifted a dustbin lid. Ellie looked down. She calmly asked: 'Do you know if there is anyone in Mr Bellot's flat?'

'What?' The woman came up the steps to the area gate and peered suspiciously through the bars. 'That flat's unoccupied,' she said. 'They're coming to take the furniture next week.'

'But I left something there. A portfolio. Could you let me in to find it?'

'Certainly not.' The woman surveyed Ellie from foot to head and back again. With her eyes fixed on Ellie's shoes, she said: 'No one's going up to that flat, not while I'm caretaker here. All his things are there, clothes and all.'

Ellie's heart jumped painfully at the thought and her calm was suddenly gone. The portfolio existed, but Quintin did not. Her voice shook as she asked: 'What will they do with his things?'

'How do I know! His solicitor's coming and I'm responsible till he comes.'

'But I must get my portfolio. I know it's there.' Ellie, in her agitation, was becoming a little shrill. The caretaker looked at her with an expression that said: 'And what's it doing there, I'd like to know.'

Ellie said: 'Mr Bellot promised to show it to someone who might give me a job.'

'Um. Well, I haven't seen no portfolio and I've been doing the place out.'

'Could you ask Mrs Bellot to look?'

'Her? She hasn't been here since he left.'

'But she was here on Monday. She answered the telephone. She told someone that Mr Bellot was dead.'

'Dead? Him?'

'Yes, he died on the day after he reached Switzerland.'

'Nobody told me that. So that's where he went off to with all that luggage. I saw him go with that party down the road.'

'The party down the road?'

'Yes, her that calls herself Lady Someone. She came here with her car and chauffeur. He looked lively enough then. Dead? Who'd've thought it!' Enlivened by the mystery of life, the caretaker was becoming almost friendly. Ellie pressed for her portfolio:

'Could I go in and look for it? The paintings are all I have. I'll need them if I have to find a job.'

The caretaker looked at Ellie and nodded her head: 'You're right. She was here on Monday. I smelt her scent. And I believe it was her burnt the stuff in the grate. You wait there.' She went down the steps to the dustbin and came back holding the charred corners of Ellie's portfolio and some pieces of drawing-paper that had fallen from the fire. 'That anything to do with you?'

It was now quite dark. Ellie took the cardboard and paper to the street-light. Her hands trembled. 'They are mine,' she said. 'But – what happened?'

'I don't know nothing. I just found them.'

'But who would burn them? Who would do it?'

'Don't ask me. I don't know. Look at the way I've been

treated after all I've done for them, him as well as her. And then they clear off like that without a word! They're a pair, I can tell you.'

'Where does Mrs Bellot live?'

'Live? How do I know? She lived here for months, him never speaking to her. I don't know where she's gone to. Well—' the woman turned suddenly and decisively away – 'I can't stay talking all night.'

Ellie wandered off with the pieces of paper still in her hand. Something at last had penetrated the fog of her misery. Klixon had called Quintin Mrs Primrose's 'boy-friend', but because she knew Klixon's idiom, she had discounted that at once. Yet, strangely, she had been stabbed by 'that party down the road'. She longed for contradiction, for reassurance, and the only one who could give her that was dead. She stopped at a litter bin and put into it the burnt pieces of her portfolio and drawings. The last contact was gone.

That night she dreamt of Quintin and awoke in darkness imagining him in the air above her. She felt afraid and, turning from him, pulled the bedclothes up over her ears. Next morning she wanted to weep from remorse, but she could not. She felt indignant with herself, unwilling to recover so soon.

3

During Ellie's second week in the basement, her mother wrote to say she and Emmy were coming to London by excursion train early on Saturday morning. They would spend the morning buying a bridal dress for Emmy, then Ellie must meet them for luncheon at the Marble Arch Corner House. They could have the rest of the day together.

'This, on top of everything else,' thought Ellie, and the more she reflected on the hours she must spend with her mother and Emmy, the less endurable they seemed to her. And how could she be sure she would not betray herself with tears?

On Friday, when the meeting was almost upon her, she rebelled. She would not see them. To make sure they could not track her down, she would go away. She would go to Clopals.

Tom had recently sent her a card from Menton. He said he was recovered, on the point of returning to England and looking forward to seeing her again. When she rang him, he had been back a week. Could she come and see him? He would like nothing better.

His pleasure warmed her like a stimulant, bringing life into the nullity of her desolation. After all, she had to live. She could not mourn for ever. Yet, when she left London on Friday evening, the journey filled her with sadness. Although she had never visited the country with Quintin, the long falling sunlight on the fields, the fleeced sky, the windless evening that gave to the scene the quiet of a painted scene – all these things seemed now a part of Quintin, a tablature of loss.

There was a go-slow strike on the line. The train crept, paused, shunted: and darkness fell. It was a chilly night. Ellie did not notice the cold or the delays. When she arrived at Clopals she looked pinched and pale. Partridge told Tom the train had been nearly an hour late.

Tom said: 'A lot of shirkers. Any excuse not to do a decent day's work.'

Ellie, too remote to restrain herself, said: 'I think they're right. They need more money. You don't know what it's like to be poor.'

Tom, raising his brows, said unbelievingly: 'And you do? Oh, well, it's the poor that suffer. I never travel by train.'

Ellie, scarcely able to listen for the distraction of her own unhappiness, stood forlornly, making no attempt to defend herself. Tom suddenly laughed at her.

'Well, well,' he said. 'They say that to be a Tory before you're forty shows want of heart: to be a Socialist after forty shows want of head. It is quite right for you to be a Socialist. Quite right. Now let us talk of other things.'

He was looking well. Restored by idle weeks in the sun, he was eager to take up his English life again. He asked what she had been doing all these weeks. She tried to make a picture of her life without mentioning Quintin or the loss of Quintin. Tom asked, had she heard from

Nancy? Yes, she had received a letter. Nancy's mother was recovering and Nancy longed to return.

'Wants to come back, does she?' Tom gave his mouth a downward twist of distaste.

Ellie said: 'Of course she does. It means everything to her.'

He laughed as though Nancy and Nancy's longing for London were equally absurd to him.

They were at the dinner table. When the butler served her, she noticed he was not Fitton. When he left the room, she said: 'Have the Fittons gone?'

'Yes. I gave them an hour in which to pack and get out.'

'Goodness! Where did they go?'

'I have no idea.' Tom lifted his chin as though on the alert to take offence, supposing Ellie would defend the Fittons as she had defended the strikers. She asked: 'What had they done wrong?'

'She made some little remark that displeased me.'

Ellie knew that closed the subject. She said: 'Tell me about Menton.'

Tom's worn old face had been tanned to a leathery darkness. She could feel his pleasure at recovery, his satisfaction that he was well and home again. She knew he was unaware of anything but himself.

'Menton,' he said. 'A nice, old-fashioned place; not at all flamboyant; no cinema stars, as they're called; no millionaires; nothing of that sort. I'm very fond of Menton. A most remarkable cemetery up on a hill, surrounded by the sea: full of poor young people who went there to die of consumption. A long time ago, of course; a hundred years or more. I always visit their

286

graves. Poor, poor young things – English, Russian, German, Scandinavian. So sad! Why, it's years since I was last in Menton. I felt full of beans: took my daily constitutional, ate like a horse, sat in the sun and slept the clock round.'

Ellie, her head bending, brooded on the young people who had gone to Menton to die, and thought of another death. Suddenly grief came freshly upon her. She let her head fall. Her tears splashed on to the table. She pressed a hand to her eyes, then she was seized in a ferocity of grief. She could make no effort to control herself. All she could do was hide her face and try to hold her body still within the earthquake of her sobbing.

'My dear child!' said Tom, shocked that his cheerful memories of Menton should produce this response.

In shame, she wept with the abandonment of the lost. Tom was silent. Some minutes passed before he quietly asked: 'What is the matter?'

She managed to say at last: 'It's my job. I'm frightened. They've taken me out of the studio. I have to work by myself in the basement. I don't know why. I don't know what's going to happen. I don't know what I'd do if I lost it.'

'Good heavens above! Is that all? Why, I'll find you another job. I'll find you half-a-dozen jobs. Now, pull yourself together. Don't spoil the party. There's a good girl.'

Ellie thought how little a thing, after all, would have been the loss of her job. How easily remedied! But there was no remedy for death. Quintin dead, was dead for ever. Never again could she come upon him on a summer evening as he leant to contemplate the river. Wherever she went, she would be looking for him, but she would never see him. He was nowhere in the world, nowhere to be found.

She gave a gulp. Seeking to spare Tom, she blundered from her seat and found her way to the drawing-room. She threw herself into an arm-chair and, wrapping her arms about her head, shut herself within the space of her affliction. She shut out everything else.

In some other dimension of existence, people entered the room, moved about: there was a murmur of voices. A smell of coffee came to her like something remembered from another life.

Tom's hand touched her hair: he spoke at her ear: 'My dear, what is troubling you? Surely all this can't be about your job?' He sounded perplexed and concerned, yet a little impatient of such preposterous grief. He put his hand on her shoulder and she could withhold the truth no longer.

'Someone has died.'

'A relative?'

She shook her head: 'Someone I loved, terribly.'

He took his hand from her shoulder. He went to his chair and occupied himself with cutting and lighting a cigar. At last, when she had no tears left, she scrubbed her face with her soaking handkerchief and looked across at him. He was watching her, his eye critical, slightly derisive, like the eye of a parrot. He said with a certain grudging sympathy:

'I take it that such an upset could be caused only by a member of the opposite sex. Were you hoping to marry this young man?'

She shook her head: 'He was married. He didn't live with his wife, but she wouldn't divorce him.'

'Dear me! that sad, old story!' Tom gave a rueful grimace that at once dropped Ellie's tragedy down to the plane of doubtful humour. Ellie could feel at once the change in his attitude towards her. It was slight, but unmistakable, like a drop in temperature. He was disappointed in her and his disappointment made his glance hard.

He said: 'I suppose young women have a great deal of freedom these days?' When she did not reply, he added: 'I can only hope they do not all use it so unwisely.'

She knew he was seeking reassurance: she had none to give. When she still did not speak, he gave her a long, reflective stare, ironical and mortified. She read his thoughts. If he had been so mistaken in her, what of Maxine? She could not care enough to defend Maxine.

Sitting up, swollen-eyed, she was exhausted of emotion. When she spoke, it was half humorously: 'Tom, have you ever been as unhappy as this?'

'I do not remember.' He had no wish to discuss the matter. He said with cool compassion: 'I am sorry for you, my dear, but I am afraid we must suffer these things alone. You probably need a good night's sleep.'

'I always sleep well.'

'Then you are to be envied.'

He rose. She knew herself dismissed. She went over to offer him her cheek, but he was looking intently at his cigar and did not notice. She mumbled 'Good-night,' and took herself upstairs.

Next morning it was raining. Tom stayed in his room. Ellie found an old Burberry in the closet and walked down to the stream. The dahlias were in flower: the chrysanthemums were budding. Soon it would be autumn. Where had this summer gone? The dark, wind-stirred wood under the dark sky was heavy with the coming winter. She passed into the darkness where the pewter-coloured sheen on the tree-trunks stood out like phosphorus in the gloom. The trees were massive and apart. Moving alone among so many static forms, she felt the relief of isolation. Now reality had lost its hold on her. At any moment now, Quintin would appear among the trees. She hurried to meet him, she put out her hand, touched, or almost touched, his hand – and yet she remained alone.

She came to a stop and stood motionless, as the tree-trunks were motionless, beneath the wildly rushing force that bent the branches. She stood for so long that her own stillness grew upon her. She had no will to move. If she stood there a little longer she would know the secret of being a tree – but the secret did not come. She was a human being. It was too cold to stand for long. She was forced to move on.

She returned to the house with her shoes wet, her fingers icy.

When Tom came down for luncheon, he seemed to have forgotten Ellie's storm of tears. His manner was abstracted. She felt he had taken a step away from her: no more than a step, but it was enough. Were she to try and move closer to him, she would find the step was a gulf.

He talked much as usual at table, but his manner was without warmth. He might have been talking to an older person whom he did not much like. The food and wine were as good as ever, but there was no pretence that they had been specially ordered for Ellie's delectation.

She accepted this situation humbly. She was conscious of her guilt. What was worse, it came to her that she had, in some way, betrayed not only herself but the other girls.

She said: 'I know you're disappointed in me, but you mustn't think that Nancy has ever done anything wrong.'

He replied with a contemptuous lack of interest: 'What do I care about Nancy? She's just an old maid.'

'But she isn't . . .' Ellie's defence started with fervour, then stopped uncertainly – 'at least, I think . . .'

'My dear child, I little care what Nancy is or is not.' Tom, impatient of the subject, lifted his head and looked from the window: 'The rain has stopped. We might take a stroll.'

When they went out, Tom led Ellie through the front gate. They walked a long way between bare fields in a rutted lane where the puddles reflected the grey cold of the sky.

Tom made a few cross comments on the shortcomings of local farmers, but most of the time he was silent. At the end of the lane they came out on the by-pass. They walked uncomfortably on the verge, beset by the smell and uproar of Sunday traffic. Why, she wondered, had Tom brought her here when they might have walked comfortably in his own garden? She supposed it was the intimate quiet of the garden or his own fireside that Tom wished to avoid. He wanted no more confidences, no more tears, nothing more of that matter that had ended their pleasant relationship. He wished her to know the whole thing bored him.

A few hundred yards down the by-pass they turned into another lane that would lead them back to Clopals. There they were approached by a family; a down-at-heel couple with four children. The father was carrying one child, not cradled as a woman would, but spread-eagled against himself, its head hanging in sleep. The woman, holding a second in the crook of her arm, pushed a third in a wheel-chair that also held a bundle of clothes. The fourth stumbled along at her heels. The whole family had the feckless, slipshod look of the incurably poor.

The man stepped in front of Tom, touched his hat, and at once launched upon his story. He was a farm-labourer who had been evicted from his cottage when he lost his job. To avoid being separated by the local authorities, the family had set out to walk into Buckinghamshire, where, it was rumoured, there were jobs with tied cottages. If the jobs had ever existed, the family had arrived too late.

Before the man could finish, Tom paid up. Ellie did not see what he gave, for it was covertly handed over, but the family moved aside to let them pass and the husband and wife spoke their thanks after them as they went.

Ellie said: 'You are kind.' Tom made no comment.

Soon after she had arrived, Tom had mentioned that early on Monday morning he was driving into London: he would take Ellie with him. Now she was not certain whether this offer held. During tea, she said nervously: 'Perhaps I should catch the train?'

'And why, pray?'

'You might not want me to drive to London with you now.'

'Don't be childish.'

Tom went to bed directly after dinner. Ellie went soon after from lack of anything better to do.

On the early drive to London, he sat at some distance from her on the wide, thickly upholstered back seat of the car. He displayed a certain self-conscious hauteur, but whether in reproof of her or in anticipation of his London visit, she could not tell. She knew she would never be invited to Clopals again. She felt a deep sadness that this friendship, so hopefully begun, was lost like everything else. Because of her long period of stress, she was heavy-headed and sleepy. When Tom lit a cigar, the scent of it made her feel sick. She thought she would be glad to sleep and never wake again, but she knew she would live. She told herself: 'At least, nothing worse can happen to me.'

Once or twice on the journey Tom glanced askance at her, then he said: 'I know you girls want to look pr'hy, but I think, don't you know, it's a pity to colour yourself up.'

At this Ellie's spirit raised its head. She said: 'If you mean my hair, it's naturally this colour.'

Tom gave it a glance of disbelief: 'Then it's most remark-able hair,' he said.

She felt she could spare herself protest. Tom would believe anything against her now. It was all part of her downfall.

Tom ordered Partridge to drive straight to Primrose's. When he dropped Ellie, he did not leave the car or kiss her forehead, or make any of his small gestures of affec-tion. When she looked back to thank him, he did not lean towards her or smile: he gave, merely, a lift of the hand that held his cigar butt, then glanced away, intent on more important matters.

When she reached her room that evening, Ellie found a note written to her by Mrs Mackie: 'Your mother rang up. Said she was disappointed. Said she wants to hear from you.'

The guilt Tom had roused in her was nothing to the

guilt Ellie felt now. She knew she had treated her mother abominably. She was stung by her own ingratitude. She wanted to write: 'Forgive me. I love you, but . . .' But what? 'But you do not understand?' Of course her mother would not understand. No explanation that Ellie could give would be an acceptable explanation. She did not know what to write. She delayed until it was too late to write at all. Mrs Parsons, hurt, no doubt, and indignant, did not write to her. For three months there was silence between them.

4

Quintin, arrived that morning by air from Zurich, was a prisoner in his club. He had come to England with the intention of making a settlement of his affairs so that he could, without worry, stay indefinitely in Switzerland. He had made an appointment with his solicitor and was about to order a taxi when he was told a lady wished to speak to him on the telephone. Had she given her name? Yes: a Mrs Valance. Quintin knew no one called Valance. It might be some member of the solicitor's staff. When he spoke into the receiver, Petta replied: 'Darling!'

'How did you know I was here?'

'I got it out of Verney. Don't blame him.'

'I do blame him.'

'I went to see him, to find out where you were. Your telegram was on his desk.'

'And why "Mrs Valance", may I ask?'

'Would you have come to the phone if I'd said "Mrs Bellot"? Quintin darling, I must see you.'

'You certainly won't see me.'

'It's imperative. Just for a few minutes. My situation is impossible.'

'I intend to regularise it. I'm seeing Verney today to arrange, among others things, our divorce.'

'Don't be ridiculous. You have no grounds.'

'I have all the evidence I want. You lived openly with Theo.'

'My dear, I've lived with you again since then. That cancels out Theo. And you deserted me! I have your letter . . .'

'Now you're being ridiculous.'

'I don't think so. What's more, you're living with Alma.'

'Oh no, I'm not. We're being pretty careful about that. You'll get no evidence against me.'

'Verney will put you right, darling. You haven't a leg to stand on. You've missed your chance . . .'

'Very well,' Quintin broke in angrily. 'You can divorce me.'

'But I don't want to. I shall never divorce you.'

'Petta, be reasonable.'

'I'm not reasonable. You've often told me I'm not. Why should I be more reasonable on your behalf than I've ever been on my own? I don't want to lose you, sweetheart. What I want more than anything is to come back to you. We must meet. You're going to Verney's. I'll see you there.'

She put down the receiver before he could protest. At once he rang and arranged for Verney to come that afternoon to the club: then he told the porter he would take no more calls and see no one except the solicitor.

He was still hopeful that the evidence he held against Petta would enable him to divorce her, yet he had been disturbed by her confidence. He had never before gone into the question of divorce. Petta might, for once, know what she was talking about. It was possible she would again get the better of him.

He took a seat in the large window overlooking Green Park and spent the morning there, on view but out of reach, half-hoping to see Petta attempt an entry. By mid-day he had seen nothing of her, but he did see Tom Claypole's arrival. Both himself and Claypole appeared infrequently in the club and this was the first time they had chosen to come on the same day.

Claypole struggled out from the plump, enveloping seat of the car, using heels and elbows with the activity of an old man who will not accept assistance. Though he was sunburnt and held himself tautly, his appearance had aged ten years since Alma's dinner-party. He was raddled and thin with the thinness of the old.

Quintin felt a momentary compassion for him, then forgot him until he saw the old fellow coming across the room. Tom made straight for the two arm-chairs in the window alcove, smiling towards Quintin with a sort of conspiratorial pleasure.

Quintin did not much mind. At that moment, anyone would serve to take his mind off things. He rose with an appearance of delight that was partly genuine, and said: 'I haven't seen you for a long time.'

'No. I had a little "turn" in the spring. Nothing much, but it made me feel a bit cheap. I've just had a spell on the Riviera. Done me good. I've picked up wonderfully. In the pink, in fact. I thought I'd just have a few days' relaxation in town.'

'Relaxation, eh?' Quintin smiled the sort of smile he felt was expected of him.

Claypole protested pleasurably: 'Dear me, no, nothing like that. In fact I am in retreat from, not in search of, feminine frailty.'

Quintin laughed aloud: 'Then, my dear Claypole, we are fellow sufferers.'

'Splendid. If you are free, let us console ourselves with a really excellent luncheon. You must be my guest. Yes, I insist. We can have another chat about those happy days at Chudleigh. What are you drinking?'

Tom took the second arm-chair and ordered drinks. He settled himself comfortably, with the expectant look of a man prepared to do the talking.

Usually when Quintin adjusted the appearance of entranced listener, he could not himself tell where entrancement ended and boredom began, but now, with this nagging doubt implanted by Petta, the entrancement soon fell away like a badly fitting mask. Behind it, he contemplated the possibility of never getting free of her.

He was roused by Claypole's tapping his knee: 'Not a serious matter, eh? I mean your "bit of trouble" with the Fair Sex?'

Quintin answered seriously: 'My wife and I no longer live together. She refuses to give me a divorce. It is an impossible situation.'

'My dear fellow!' Tom looked concerned. There was no doubt all his sympathy was for Quintin and his look conveyed that he had not forgotten how difficult Petta had been during their one meeting.

Quintin smiled and asked in a lighter tone: 'And you?'

Tom shrugged his shoulders: 'A little disappointment. Shall we say – a little ideal fallen? Not important.' He glanced reflectively aside, then started to laugh. 'Women!' he said. 'I fear, had we to suffer their monstrous regiment, there would be complete moral anarchy.'

Quintin gazed across at Tom, encouraging him to talk

with an expression of sympathetic interest that gave his face a compelling charm. Tom, settling himself more deeply into his chair, had a look of contented relaxation, like one under hypnosis. The conversation seemed fixed upon feminine frailty. Tom, though he deviated to mention his Menton visit, almost immediately recalled a meeting he thought would amuse Quintin:

'Once, in Nice, not so very long ago, I met a most charming young creature whose frailty, I may say, was of international repute. Her hotel bills had been paid by gentlemen of every nationality under the sun. After I had done my best – such a reputation is, after all, something of a challenge – I asked her how she rated the prowess of the different races and colours who had sought her – um – favours. What do you think she said? Um, um?' Tom laughed ruefully. 'She said she'd never found anyone to equal a well-fed Turk.'

'A Turk, indeed!'

'A *well-fed* Turk, my dear Bellot. That reminds me of another little lady, much sought after – I must confess I could not at first see why. Quite a nice little mug, don't you know, but no beauty; nothing remarkable about her. However, I was soon to discover the secret of her success. As soon as . . .'

At the approach of the waiter, Tom dropped his voice and finished his anecdote in a rapid whisper. Quintin's appreciation caused Tom's old cheeks to redden. He said: 'Shall we repair to the dining-room? One of the finest in London, I always say. By jove, Bellot, I'm glad I ran into you. You've cheered me as few people could have done at that moment.'

He led the way to the dining-room, walking with a

little back-thrust of the shoulders, a strut, masculine, self-sufficient, yet defiant.

Quintin, a step behind, noting the defiance, thought: 'To grow old! There is no greater tragedy.'

5

After the disastrous outburst at Clopals, Ellie did not cry again. That stage of her grief was over. She simply told herself that, if she lived another eighty years, she would never know happiness, never care whether she was alive or dead, never love another person. Her life, in short, was finished.

Meanwhile, she began to feel acute exasperation with her position at Primrose's. She hated her little window-less basement room: she loathed the disgusting little blotters and boxes stacked up about her. She worked on them in a frenzied way, slapping on white paint and antiquing mixture, covering them with varnish; all at conveyor-belt speed.

As she worked, she thought only of Quintin and the disappearance that is death.

By the beginning of her third week in the basement she had completed all the boxes and blotters. As soon as she heard Klixon's voice on the stairs, she ran out breath-lessly to him: 'I've finished work. Can I go back to the studio? Could I go now? Straight away?'

His smile had disappeared at the sight of her. He seemed discomforted. He said irritably: 'I don't know, kiddo. Why ask me? Why don't you ask Mrs P.?'

'I can't. She just ignores me.'

'You never treated her right, from the start. You ought to have jollied her along.'

'I'd like to see her face if I jollied her along. She doesn't like me. I expect she doesn't like girls.'

'I don't know. She's got a smasher in the studio at the moment.'

'In the studio? A new girl?'

'Didn't you know? A luscious piece. Primrose's Perfection Pink! Schiaparelli overalls and mink sandals.'

'No?' said Ellie, hoping this was a joke.

'Yes,' said Klixon seriously. 'Not a word of a lie. Says she's been to the Beaux Arts. Lived for three years in Paris. Speaks with an American accent. Quite a dish, I can tell you.'

'And her designs? Are they any good?'

'Brilliant.'

Ellie rubbed cold sweat from the palms of her hands. Suddenly she was flooded through with relief: 'But she won't do "antiquing"?'

'That's being done in the paint-shop now.'

'I bet they're making a mess of it. Please, Mr Klixon, let me go back to the studio!'

'"Fraid you can't. You're to stay here.' Klixon edged past her. 'Daze wants to see you for something. He'll be sending down.' He hurried away.

The call from Daze came late in the afternoon. As Ellie entered his office, he was sitting with his head on one hand, picking paper-fasteners from a dish and dropping them back again. When he saw her, he said 'Ah!' and sat upright in a businesslike way, but he seemed to have nothing to say.

Ellie said: 'I've finished the job in J50.' She spoke eagerly, trustingly, with an innocent air of willingness to do anything, go anywhere, in the service of Mrs Primrose. Daze gave her a suspicious look.

'Well, I'm afraid that's the lot, Miss Parsons,' he said.

'Do you mean I can go back to the studio?'

'No.' He threw down the paper-fasteners in his hand, then fixed his eye on an ink-pot as though by closely watching it he might turn it into something of more use to the present situation. 'The thing is . . .' he said and paused for a long time. 'The thing is . . . Mrs Primrose fears you have become redundant. There simply is no more work to be done in J50.'

'I'd much rather be in the studio,' said Ellie.

'You no longer work in the studio, Miss Parsons.'

'But why? I don't understand. Why did they ever take me out of the studio? I had a lot to do there. I was decorating a little table. It was my first decorating job. Bertie Hawkins promised to show it to Mrs Primrose if he liked it. I still have to finish that.'

Daze shook his head. He began to tap on his desk with his thin, red fingers.

Ellie persisted desperately: 'And Miss Claypole's still away. Surely I could stay until she comes back. I'm quite useful for "antiquing".'

Daze let Ellie plead, but the droop of his shoulders told her her case was hopeless. When she was silenced, he said:

'Your job in the studio came to an end three weeks ago. Didn't you realise that? Mrs Primrose found you that work on the blotters and things because she wanted to help you. She's very good that way.'

Ellie, confused, could not cease to protest: 'But why did my studio job come to an end? I had lots to do.'

Daze sighed and leaned back in his chair. 'Mrs Primrose did not employ you as an artist, Miss Parsons. When you first came here you were working in the packaging department.'

'But I am an artist. I only took the packaging job until I could get my own sort of work. Mrs Primrose did not complain about my work. I thought I was doing well.'

Daze began to look as though Ellie were becoming a nuisance. While she talked, he leaned forward again and placed the paper-clips in a row on his blotter. When she stopped, he cleared his throat and said: 'You know, Miss Parsons, London isn't your home. You're not forced to earn your living here. Your mother wants you back. Why don't you return to her?'

'Has my mother written to you?'

'No. Mrs Primrose told me about you. Why don't you go back, eh?' Daze urged her kindly enough.

'I won't go back. I've come to London to stay.'

Daze put his hand down flat on the paper-clips and pushed them off the blotter: 'That's all, then, Miss Parsons, I'm afraid. We don't usually give leave in the first year, but you've been here nearly a year, so Mrs Primrose has kindly agreed that you can have next week. Miss Senior will give you two weeks' salary on Friday evening. That's by way of a helping hand. You need not come in again after that.'

He looked at Ellie expectantly. She said: 'Thank you.'

He nodded dismissal, but as she went he added: 'If you're in difficulties in the autumn, there may be another vacancy in the packaging department.'

She did not reply.

During her last days at Primrose's, when, from habit, she kept up a show of being occupied in J50, Ellie saw and heard nothing of Bertie. She never saw the girl who had displaced her in the studio. Only Klixon came once or twice to speak to her. When she found he had come to commiserate and not to say 'I told you so', she was grateful. She knew she had never appreciated Klixon.

He said: 'What are you thinking of doing when you leave here, kiddo?'

'I'll go to the labour exchange. They'll give me something to keep going.'

'Did Daze tell you you could come back as a packer?'

'Yes, but I'm not coming back.'

'Now, don't be a silly girl . . .'

'I'd never come back here, Mr Klixon.'

'That's up to you, of course. Here, kiddo, cheer up! I'll tell you something funny. This'll make you laugh. You know how Mrs P. thought her boy-friend had died? Well, he isn't dead at all.'

'Not dead? You mean Quintin Bellot?' Ellie's expression caused Klixon to burst out laughing.

'You don't believe me, do you? Well, it was Mrs Q.B. – she was just taking a slap at Primrose. No doubt well-deserved. I know our Mrs P. Bellot, it seems, had cleared off with a rich girl-friend. He knew how to line them up. Mrs Bellot was in such a state, she took it out on Primrose.'

Ellie was slow in realising what she had been told. After a long pause, she vaguely asked: 'You mean he is not dead?'

'No more than me or you. He just cleared off. He's

living abroad somewhere with this rich floozie. But the whole story's damned funny, don't you think?'

'I suppose so. Was Mrs P. upset?'

'Upset? She was hopping mad. She'd been made to look such a fool.'

'How did she discover the truth?'

'She rang his solicitor. She thought, after a decent interval, she'd better find out what was happening to Bellot's shares in the firm. The solicitor hooted with laughter at her. You can imagine how she took that.'

'Mrs Bellot said he was dead? How could anyone do that?'

'She was crazy. I'm told she's a bit off her nut at the best of times. She wanted to give Gem Primrose a slap in the eye. And she did it! Bellot had been too great with our lady boss. Everyone knew that.'

'Still, it was a strange thing to do.'

'Ah!' Klixon's lips went suddenly askew with disgust. 'I could tell you some funny things about that lot.' He exited effectively as he finished speaking.

Ellie sat down. Contemplating Klixon's news, she said to herself: 'Of course he wasn't dead. The story didn't fit together.' She tried to imagine she had known that all the time, but she had not known it. For her, he had been dead. She had been emptied by grief.

Now her grief was gone completely: she had nothing now but a bitter flavour on the tongue. She knew why she had been turned out of the studio. She knew why Mrs Primrose had resented her: why she had no job now.

She felt she had been injured by people much more powerful than herself. They had had knowledge and power. She had never stood a chance against them. But it would not always be like that. Already she felt herself changed. Something warm and molten in her had hardened as though from cold. She told herself: 'They will not defeat me in the end.' Contrasting the behaviour of the Bellots and Mrs Primrose with her mother's sombre morality, she thought with pride: 'I come from a different world.' Someone who had grown up pampered, in comfort, might be destroyed: she would not be destroyed.

When she considered how she had treated her mother, she burnt with remorse. And she could never return to her home! Maybe they would never meet again!

Klixon paid his second visit to J50 on the day Ellie was leaving Primrose's. His manner had changed. He spoke quickly and importantly as though too busy to waste much time on her: 'Would you like to make a bit of lolly? Bit of lolly?' He rubbed together his first finger and thumb so Ellie would understand what he meant.

'Of course.'

'It's a lady, see! Lady of title. A customer. Wants a bit of work done on the side. She happened to have a word with me last time she was in and I said I'd see what could be arranged. I'm doing this for you as a favour, mind, so keep your trap shut. Name's Countess Slanski. Here's her number. Give her a tinkle and tell her you're free.'

Into Ellie's breathless thanks Klixon broke with: 'Well, so long, kiddo. Be good. Be seeing you,' and he passed out of her life for ever.

Looking at the telephone number on the paper, Ellie said: 'I shall survive.'

6

Monday, the first day of Ellie's enforced freedom, was as brilliant as mid-summer. Exhilarated by the weather, she began to believe that a new liberty must bring a new life. Because she had nothing, she could hope for anything. There was no knowing what the future might offer.

She telephoned Countess Slanski and was told to call at three o'clock. After the heat and sunlight of the streets, the countess's Belgravia flat seemed very dark. It was on the ground floor of a modern block. Light and air were excluded by the balcony of the flat above. In the sitting-room where Ellie waited, the gloom was deepened by the ponderous Spanish furnishings. Looking at the wrought-iron work, the high-backed chairs, the dark decorated leather and velvet and the fringes tacked on with ornate tacks, Ellie was surprised that anyone who could afford to furnish as she pleased should choose any period but Mrs Primrose's 'Regency'. After waiting for half-an-hour and finding nothing to read but the *Financial Times*, Ellie was discouraged by so much gloom and began to feel fearful of the countess. The countess, when she arrived, was reassuring. She had a soft, dimpled prettiness that seemed especially sweetened and dimpled for Ellie's sake.

'Poor darling, you've been waiting so long,' she said,

her voice and manner revealing that, in spite of her babyish prettiness, she was an experienced woman of thirty. She was dressed in a suit of cream silk and her boater hat, set on hair the colour of pinchbeck, was decorated with a row of crimson velvet rosebuds. 'This luncheon party went on and on. It's such a darling day, isn't it? The end of summer – but quite perfect.'

The countess gazed deeply, with intense pleasure, into Ellie's face: and Ellie felt as though delight were being drawn from her towards the countess, whose eyes were flecked green and brown like mignonette.

'The thing is this,' said the countess: 'we have a spare room that I'm doing up. I just want something painted on the walls. Some little thing. You see, it's only a guest room. Make it fun. Of course, I mustn't be naughty and spend a lot of money. Come and look at it.' The room to be decorated was some sixteen feet long and ten wide: it was painted white and looked out bleakly on to brickwork. 'You see it needs . . . well, just something to make it distinctive. How much do you think it would cost?'

Ellie, forewarned, was afraid of asking too much. She put off the moment of naming a sum. Looking with longing at the bare white walls, she said: 'A jungle. You know, lions and tigers and dark trees. Like Rousseau. I'd love to do it.'

'Oh yes – a jungle!' The countess clapped her hands. 'That would be darling! But wouldn't it be rather – expensive?'

'It would take a lot of paint, and I'm afraid I haven't much money. Mrs Primrose let me have two weeks' wages, but I'll have to live on that.'

'Two weeks' wages! Is that all you have in the world?' The countess gazed at Ellie with pained and sympathetic surprise. 'You poor thing! How will you manage? I know! You can have your luncheon with Miss Horsepin in the nursery: and we can get the paint on my account at Harrods. Now, it shouldn't cost too much, should it?'

Ellie reflected and nervously suggested: 'Eight pounds?' When the countess looked vague, Ellie quickly said: 'Or six pounds?'

'I know!' the countess, neither agreeing nor disagreeing, broke in. 'Let us go straight to Harrods and buy lots of gorgeous reds and greens and yellows. I've just got time before tea.'

They went out to the car. 'This is Mottram.' The countess waved at an ugly little man in chauffeur's uniform. 'Mottram dear, just drive us to Harrods, will you?' She smiled as though asking a favour, and Ellie, catching the sweetness of the smile, thought her the most delightful woman in the world. As they drove, she questioned Ellie with sympathetic interest about her work at Primrose's – how long had she been there? Why had she left? Where did she live in London? Where was her family?

Ellie answered eagerly.

'But how brave!' said the countess when she heard of Ellie's move from Eastsea to London: and 'What fun!' when Ellie described her room in Chelsea: and 'How horrid! How really horrid!' when she learnt how Mrs Primrose had deprived her of the studio job. Ellie thought if only Mrs Primrose had been like the countess, the studio job would have been hers for ever.

'Now,' said the countess when they reached the counter. 'Some of those large, beautiful tubes – the best, of course.

But, no! It's only a spare room. Student's Colours! What are they? Won't they do?'

'The colour isn't so brilliant,' said Ellie, holding to the pure madder, the viridian, the carmine.

'I'm sure they'll look lovely.'

On the return journey the countess became silent. She pulled off the little white hat with the velvet roses and leant back in the corner of the car as though exhausted. She threw aside the hat and did not pick it up when she left the car.

'Your hat,' said Ellie.

'Oh, leave it. I'm bored with it. I shall throw it away.'

Ellie held it, gazing at the velvet rose-buds that perfectly imitated reality, her desire showing on her face so that the countess laughed and snatched the hat from her and carried it into the house.

In no time, Ellie saw herself as part of the household. She knew Miss Horsepin, the 'nanny', Mottram, the chauffeur, and a large, strong-featured girl called Désirée, the housemaid, to whom Ellie had to apply for step-ladders, dusters and papers for the floor. Whenever Désirée brought what was needed, she looked as though Ellie were committing some inexcusable folly: 'Painting the spare room walls! I don't know, I've never been in such a place. And I'm not here now because I have to be. I've got a young man. I'm getting married. I'm just here for my own convenience.' She threw down a bundle of newspapers: 'You see that floor's all covered up. I'm not cleaning off no paint.'

Ellie was not much moved by Désirée's attitude. Life had taught her that disapproval was the common attitude of the employed towards the employed. She took the bundles of *Daily Telegraphs* and *Financial Times* and carpeted the floor. Her mind full of paintings by Gauguin and the *douanier* Rousseau, she sketched a jungle on one wall before the bell rang for luncheon. She was extremely hungry, too hungry to work any more. She moved around restlessly, longing for someone to appear and invite her to eat in the nursery. When no one came, she set out through the dark passages of the flat to find the nursery for herself. The first door she opened showed her a black, sunken bath whose taps were golden dolphins. In the same room there was a black water-closet with a yellow seat and this seemed to Ellie more astonishing than the bath. The next door discovered a bed of taut pink satin shaped like a scallop shell. From the other side of the passage came the sounds of the dining-room. Ellie hurried across the hallway and at last opened a door to meet the pale, blank eyes of Miss Horsepin, who was at table with the small boy Peter.

'Countess Slanski said I was to have lunch with you.'

'You'd better tell Désirée.'

Désirée, with the look of someone reminded of something forgotten, went off angrily and returned more angrily. She put down a plate containing a chop, potatoes and cabbage: 'Cook says that means no second helpings,' she said.

When the door slammed after her, Miss Horsepin said with scorn: 'Perhaps they get second helpings, but I never get second helpings. Not that I want it. This nursery food's not up to much.'

To Ellie it seemed so richly flavoured that she thought back on canteen fare as a mere imitation of food. Miss Horsepin pushed her plate away fretfully. 'I can tell you,' she said, 'this isn't what they get in the dining-room. There it's just a question of "What d'you fancy today, dear?"'

'What d'you fancy today, dear?' Peter yelled and threw over his glass of milk.

'Oh, look at that!' Miss Horsepin dragged herself to her feet and, with painful dilatoriness, began mopping up the milk with a bath towel.

Peter sustained his bellow on a diminishing note until he caught Ellie's eye, then he squirmed down, giggling, into his seat.

Ellie said: 'Isn't he like the countess!'

'He's the spit of his father, ac-tually.' Miss Horsepin spoke reprovingly, then, with sudden surprising strength, she hoisted up Peter, carried him into the next room and shut the door sharply.

The next morning Countess Slanski came to the spare room. She brought with her a small, sharp-eyed, darkly dressed, elderly woman who was her mother, Mrs Harris. Mrs Harris had a stiff, suspicious atmosphere about her that oppressed Ellie and made the countess's gaiety ring false.

'Isn't it fun?' The countess surveyed Ellie's mural. 'Look, a lion! What a funny face! And monkeys! How darling! Aren't they all fun?'

Coldly, Mrs Harris said: 'Yes.'

'Oh, do tell Mamma what you told me about Mrs Primrose. Mother knows her, you know.'

Ellie was unwilling to tell Mrs Harris anything: her instinct was against this woman. When the countess insisted, she told the story in a self-conscious, unsatisfactory way, with her glance on the floor. When, at the end, she looked up, she found Mrs Harris watching her

313

with eyes shrewd, critical and sharp as ice. She turned quickly and surprised in the countess's beautiful green-brown eyes a shadow of the same ice-sharp shrewdness. Mrs Harris covered her expression with a thin smile, and the countess dropped her eyelids and said: 'There! Isn't it a horrid story?' Then she looked at her watch and said: 'Lunch will be late today. Cook's being tiresome.'

'If that's so, dear,' said Mrs Harris, 'I think we should drop into Pragner's for some chicken broth and a sandwich. I expect Miss Parsons wants to get on with her work.'

Ellie had started on the jungle with excitement, trying to reproduce the effect the *douanier's* paintings had on her. To the countess her work was a joke:

'It's so funny. I'm sure all our guests will roar with laughter.'

Ellie, feeling a chilly drop in confidence, said: 'I'm afraid it's not very good.'

'Oh, I adore it. How long will it take? You must finish it before I go away.'

The countess came once or twice every day to see the mural. Sometimes Mrs Harris came too, but she came without enthusiasm, her attention only for her daughter, whom she watched with a sort of bleak satisfaction. On Saturday morning the countess brought her husband, a tall man, pallid and very fair, already growing stout. She squeezed his arm and whispered: 'Really, isn't it funny? Look at this one—' she pointed to one of the monkeys and leant her head against him and laughed. The count smiled gravely. Before they left, he gave Ellie a single, brief glance that seemed to hold compassion but may not have had any reference at all to her. When the door closed

314

behind them, Ellie heard the deep, wordless murmur of his voice: the countess's reply rose clear as the luncheon bell: 'But, darling, it costs almost nothing.'

Ellie felt relief at this reference to cost, for the countess had made no other. Ellie had paid two weeks' of her rent in advance, fearful of owing anything. She had had to buy her week-end meals. After the first week her money was so low that she walked to and from Belgravia. It did not occur to her she could ask for payment until her work was completed. She began to wish the countess would not delay her with so many visits, but the countess found the mural diverting and, when her mother was not with her, would often spend half-an-hour chatting.

'I love all this sort of thing,' she said. 'I've often thought of opening an antique shop, or an interior decorator's, or a shop for beautiful materials. What fun if you could run it for me!'

'Oh, I should love it. I should *love* it.' Ellie blushed and sparkled at such a solution to her fortunes.

They talked about the shop for an hour – what it should sell: where it should be situated: how it should be decorated. They decided the walls must be lobster-pink and the carpet the colour of green Chartreuse.

That night the wind changed. Ellie was awakened by the cold air pouring in through her open window. Summer, it seemed, had gone in a day. Next morning the pavements were wet and cold beneath the slate-grey sky.

The countess, who had been wearing a silk dress the day before, now appeared in a coat and skirt and shivered in the bleak, north-facing room. Her mood had changed with the weather. She looked at Ellie's jungle as though the joke had ceased to amuse. She scarcely spoke, and when Ellie, who had thought of nothing else, made a mention of the shop, the countess said vaguely: 'Oh, it's all very well talking about it, but who could you get to run it for you in your own interest and not in theirs? You know what people are like!'

Ellie said earnestly: 'I would run it in your interest. I really would.'

The countess laughed. 'Have you any experience of running a shop? It's quite a job, you know.'

'I'm sure I could do it.'

'Nonsense. You're much too young.'

Her tone wiped the shop out of existence. Ellie knew then it had all been fantasy. The countess shivered and said: 'The horrid winter. Oh, to get away!'

After that, Ellie's only visitor was Miss Horsepin, who, for the first and last time, entered the room to look at the mural. She peered at it peevishly: 'What's it meant to be?'

'It's a jungle.' Ellie made a half-hearted attempt to explain it, but Miss Horsepin was not interested. She broke in to say:

'I wish I could do work like this. I'd like a bit of extra cash.' She fixed her washed-out eyes resentfully on Ellie's materials as though the secret of their use had been unfairly withheld from her. 'Where did you pick it up?'

Ellie, not over-pleased at this attitude towards her art, opened her mouth to speak, but Miss Horsepin held up a hand for silence: 'There!' she fiercely said. 'Did you hear that?'

The countess had been speaking on the house-telephone. The receiver was replaced as Ellie paused to listen.

'What was she saying?' asked Ellie.

'She was ordering dinner. She said: "A pheasant for the dining-room and a pork-pie for the nursery". You see! They get pheasant: I get pork-pie.'

Ellie said: 'I wish I had a pork-pie to go home to.'

Miss Horsepin looked displeased. She left the room without speaking again. Perhaps because of this, Ellie was not told that Peter and his nanny were leaving next morning for the Slanskis' country house. When Ellie went to the nursery, it was empty: no meal awaited her. She rang Désirée, but Désirée did not come to the telephone. At last, driven by hunger, Ellie passed through the green baize doors to the kitchen quarters.

Désirée and Mottram were eating at the kitchen table. Désirée looked so fiercely at her that Ellie made to retreat, but Mottram said pityingly: 'She wants her grub.'

'You still eating here?' Désirée asked in disgusted disbelief.

'The countess said I could till I'd finished the mural.'

'When will that be? It's cook's day off and it's all extra work for me. You'd better sit here.' Désirée went to the pantry. 'There's no more pheasant, but you can have this bit of pork-pie.'

Mottram, watching Ellie eat, asked: 'How's the job going?'

'Nearly finished.'

'Managed to cadge a bit of cash yet?'

'Oh, not yet. I haven't finished work.'

'If I were you, I'd just ask for a bit on account.'

'Do you really think she'd let me have it?'

'No,' said Mottram with a bellow of laughter.

'Her!' Désirée's voice was a moan of weary bitterness. 'And that old what's-it, her mother! I'd like to know what

Mrs Harris was before she got her daughter married to a lot of cash.'

'The countess . . .' began Ellie.

'"Countess", my foot!' said Mottram. 'You ever heard of one of them Polish nods doing an honest day's work? *He* works like a perishing nigger. No more a count than I am.'

'I'd like to know how she landed him,' said Désirée. 'She's not got all that "glam".'

'I don't know about "glam",' said Mottram, 'but I do know she can have yours truly any time she likes. Ever notice the way that woman walks?'

'I can't say I have.' Désirée's small mouth, heavily painted, was a patch of indignation on the lower half of her face. 'But I do know what I think of her! "Insolent" she called me. What does she think she is? I've worked for better than her and stood no nonsense. And when she writes my name on instructions she leaves off my accents – now, that's insolence, if you like.' Désirée, throwing the plates together, seized on Ellie's plate from under the last morsel of pie: 'You finished?'

'Yes. What about tomorrow?'

'I'll bring you a tray.'

Ellie's mural, so vivaciously begun, was ended in cold, solitude and silence. Désirée brought her tray but was not willing to talk. Oppressed by lack of company, Ellie now only wanted to finish the mural and find a job, any job, that would bring her a living and contact with life. She no longer thought of Quintin. If, inadvertently, he came into her mind, she thrust him out again. In this matter she would stand no nonsense from herself. She had begun to think she might be a natural unfortunate in love: that

318

she might never marry. This made more pressing her need for a livelihood.

On Friday afternoon the mural was completed. She leant against the opposite wall and gazed at it with a pang of fulfilment. The lion, that had been 'lifted' from a post-card reproduction of 'The Sleeping Gipsy', seemed to her peculiarly satisfying: the monkeys less so – but the whole conveyed something of the Rousseau quality that for years had possessed her imagination.

The countess must see it. She ran to the sitting-room, but knew from the silence of the flat that the countess was not in it. She rang through to the kitchen, but no one replied. In the end she wrote on the note pad:

'Dear Désirée, would you please tell the countess the mural is complete. Would you please ask the countess if I can have the paint left in the tubes.'

She wanted to mention the money due to her but could think of no tactful way of doing so. She finished: 'Yours sincerely, Ellie Parsons.'

She left a few days for this note to be digested, believing the money might be more freely given if over-due, then she telephoned the flat. Désirée replied with an accusation:

'You left all that newspaper on the floor.'

'I'm sorry. I forgot about it.'

'Well, Mrs Harris says you'll get nothing till you've cleaned the floor up.'

'Cleaned it up?'

'It's in a shocking state. I can tell you, I'm not touching it.'

Désirée put down her receiver. Ellie felt a furious unwillingness to clean the floor. She left the house to walk off her anger, and met Denis. A tear rolled from her eye: he noted it without patience:

'What's the matter now?' he asked.

'I've had the sack. I owe a week's rent.'

'For crying out loud! I owe six weeks' rent, and the last flat I was in, I left owing three months.'

'I didn't know you were so hard up.'

'I'm not hard up. I just haven't the ready. Tell them: "I'm out of work – to hell with you," and if you need to eat, get Castiglioni to chalk it up. That's what I do.'

'I've never been inside Castiglioni's.'

'My dear child, you must make contacts. Get around. Get credit. Learn how to live.'

She sighed, fearing nothing in her upbringing had taught her how to live. To avoid admitting this, she told the story of her employment by the countess.

'And how much were you to get for that little job?'

'Well, I said eight pounds and she didn't say anything: so I said six pounds and she still didn't say anything, so I suppose she'll give me what she thinks.'

'Like hell,' said Denis. 'If you said eight pounds, stick to it. Go and clean her bloody floor – it won't kill you – then say "I want my eight pounds and I'm not leaving without it." Tell her you'll sue her.'

'I couldn't do that.'

'Rubbish. Stand no nonsense. If you let people kick you around, they'll do it.'

Uplifted by Denis's advice, Ellie walked on to Belgravia. Désirée opened the door. When she heard Ellie had come to clean the floor, her manner softened. She brought in a bucket of water and a packet of detergent. 'Use plenty,' she said. 'It'll make it easier.'

When Ellie finished, the floor was cleaner than it had ever been. She looked up at Désirée, who had watched her, and said: 'Now, what about my money?'

'You don't think I've got it, do you? She'll send it to you – if you're lucky.'

'But I need it now. Can't I speak to her?'

'Her? She's not here. She went off to Majorca days ago. You can have her address, but that won't do you much good. She never pays till she gets a writ. Why, they've put the bailiffs in twice since I've been here.'

'Haven't they any money?'

'Pots of it. She just doesn't like paying for things, that's all.'

'What about the count?'

'He's a dead loss. He never comes in till dinner-time: and at week-ends he mustn't be disturbed.'

'What am I to do? I owe a week's rent, and I haven't any money at all.'

'You could ring the count,' said Désirée. 'I'd ring him. Other people have done it. Get him at his office. Tell him straight. He knows what she's like, all right. There's always trouble here.'

Walking back to Chelsea, Ellie saw Simon Lessing on the other side of the road. He was looking at her, but when she returned his glance, he looked abruptly away. It was evident that he thought she wished to avoid him. She told herself she had only herself to blame.

7

At first Petta had barely noticed the shortcomings of Arnold's flat: now they disgusted her. Had she had the energy to arrange a move, he would willingly have gone with her, but she had no energy: she cared about nothing. She lived in these quarters as a refugee lives, uncommitted, temporary, without expectations.

They arose late. Arnold spent most of his days in the British Museum library. Petta lay around the flat as she used to lie around Quintin's flat. Often enough, when Arnold left, she returned to sleep as to a familiar resiance where nothing was expected of her.

On an October afternoon, while rain poured into the weed-filled garden beneath the window, she sprawled uncomfortably in a Victorian arm-chair, her cheek against the plush, her mouth open. The fire was sinking. Only an orange glimmer remained beneath the fur of ash.

As she grew cold, apprehension touched her. The clock gathered itself to strike. In the interval of silence, the canal of her dream turned into an asphalt road. The board on which she had been carried along by an inner urgency now moved with difficulty as though caught in treacle. The single, cheap ping of the half-hour threw the dream into confusion. Traffic appeared and cut across her path:

a policeman rose before her, requiring her to stop. As a circular car hurtled towards her as a ball towards a batsman, she was saved by a last-minute change of scene. She found herself alone in a room at the top of a building; in darkness, not complete, rather the darkness of a film where important objects and faces are limned by an artificial moon. As she felt her way cautiously through this polished night, she heard, below, the clump of running feet. She leant from a window and gazed over a panorama of steep house sides and deserted streets. A line of round, lighted globes, white as bryony berries, threw a channel of light on the gloss of the tarmac. She could see no one, although the runner was passing directly beneath her. The sound diminished. She called: it ceased. Now she knew who was there. She knew that at the sound of her voice he had flung himself out of sight. She felt him standing there, somewhere below her, flattened in a doorway. She could hear his breathing so clearly, it might have been her own.

Her eyelids opened. Her head had dropped so that her neck was aching. She had been breathing heavily. Before she could wake completely, she buried her face in her arms, but it was no good. She had been skimming the surface of consciousness too long to escape again. Her mind began to work. Boredom forced her to open her eyes. She felt for the switch of the reading-lamp.

Because the rain-dark was not night, but a sort of sordid half-night, like a rag pulled over the sky, the bulb shone bleakly. It enhanced the wretched disorder of the room. Petta had made no attempt to charm Arnold's charwoman, who, disapproving of Petta's presence in the flat, her lying a-bed, her hopeless untidiness, had left without notice a week before. After that Arnold did what he could. He threw the bed together, cleared the grate, washed a dish or two when all were dirty, emptied the ash-trays, and sometimes murmured: 'You might give a hand.'

Petta said: 'Housework depresses me.'

'Then you might find another woman.'

Petta had not the energy to do even that. An indifference, like paralysis, had come down on her since Quintin's escape. This was the first time she had completely lost hope of recovering him. Now she knew he would divorce her if he could. She believed he could not – but he had placed himself out of her reach. Their relationship was at an end.

All the false moves of her life had, together, reduced her to this. She believed, now, she had only to move, to err.

When the clock struck the three-quarter-hour, she remembered the evening post. She had written to Quintin, through Verney, begging him at least to write to her. She had forgotten how long it was since she posted the letter. Though he had not yet replied, he might take pity on her in the end.

With an effort she started to make the journey downstairs.

As she reached the lower landing, she saw someone move in the darkness of the hall below. She knew at once who it was – a man whose room was on the ground floor. She had seen him several times, a foreigner of some sort, probably a German. His eyes, small, of an indefinite yellow-blue, looked shallow as a pair of lenses: his thin, short nose had a turn to one side that gave vulgarity to the whole face. Beneath his nose there was a scrubby patch of hair; beneath that, a thin, long mouth that ran into puffy cheeks. On his head there was a fawn-grey stubble. She imagined he gave off an unpleasant odour, but she had not been close enough to him to know.

When she had to pass him, her one idea was to get away from him, yet her instinct was to observe him, believing it in him to commit some disgusting crime against life. Once or twice, descending the stairs, she had seen him fingering the old letters that lay on the hall-stand unclaimed by past tenants – the word 'fingering' came into her mind because it expressed her disgust at his existence. Her impulse had been to make some insulting remark to him. She had looked at him as though he were a decomposing carcase, or some other object that repels yet draws the sight. He always met her stare with a slight, placating smile, moving aside from the letters as though to imply they were hers if she wanted to examine them.

Once she saw he had pulled out the drawer of the old-fashioned hall-stand. That, too, was stuffed with letters. The house was dirty, neglected, full of people whose rent was overdue. No one bothered to forward letters, but the envelopes had been slit open in a search for postal-orders.

Now, looking down on the discoloured grey of the man's suit, she asked herself with disgust: 'Why must he hang about in the hall?' knowing he did so from an unbearable, helpless and supplicating loneliness. She thought no human creature had a right to exist whose unhappiness so infected the air.

As she reached the last flight, she heard him strike the wall with his shoe. She peered at him. He was standing close to the wall, his hand spread on the dirty paintwork.

Something furtive in his pose alerted her: anger glanced through her. She saw he had cornered a mouse and was trying to kill it.

'What are you doing?'

He looked up, not replying. The mouse made off. In a tone of loathing so intense it surprised her, she said: 'You criminal! You disgusting butcher!'

The man started: his mouth fell open: his weak, shallow eyes filled with fear. After a moment, he said gently: 'Why, it was a mouse; no more. Would you have mice here, everywhere?' He had a foreign accent, very slight, that completed for her his degraded repulsiveness.

She gave a quick look at the letters, saw there was nothing for her, then went upstairs. When she reached the room, she fell trembling into the chair. Her rage at that moment was such that she could have murdered, had she had strength to murder. Her anger turning against her, she started to weep, but she wept angrily, telling herself: 'Those who have no compassion for the beasts will destroy themselves.' She cried herself into a stupor from pity – but she did not know what she pitied. She did not like mice. If one came into her room she would set a trap for it, though she would prefer someone else did the killing.

When she could cry no more, she looked about her at the litter of newspapers, the heaped ash-trays, the dusty, sticky table-top, and said aloud: 'Quintin has driven me to this.'

She remembered the house in Culross Street where she had lived with Henry: she thought of her daughter, Flora, whom she had not seen for two years. She tried to think of them with regret, but she could not deceive herself for long. Even had she never met Quintin, she would have left Henry. She had suffered with him, as she suffered now, a sloth of the spirit that had made her existence intolerable. Quintin had saved her then, but who could save her now? This time, perhaps, the condition was incurable, a process of age. The sensual exhilaration that had once been a glow through her whole body might never raise itself again. Perhaps that evening in the public-house, when she had caught Arnold's eye and seen the young man, Simon What's-his-name – perhaps then the last glint of it had been running out like the last upswirling glint of bath-water down a plug-hole. If that were so, she might as well turn her face to the wall and die.

And she would die. There had been a time when she scarcely believed in death, but now she believed in it all right. Her desolation, her physical weariness, her indifference to life – all those were a part of death. It was as though death were getting on to terms with her, giving her a jog now and then, as though to say: 'One day we'll know one another better.' At night, though she longed for sleep, she lay in a stupor of half-waking, conscious of the route to non-existence as of a tangible boredom, an eternity infinitely insipid, neither to be comprehended nor evaded. This, it seemed, was the meaning of existence. There was nothing more.

When Arnold came in he gave her a glance and she saw pity in his eyes. He asked: 'What is the matter?'

'Why?' She was indignant that he should pity her.

'You have been crying.'

'No. I was asleep.'

'You need some fresh air. Let's go out for supper.'

'If you like.' She took out her powder-case and looked

into the glass. Before she could absorb the fact of her face swollen with sleep and tears, she slapped the puff over it. The powder accentuated the uneven contours of her cheeks and gave to their flush a tinge of violet. With a defensive stare she faced her own reflection, then closed the case angrily. Her growing age seemed to her a personal affront: she could not bear to seem pitiful.

Arnold was putting on the kettle and getting out the teacups.

She said: 'And how was the hack-work today?'

He answered mildly: 'Coming to an end. When I've finished this, I'll do something of my own. To write! – but what to write about?'

'"Look in your heart", as the reviewers say. Just write about life.'

He answered as though unaware she was baiting him: 'No, I couldn't be bothered to write a novel. Novels are *démodé*. No important reviewer will notice them.'

'A political piece, then. Surely that would be modish enough!'

'No. Politics may be serious enough to destroy us, but not serious enough to be a subject for literature.'

'Darling, how Wildean! Then, why not a biography?'

'Yes, but whose? They've all been written.'

'A new person, recently dead. Get in on him quickly.'

'Someone else would get in more quickly. It's quite indecent these days, the scramble for the body.'

'Then why bother? It's not as though the libraries are short of books.'

Watching him closely, she saw his equanimity falter. Hide the fact as he might, he was fool enough to take himself seriously. She watched his movements with indifference. Already their relationship was like an exhausted marriage. They lived together with a contemptuous tolerance: they seemed to know one another through and through. She thought: 'I must have been married to him in a past life: married in a dozen past lives: married and remarried until now I'm sick of it.' Yet the relationship had its shabby comfort, fitting like an old shoe.

When he had made the tea, he placed it on the table between them, sighed deeply and let his large, soft body relax into the largest chair. He had a natural elegance of pose. With his massive face and body above slender legs that ended in long, slender, delicately shod feet, he had a look of importance, even of grandeur. She felt it ridiculous that he should look like that.

She said: 'From your appearance one might think you were somebody. And what are you? A man of possibilities and no achievements.' She thought of him as she had now seen him innumerable times, abandoned to sleep, snoring, the small mouth pocked open. She said: 'A self-made nonentity.'

As he lifted his sombre, defeated glance away from her, his annoyance flickered out.

She said: 'What does it matter? If we fail, we return again. Life is not inflicted upon us. We choose our own difficulties the way a rock-climber chooses a rock face. We're not pressed for time.'

'You mean we spend eternity fooling around here? You don't expect me to believe that?'

'Why not? One has such a great longing to escape the limitations of life – surely there must be somewhere to escape to!'

He said: 'I remember when I had a minor operation

once, I was given pentathol. I did not feel the needle being drawn from my arm. When I woke up some hours later, I knew I had been nothing during that time. On other occasions, when I'd had cocaine or ether or one of the old anaesthetics, I'd wake up with a memory of dreams, but that time I knew oblivion. I realised then that death really was extinction. I would never know the origin or purpose of the universe. I would never know more than I do now.'

She listened to what he said but let it pass over her mind. After a long pause, she said: 'I must believe in something. What can we do? – saddled with our accursed mortality.'

'There's much to be said for it.'

She dropped her head down on to her arms and saw against her eyelids Quintin's face – a face that touched the imagination, made infinite promise, yet was the face of a man who left one empty-handed in the end. Probably other women had been caught by that amenable look. She wondered how many of them had discovered what she knew – that there was nothing to him at all.

She began to smile, then she burst out laughing. As she turned to Arnold, her face was revivified. She said: 'I remember . . .' She paused and turned her face sideways to look into the fire. When she said nothing else, he asked patiently:

'What, my dear? What do you remember?'

She smiled for some minutes into herself, then she told him of the early days of her affair with Quintin when, soon after meeting him, she had gone to stay with Henry's sister at Cheltenham. Quintin had followed her there. Indifferent to everything – her sister-in-law, Flora, the expected arrival of Henry, the scandalised attention of her sister-in-law's friends – she had given all her time to Quintin: and when Henry arrived, she had simply disappeared. Quintin had hired a car and they had driven without direction about the winter countryside. Shut together in the car, the rain blinding the windscreen, their senses heightened by nearness and a constant consciousness of one another, one or the other would whisper: 'What shall we do now?' and the other reply: 'Make love.'

Then they would drive at maniac speed to the nearest hotel, and take a room, whatever time it might be. Sometimes they would lie in bed all day and drive all night, their headlamps flicking over bare avenues of trees that disappeared behind them, for ever, into darkness. They sped through villages that never had a name for her, past sleeping cottages, through towns as deserted as those waterless desert cities that stood for centuries unvisited. There was no traffic on these country roads at night. Sometimes a rabbit crossed in front of them, but they seldom saw any other life. The car was a large limousine, heated, silent, insulated from the outside world that seemed to have emptied itself in respect for their intimacy.

Early one morning they had crossed the Welsh border and at daybreak reached the snow mountains. Quintin had stopped the car and they had stepped out into air that touched the skin with the fine iciness of crystal. At first they could not breathe for the cold, then, breathing, they felt a wild exhilaration at the perfect whiteness and silence about them. The mountains hung over them like giant icebergs. There was no sign of human life.

Quintin said: 'We are the only people left in the world.'

She had laughed at him and flung her arms about him

so that they fell together to embrace within the swans-down pillows of the snow.

While she talked, Arnold kept his eyes on her face and said nothing. She felt so remote from him, and from the room in which they sat, that she stretched her arms above her head, possessed by the almost unendurable sweetness of life. It passed in a spasm through her body and she turned, as though in pain, and put out her hand, imagining she was being offered all she could wish. But the sensation passed and she closed her fingers on emptiness. She looked at the room about her and said: 'I'll end in the gutter.'

Arnold made no comment. After a pause, he asked: 'And after this *tour passionel* – what happened then?'

'I returned to Cheltenham. Quintin went to London. I suppose he imagined it was all over. I knew it was not. One night, when I could bear the separation no longer, I went to Quintin and said: "I've come to stay."'

'He was agreeable?'

'Not at first. We argued all night. I knew I could not go back to Henry. If Quintin would not have me, then . . .' she made a small movement with one hand.

'What?'

'Oh, some way out. Sleeping-tablets, the river, or something. In the morning he said: "All right. Stay".'

Arnold nodded as though the whole situation had been perfectly revealed to him. He said with what seemed to her insulting complacency: 'These furious affairs die quickly. We can't expect them at our age. They're a part of youth.'

'That was not so long ago. I could still live like that – but not here, not with you.'

332

He looked down, accepting this as he had accepted much more. He said: 'Get your coat on. Let's go.' But she was not finished: she never could finish. Her mind crowded to the attack.

'I've never been afraid of life. I've rushed forward to meet it. I have involved myself. I didn't care what happened. But you – all your life you've avoided ties and responsibilities: you haven't even married.'

'And what have you to show for it all?'

'I? I – I have a child, a daughter.'

'Whom you see – how often?'

'That doesn't matter. She's mine.' Petta jumped to her feet, given energy by anger that was like blood returning to a benumbed limb. Arnold eased himself from his chair. Collecting the tea-things, he limped over to the sink with them. His forbearance, his meekness, touched her. She knew that in all her life she had defeated herself with her own nature. She went into the bedroom. When she stood under the hard, central light and looked at herself wrapped in her rich coat of geranium-pink, she spat at herself with disgust: 'You look like some old bag slipping out for a pint.'

8

The next morning, Petta wrote to Henry's sister, Diana, and asked if she might see Flora. She was invited to take tea in Charles Street a few days later.

Petta had seen Flora less than half-a-dozen times during the years following her separation from Henry. The last time, she had suffered an edgy hour at Gunter's with a strange girl, no longer a child, whose shyness had seemed resentment. Petta had wanted no more of it. She told herself she had no aptitude for motherhood.

Flora looked like Henry. She had Henry's slow speech and manner. Petta remembered what a burden the child had seemed to her at Cheltenham when she was planning her escape with Quintin. Her feeling for Flora then had been nearer hatred than love – yet, when Henry's divorce went through and the court deprived her of all rights in the child, Petta was suddenly inflicted with so profound a sense of loss that she had cried herself to sleep.

As she journeyed towards Mayfair, she remembered that bout of remorseful longing for Flora, and wondered if the lost relationship might not be reclaimed. She suddenly saw for herself a renewal of life, and interest in life. Flora was growing up. Soon enough it would be for her to choose whether or not she saw her mother. And a beautiful, amusing, knowledgeable mother, a mother who knew her way around, had surely more to offer a girl than had Henry and that god-awful widowed sister of his, Diana.

Petta felt a new vitality as she saw her life's focus change. Now she saw the pleasure with which a mother could step back, giving the centre of the stage to the young beauty. As the taxi turned off Berkeley Square and came to a stop, she decided that, should Diana intrude on them, she would demand to see Flora alone. She would probe the girl's heart.

She arrived early. A maid asked her to wait in the drawing-room. Flora and her aunt were out shopping. Petta moved round the panelled, low-ceilinged room that had, despite its size, a dolls'-house air. It was an eighteenth-century house that some time before the first war had been refaced with ornamental terra-cotta and fitted with bow windows. The panelling was painted with a shade of green that Petta disliked. She found its vapidity vulgar. She saw vulgarity everywhere – in the new green silk brocade of the upholstery, the small walnut tables and cabinets, the silver card plates and cigarette boxes, the latest best seller marked with a Times Book Club marker. All over the place, in silver frames, stood, large misty portraits of Diana in her heyday. The placid 'county' face, wreathed in floating gauze, was pretty and dull as a shop carnation. There was one of the late husband – Arthur in major's uniform: the straight, narrow features, the moustache, the heroic stare, the ideal 'soldier daddy', only he had never been a daddy and the only fighting he had done was a wrangle with the War Office over his establishment Cairo Headquarters.

There were no up-to-date photographs; nothing of Flora. Probably they cost too much these days. Diana had always been given to economy.

There was a window-seat in the fake Queen Anne bow of the window. Petta sat on the hard cushion and watched for Flora's return. Most of the passers-by were women; rich women. Nothing the high-glossed perfection of hair, skin and dress, Petta realised she was neglecting herself. Her nails needed filing, her heels needed levelling, her suit needed pressing: she did not care. Her appearance had begun to bore her.

Diana and Flora returned in Henry's car. Petta did not recognise the car, a new one of enormous size, but the chauffeur was an old friend. She felt an odd, unexpected pang at the sight of him. She moved to where she could see without being seen. While Diana gave the man instructions, Flora stood on the pavement, smiling humbly – a short, stout girl dressed in a princess coat, holding her little handbag with both hands and turning her face from the passers-by as though it called for apology. Petta felt sorry for the girl's youth and uncertainty in the world. She was prepared to receive Flora with tenderness.

When Flora came into the room, there was nothing in her manner that should have discouraged Petta. The humility was still there. Her round, soft-featured face beamed on her mother with kindly compassion.

Petta, about to reassure the girl, realised the girl was attempting to reassure her. Of course Diana, priding herself on some sort of 'officer class' loyalty, had represented Petta not as a rake, a runaway, an irresponsible baggage, but as an object of pity.

Petta immediately reversed tactics. Showing no

336

emotion, she kissed the girl, then gave her a little push towards a chair, discouraging her with a show of dignity. 'Sit down, my dear.'

The girl sat obediently, her confidence gone. After some enquiries about health, Petta asked if Flora had left school. Yes, at the end of last term. And what did she want to do now?

Flora blushed, sitting forward in a round-shouldered, uncomfortable way. 'Well . . .' she gazed down at her hands, that were her chief beauty. 'Aunt Diana wants me to "come out", of course.'

Of course; a new round of amusements for Aunt Diana.

'But . . .' Flora had a slight, hissing stammer that now overwhelmed her.

So there was a 'but'! Petta, like a polite stranger, murmured encouragement.

Flora ended with a rush: 'I want to study medicine.'

'*Medicine!*'

'Yes, and Daddy is backing me up.'

Did Henry really imagine this girl had the intellect and staying-power to enter one of the learned professions? Petta was astounded. Then she was angry, certain that Henry was encouraging Flora into the fellowship of students so that her interests would place her beyond Petta's reach. And the move would be effective. It would displace Petta altogether. She could no longer offer herself as guide and mentor to a novice of the social whirl. She would simply be a silly feather-head of an erring mother.

Petta deprecated the idea: 'It means years of study.'

'Oh, I know.'

'But would you like that? Did you take your School Certificate?'

'Yes.' Flora looked up, smiling with her same natural modesty but with a new assurance: 'I got four distinctions.'

'Did you!' Petta looked at her daughter as though she were a stranger. Henry had given no details of Flora's school career, and Petta had asked for none. It had never entered her head that a child of hers would want to learn more than convention required. After a long pause, she could only think to say: 'So you want to become a doctor?'

'Yes, but not a general practitioner. I want to specialise.'

'And your Aunt Diana disapproves?'

'Yes.' Flora laughed a little. 'But Daddy and I can manage her. As a matter of fact, he's already in touch with the Royal Free.'

'What on earth is that?'

'A hospital. The school's the best for women doctors.'

Petta noticed that Flora made no appeal for her backing. She was an outsider. She could influence no one, except, perhaps, Flora herself. Now that her first surprise had passed, she felt a sudden acute envy of the girl. It seemed that all she had been given herself – beauty, an unexpected fortune, the attention of countless men – was as nothing compared with the intelligence that would enable this plain girl to turn her back on a world where beauty and money held all the cards. She was simply side-stepping the whole damn-fool set-up.

'You don't know how lucky you are,' said Petta.

'But I do. I know I'm lucky to be able to afford to do what I want to do. Lots of girls can't.'

'That's true. I grew up in poverty. (Perhaps you did not know that?) When my uncle in America died and left me the income from his capital, I too might have done something worth doing, but I had had no real education. It seemed too late to start. Besides, I thought my looks were enough. So they were, while they lasted. One day that income will be yours. I haven't done much for you, but I can give you independence. Now I must be going.'

'But you're staying to tea. Aunt wants to see you.'

As though at a signal, the door opened and round it came Diana's withered carnation of a face. She switched on the lights. 'May I come in? Tea's ready.' Behind her the maid wheeled a trolley.

'I'm afraid I must go.' Petta was determined to get away, but politeness forced her to spend a few minutes in conversation with Diana. She said: 'I am glad to hear Flora has decided to study medicine.'

'Oh!' Diana's laugh was not as light and scoffing as it was intended to be. 'That's not decided at all. That's some silly idea of Henry's.'

'It certainly isn't, Aunt.' Flora spoke quietly but with a decision that showed Petta that, if need be, the girl could fight her own cause.

Petta pretended to look at her watch. 'I am late. I must fly,' she broke in on the argument developing between Flora and Diana, and took herself off before either could detain her.

She wandered through Berkeley Square and stood for a long time gazing into the brilliant windows of a flower shop. She did not know what to do. She had an impulse to go at once to her solicitor and alter her present will that left all her income to Quintin – but what was the hurry? The office would be closing. There was time enough. She might live another fifty years.

Fifty years! Half a century! She was desolated by the

thought of so much time. There seemed nothing she could do with it. She thought: 'If I could sleep through it!' and then: 'If I could sleep for ever!'

The air was damp and chilly with winter. In Piccadilly young men and women were crowded at the bus stops, thrusting indifferently against one another in the rush-hour fight. Men, hurrying into the Underground station, dodged irritably about her as though she were an exasperating impediment. She crossed the road and turned down Arlington Street to avoid the crowds. Beside the Ritz, some unfortunate in an old car had failed to start when the lights turned green. As he peered, shame-faced, under the bonnet, the blocked traffic set up a frenzied clamour. She followed the line of cars through to St James's Street, where it stretched out of sight.

She crossed the road again and escaped from the uproar into King Street. She had once lived near here: then the district had seemed to hold all the delight and fashion of the world. Now she found it repellent; trampled upon, agitated and rowdy as a bank holiday fair.

She did not know where she was going. She walked because she could not face so soon the return to Redcliffe Gardens. She would spend this evening alone. She turned a corner and made her way towards a hotel in Jermyn Street where she and her friends had met before the war. She had a curious hope that someone there might claim her: draw her from the empty and purposeless present, back to the past that in her memory held the flavour of perpetual summer. She was surprised by her own nostalgia. She remembered how, a few evenings before, she had described to Arnold her first weeks with Quintin. She had described them with longing, knowing the past had given her something the future could not give. She told herself: 'My end is nearer than my beginning.'

She reached the hotel. She had not been inside it for years. During the late '30s it had become unfashionable: its reputation had fallen. Then she had already broken away from the raffish and extravagant set that had once been the centre of her life. She had fulfilled her mother's wish. She had married Henry.

The hotel was unchanged. The black and white chequered entrance hall, the polished mahogany pillars, the mahogany panelling, the vast steel engravings, the Turkish carpets – all were as she remembered them. Only, the people sitting in the entrance hall were not the people she had known. She took a seat and ordered gin. When she had lit a cigarette, she glanced about her at the pearl-smooth girls, the brisk young men newly come in from offices. Their behaviour was conventional: none of the outrageous attention-getting that had characterised her friends. These young people probably all earned their livings. When the money spent here had been inherited or begged from father or borrowed from anyone who would lend, then it was correct to assume a languid indifference, an acid wit, the slender and faded air of a dying aristocracy. These young men looked tougher but were armed with good fellowship, good humour, a tendency to 'look on the bright side'. No one could afford an acid wit these days.

Soon the girls and men were leaving. From outside came the sound of cars starting off. By eight o'clock the hall was empty. Petta looked into the dining-room, but its forlorn show of empty tables and ancient waiters discouraged her. She wondered how the place kept open.

She returned to her seat and ordered sandwiches. For nearly an hour longer she remained there alone, held by inability to take herself elsewhere. In the past, bored with circumstances and feeling the need for change, she would have looked to events to claim her. There was a time when, whenever she went out alone, her personality compelled pursuit: she had so burned with life that every-one who approached her caught fire from her. Not now. Not now.

She thought 'My time is over,' and she did not really care. What did it matter if one were page 20 or page 200 in a book? – all the pages would be turned in the end.

Some time after nine o'clock, people came in to drink again. These were not the people who had been here earlier. They looked older and harder: there was no friend-liness among them. She decided to go, then saw a man enter whose face was familiar. She watched him and suddenly recognised him – Dinkum James. She made no attempt to attract his attention. He seemed to be looking for someone. As soon as he saw her, he smiled and crossed to her as though it had been she for whom he was look-ing. He stretched out his hand. She took it affectionately: it collapsed in her fingers like the skeleton of a bird. He did not speak.

After several arrests, he had been forcibly cured of drug addiction. He looked now as though there was nothing left in the world for him. He stood smiling by the table until she patted the chair beside her. He shook his head, but did not move away. His ghostly paper-mask of a face had still the imprint of his once remarkable good looks, but his body jerked about with the angular indecision of a ventriloquist's doll.

She had been fond of him in the past. He had been a gentle creature if you met him alone, but with the others he had never been able to stand apart from their convention of aggressive bad manners, and that howling persecution of outsiders that made them so formidable. Their confidence – well, anyway, their show of confidence – in themselves and in the rightness of everything they did, said or thought had frightened her and everyone else. Yet, now that they were scattered, moneyless and out-of-fashion, they were as ineffectual as rabbits.

She realised why Dinkum was standing there. She called the waiter, ordered gin for herself and asked Dinkum what he would drink.

He made a noise in his throat, pulled himself together, seeming to creak as he did so, and attempted speech. The waiter, a very old man, stood patiently by until Dinkum had stammered out: 'Brandy' and crumpled into the chair.

'Do any of the others come here now?' Petta asked.

Dinkum looked at her as though trying to read from her face what she had said: after some moments, he shook his head. When the drinks came, Dinkum had swallowed his before Petta had had time to settle with the waiter. She ordered him another: he smiled pathetically and made a little gesture that said: 'My dear, how kind! It should be I who . . .' The movement of his shoulders indicated the helplessness of his poverty. She touched his arm and smiled, then asked: 'Do you ever see any of the others?' Dinkum nodded.

'What's become of Ba-ba Poulsen?'

Dinkum's smile broadened: after some effort, he stuttered out: 'Had D.T.s,' then to please Petta he managed to say: 'Fat – like an imbecile baby. Hair dyed yellow. Poor old hay-bag.'

Petta, was not pleased. She and Ba-ba were much the same age. How would Dinkum describe her? She said: 'Ba-ba used to be lovely. And Eddie – where is he?'

'S—still s-sponging about Europe.'

'And Hartley?'

'D-dead. S-shot in Marrakesh. S-some trouble in a café.'

Remembering Hartley as she had seen him two years before across a restaurant – the plum, plush skin, the white hair, the violently shaking hand that held the whisky glass – she said: 'Lucky to have made an end of it.'

Dinkum nodded. They went on through the list. Only one of them had been killed in the war they had all feared so much.

She said: 'We could not afford to grow old.' She stretched out her hand and rubbed the wrinkles that formed in the skin over her knuckles. 'I'm doomed, like the rest of them,' she said.

Dinkum caught her hand and bent his face towards her: 'No, no,' he reassured her. She knew he was rewarding her for the drinks. 'Y-you have not c-changed. S-still young. S-still beautiful.'

She laughed in spite of herself: 'I wish I could believe it.' Yet she believed it and, waving to the waiter, she ordered more drinks and began to talk. 'The trouble with Eddie and Hartley and all of them was they were vaguely creative. A bit of writing, a bit of painting, playing a bit on the piano – nothing good enough. They came up against their own second-rateness. Mediocrity is an incurable disease. One way or another, it kills you in the end. Now I – I never tried to do anything.'

She looked for agreement at Dinkum, but, of course, he could not listen for so long. He had swallowed his third brandy down and now was rising, with an air of secretiveness and urgency. He whispered: 'Must steal away,' and with a smile of extraordinary sweetness, stammering some unintelligible apology for his departure, he made out as though he feared everyone in the bar would note and impede him.

She sat looking after him. The door opened and a man entered who looked like Quintin. It was not Quintin, but in the instant of her agitation she upset her glass. The gin spread and dripped on to the floor. She did not right the glass but sat for a long time as though she had lost the power to move: then, dragging a finger through the pool of gin, she wrote on the table-top:

> 'Shall I abide
> In this dull world, which in thy absence is
> No better than a sty?'

When she could make the effort she left the hotel. It was nearly closing time. She felt a deep unwillingness to return to Arnold's flat. In the bar she had thought she might go to some small hotel and live on hope of Quintin's return, but the outer darkness, the indifference of the passers-by, the cold, the strangeness she must meet and overcome in strange rooms, defeated her. Perhaps if it had been summer! – but the air was bleak with the coming winter. Like a domestic animal, she needed more than shelter.

She walked up to Piccadilly. As she sauntered in a purposeless way beneath the colonnades of the Ritz, she was accosted by a man a few years younger than herself.

She stopped and watched him as he mumbled at her in the shadows. Perhaps she should expect no more than this. On an impulse she caught his arm and drew him into the light. His face was neither brutal nor vicious, it was merely paltry. She pushed him aside. When she saw a cruising taxi, she caught it and drove to Redcliffe Gardens.

Entering the sitting-room, she saw the bedroom light shining beneath the door. Arnold, as he usually did when alone, had gone to bed to read. She sat down and waited for the light to be turned out. She had no wish to talk to him. When, at last, the light went out and she judged he was asleep, she entered the bedroom silently, undressed and slid into bed. He rose towards the surface of consciousness and, moving towards her as though from long habit, wrapped her in his arms.

9

The labour exchange had nothing to offer Ellie. Even during the year she had been in London, prices had risen, jobs for the unqualified had become fewer and more people were seeking them. Ellie said she was willing to wash dishes in a hotel. The labour exchange official was unimpressed. Students and out-of-work actors were queuing up to wash dishes in hotels. The work called for stamina. The official, eyeing Ellie, seemed to imply that stamina was just what she lacked. She was advised to wait for more suitable employment.

That evening she was telephoned by Nancy. This was a restored and exultant Nancy who had come to London to see Terry, reclaim her room and prepare everyone for her speedy return. She had rung Tom on her arrival and been invited to Clopals for the week-end.

'It was lovely. Clopals is lovely in the autumn.'

'Did Tom speak of me?' Ellie asked.

'Didn't even mention your name. And what do you think? Terry has taken the room above mine. I'll be able to hear him walking about. Isn't that marvellous? I'm so excited, I could cry. Now I must rush for my train.'

Ellie did not try to tell her own story. Nancy could do

nothing for her. She believed she would soon find work. There was no need to worry anyone about it.

The next afternoon, envious of Clopals, knowing she was unlikely ever to go there again, she took herself to Battersea Park, where the haze from the river hung like dust in the tepid sunlight. The grass was brilliant, but spongy with rain. The mower had pulled it bare in patches. There were flowers – clumps of Michaelmas daisies, some ragged chrysanthemums, some ostentatious dahlias, their heads hanging heavily from their stems, even a few imperfect roses – but they were all like late-comers at a party. The festivities were over, the room trampled upon, everyone else had left.

Wandering about as evening came down, she suffered the memory of her first autumnal evenings with Quintin. Then, as now, the air was full of the smell of autumn: the sugar-pink light from the streaky sunset turned the smoky distances to violet. Then, it seemed, she had had everything she could want in the world. She did not believe, now, she could ever be so happy again. She had lost the trick of it.

When she left the park, the lamps were coming on along the Embankment. They shone among the thinning leaves. This was the teasing, disturbing season when rooms were lighted early and those who passed outside could look into the lives of others. Ellie took a roundabout route to Oakley Street. In Flood Street she stood a long time watching a woman dressing her hair before a gilt looking-glass. The walls of the room were red, rubbed and shabby, yet seeming to enclose the elements of ardour, as though love had lived itself out there a thousand times. The woman put down her comb and started to rouge her lips. A few heavy, fallen leaves moved on the pavement. The woman glanced towards the window: Ellie hurried away.

At the end of the week she was given some unemployment pay. Having reached an abandonment of hunger, she spent a quarter of her money on a meal: then, in the relief of feeling well-fed, her spirits rose and, with new confidence, she went to a telephone box and rang the Slanskis' to ask if the countess had returned. Désirée had left. The new maid behaved as though the information for which Ellie asked was valuable and not to be given away.

'Can I speak to the count, then?' Ellie boldly enquired, knowing the count would not be there.

The girl's front was shaken: 'The count's not in.'

'And the countess is still away?'

'Yes.'

'When will she be back?'

'Nobody knows.'

In the weeks that followed, Ellie could eat irregularly so long as she did not pay her rent. As she had paid so scrupulously in the past, Mrs Mackie was lenient with her at the end of the first week. At the end of the second week she said: 'You know, Miss Parsons, this can't go on,' and Ellie took to avoiding her on the stairs.

At the end of three weeks Ellie had no more hope of paying than at the beginning. She had never been in debt in her life before. She was filled with fear and guilt. Added to that, she had broken a rule of the house. Tenants were permitted to make tea in their rooms, but not to eat in them. Ellie had hidden on her wardrobe shelf a loaf of sliced bread, a piece of margarine and a pot of jam. Often she brought in half-a-pint of milk and made her own midday meal. She had to keep her wardrobe locked and pick up every crumb.

On Sunday, imprisoned by an autumnal downpour, she reviewed her position and decided it could not be worse. She owed rent. She was unemployed. She had lost weight. Her clothes were worn out. She had cut herself off from her home.

One thing remained to her: she could appeal to Tom Claypole. He had said he could find her half-a-dozen jobs. For fear of being snubbed, she had put this possibility from her mind. Now she started composing a letter: '. . . I know I have disappointed you, but I badly need your help. I have lost my job and . . .'

Suddenly there flamed up in her the hope of success. Tom had been kind to her once. Surely he could not now be so cruel as to refuse her the help he could easily give! In her excitement, she determined not to write but to telephone. She sped down the stairs, asked for the Clopals number, put one and sixpence into the machine and, in return, was connected to the voice of Maxine.

Ellie asked if she might speak to Tom. Maxine, with cold dignity, said she feared not. Tom had had a second stroke, more serious than the first. He was too ill to speak to anyone.

'Oh, please,' Ellie begged. 'Just for a moment.'

'It is out of the question.'

Fearing Maxine would put down her receiver, Ellie rushed on to ask, desperately, knowing she asked without hope: Could Maxine not help her? She had lost her job and Maxine worked for a large firm . . .

Maxine interrupted to say that the firm for which she worked employed artists only with the highest qualifications. Ellie would not stand a chance.

'Tom said if I lost my job, he would find me another.'

'He talks like that. Anyway, he's too ill to do anything now. The doctor says he won't be himself again for months.'

At that, the telephone exchange broke in to demand another one and sixpence. Ellie said a rapid good-bye.

Ringing Clopals had been a desperate measure enough, but now an even more desperate and frightening intention possessed her. She would telephone Count Slanski. She did so before she had time to think again. She was prepared to fight past the obstructing parlour-maid, and was brought to a pause when it was the count himself who answered the telephone. She put her request for payment with such diffidence, and, from dryness of throat, her voice died in so futile a fashion, she was surprised to find she had convinced him of her need and right. He asked what was the sum owing. She replied: 'Eight pounds.' He said: 'If you come round this evening, I will give it to you straight away.'

She returned to her room astounded, still hearing his distant, expressionless voice, the voice of someone to whom the matter was of no importance at all.

Towards evening the rain cleared. She set out in nervous triumph and walked the length of the King's Road as though transported in a disembodied state from point to point. Yet it was dark when she arrived in Belgravia. The servant admitted her without a word. She entered the vast drawing-room, where the count sat alone at his desk. The desk-lamp was the only light in the room. Ellie crossed towards it. The count rose, a tall, pale man in a dark suit, and handed her an envelope.

'The money is there,' he said.

She said: 'Thank you,' and thought she should say more. She felt sorry for him because he was alone there in the dark room, a sad, solitary, unsmiling man, but he merely waited for her to go. She left without another word.

As soon as she entered her own house, she called to Mrs Mackie and gave her the eight pounds. She went to her room rejoicing – a girl who was defeating adversity, who knew that tomorrow or the next day her troubles would be at an end.

Another week passed, then Nancy telephoned her again. It was a Monday luncheon hour. Nancy had returned to the studio that morning, to find Ellie had been dismissed.

Ellie felt an anguished happiness that Nancy should have telephoned her at once. Her eyes filled with tears, her voice broke.

'For goodness sake!' said Nancy. 'Come and meet me for coffee somewhere.'

Ellie left the house at once and ran all the way to their meeting place. Nancy was indignant enough when told of the moves by which Ellie had been expelled from the studio, but when she heard of the telephone conversation with Maxine, her indignation became wrath.

'This,' she said, 'is *the end*. And, what's more, I don't believe he's ill at all. Why haven't I heard about it? He was perfectly well when I was there. She's just taking possession. I suppose if *I* rang up she'd tell me *I* couldn't speak to him. She must be staying there, going up on the businessman's train and coming back at night. I know what I'd do if I were you – I'd go straight there and see him.'

'But, Maxine . . .'

'She can't be there during the day. She must go to her job.'

Nancy took out a ten-shilling note for Ellie's fare. 'And get something to eat.'

Ellie was to visit Clopals as Nancy's emissary and her own advocate.

IO

Ellie reached the country station late in the afternoon. She waited an hour and a half for the bus that passed Clopals. The wintry twilight turned to darkness. Everything was shut. Neither girl had visualised this wait for the bus. They had somehow imagined buses came and went much as they did in London. Wandering about the village, Ellie wondered if Tom would ask her to stay to supper. Perhaps he would let her stay the night.

The bus appeared at last. She was put down in the dark country road a few yards from the house. The only light at Clopals was in the hall: not the rich glow of her first welcome there, but a single pale bulb. She was disturbed by the smell of the damp earth, the bitter scent of rotted leaves. She began to feel frightened.

The door was opened by the new housekeeper, who had barely time to speak before Maxine called down from the landing to ask who was there. When she saw Ellie she came downstairs. She dismissed the housekeeper, then faced Ellie as though dealing with an animal in which she was surprised to find fight. Ellie had become dumb at the sight of her.

'Well?' Maxine waited with the look of someone up-raised above the vulgar emotions. She said nothing until Ellie found power to speak:

'Can I see Tom?'

For reply Maxine ran back up the stairs and called in a high whisper: 'Nurse Rogers.' When the nurse appeared, Maxine said: 'This young woman insists on seeing Mr Claypole. I have already told her he is too ill to see anyone. Apparently she is not willing to take my word for it. I think you had better deal with her.'

The nurse, authoritive and disapproving, came halfway down the stairs and looked sternly at Ellie. 'Mr Claypole can have no visitors at all. Not even family.' The matter dealt with, she returned to her patient.

Maxine began to move towards the door. Ellie looked vaguely about her, scarcely able to believe she must go so soon. It still seemed to her that somewhere in the house there must be help for her, but Maxine was opening the front door, inviting her departure. She caught the sharp scent of apples and now noticed some baskets of pippins on the floor. It was as much as she could do not to pick one up.

'If you don't hurry,' said Maxine, 'you may miss the last bus to the station.'

Ellie went. The door closed after her. It seemed she had not been inside a minute, and now she was outside again. When she stood at the bus stop in the lane, all the excitement of hope subsided, she felt the country silence, as deep as the country darkness. She waited for a long time, barely aware of the passing of time. In this darkness and silence, her own feet invisible to her, she felt disembodied, existing only in her own poignant sense of failure.

What would Nancy say? – her ten shillings lost. How could Ellie excuse the fact Maxine had overridden her so completely? She might say it had not been Maxine but the nurse, but it was Maxine who had defeated her – if anything so easily achieved could be called defeat. She leant against the bus-stop post, stupefied by her own helplessness and frustration.

The world, it seemed, was full of cunning. The experienced met intrigue with intrigue: the serpent respected the fox. She saw her own innocence as idiocy. No wonder Quintin, Mrs Primrose, Maxine and Countess Slanski treated her as a nonentity. How could anyone so foolish be thought to feel?

'But I am learning. I shall not always be despised.'

Then she began to realise how long she had been standing by the bus stop. There was some frost in the air. The cold was growing. In all the black reaches of the countryside about her there was no hint of sound or movement. The last bus must have gone while she was in the house. She started to walk to the station.

The sky was covered with cloud. Unused to this darkness that seemed impenetrable to her unaccustomed sight, she stumbled into brambles and felt the verge's chilly grass through her shoes. A wind had risen. The clouds began to pass over. She saw with relief the first stars appear beyond the cloud's edge. Slowly the whole firmament was revealed, the stars not shrunken and befogged like London stars, but great crystals, flashing and trembling upon the blue-black night. The countryside took form beneath this clear and spacious sky.

Now she could see the road, she walked quickly for a mile or two, then paused to rest against a gate. She looked across the fur-thick darkness of the fields to where the sky began. Lifting her face, she found the Dog Star. As, years before, they had walked along the dark sea-front, her father had shown her Orion's Belt, the Plough, the Bear, the Pleiades. Now she sought the great star Betelgeuse. She had no knowledge where it was, but, fixing upon the brightest in the sky, she pictured that vast, cold, silent world turning with weighty slowness just above her head.

During all the time of her grief for Quintin, during these last weeks when all her thoughts had been given to unemployment, hunger and halfpence, these frozen worlds had turned in silence as they had turned a million years.

As she considered the substance of a million years, the nerve-ridden chaos of her life shrank out of sight. It seemed to her that, passed beyond the bickering household of the world, she was defined in silence like a turning star.

The wind awakened her. It blew in coldly from the fields as from the sea. Shivering, she returned to the pathetic disorder of the world. A pity of it all possessed her. She pitied the wood beneath her hands.

'Poor Tom,' she thought and imagined that old and ugly face dark among the linen of his bed. He was indifferent to the windy brilliance of the night; indifferent to the universe. All he could know was an ignominious weakness, the smell of medicine, the narrow confines of suffering. He admitted only the material world, believing his life shrank and ended like the spark that dies on burnt-out paper.

She walked on, too tired to keep account of distance, and came to the town. The clocks were striking eleven. A train stood at the platform.

She asked: 'Does this go to London?'

'The last train,' shouted the ticket collector. She ran

and was thrust by the guard into a moving carriage. At this final effort, her legs collapsed: she lay on a seat and slept until she reached St Pancras Station.

When she left the station, she was in unknown territory. As she walked down the steps she looked back at the hotel that seemed empty, unlived-in, its windows dark. Below the steps, the empty drive swept down to an empty street. The street lamps did no more than make islands in the dark. To the uneven buildings, patched with advertisements, they added a jaundiced dilapidation.

She started to walk to the left. She wanted to ask the way, but people were few and scattered. The faces that came towards her in that desolating light seemed inhuman. As she hesitated to speak, they passed indifferently. She came to a coffee stall and spoke to the owner. Where could she find a 19 bus? He thought it too late to find one anywhere. He recommended the Underground and pointed vaguely towards a muddle of neon and traffic lights somewhere in the distance. Her instinct was against it. She preferred the bus: it was a part of home. Well, then! He sent her back to St Pancras church. If she turned left there and walked ahead she might come on a 19 bus in time.

She rounded the formidable grandeur of St Pancras church. Movement now required no effort: it came from a habit of movement. Her legs, passing and repassing each other, felt limp, as though the bones might bend. Yet they kept going. They brought her into an area of vast and sombre buildings. One ran the length of the road, blank-faced, two lions at its door: another rose in the distance to a great height, narrowing as it went, an array of windows, and not a light in one of them. No one was in sight. The sky and its stars were hidden behind the city's atmosphere. Ellie was shrunken again to the scope of her own anxieties.

She was lost. She could not find a bus stop. She walked a long way before she met an old woman coming up from a basement. The woman said in an Irish accent: 'Come along with me: I'm going that way myself.' She showed Ellie Bloomsbury Square and the direction from which the bus would come.

'Do you think there will be one?' Ellie asked.

The woman spoke comfortingly: 'I think there will. I think there will,' but her face had a worried look and she hurried away before Ellie could ask anything more.

Ellie, gazing down the deserted road, thought that no sight in the world could be so glorious as that of a 19 bus. But no bus came. She gazed for so long in the direction of Theobalds Road, she almost conjured one out of nothingness. Once or twice a human being passed on the horizon of her sight, then disappeared. Cars sped out of sight. In the end she seemed to be alone in a sleeping world. She knew she should start walking home, but she was uncertain of the direction. Worse than that, her feet, having come to a stop, would not start again. At last she slid down the bus post to the kerb, meaning to sit for five minutes before setting out, but as soon as she propped her head against the post, she fell asleep.

Some time in the middle of the night she was awakened by a policeman, who wanted to know what she was doing there. She said she was waiting for a bus. He looked at her without humour. 'You move on,' he said. 'You know you can't sleep here.'

She had never before met a policeman who had seemed

to her anything but a friend. She went on with an acute fear, not that she had broken the law, for she was sure she had not, but that, by being moneyless, shabby and unemployed, she had dropped out of the protected regions of respectability into an underworld where human beings were open to insult. How appalled her mother would be to know it!

'But she'll never know,' thought Ellie. 'I'll never go back.'

Though Mrs Parsons would welcome the return of the transgressor with righteous satisfaction, she would never let the fall be forgotten.

Walking westwards, Ellie came on Oxford Circus. Now she knew where she was. She turned down Regent Street. As she descended the steps to the Mall, she saw the east growing green behind the pallid, cardboard shapes of Westminster. Above the park the constellations were askew, not flashing and trembling now, but sinking back feebly, as though into a solid sky. The trees were taking shape from the shadows, the façade of the Palace grew white, beyond it the uncertainty of Pimlico was settling down into substance. Here and there tramps lay like bundles of rags.

For whole minutes she could grasp what she saw exactly, in detail, then, with a barely visible movement, it would shift into a region of unreality oddly connected with the pain in her head.

In Victoria Street she passed a number 11 bus because she had ceased to believe in buses: then she looked back. It was standing at a bus stop. She ran to it and asked: 'Do you go down the King's Road?'

Yes, it was a genuine number 11 bus that had started

out with the dawn and would come eventually to the Chelsea Town Hall.

She sat on the front seat and watched the streets go by. She was in a physical stupor but her mind was awake. Indeed, as the light grew, things seemed too clear, too brilliant, as though they had turned to silver and crystal. Perhaps she would never sleep again.

When she left the bus at the Town Hall she saw Simon Lessing coming from a doorway among the shops and crossing the pavement to a dilapidated car. She knew at once that this was the one person in the world who could and would help her. He was about to pull out the brake when she reached him. In a moment he would have gone. The car was an open Ford. She leant over the side and looked at him with the calm seriousness of someone who has encountered tragedy. 'Will you help me?' she asked.

He answered in her own tone: 'What do you want me to do?'

Her need, for all its simplicity, was suddenly too complex to explain. She did not know what to reply. As she tried to speak, her eyes swam with tears. She dropped her head to her arms and sobbed.

Simon was not disturbed by her tears. He left the car and led her back to the place from which he had come – a large studio, shabby, crowded and rather cold. He sat her on a sofa beside the stove.

'Put your feet up,' he said.

'But you were going somewhere?'

'Only meeting a man for breakfast. I'll ring him later.'

Seeming to float a little above the confines of her body, she lay and watched him as he boiled water and made toast and coffee.

361

He said: 'What's the matter? Anyone would think, to look at you, you'd been wandering about all night.'

She smiled, too tired to answer, and thought of the dark, windy country through which she had walked. She could not believe it still existed. She could no longer believe in Betelgeuse and the silent movement of stars. It was as though she had taken a step from outer darkness and found herself at home. Simon Lessing looked as familiar as an old friend. She watched his movements as he poured boiling water on the coffee and she seemed to know all of them.

He set out a tray. When he brought it over, she asked: 'What age are you?'

'Twenty-five.'

'Then you're quite grown up.' She roused herself to take the cup he was offering her. Her tiredness was gone in a moment: she became suddenly talkative. 'What do you believe – about religion? about politics? Is the world overcrowded? Will people starve and gnaw one another's thigh-bones? Is it all nonsense about love and God? Are we going to be destroyed? If not, what is going to happen to us all?'

'I don't know.' He sat on the edge of the sofa. 'Everything's been proved and disproved, so now we only know that we don't know.'

'So you didn't grow up believing in civilisation?'

'I suppose not.'

'Other people did. I was afraid I'd overlooked something important. So we can't be certain of anything?'

He took away her empty coffee cup. 'If we could believe in one another,' he said, 'we would have as much certainty as we have any right to expect.'

As he leant towards her, smiling, she stared up at his face and felt for him a sudden vivid tenderness. Knowing herself in love again, she raised her arms and placed them round his neck and said: 'If only I could live for ever!'

I I

Petta and Arnold were eating at 'The Passport to Fortune'. This was a new restaurant, decorated with trophies of the bull-fight, and lit with pink and yellow lights. It offered little but an appearance of being more expensive than it really was.

Petta was in her sublimest mood. It had occurred to her that evening, not for the first time in her life, that the experience she sought still lay before her. Now, almost at any moment, she would find the ultimate response to her own exaltation. Love, she sometimes said, was a light that could not be held in the hand. It existed and burnt of itself and died when it could burn no longer. But, surely, in every life there was one love that did not die? Then there must be one still due to her.

To each glance that came her way she responded with brilliant, provocative eyes, elated by anticipation, knowing that at last her life was about to begin.

She looked at Arnold, who was eating gloomily. She wished he were not there. She feared loneliness, yet desired separateness. She needed Arnold, but resented his presence. He had little to say to her. His intellect had to be set in motion by the friction of other people's talk.

An expression of desolate disgust came over his face. She said: 'What's the matter?'

'This filthy food. Nothing tastes as it used to taste. Nothing means anything. What are we alive for?'

She leant back in her chair and stretched her shoulders deliciously. 'Adapt yourself, darling,' she said, her voice full of inner satisfaction. 'Why come to a place like this? It's nothing but a compromise. Stop thinking you're something special and accept your new position as part of the crowd. Enjoy it. If you can't afford good food, good wine, then change your tastes. Learn to like what you can afford.'

'Such as what?' he asked, in a low tone of direst despondency.

She laughed in a series of excited ripples, attracting the attention of everyone near. 'Whelks,' she said. 'Or fish and chips.'

'Both pretty expensive these days.' He turned sideways in his chair and pushed his plate away.

Petta watched him with amusement. 'The trouble with you, darling, is that you've never tried to adjust yourself to whatever comes. In life you can do one of two things – retreat into a private world and admit you're done for, or face it like a swimmer who cuts through a wave and comes out on the other side ready for whatever he finds there.'

Arnold sat as though he had heard nothing, but after a while he said: 'It's not that I can't adjust myself: I simply don't want to. I have no use for poverty and middle-age. I don't like the common man: he bores me. I want things to change, but I'm not such a fool as to think they're going to.'

'Well, that's something.'

'I envy the young. They expect nothing.'

'The world will change again before they're dead.'

'But they don't know it.'

'They soon will.' She leant towards him, gently smiling, and squeezed his hand: 'Poor Arnold, you're an unhappy man.'

'No, I'm past unhappiness. Nothing can touch me now.'

'Then you've no cause for complaint.'

'Cause enough. When your unhappiness goes, everything goes with it. Each time you're wretched and make a recovery, some part of yourself has died. In the end you've nothing left but your aches and pains and a tired feeling in your belly, and your brain going on like a machine that's got into the habit of it.'

She squeezed his hand again, but now she had lost interest in this analysis of his condition. She wanted to talk to someone else. She pulled her fur coat up over her shoulders and said: 'Come on. Let's go to the "Rose".' She imagined Robert would be there. She looked across the restaurant into a pink looking-glass and saw her face a-glow, as lovely as it had ever been. She would give one look at Robert, then look away and fail to notice him again.

Arnold said wearily: 'Oh, not the "Rose". Let's go back. I feel like an early night.'

She went impatiently ahead: 'One drink. Come on. I'm sick of this place.' She danced a little as she moved, turning about on her heel as Arnold paid at the counter: then they passed into the cold street.

'Almost Christmas,' Arnold sighed.

'How do you usually spend Christmas?'

'In bed.'

'I did that last year. I . . . I'd been ill. This year, let's have some fun. Let's give a party.'

Arnold grunted, neither agreeing nor disagreeing. They walked down the King's Road to the public-house. Denis Plumley and his friends were sitting near the door. Petta gave a look round but could not see Robert. She put her hand under Denis's chin, tilted up his face and, gazing into it, said: 'Darling Denis, let's get drunk.'

Denis smiled, but looked to Arnold for succour. Arnold said: 'What is everyone drinking?'

'I don't want anything,' said Petta. 'I don't need to drink.'

When Arnold came back he brought her a glass of ginger ale. She had been talking excitedly while he was at the bar, but already her exhilaration was passing. When he and Denis started some arguments about books and films, she settled back into silence. Robert did not arrive. A stupor of boredom came down on her. She began to think about Quintin: of the days of their early acquaintance when she had longed for him and it had seemed he felt no interest in her. Then she had told herself: 'Bear it: let it pass. The day will come when you will see him and it will mean nothing.' In the end she had had all she wanted from him, yet the day of indifference had not come.

She felt an almost unendurable intolerance of the voices about her and the flat, tepid liquid she was drinking. It occurred to her that she was the cause of her own failure. When she reached that point, knowing where it would lead, she came to a stop. She sat, trying to think of nothing, feeling herself hedged in by the edgy limits of the minor anxieties of life. When she sighed, Arnold caught her arm.

'Very well,' he said. 'We'll go.'

'Go where?' She shook his hand off irritably. 'It's not closing time.'

'We're all going. Denis is taking us to a party.'

'I don't want to go,' she grumbled, but did not really care. After all, there was no knowing. She might meet someone. She let herself be led off. She felt sleepy. She stumbled on the kerb. Arnold pulled her up. As they crossed the road, the wind blew her coat open. Fog was coming up from the river. She walked blindly, not knowing why she felt so cold, and grumbled as she went: 'This world is hell. There's no possibility of happiness: it's not intended, of course. It's either the misery of youth or insufficiency of age. All I can look forward to now is dying.'

'Nonsense.' Arnold half-carried her along. 'You're too young to die.'

She wrenched her arm from him and said angrily: 'No one's too young to die. But who cares? To die young is simply to get away before the bills come in.'

As she swung away from Arnold, she bumped into a little group of people. She shouted: 'Crowds everywhere. When I was young the world was comfortably filled, now there's no room to move. It's all queues and crowds and bad temper and noise.'

Arnold pulled her along, trying to catch up with Denis, who, walking ahead with his friends, clearly wished to disown her. They turned into a doorway beside the Town Hall.

Denis said: 'The light's always broken here.' He led them in darkness along a passage, up stairs, along another

368

passage, to where a door stood open on a lighted room. Arnold, who took the stairs slowly, soothing Petta's complaints as they went, arrived a long way behind the others. In the doorway she looked round and said aloud: 'What a place! God save us!'

Arnold led her over to a divan covered with a torn rug and settled her on it. 'What will you drink?' he asked.

'Water.'

'Have some gin. It will wake you up.'

'I don't need waking up. Who's giving this bloody party?'

'I'll find out.' He moved away to a table where drinks were being distributed. Most of the guests were gathered round it. A standard-lamp and some reading-lamps lit the packed-up easels and drawing-boards. There were several broken-down divans against the walls. The oddments of furniture were scattered round a stove, the heat of which did not reach the point where Petta sat. Between the ranges of the lights there were areas of darkness that might, for all she could see, stretch into infinity.

Of course the party was crowded with young people. A little while ago she had not noticed them because she seemed to be one of them. Now, wherever she looked, there they were, thrusting her out of life, taking possession of what had been hers.

There was an atmosphere of congratulation at the end of the room. Arnold, making no attempt to return to her, was talking to a young man and beginning to laugh. Her sight was not very good. She narrowed her eyes and saw the studio like a park in a fog. She gave it up. She had lost her sense of time. She could not have told whether she had been sprawling there five minutes or half an hour when a young man came in her direction, moving at an angle that permitted him to by-pass her if her appearance proved discouraging.

She stretched out her hand to him, fingers apart as a baby stretches for a rattle. 'Here,' she said hoarsely, 'come and sit here.'

He laughed as though she had made a joke and sat on the edge of the divan.

'What sort of party is this?' she asked in the same hoarse, intimate voice.

'It's an engagement party.'

'Do people still get engaged in Chelsea? How "old world"!'

He laughed again, uncertain how to take her, and seemed about to move away. She leant forward and held to his arm, whispering conspiratorially: 'Show me. Show me the engaged girl.'

'She is behind the table pouring drinks.'

Petta narrowed her eyes again and saw the girl pouring drinks with the lavishness of an amateur: 'And the man? Ah, that one. I've seen him before somewhere. I hope she treats him properly.'

'I think she will. Can I get you a drink?'

'Someone is getting me one.' She held to his arm, preventing him from rising: 'Don't go. Tell me about these people.'

He looked as though he did not think there was much to tell: 'They're just people who live around here.'

She felt his detachment, noticed his glance move again and again to the door. Perhaps in the past young men had behaved in this way in her company, but she had not noticed it. 'All right. This is where the strong swimmer cuts through the wave. Be a brave girl. Stick it. Come out on the other side.' The trouble was, she could not see the justice of her state. She was not old: she was a girl hidden behind a mask. Now that she had realised she was no longer young, she did not know how she should behave. She had become a stranger in her own life.

She thought: 'He is afraid I'll make a pass at him.' Withdrawing all the tendrils of her attraction, she coldly said: 'You seem to be looking for someone. I must not keep you talking.'

'As a matter of fact,' he said, 'I'm looking out for my wife. Our baby-sitter was late. I came on ahead.'

Arnold brought Petta a glass: 'It's only beer,' he said. 'That's all there is.' She took it without comment. Seeing she had a companion, he went back to the crowd round the table. The young man could have made a get-away, but did not do so. Petta, reassured, rallied him a little nervously, fearing her old power to enchant might turn against her:

'Why, how respectable you are nowadays, you young people! Marriage and babies before you've even started to live.'

'But isn't that living? What else is there?'

'Oh, lots of things. At least, there used to be. Travel, for instance: in my day you could live abroad for next to nothing: you could spend months in the sunshine. Then there were parties that went on for days. And people were amusing; so witty: they didn't give a damn about anyone or anything. They just did and said what came into their heads. We enjoyed life so much, we weren't in a hurry to marry. As for having a family . . .'

'Have you no family?'

371

'I had – I have a daughter. It doesn't mean much. I saw her the other day: she's a complete stranger. I expect you think you'll get your rewards when the kids grow up? Believe me, you won't. There are no rewards.'

'We weren't thinking of rewards.'

Petta did not listen to him. She grumbled on irritably: 'Why is it all so dismal now? What's happened to life? What's missing from it? It used to be such fun. It's true, conditions were different. Money bought things then. Everyone had country cottages: they picked them up for a few pounds. Other people did the work for us – but it wasn't all that that made life fun. I know you have plenty to worry about – still, why don't you enjoy yourselves any more? You can't blame conditions. I've had to accept them, and I've more to lose than you. My money's scarcely worth a thing these days. "Come on," I say to myself, "Life's still fun . . ."'

The young man listened, bewildered as though he were being accused of a crime he did not know existed. He laughed, shook his head slightly, then seemed to give it up. He protested: 'We're quite happy.'

Petta, propped against the wall, sniffed at her glass and said in surprise: 'Beer!' At any other time she would not have drunk it, but now she sipped it as she spoke. 'The human situation,' she said, 'sickens me. I don't want to be an animal. I don't want to be a machine for breeding, but if I have children, I don't want to love them simply because a gland is secreting mother love into my system. And when I'm middle-aged – as I am, of course: no need to tell me – I don't want to feel depressed and defeated because some other gland isn't doing its job.'

The young man, watching her, seeming to hide whatever he felt beneath a look of laughter, asked: 'And love?'

She considered the question sombrely, and sombrely answered: 'That's a trick, too.' After a moment, she said: 'I resent the whole set-up. I want my emotions to be attached to something bigger than biology. I object to the limitations of the human creature. I want to be something different.'

'What, for instance?'

'God knows. I don't. I don't suppose I shall ever know. I suppose I shall die and come to an end without ever knowing what it is I have wanted to be, but . . .' she suddenly thumped the divan, 'I put it on record here and now, that I am dissatisfied with my human state. I ask for more.' She looked accusingly at the young man for some moments, then pointed angrily at him: 'But you, you're satisfied, aren't you? You're all cosily settled in your little hole – wife and children cuddled up together. It's easy for you. You're young.'

She was holding her glass so that it spilled on to the rug. He steadied it for her, saying as though to a difficult child: 'Did you think that when you were young?'

She caught her breath, slighted, but he noticed nothing. He said: 'Perhaps it is easier, being young. I don't know. I can't tell till I'm old – but it doesn't seem so easy.' As he spoke, some instinct drew his eyes again to the door. At once he put down his empty glass and rose, excusing himself.

She watched him go, not caring. To hell with the young! What a pack of fools they were!

The girl who stood in the doorway was large and pale and round-bosomed – not a beauty: not a beauty as Petta

373

had been at her age. The young husband lifted her hand and pressed his lips into her palm, then they smiled at one another. Sliding his arm round her waist, he led her into the room. They went, not towards Petta, but over to the engaged couple, who, in imitation of their visitors, encircled each other's waists. The two couples exchanged looks of congratulation and pleasure as though they believed themselves bound safely for ever in content and love.

Petta, swallowing in her throat, drew her glance from their illusioned world: 'What does it matter? It lasts so short a time.' She looked about her for distraction and saw an old magazine wedged down between the bed and wall. She drew it out: a thick, glossy American magazine, the cover missing. She opened it at a picture of a serious-faced young man in uniform – the first American killed in Korea. That forgotten war! How old was this periodical, for goodness sake?

An American called Kenneth: and here were his mom, dad, sis, the family dog. The father was a coal miner, not at home on the upper crust of the world where the wars were made. When a reporter asked him why the boy had given his life, the father replied: 'He was fighting against some sort of government,' and then: 'That boy was in here every night by dark. Never caused us a mite of worry.' And Mom said: 'He never saw a bad day in his life. Never bothered nobody any time.'

The rest of the article had been washed off. It seemed as though someone had dropped the magazine into the bath. Half the thick, glossy pages were stuck together solid as cement. Petta threw it aside. 'They all die,' she thought with morose satisfaction and she looked about her blackly.

Seeing she was alone, Arnold came over, bringing Denis. He said: 'Why not come and meet some of the others?'

'Why should I? What are we doing here among the young? They all look so damned pleased with themselves.'

'Let me get you another drink.'

'No.'

The engaged couple crossed over to the three on the divan. Denis caught the girl's hand and said: 'Ellie darling, you've met Arnold Valance. This is Mrs Valance.'

Petta smiled vaguely and made no attempt to correct him. As the girl bent towards Denis, her hair, that had seemed black when in shadow, was seen to be a dark red. Petta found this colour disturbing, though she could not remember why. She watched the girl playing hostess in an earnest, painstaking way, like a child at a dolls' tea-party.

'And what will you do when you are married?' asked Denis.

Simon Lessing, putting his arm protectively round Ellie, said: 'I'm sending her to the Polytechnic. She must learn to draw. I don't want any regrets.'

'Why bother' said Petta. 'She'll be producing babies in no time.'

'Women have no regrets,' said Arnold. 'They're a lazy lot. They're only too glad to use someone else's talents instead of their own.'

The girl smiled, denying nothing. As Denis pulled her closer, questioning her confidentially, Simon returned to the guests round the table.

'Tell me, darling,' Denis asked in a half-whisper. 'Are you living here?'

'Yes. You see, it's cheaper and we'll soon be married.

And it's so wonderful. I've always wanted to live in a place like this.'

Denis looked up at the crumbling plaster and down at the bare floor, and said: 'Delicious, darling! Just like a French film or something.'

Petta watched the girl answering questions, taking no offence, all the time holding the heavy jug of beer, waiting for their glasses to empty. Arnold held his out. As she leant forward, filling the glass with a careful, steady hand, he touched her glistening hair.

'Like silk,' he said.

Simon had returned to the crowd round the table. The girl glanced about for him, uncertain whether to leave her present company or not. Denis gave her a little push, dismissing her: 'There's a good girl! Go and fill them all up. Let joy be unrestrained.'

She smiled and went.

Petta realised Arnold was drunk. There must be more than beer over at the table. She said: 'This is a boring party. Let's go.'

Arnold did not answer, but started one of his tedious literary arguments with Denis. A heavy, uncomfortable sleepiness hung over Petta so that she longed to be away from the place. She shook at Arnold's arm and said again: 'Let's go.'

'No.' He stared irritably at her as though she were trying to deprive him of something desirable: 'The party hasn't begun yet. I don't want to go.'

'I'm very sleepy.'

'You can lie down on the divan and go to sleep.'

'Thank you. I'm not drunk.' In her present mood, the suggestion seemed to her an insult. She shuffled to

376

the edge of the divan and sat there, about to leave and yet not leaving.

Someone was putting records on the gramophone. The young people were dancing, not as Petta had danced when young, but fiercely, as though the intention was to rid themselves of an incubus of energy. Some of the girls had thrown off their shoes and were dancing in bare feet. They moved wildly, turning their feet in and out, flinging their thighs to one side and the other, clutching at their partners as in an orgasm.

This was a party, but it seemed to Petta no one was dressed for a party. The girls, who wore wide skirts, made great play with them, but several did not even wear skirts: they were dressed in jeans and jerseys. Petta followed with her eyes one youth who, having the imbecile look of a drug-taker, danced as though he had lost awareness of everything, even the insanely jerking automaton that was his body.

She edged still further off the divan and managed to get to her feet. Why should she stay here to watch the appalling good fortune of the young?

She said to Arnold: 'If you won't come, I'll go alone.'

This threat usually brought him to his feet. Now he simply lifted his glass and said: 'Just as you like. I won't be late.'

She pulled her coat round her, saying nothing. He added in a gentler tone: 'You don't mind, do you, dear? I'll drink this and be back in half-an-hour.'

For the first time since their relationship had started, she went home without him. Feeling her way through the unlit passages, she stumbled and grazed her shin on the stair. The street, when she reached it, was full of a shrill and foggy damp. Damp glistened on the pavements. It filmed over the ironwork of street-lamps and railings. The fog drifted like smoke across the road.

The cold, the pain in her leg, the bleak emptiness of the street, filled her with a sense of injury. Why had Arnold chosen this night of all nights to treat her with such callousness? It seemed to her that all her suffering came from the fact that her youth was passing and her beauty fading. She felt martyred, as though age were some horrible and incurable sickness imposed on her and on no one else.

She thought of a young man she had known years ago in Ireland, the first to love her. He had said: 'You seem to have a light about you.' She wondered where he was now. Young no longer, she supposed, but perhaps he still imagined her as she had been, young, and so beautiful it seemed she had a light about her.

In those days she had thought her beauty must bring her everything – yet what had it brought? That plain, pale girl, Ellie – she might, in the end, be given more than herself had ever been given.

As she remembered Arnold's hand stroking the girl's hair, tears came into Petta's eyes. It seemed to her she had no one. All her life she had most feared the moment when she would be thrown dependent on herself. How had she failed? Had she possessed some talent and kept it hidden? Some creative power that, aborted, had destroyed her?

Well, if she had, she had lost it. She could do nothing now.

In Fulham Road she stopped a taxi. The cold had wakened her. She was afraid she would not sleep. It was in her mind now to leave Redcliffe Gardens. She could keep the taxi waiting while she packed. When Arnold returned, he would find her gone. 'That will give him a jolt,' she thought. Then she decided she would not take her luggage: only a few things in a make-up box. Arnold would not know what had become of her. She might be dead.

For a short time this intention enlivened her. She thought with contempt of Arnold: 'That withered windfall,' she said to herself. He had stayed at the party imagining himself young because he had never matured! Well, he'd come back to an empty flat! But by the time she reached the house her intention had weakened. As she left the taxi, she looked about the empty street. What place was there for her in this homeless night? She paid off the taxi, knowing the move was beyond her.

If only Quintin were in England! She imagined herself flying to him, throwing herself into his arms . . .

Someone came in at the front door. She looked down to the hall, imagining it would be Arnold. Had it been he, she would have run to him, remorseful, weeping – but it was not. It was the man on the ground floor, the disgusting mouse-killer.

She went upstairs in an agony of resentment that Arnold had not come at the moment she needed him. She ran into the flat, possessed by a desperate and bitter purpose. Acting quickly, expecting him to come at any moment, she wrote:

'Sorry Arnold, but I'm tired of everything. This is not the world I want, but I have not the means to change it. Forgive me. I really long to die. Please ring

379

my husband's solicitor (number below) and ask him to tell Q. what has happened. Petta.'

She rummaged wildly through her papers, seeking the solicitor's telephone number, found it at last and added it to the note, which she pinned to Arnold's pillow.

She filled her hot-water bottle. When she had undressed, she propped herself up on pillows and placed the hot bottle on her belly. She had lit the reading-lamps on either side of the bed. In the drawer of the table beside her she had a dozen or so boxes of sleeping-tablets. She looked them over and took out a box of a hundred she had bought a couple of years before in Paris. With these in her hand, she looked round the room, seeing it a place she was leaving for ever.

The fog-coloured wall-paper was peeling off at the corners near the ceiling. The ceiling had been white once but now it was darker than the paper. There were no pictures: pictures meant nothing to Arnold. The fireplace and shelf above it were heaped with books. So were the pieces of late Victorian mahogany furniture on either side. Books were stacked against the walls, on chairs, on the window ledge, all spine-broken, torn, faded to an even greyness. Every day she had been there, Arnold had come in with more books, picked up for a few pence 'for reference'. He never opened one of them.

The room smelt of books. This concourse of books produced no show of culture, only a desolate squalor. And here, she thought, is where I am to die – 'the worst inn's worst room'.

She took three sleeping-tablets and washed them down with water: she took three more. Then, in a sudden fear that death would miscarry again, she emptied the box into her hand and began cramming the pills into her mouth, taking gulps of water to clear away the acid powder. When she had swallowed all but a few that fell on the floor, she flung the box across the room.

She lay down among the pillows, waiting for the first premonitions of sleep. Nothing now could keep her from unconsciousness of life. She pressed her face away from the light and felt, sensuously, through all her nerves, the heaviness of her body relaxed against the bed.

She had imagined the tablets would act at once, but she remained awake. Bored with waiting, she stretched her arm down among the books beside the bed, lifted one and knocked off the dust. It fell open and she read:

'. . . we carry within us the wonders we seek without us: There is all *Africa* and her prodigies in us; we are that bold and adventurous piece of nature, which he that studies wisely learns in a *compendium* what others labour at in a divided piece and endless volume.'

Her eyes, blurring, passed several times over this passage, then remained on the lines: '. . . we carry within us the wonders we seek without us: There is all *Africa* and her prodigies in us,' until a fog of sleep came between her and the page. The book fell from her hand. If she had made a discovery, she had made it too late.

It was as though her own weight was carrying her down through folds of darkness, each more compacted, till the last was dense enough to hold her. There, in the darkest recess, was to be found velvet oblivion.

At the last moment of consciousness, she stirred, stretching her fingers, as she felt the voluptuous sweetness of life where it bordered dissolution. She sighed, the moment passed: she slept, certain she would not wake again.

She returned to consciousness some time after nine in the morning. She opened her eyes to the delicate topaz light of the winter sun. The light crashed at her like a blow. She closed her eyes: her mouth fell open in pain and nausea. She must have a hang-over. As she tried to move, an excruciating sickness was set in motion. She lay still, but let her eyelids part again. She had not drawn the curtains: a reading-lamp was switched on. The whole room was a shifting dazzle of light. She could make nothing of this awakening. No hang-over could be as bad as this.

She waited for the nausea to pass off. There was a sour smell in the air, like vomit. She imagined it came through the window. She turned her head distastefully and felt something wet and cold on her cheek. When she was still, the pain was no more than a twitch in her brain. After a while she managed to lift her hands and press them to her head. This darkened her consciousness, but the twitch remained. Worse than that, the sickness was becoming active, flooding up through her blackly until, at the last moment, she flung herself from the bed, reached the window and pulled up the lower frame. As she knelt, vomiting upon the weed beds below, she felt the luxury of relief. She closed her eyes and lay with her head on the window-sill until the cold saturated her and she began to shiver. Her head throbbed, but now, at least, she was capable of movement.

In the pit of her body the waves of sickness were moving again. She wrapped herself in a dressing-gown and went down to the bathroom. She moved carefully, holding her head as though to hold it together, and reached the bath-room with a sense of gratitude for its existence. She had scarcely bolted the door when the walls began to jerk and spin about her. The air turned yellow. She could not stand. She slid down beside the water-closet, that had a sickly urine smell, and, propping herself against the seat, she let her mouth hang open and waited.

12

Some time after nine o'clock the dozen or so persons who had spent the night in Simon Lessing's studio began gathering themselves up from the floor, from chairs, from the divan beds, to follow Simon and Ellie out to the car.

Simon was carrying the suitcases. Each of the others, in imitation, picked up some object as they passed. Arnold Valance, the only one among them who was no longer young, cradled in his arms a plaster bust of Venus.

The car doors were held open. Ellie and Simon were solicitously packed into the front seat. The luggage was placed in the back and on top of it were piled a wash-jug, a T-square, the top of the stove, several cushions and picture-frames, and two plaster cones.

Arnold, swaying and smiling on the pavement, held to the bust as though it were part of himself.

'Take them all back,' said Simon, and the company, in a state of obedient torpor, a step beyond drunkenness, repossessed themselves of all but the plaster cones. These, rolling unseen into a corner, were carried down to Eastsea.

The car started off. Arnold, with a vague and sleepy smile of good-will, waved until it was out of sight, then, with the bust in his arms, set out in a dream state to walk to Redcliffe Gardens.

The car passed from London into the clear sunlight of the countryside. It was Christmas Eve. Ellie had not written to her mother to tell of her engagement. She had half expected Mrs Parsons would write inviting her home for Christmas – but Mrs Parsons did not forgive so easily.

Now Ellie went home with confidence, taking with her, as she did, that most desirable of peace offerings – a future husband.

The car could not travel at speed. They stopped at Tunbridge Wells for luncheon and reached Mrs Parsons's restaurant as the sun was setting. The lights were coming on along the Eastsea promenade in a sad, wintry sunset. Ellie looked indifferently at it all. Nothing could touch her now.

As the door-bell pinged, Mrs Parsons came out through the bead-curtains that hid the kitchen. At the sight of Ellie, her eyes narrowed, with resentment, yet with gratification. They moved to the male figure behind. She did not smile or speak. She awaited explanation.

Ellie smiled. With as much triumph as pleasure, she said: 'This is Simon Lessing. We're engaged. We thought, if you approved, we'd get a special licence and be married down here.'

Mrs Parsons raised her eyes again to Simon's face, which, with its look of transparent simplicity and good-will, smiled over Ellie's shoulder, then her lips shook, her face crumpled and tears welled into her eyes.

Ellie put her arms about her mother. Embracing her daughter, Mrs Parsons choked back her sobs to say: 'Both my girls married before they're twenty. I never dared hope for such happiness.'

13

Tom Claypole died in the new year, during a period of unusual cold.

When Ellie left the Underground station, snow hung like swansdown in the air. It did no more than drift on the air's currents, yet the roofs were already white and cars were cutting tracks in the lace-film on the road.

As, directed by the ticket collector, she found her way from the station to the crematorium, the distances disappeared in a fog of gun-metal grey. The light was without shadow.

This was Golders Green, the place she had once imagined to be in the depths of the country. Remembering Rhoda's lily-pond and lawns and vine, she saw them now reduced to the stature of this red-brick suburbia where there was no brilliancy but the snow.

A great many things had been reduced in her mind since her first days in London. Many mosaics of shadow and unsubstantial wonders had hardened now into fact.

She thought: 'I am growing old. A friend has died.' This death seemed to her a step towards maturity, bringing her own death nearer and into perspective. That, she supposed, was how people came to accept death. Friends died and their presence there made a home for one in the grave.

The softly tangling powder grains of snow were growing into flakes. A silver iridescence filled the air. Dazzled within this glass snow world, she remained on these new terms with death until she reached the crematorium church, then death took on a leaden look. The church was cold; its light livid from the snow. How desolate to be old and dead instead of young and married!

The service had already started; a secular service. Verses and songs – agnostic but hopeful – had been chosen by Tom's solicitor. Ellie tip-toed down the aisle to where Nancy sat.

Nancy moved the black-gloved hand that shaded her face and whispered: 'She hasn't got a thing.'

'Who?'

'Maxine.'

'Not *any*thing?'

'Not a bean. He's paid off her overdraft, but who the hell wants money already spent?'

The elderly gentleman beside Nancy shuffled in his seat. Silenced, she gave Ellie a grin of triumph. They bowed their heads.

The coffin, hidden beneath chrysanthemums, began to slide out of sight. Did the flowers die in the flames? Ellie imagined Tom's dark, folded face within the box. Because he had believed himself mortal, she felt him the more dead. He was shut in, immobilised by his belief in his mortality, a figure of clay. The coffin had gone. The doors closed on it. She pictured its journey into the furnace. When she supposed the clay body must be consumed, Tom seemed to her more dead than were the buried. Such non-existence did not leave space even for compassion.

Someone was reading verses in a flat, dispirited voice.

Ellie had never attended a funeral before, but she had once heard on a gramophone record the Russian Kontakion for the dead. She had come prepared for grandeur, supposing they would be caught up from their thoughts of past and present in the brilliance of a moment and a triumph of sound. Apparently that was not to happen.

She whispered to Nancy: 'Did he leave you anything?'

'Only my allowance: that goes on.'

Nothing for Ellie, of course. She had expected nothing. The service came to an end.

When she turned to face the people who were filing out of the pews, she saw, for the first time since they parted that summer evening, Quintin Bellot. She came to a stop, growing faint.

Nancy pushed her on: 'Hurry. Get out before Maxine.'

Partridge, who had sat at the back of the church, was standing beside Tom's car.

'Come on.' Nancy caught Ellie's elbow and rushed her to the car door. Partridge saluted and opened it. They took their places on the back seat. Through the rear window they could see Maxine, black-clad, with the air of a widow, talking to one person and another, making a leisurely exit from the chapel.

Nancy said: 'You can drive on, Partridge.'

He looked uneasy: 'Miss Maxine said . . .'

'That is all right.' Nancy spoke with authority: Partridge obeyed.

As they started off, they watched, until they passed beyond her sight, Maxine's furious awareness of their departure.

'Does she know?' asked Ellie.

'Not yet. The solicitor rang me because I'm the only relative. He thought he ought to soften the blow. I was so damned glad she hadn't got it, I didn't care who had. At least, not much.'

'And who has got it?'

'An heir. His wife's nephew. Perhaps he intended that all along.'

'And you don't mind?'

'Well, Tom believed in the male heir.' Nancy looked a little smug, as though, against all reason, she felt something glorious in the belief.

'What was Mr Bellot doing there?'

'Bellot? The heir? How do you know him?'

'He used to come to Primrose's. He's a friend of Mrs P.'

Nancy found this coincidence remarkable and, talking about it at length, she permitted Ellie to remain silent.

Ellie watched the heath running whitely away into the violet snow mist that filled the bowl of grass. In the distance the roofs and spires of Highgate rose above fallen cloud. 'I must come here with Simon,' she thought.

Suddenly she asked: 'Will Mr Bellot be at the house for sherry?'

'Of course. He's been especially asked to come because he's the heir.'

When they reached South End Road, she said: 'Put me down here. I don't feel like sherry.'

'Nonsense,' said Nancy. 'You look as though you need it.'

The car turned into Keats' Grove. They were the first arrivals. The snow, no longer falling, lay untrodden on the neat, small garden behind which the house of Tom's solicitor stood like a doll's-house. A maid showed them into the front room. They were left alone with plates of sandwiches and several decanters of sherry.

'Fall to.' Nancy took a sandwich in each hand.

Ellie, watching from the window, felt sick at the thought of meeting Quintin again. 'They're coming,' she said fearfully.

'What do I care?' said Nancy. 'He was my uncle.'

Maxine entered first. She gave Nancy a stare of threatening calm, then turned the full force of her vivacity upon the men behind her. Among them was Quintin. Ellie saw him responding to Maxine as he responded to every attractive woman. She moved into the bow of the window, willing to remain unseen, but Quintin saw her and crossed to her at once. He looked as though this were a meeting too long delayed. His face was alive with pleasure, and with astonishment at finding her there.

'My dear child, whatever are you doing here? Did you know old Tom Claypole?'

Ellie at once set about explaining her presence. Her apparent casualness was enhanced by the fact that she felt as though she were being throttled. While she talked, Quintin gazed down into her face with an admiring amusement, his hand hovering to take her hand, to restore them at once to their old intimacy.

Ellie took a step away and kept her hand out of reach. The spell no longer worked. That was a relief: and equally a relief was the fact she no longer felt angry with him.

When she had nothing more to say, he started explaining his sudden departure to Switzerland. He seemed unaware of her new indifference to him. Watching him dispassionately, she saw him more charming, more elegant, better-looking than anyone else in the room. The other men had been old friends of Tom. They were commonplace men who had given their lives to commonplace employments: Quintin was of another order of human being. He had been free to be anything, and he had chosen to charm. It seemed to her right that Tom's money should have gone to him. She could not imagine he had ever manoeuvred to obtain it as Maxine and, she feared, Nancy had done. She told herself that Quintin would own the money, not the money Quintin. Somehow these reflections tidied away her past relationship with him. He was rewarded. Her reward was elsewhere.

He managed to catch her wrist and give her hand a shake to gain her attention. He had mistaken the remote gravity of her face.

He said: 'You must not be cross with me. You took it all too seriously, you know. It was just a little *affaire* – not to be taken seriously.'

She opened her eyes at him and laughed. 'Are you sure I took it seriously? One can play even at seriousness.'

His smile widened: he raised his brows and stared at her as though transported by admiration of what he saw.

'You remarkable girl!' he said. 'You reawaken all my old interest.'

'I hope not. It would be such an anti-climax. You see, I'm married now.'

'Married! At your age!' He turned over her hand and looked at her ring. 'So you are! Why, I am delighted.'

She had not expected him to be as delighted as that. The atmosphere between them flattened somewhat. There was a pause, then she asked: 'Where is your wife now?'

'Carrying on some squalid liaison somewhere. The usual thing.'

'And the lady with whom you went to Switzerland?'

He nodded, amused that she was so well-informed: 'Alma? She intended marriage and left me when she found my wife would not part with me.'

'And Mrs Primrose? Are you still attached to her?'

'Oh, that! – that was nothing. I thought it would be entertaining to stretch up to an apple just out of reach – and lo and behold! I made a little movement and it fell into my hand. Naturally I did not want it then.'

Ellie smiled her disbelief. 'What will you do with Clopals?' she asked.

'Sell it. I believe it's terrible; a sort of super-suburban Kozy Kot; all mod. con. and so on.'

'I thought it was wonderful,' said Ellie.

Quintin touched her under the chin. 'When are we going to meet again?'

Smiling, she turned her face away and shook her head.

'But, my dear child, surely you are not going to deprive yourself of all sorts of fun? These days, marriage is no more than the permanent set against which we play out our romances. It's not a binding contract.'

She said quietly: 'I think it is a binding contract.'

'Oh, oh!' He shook her hand while she held herself stiffly from him. 'What a little prude! You used not to be like this. Do you imagine your husband will remain faithful to you?'

'Yes. Why not?'

Quintin laughed at her: 'My dear child, husbands just don't remain faithful.'

'Perhaps some husbands do.'

'You'll learn better. And, don't forget, life is short: you will grow old.'

She thought of Simon and smiled: 'I'm prepared for that.'

He tilted back his head, narrowed his eyes and drew down his lips in a smile that would once have enthralled her. Now she was acutely aware of the marks of age on him. She thought of Simon's strong, young body and smiled into herself, a smile secret and expectant.

Quintin said: 'Perhaps I made you unhappy? If I did, I am sorry. But we are all victims, one of another.'

She was not sure he was not laughing at her. She smiled, guardedly, but his face remained sad. Ageing and sad.

'I must go,' she said.

'No, no. Don't go.'

'The will has nothing to do with me. I'm not meant to hear it.'

Snow had been falling again. A white light was reflected from the lawn on to the ceiling. Now the motion of snowflakes was thinning into nothingness. When the last flake fell, the outside world was still. To her it seemed to have been renewed by snow as by the supernatural agency of love. She longed to walk into it.

Quintin, holding her wrist, was trying to detain her. Gently, but with determination, she detached herself. 'My husband is expecting me for tea.' She spoke rather proudly – a married woman, a woman with a secure background.

Quintin gave his little, comic bow, turning his lips down as though to say: 'I acknowledge my error.'

When she said good-bye, his only reply was a small, regretful movement towards her. She hurried away.

Nancy had been cornered by Maxine. Ellie signalled that she was going, and went without speaking again to anyone.

Down in the square she boarded a waiting bus. The air was cold and brilliant as crystal. The trees were snow-heavy as with blossom. When the bus moved off, it passed in spectral quiet through the twilight of Kentish Town and Camden Town, journeying westwards into the transformed city where Ellie had her home.